# The Dogs Are Curling Up Again

Margaret H. Townley

**BALBOA.**PRESS

A DIVISION OF HAY HOUSE

Balboa Press books may be ordered through booksellers or by contacting:

Balboa Press
A Division of Hay House
1663 Liberty Drive
Bloomington, IN 47403
www.balboapress.co.uk
UK TFN: 0800 0148647 (Toll Free inside the UK)
UK Local: (02) 0369 56325 (+44 20 3695 6325 from outside the UK)

Print information available on the last page.

ISBN: 978-1-9822-8638-5 (sc)
ISBN: 978-1-9822-8639-2 (e)

Balboa Press rev. date: 10/03/2022

*To my sons Tim and Andrew*
*and to Archi and all my Chilean friends*

# Chapter 1

er mother had begged her not to join the funeral march. She'd said it was too dangerous, a foolish risk, the military coup being less than two weeks old. Everyone, she had insisted would be picked up or photographed for future action on 'subversives'. Isabel had weighed all this up beforehand and had made her decision. Her mother had always called her stubborn – now she would show her. "Anyone who doesn't go," she remembered replying to her *mama*, "was either a coward or didn't love their country and its people." She'd known that day would be more than a funeral procession for the second Nobel Prize-Winning Poet of her own little country – the land of poets, it would be a protest against the military Junta, the destruction of Chile's freely elected government, the death of its president, the rounding up of so many loved ones, and the fear and terror injected into all its people.

Now it was an unbelievable twenty years on and so much had happened that she had never anticipated would ever occur in her life. Isabel had lived for fourteen of those years in England. She was now back in Santiago again for her first visit after going into exile, years after the coup d'état. *There must be a million of us here today,* she remembered she had thought when she followed the massive procession through the streets of Santiago de Chile in September 1973. Like everyone else marching at the funeral of their most acclaimed poet, Isabel had nervously watched the soldiers lining the route and anxiously thrown sideways glances at the tanks and armoured cars waiting in every side street. *How could it all have come about*, she remembered pondering and how she had agonised.

Isabel could answer that question better now than she had been able to then but it seemed in some sense as unbelievable now as then. Now she knew the evidence of the North American involvement and the traitorous upper echelons of Chilean society that had together instigated the coup and its preconditions. All Isabel had known at that time was that what was happening had to be opposed. She remembered the slow processing along the packed streets - that crowd must have astonished and frightened even the military Junta. They'd not had time to consolidate their power and here were hundreds of thousands of people on the streets in protest. For a day the *golpistas* must have felt helpless, obliged to accept the march, even though they had declared there would be no public funeral. The whole world was watching but they would bide their time.

"Let the fools have their day" – the generals must have thought, mused Isabel as she trod the same streets again. They had the guns, the power and the CIA backing. She wondered too if the sheer immensity and sadness of the military coup must have killed Pablo Neruda, despite his great courage in the past. He must have felt he could no longer live with such a broken heart. His close friend President Allende, on whom so many hopes had been placed, was dead. Many colleagues and friends had been killed, thousands of ordinary people had been arrested and all the hopes and longings of a people smashed under those ugly jackboots. Neruda had been ill and getting old, too old to face again a popular movement being destroyed in what he had called the "permanent war" – the repetition of bloody actions of an elite against their own people, "which the powerful call 'order', and which was paid for with a journey to Washington."

"I want to just weep and hide," Isabel remembered she had told her mother back then, "but I can't. What about Raúl, Jorge, Pedro and Luis and Marta?" Their families hadn't known where they were. Raúl had been her boyfriend and the others were friends of the family from Isabel's own neighbourhood. "What about my friends in Manuel Rodriguez?" Her mother hadn't liked her going to that *población* to do voluntary work. She had insisted that nothing good would come of it and that Isabel had best stay away from those people.

"Are you going to stop being friends with Pedro's mum or Luis's now? Aren't they respectable enough for you now?" Isabel remembered she had retorted. And so the arguments had raged, heightened by the fear and dread of what might happen next. They had been arguing since Isabel had joined the campaign to help *Popular Unity* to power in 1970. She had only been fourteen then but was swept up with excitement at all that was going on politically in her country. It had felt like everyone was participating in creating a brave new world. It was to have been an example to the world! Milk and free schooling for all children, literacy campaigns, she'd been helping with those - caring for the children whilst mothers went to classes - the end of poor housing and encampments like Manuel Rodriguez. Changes had been underway, the whole world was interested in its first freely elected Marxist government, and it was in her own beloved country - Chile.

Now Isabel found herself still arguing with her mother. She hadn't wanted to spoil her first visit back from exile and the first time she'd seen her mother in 14 years, by arguing with her. But did her mother do it deliberately to provoke her? *Did she have to caress that photograph of General Pinochet in the newspaper? How could she after all that has occurred? How could she still believe the propaganda and the lies? After what happened to my own father?* Isabel's parents had not been together for 10 years before the coup. Her Papa had understood what Allende and Popular Unity were trying to achieve. He'd been a teacher and active in the teachers' union. He'd been at Neruda's funeral march and was arrested a few days later. It had been dangerous to go to the march but her father had courage because we had to show our opposition to the Junta. But she had lost her father. Was it worth it? Wouldn't they have caught up with him anyway? How she still grieved for him. He was such a good man.

Perhaps her mother was still angry with her for choosing to go into exile with her stepmother. Isabel had felt she had to go because for her the situation had become unbearable. Her father had been one of the detained who was never heard of again. Six years she had spent searching for news of him. Thousands had disappeared and rumours were rife of mass burials in the desert or bodies thrown in the sea. Neighbours had talked of bodies seen in the Mapocho River, but still, her mother didn't get it. Her mother seemed even more now to believe all that propaganda of the dictator's government or she had forgotten and blanked through fear, what had happened to people around her.

*The country has only partially emerged from that dictatorship, and it is as if a blanket of silence has fallen over the land,* thought Isabel. *How am I going to find out what is really going on? No one seems willing to talk. No one can celebrate the end of the dictatorship because Pinochet is still Head of the Armed Forces and he still has power and influence, tied up in the Constitution he imposed. But why are the people I've talked to so far, so frightened still to speak?* Isabel hadn't expected to find the people so fearful and so divided. Some claimed it had all been necessary but they would not debate why or how the dictatorship could be justified and they were in denial about the cruelty and killings it had perpetrated. Still others, equally mistaken, said it was best not to stir up the past, not to talk of painful memories and that this was the only way to heal the massive divide in the country. That was another argument Isabel had had with her mother that morning.

"How can you have reconciliation if you haven't examined what happened?" she had shouted, telling herself to stay calm, but getting more furious every minute. "How can you have peace without the truth first?" But her mother walked away muttering about it only making things worse.

When she returned to her mother's house that evening, Isabel threw herself into an armchair, feeling very alone and depressed at how distant she seemed from her mother and from her country. Right now she felt a long way from her English partner Julian and her *Mamadre,* as Neruda had called his stepmother and Isabel had followed suit with hers. She'd come to love her stepmother, Constanza, very much and had needed her tender affection so much in exile. Isabel had left her, her step-brother and Julian in England, for her first visit back to Chile. She had come to Chile in 1994, the first possible opportunity for her after Pinochet had stepped down from the Presidency. She had yearned to return to her land for years and once it was actually safe for her to come and the Chilean Embassy would grant her a visa, nothing was going to stop her. Like other refugees she previously had a British Home Office Document, in place of a passport, that declared itself: 'Valid for all countries except Chile.' She'd wanted to scream or cry every time she saw those words and, despite their claim, she had endured maddening waits and questioning whenever she re-entered Britain from very ordinary holiday visits to European countries. Did the immigration officials have to repeat the same questions every time, the answers to which were before them on their computers anyway? Isabel could barely contain herself on such occasions.

4

It reminded her of the offensive checking and six-hour wait in Immigration upon her family's first arrival in Britain from Chile. Did she have to relive that every time she went on holiday?

Julian had been very patient with her, she had to admit. He had wanted to go to Chile with her but she felt he was not part of the reality that Chile was for her. *It wouldn't feel right, for him to be here with me now, not this first time anyway,* she had said repeatedly to herself. She wanted to find **her** Chile again and she could not yet recognise that she needed to find herself. She was not even sure of where in the world she wanted to be and whether she should be with Julian or not. Isabel felt she needed to see what she could establish in Chile, what contacts she could restart and what opportunities she could make. She was planning to make a documentary, so she was going to have to work hard to find the people who would really know what was going on and be willing to articulate it on film. All those years waiting for this chance to come back, all those years constantly playing the music of the *New Chilean Song Movement*, waiting, initially for a quick return and when those hopes faded, waiting anyway, waiting loyally, centring all hopes for her future on being in Chile again. Then she had changed direction to be with Julian. It was an intense and very powerful draw. He seemed to her to be the love of her life. But here she was at last in Chile and she knew she didn't want to be inhibited in any way in her search for what she called the real Chile.

When Julian had wanted a serious relationship with her and they talked of a long-term commitment, she had told him she was prepared to live in England forever. She believed she did mean it after long, soul-searching thought. But if she was honest now with herself, she knew she had always hoped to come back to live here again. She tried to be sincere with Julian. She thought she did mean her promises and was truly, deeply in love with him. She had only come to Chile with the intention of a visit, to make a video and to see the place again. Right now, despite disappointments and disillusions, she couldn't imagine leaving Chile again and England seemed a very distant other reality. Perhaps she had thought she could turn the clock back and return to the old Chile. She knew now that she had changed and that her country had changed too. She was beginning to feel as though she could no longer feel at home in Chile just as she had always felt not at home in England. It was painful for her to begin realising that she may have to remain an 'outsider', an observer forever. Isabel was clear on one thing only. She must come here often and spend a lot of time here, whatever happens. She was not clear about her feelings towards Julian. He was a good man who clearly loved her but could she give up her homeland for him now?

It hadn't been easy to explain to Julian why she wanted to come alone for this first visit but perhaps she hadn't really wanted to admit why to herself. Julian had always desired to share the emotional experience of her return but he had tried to be understanding. Why had she pushed him away like that? He would only have stayed a few weeks and she wanted to be here much longer. Had she lost the love she had for him? Would she go back to him? She was glad she did not need to decide that yet. There was plenty of time to think about that. For now, she couldn't believe that he could possibly imagine her pain and how she was going to confront the tragic history of her country, her father and her friends. She said to herself that she couldn't face having to explain every detail to an outsider.

*Or was I making an excuse*, she wondered? Communication between them had been an increasing problem in recent times. She knew she welcomed a break to give space to decide if she was committed to the relationship or not, though she had hardly wanted to admit it to herself and certainly not to Julian. She wanted to see neighbours and school friends with whom she had shared her childhood. *You can't share intimate thoughts with old friends with an outsider, a foreigner standing helplessly on the sidelines with not much Spanish,* she'd told herself. She wanted to be free to travel to areas she'd not been to before and to know her country more fully. She already had invites from two old school friends who now lived in the south, where she had never travelled. Then, there are places in the north to visit, where the oldest known mummies in the world are, which she needed to see, as she had never had the opportunity before. In the south, there are the Mexican Mayan-style murals promoted by Diego Rivera, which some fellow artists of his had done in Concepción and nearby. Isabel had written about these in her History of Arts degree in England, but she had never seen them in real life and one school friend lived now in Concepción. While in the south also she wanted to see her closest childhood friend who now lived near where Pablo Neruda had grown up.

*All this visiting is going to be easier and less of an imposition if I'm on my own,* she had told herself. *And the conversations and memories shared will be easier if I'm visiting alone.* Then there were new contacts she wanted to make and she anticipated some would have to be subtly done if she was truly to find out what was going on. She hoped she could make contact with political groups who were actively seeking change by whatever means. She knew from them she would learn the fullest critique of all that was taking place in the country. After a few weeks with her mother and her brother's family, it was time to get on with planning the task she was here to achieve.

Isabel's purpose was to make a documentary film, five years into the so-called 'transition to democracy' from the dictatorship, as the government referred to the present period. She had done some freelance filmmaking with others in the UK but now she would be on her own. She did not have a commission but she had worked in a documentary film agency and had contacts with various broadcasters. She hoped she was going to be able to make a film good enough to gain acceptance. She wanted to follow the clandestine filming of her great hero film-maker Miguel Littín had done in the dictator's time. He had wanted to inform the outside world of what was going on in Chile. He was in exile and was on the list of people who could not return to Chile. He entered secretly and his courage was honoured by the writer *Gabriel García Marquez* writing a report: *Clandestine in Chile - the Adventures of Miguel Littín in Chile. At least I didn't have to come to Chile with a false passport and false identity, as Littín did. What a risk he had taken.* Lattín had gone in with a false wife in the hopes of avoiding detection and he was successful in his deception. Isabel wanted to get to the heart of what was going on now. There were many people in Littín's time conspiring to overthrow the regime in any way possible. *Who could blame them? Today in the 'transition' there are people who take risks to make a stand and get detained and shot with rubber bullets because they know there can be no transition to real democracy under Pinochet's unjust constitution.*

-oOo-

It took a while to find the right buses to cross the city to another neighbourhood where Isabel had decided to look up the parents of Raúl. Stopping passers-by to ask for help, she found them as friendly and ready to assist as she remembered Chileans had always been. Isabel turned the corner into the long street that lead to Raúl's parents' home and she was shocked at the changes. Some of the old houses remained with their elegant heavy wooden doors and wrought iron railings, most of them now in desperate need of revarnishing and repainting. But it seemed like every alternate house had been torn down and a modern monstrosity put up in its place. They were heavy, dominating, characterless examples of modern design, some in brick, some of painted render, but all irregular and spoiling the beauty of the traditional street. Isabel felt she had to be fair, some were quite exciting, imaginative, designs with whole walls of glass, but they were all in the wrong place. Why were they intermingled with the old, making the whole street look so untidy? *Lack of proper planning laws. At least that is one good thing about Britain.* More and more of the old houses, as she continued up the road, looked dilapidated and abandoned - just waiting to be pulled down and replaced. Suddenly Isabel realised she'd gone too far. *How could I miss the house that used to be so familiar to me? Could it be one of the ones torn down?* The changes made it really hard to see where she was, the numbers and their inconsistency were baffling. Then she saw the old familiar house - now with its flaking paintwork, its dusty steps and its dried, cracked wooden window frames and shutters. Isabel's heart sank. *My first search for the old Chile and it's going to end in disappointment. No one could be living here, it seems so dirty and abandoned.*

She tried knocking the door because it appeared wrong not to bother to knock after such lengthy bus rides to find this family. They could not be here, however. Not a sound came from the house. She rubbed her finger to clear the dust from the corner of a windowpane in the once-grand front door and peered through. For a moment she saw Raúl walking in front of her, holding her hand and taking her to meet his parents for the first time. Noisy laughter in the house, the smell of cooking, all rushed back to her. She felt faint and sick and wanted to collapse onto the dusty steps. She steadied herself on the railings and just stood still, feeling a deep sad ache in the bottom of her stomach. She had lost the will to go anywhere else that day. She couldn't even think of what she could do next to track down this lovely family. Asking the neighbours didn't even occur to her. Every old house seemed silent and deserted and the new ones uninviting. They all made Isabel feel frozen inside.

After a wait of several minutes, Isabel finally dragged herself to a little corner shop with a few Formica tables and she sat herself down. It seemed to her that she didn't want to leave the neighbourhood. She felt she wanted to be around this old familiar haunt a while longer, hoping for what, she couldn't quite define. Her thoughts were interrupted by the assistant, who asked to know what she wanted to order. Isabel mumbled a cup of tea would do her and she scooped in three spoonfuls of sugar when the tea came. This was a normal amount of sugar for many Chileans she had noticed but an amount that she would never have dreamt of having in England. What scorn that amount of sugar would pour forth in Britain. Tea without milk being the norm in Chile, Isabel decided she needed the glucose right now as she was picturing Raúl with his mop of dark, curly hair, quite long as the fashion was then, his attractive smile and she ached deeply again at his loss. She had never heard anything definite or official of what had happened to Raúl when she'd finally left for England, and she had searched and searched with his mother for news for years, together with hunting for her own father. They went to all the hospitals and morgues they could, many times over. Isabel hadn't wanted to go to England without knowing what happened to Raúl but nearly six years had passed and when they had confirmation of her father's death, her stepmother insisted they must take the opportunity to get out without further delay. Isabel had kept in close touch with Raúl's family for those six years. She remembered his distraught mother, his sister María Paz bubbling over every time they met. His brother Javier, who had seemed so full of life and happiness before Raúl was taken and afterwards, she had only seen Javier with his head hung down and in silence as if deeply depressed. Isabel wondered what had happened to him too. Sadness seemed to paralyse her again. She sat motionless, staring.

The young waitress began to sweep the floor and Isabel roused herself and sipped her tea. She'd have to move soon but couldn't think what to do. After paying, she stepped into the street. There were few people around but Isabel saw a greatly stooped elderly lady tottering along the pavement towards her. The old lady steadied her every step with her stick and had difficulty looking up to see ahead of herself, she was so bent. Dressed in black except for a grey scarf around her head and tied under her chin, Isabel thought she looked like a black and white photograph. Her face was as pale and as grey as the scarf and the little wisp of grey hair that covered the corner of her forehead. Isabel puzzled over the face when she could, as it looked up to check the direction. There was something familiar about that face. Isabel stepped forward intently trying to study the face. Now close to Isabel the old woman lifted her head and her eyes met Isabel's. Isabel gasped and put out her hands. It was hard for Luisa to smile, she seemed to have so little muscle to use but her toothless mouth opened and tears ran from her eyes. Isabel embraced Luisa's strange angular form and hugged her as hard as she dared. Isabel knew that she'd been recognised by Raúl's grandmother.

The slow walk with Luisa back to the house seemed to last an eternity. Isabel longed to ask a million questions but couldn't really talk with the shrivelled old lady clinging to her arm and seeming half her height. Cars noisily passed and blocked out the words Luisa was muttering and whatever Isabel tried to say to her. They communicated by the constant squeezing of each others' arms until finally, they reached the old house. When sitting down, with the kettle on and Luisa's tears slowing a little, Isabel asked if there had ever been further news of Raúl. In confused, disjointed sentences Luisa explained that Raúl's mother María had had lots of contact with the Association of Families of the Detained Disappeared but never any news of Raúl. His father too had later been arrested, probably, thought Isabel, to stem his efforts to find his son and he had spent four years in prison. In 1983, ten years after Raúl's disappearance, María, her husband Pedro, Javier and María Paz had gone to live in Spain.

"They wanted me to go with them but I was too old to leave my home," stuttered Luisa through her toothless gums and she began to cry again. "I told them they must go and give the children a new opportunity. There was nothing for them here and Spain had made a new start after Franco." Luisa went on to describe how hard Pedro and María worked running a restaurant, serving lots of Chilean food. "They work terrible hours…"

"Have you lived alone since they left?" Isabel asked, wondering how she was going to manage much longer without being cared for.

"My sister lived with me until last year when she died and now her daughter comes to see me several times a week and she brings meals she has prepared." Greatly relieved at that news, Isabel began to appreciate that she wasn't going to have to pass all her time in Chile caring for this little lady, lovely though she was. She had begun to think she'd never be able to leave her despite Luisa's insistence that she was doing fine. As they talked Isabel saw how tough Luisa was and how aware still she was of all that was going on.

"I remember when you and Raúl used to go to the countryside helping the people. What tales he used to come back with!" mused Luisa.

"We believed it possible then to make a new world."

"Today the young people seem as frightened or as disinterested as the parents that are left. I suppose it's all they've been brought up with. Fear has eaten away at the soul of this country." Luisa's eyes watered again. "It's not only that they don't do the things you and Raúl used to do, helping build houses, teaching reading and the rest, but it's also that they don't want to help others, they don't see why it matters. They don't care or they're frightened or they say they are, but it's a good excuse for doing nothing. The fear cuts people off from each other, which I suppose is what the military regime wanted. Fear is corrupting. We used to have a sense of community but it's not like that nowadays. I know, I talk to the young people coming along the road from school. Some of them laugh at me and call me names. It never used to be like that. Old people were respected and the young were kind to them. But nowadays, those that will talk to me, tell me they can't do anything. When I ask them to get some shopping for an old lady or help a mum down the road, they say their parents wouldn't let them. They weren't interested when I talked to them about the plebiscite and getting the 'No' vote against *el hombre.* It's just as bad still."

"*El hombre,* you mean the General?" inquired Isabel, not having heard all the Chilean jargon yet.

"*El huevón,*" replied Luisa, which surprised Isabel. She hadn't expected this sweet little lady to use vulgar modern slang, even if she was referring to the hated dictator. However, it was the normal parlance of those who were against him and with reason. Luisa reminisced some more about the time before the military coup and Isabel, who had been thirsting for such talk, indulged herself in sharing many old memories. Luisa had even been to a few *peñas* by artists of the *New Chilean Song Movement* - with Raúl and his friends. "It wasn't only you young people who liked the music, you know. I saw Victor Jara and the Parras. And I saw Los Jaivas in concert. There were others of my generation there too. We loved the sound of the old native instruments mixed with the guitars in a new way. We were proud of what

11

Violetta Parra achieved. We liked what they were trying to create: a Chilean cultural sound in place of the domination of North American commercial pop music. It was part of what we were all trying to achieve."

Isabel was almost in tears herself by this time. This was the music that she had listened to constantly in exile. She had seen and heard how these groups went on developing their music and incorporating new influences from their wider world experience in exile but she knew they were still very conscious of their origins and their hopes for a free Chile, waiting to be able to return again.

"Did you hear what happened to Angel Parra, my favourite singer?" Isabel asked, realising Luisa might not ever have had the chance to know anything more about him after the coup. "After a time in prison, Angel Parra and his sister Isabel were in exile in France and they travelled Europe trying to keep alive the *New Chilean Song Movement*." Luisa did know that Victor Jara had been brutally murdered but she did not know of the poem he had written in the Chile Stadium in Santiago where 5000 had been imprisoned in the first days of the military coup. "His poem was smuggled out with news of what had happened to him. His hands had been broken and crushed so he knew he would never play the guitar again and he suffered many other injuries. But he wrote about the 5000 being held there and Victor's English wife Joan recited the translated poem on the first posthumous release of some of Victor's songs." Isabel realised that Luisa would never have heard that poem because of the ban, and she tried to recall some lines of the poem for Luisa:

*There are 5000 of us in this small part of the city. 5000 of us here.*
*I wonder how many of us altogether in the cities, in the whole country.*
*In this place alone there are 10,000 hands which plant seeds and make the factories run.*
*How much humanity exposed to hunger, cold, panic, pain, moral pressure terror and madness.*

*Trapped between these four walls we are just a number*
*A number which cannot grow*
*Its longing for death gradually increasing*

*But suddenly my conscience wakes up and I see this tide of murder has no
heartbeat*

*The blood of our president, our Companero, will strike more powerfully than
bombs and machine guns
That is how our fist will strike again
How hard it is to sing when I must sing of horror,
horror in which I am living,
horror in which I am dying.
Seeing myself amongst so much horror and so many endless moments
Silence and screams are the end of my song
What I see I have never seen before
What I've felt and what I feel now
will give birth to the moment....*

Isabel had always wondered at the courage of this man, who never
mentioned his own torture, only the deaths of others in that terrible place and
how he had been able to anticipate a new future that would one day come,
knowing he would never see it. When she could recover herself a little she
tried to sing for Luisa Victor Jara's last song which he called his *Manifesto*:

*I don't sing for love of singing
or to show off my voice
but for the statements
made by my honest guitar
for its heart is of the earth
and like the dove it goes flying....
endlessly as holy water
blessing the brave and the dying
so my song has found a purpose
as Violetta Parra would say.
Yes, my guitar is a worker
shining and smelling of spring
my guitar is not for killers
greedy for money and power*

*but for the people who labour*
*so that the future may flower.*
*For a song takes on a meaning*
*when its own heartbeat is strong*
*sung by a man who will die singing*
*truthfully singing his song.*
*I don't care for adulation*
*or so that strangers may weep.*
*I sing for a far strip of country narrow but endlessly deep.*

Isabel and Luisa cried and hugged each other at length, then finally they faced each others' tear-streamed faces and found themselves smiling, smiling at each other at being together again, arms outstretched holding each other by the shoulders.

Luisa wanted to know all about what Isabel had been doing in England and what her future had in store and Isabel soon felt she'd talked too much of herself and not heard enough about Chile. At least Luisa could really understand the struggle she'd had, first to overcome the loss of her father, her homeland, her friends and her mother, then to conquer the English language and to recover her education. *Luisa must be the most empathetic person on this earth. She knows, she feels, she communicates with me in a way others don't or can't. Luisa understands without having to have everything spelt out.*

"When you're stumbling on how to express an idea in a foreign language, you sound less intelligent and articulate than you really are and you know you look a fool," she said. "It takes a while to have the confidence to speak out, especially in a group, like a seminar or a work meeting. I had to really push myself. I tried to be very supportive of my work colleagues at the documentary agency. I was always willing to research bits of information for them, make them coffees or get rolls for lunch."

"Very Chilean," said Luisa.

"I think it helped them to be patient and helpful towards me. My English wasn't bad by then but I needed them to explain some colloquial expressions sometimes. I tried to make jokes, but I had to ask them the meaning of jokes I heard. If the expression had a sexual innuendo, I needed to get at what they really meant. I've one or two good friends there now and they understand what I want to do in Chile and I think they will help me when I get back with the documentary I want to make here." Luisa wanted to know more of what her film was to be about and she suggested that families broken up, like hers, should be one theme and the families returning now another.

"I heard from a neighbour about her son's family returning recently and things have not been easy for them. The son has not been able to get the sort of job he wanted. The children are young people now and they still are complaining about leaving their friends in Australia."

"Lots of us are thinking about coming back to Chile now that we can. The older ones want to most of all but what do they do for a pension? What work could younger ones get? It's not easy and children born in Britain or other parts of Europe don't want to come here. They've their own lives and relationships, they are studying or they've started careers. You're always torn. Wanting what you've waited for, for so long but at the same time not wanting to leave what you have. I'm not even sure how well we'd be received here by many Chileans. Getting a job will be hard for many because they need a *pituto* to recommend them - or they've no chance of getting the post. In addition to not having the right contacts, there is likely to be prejudice against an exile. I've heard people talk in Chile as if we were lucky to be in exile. I know things were hard here, especially in the early years but they've no idea of the empty hole you can feel every day of your life in exile, the discrimination you face, the menial jobs most exiles do although they were well educated, mostly professional people who went abroad. I went to England maybe at the best age, if I had got to go at all. I was old enough to remember and love my country but young enough to get good at English and to get an education there and to start a career only a few years late."

"It was hard for your stepmother, I imagine."

"Yes, I only realised how hard, with time. Mamadre had gone to university in Chile and had become a journalist. But I saw how studying a foreign language in midlife is not only much harder than when you start young, but her English would always have a heavy accent. I don't think she could reach the capacity she had in her own language and Mamadre had loved her fulfilling career, so losing it was a deep blow for her. But it was only one of the many losses and she complained of none. She has been wonderful. She ended up teaching Spanish in England and she says she found it challenging and interesting, but it wasn't her first love and wasn't what she really wanted to do. She'd had to start with factory work too, doing shift work in unsociable hours. That experience must have been hard for an educated woman and it was poorly paid. At last, now Mamadre is gaining some publishing opportunities in Spanish and putting her writing skills to more use.

"You remember when we finally got to know Papa was dead, Mamadre applied to do a post-graduate course abroad through the World University Service as a way of leaving the country and she told us she would take whatever offer came through first. The London School of Economics offered a place first and she wanted us all to be off. Mamadre started an English class immediately, organised by the Refugee Council. Eventually, reluctantly, I went as well. I could see Mamadre was learning slower than me and Eugenio. She needed things repeated much more often and she couldn't remember vocabulary as well as we could. She couldn't so easily go out to meet people like we could either, although it wasn't all that easy for us to talk to British young people. London is very multicultural but many stick to their own kind. People thought Eugenio and I were a couple and left us alone. When we tried to talk and try out our English, we'd get laughed at or people would walk away. It wasn't easy to meet English girls or boys. Sometimes a girl would seem friendly to me and then make some excuse to go away and she wouldn't return. It was like they were always looking over their shoulders wondering what their peers would say. We were outsiders and made to feel it. It got better when we got to University and our English was much better. At Uni there were more social opportunities, of course, there were classmates to get to know and society meetings to attend, but we had to pass English exams to get that far and we had to work really hard for that. We often had to practice only with each other. It's hard to keep up speaking in English with your own brother when all you want to do is rattle off some remark in Chilean slang, as you normally would talk with him.

"We had some wonderful Chilean parties for *Fiestas Patrias*, for New Year and other occasions. Eventually, our Association for Chilean Refugees began to organise little holidays at a big old house in the Peak District, owned by the local Borough Council. We could hire this old Boys Remand Home, a run-down institution of a place, no longer used, for long weekend stays.

They were good times. We loved being together in all those years when none of us could return to Chile. We'd sing traditional Chilean songs and play the music of the *New Song Movement* and of course, we'd eat Chilean food. We all prepared it together."

"I don't think there are many Chileans in Spain and I think Maria and Pedro were very isolated when they first went there. The children seemed to meet Spanish people more easily. Their parents work kept them isolated too. They had to rent a flat with a restaurant to get started in Spain, so it was tough working every evening to make enough money to cover the rent. How did you get housing and finance yourselves in England?" asked Luisa.

"We had state benefits until we could work which was so good of the country but the housing was another matter. Luisa, you should see some of the municipal housing in London that the refugees were allocated. They were given the houses that were the very oldest. They were damp and dilapidated and they had no insulation which is vital in that climate or the condensation just runs down the walls. I've seen council houses in London where the walls were covered in mould and freezing cold in winter. You can't imagine how cold the winters are in England. Our first house was cold like that. The gas fire in the living room burned you if you sat near it but it didn't heat the other side of the room, let alone the freezing cold bathroom, kitchen and bedroom. Everything was so squalid in those houses but we weren't the only ones. People in Chile don't believe that there is poverty in England but there is. I've seen it. Our second house was better than that and though it wasn't posh, it was adequate. It was a house on an ordinary street but owned by the University. At least it wasn't damp although it was dirty and needed painting when we got it. We were really pleased to clean it all up, paint it everywhere inside and put out our little Chilean souvenirs, our Mapuche rug and our Andean throws. The women in Manuel Rodriguez gave me a collage they'd made, which I shall always treasure and have in my room. I took it to Warwick University with me and hung it on the wall of my room in the Hall of Residence. It shows women sewing, building little wooden houses and growing vegetables. I know the story behind the collage - that their men had been taken away by the military and they had to do all the jobs in the houses and gardens themselves as well as sewing at home for a pittance, as a way to try to survive. But they made the collage very 'pretty,' with spring wildflowers, so it wouldn't arouse the suspicion of being 'political' if my case was searched when I was leaving Chile..." After a brief indulgence in her memories, Isabel said firmly, "I'm going shopping to get some lunch for us."

When she came back with the food, Luisa had made a typical tomato salad and laid the table. Isabel had spotted some Chinese Soy Sauce and some noodles in the supermarket and thought Luisa might be willing to try a Prawn Stir Fry. It would be quick, thought Isabel as it was already very late for lunch. Isabel had learned in England to do quick meals to keep pace with the way of life. Luisa might be horrified, it's not the Chilean way at all, *but needs must, as the English would say.* Isabel was quite proud of all the colloquial English she'd learned. She bought some fresh vegetables which the English would call 'Mediterranean', together with prawns, lime and fresh coriander and created a pleasant dish in no time.

After they'd eaten and Luisa had been quite impressed with Isabel's Stir Fry, Isabel began to ask about the life of the family before they went to Spain. Luisa began to cry again when she recalled how devastated her daughter was when her husband was arrested and her son was still missing.

"It was hard to keep hoping when every day it seemed more hopeless. Normal life was impossible because every day she was trying new places to ask for them. When Pedro was arrested, María had to find work as well as continue searching for Raúl. She went to cook and clean in a house in Los Condes and I tried to do everything here so she didn't have to come home to housework and cooking all over again. Javier and María Paz were very good at helping me, especially as my arthritis became worse. They were studying and I wanted to do more for them. It was hard for them to concentrate very often, with all that was going on." Isabel thought she shouldn't be pressing Luisa to tell her all that had happened as it was so upsetting but Luisa insisted that it was better to remember, to talk about her memories and to never forget.

"Too many people are trying to pretend it didn't happen now and the economic miracle has made it all right. They are just willing to believe all the propaganda but the miracle is only for some, not for all. Javier and María Paz have made a success now in Spain. I'm glad they went, it was for the best. María Paz is married now and is expecting her first child."

*Luisa is right,* thought Isabel, *it's healthier to remember although it is painful.* She began to recall memories of Raúl that she had hardly allowed herself to think of for a long time. They were painful thoughts but beautiful as the innocent young love she remembered. She felt a deep longing for Raúl but the memories of not knowing what had happened to him overwhelmed her again. At least with Luisa she could cry and be understood.

*I couldn't admit it to Julian but I see now I carried a constant rabia inside of me. I buried my anger and my grieving but it would escape at times when the slightest thing didn't please me. What I have to do now that I am here in Chile, is to try to complete this grieving process.*

"Going into exile was like a second grieving after the first loss of my dad and then Raúl. The first losses are long and drawn out because you don't believe that the person has really gone for good. You keep hoping and waiting, believing it can only be temporary. Exile is a sudden shock and I grieved then for my country, my home, my mother and for my father and Raúl.

"I remember the initial shock, the numbness when you can't think straight or do anything, at least in exile, I couldn't do anything. When I was here I had to get on with the searching. After that stage, I pretended to everyone I was perfectly all right but I feared breaking down and I felt a bit false. I knew I was putting on fake smiles and I knew they couldn't seem true but I couldn't stop myself from a sort of grin when I didn't feel like smiling and the rest of my face didn't match the grin."

"The tension of living a pretence must have made you oversensitive and ready to explode."

"It must have been hard on those around me. I was angry."

Isabel recalled the periods of hyperactivity after the Coup and her desperate need to search for the missing. Luisa remembered the planning and Isabel and María setting off for new venues to ask for their loved ones and the bitter disappointments on their return. When all hope was lost and Isabel had finally conceded to the idea of exile, she knew her anger had come out in the arguments with her mother. She confessed to the conflict she was still having with her mother.

"You need to make peace with your mother while you are here, you know."

"Yes, I do know, but it's not easy. How can I make peace with someone who doesn't accept the atrocities of the regime?"

"I think she must do, but she doesn't want you to keep going on about them. She wants all that tragedy to be left behind. You are stirring it all up again. Many people feel that and it's not good. But be gentle on her."

"But I am here to try to face what has happened and she wants to deny it or so it seems. But maybe you're right." Isabel thought perhaps it was another subtle nuance she should bring into her video, but right now she wanted to go on telling Luisa how unhappy she had felt in exile. She was one of the few people who would listen and show empathy. "In exile, I was still angry, I can see that now. Everything had to be questioned, I believed, from the important issues, like racism and British government actions down to every little niggle in ordinary life. Everything molested me in that strange culture in which I was forced to live." Now she could reflect that her exasperation was never far below the surface, even by the time she had begun the demanding task of adjusting to a new relationship - with *el inglés* - Julian. Isabel decided, however, that she didn't want to return to that subject again with Luisa. "I want to go back to being the happy, carefree person I was before the coup in Chile. I know I can't in many ways but somewhere approaching that. Is that so much to ask?"

"The reality of what has happened can't be undone. The future is up to you."

"OK, I know. We make ourselves and we make our future. We all know that but it's not always easy to do what we desire." Isabel cried a little more. "Luisa, it's very late and getting dark. The buses don't run late as they used to in the good old days. I must go but I promise to return soon. Do you think I could talk with the family who went to Australia and have returned? Their experience would be helpful for my documentary. I'll write to María in Spain." Luisa and she hugged each other again at length. The city seemed very quiet as if still under curfew although it no longer was and Isabel pondered whether people had lost the habit to go out at night because of the many years of military rule. As she made herself as comfortable as she could in a seat of the noisy old bus, Isabel indulged herself in some happy memories of this friendly, innocent city when she was a teenager but she also reflected further on what she had talked to Luisa about just

20

before she left. She knew she had taken her anger out on Julian and had made him suffer, unconsciously but sometimes consciously, she had to admit. Now she could see it took its toll on the relationship. She regretted in many ways that they were apart and wondered if the joyful good times could ever be recovered.

# Chapter 2

When they were at school together, her friend Miriam's house had been only three blocks away from her mother's home in Santiago. Miriam had been a good friend from primary school times, through secondary school and Miriam's parents' home, if they were still there, was a good place for Isabel to begin to seek out old friends. They might help her on her 'other' journey, as she had begun now to call her search. She had seen the new skyscraper buildings in Santiago. She'd seen the signs of the growing consumer society, she'd seen the superficiality of the TV programmes, and now she was going to search underneath for the old Chile. She knocked on the familiar front door. After a moment of staring incredulously, suddenly the wrinkled but recognisable face of her friend's mother broke into an enormous smile. Her arms shot out and Isabel was pulled towards this chubby, warm body, which was letting out shouts of welcome. Finally, Gladys let her go and began to jump up and down as others rushed forward to give her hugs.

"Izzy! Izzy! It's you, Izzy!" With Gladys's arms around her, Isabel was projected into the living room and to the large armchair where was seated a very wizened old lady, whom Isabel found it hard to recognise but she knew to be Miriam's grandmother. Isabel kissed the dry-skinned, bony face and was frightened to hug her tight as she seemed so delicate and fragile. Two young men, much younger brothers of Miriam, began to ask her all kinds of questions together with their father. Gladys telephoned Miriam at her home two streets away and then disappeared into the kitchen, deeming it essential to serve the now larger party with a grand array of food. The men wanted to know all about life in England and the young people spoke of British music groups Isabel had never heard of. Isabel only listened at home in England to the music of the *New Chilean Song Movement* and the later expressions of its famous groups in exile. These young Chileans will hardly know my music, she thought. You could get arrested for having a guitar on the wall in your house, she remembered, let alone caught playing this music. The overwhelming feeling of her experience of exile flooded back to her. She suddenly felt deeply sad and tearful and wanted to run away.

*I can't tell them what it was like and they won't believe me anyway,* she thought. *Getting to the United States or to Europe they think is a sign of success and what all young people dream of. To live in London you had 'arrived' and you must be rich,* she knew the boys were thinking, and that she had achieved all that anyone could desire. *They can't imagine what exile really involves. Of course, there were happy moments, moments of success or joy or satisfaction. But overall the aching hole of loss never leaves you.*

Isabel was desperate to wipe her immediate feelings from her mind. She determined she had to pull herself out from what seemed as cold and unpleasant a feeling as a foggy snow blizzard in a London street at night. She tried to answer a few questions with superficial remarks and her oft-used sarcasm about exile came out. She hadn't gone to England for the weather or because the English are so good at making cheeses. Isabel regretted immediately the bitter sting in her voice and knew she was dragging out the old shields to protect herself. The immediate tension she felt was alleviated for her, though the others felt the sharpness. She hoped she would be able to express a bit more to Miriam later.

Just then a voice was heard from the hall screaming her name. Miriam rushed in and hugged her tightly. Tears poured down both their faces. The questions began again. How was she? What was she doing for her work? How was her life? Was she married? Had she any children? Why had she come back? What was the point? She'd made it out, why should she want to come back?

"You don't understand that I was desperate to be in my country again," snapped Isabel, but she felt she had better not continue. She knew they couldn't see that she had grieved every moment of her waking life for what she had lost, what she had left behind, what she had hoped for, for her country and for her own future. In the uncomfortable silence that followed her outburst, Isabel began thinking that they did not know what it was like if they were not touched directly by the violent repression or perhaps they don't want to know. *They've kept their heads down, got on with their lives and they still think that's what they must do. I must calm down. Who can blame them? At least their father is alive. Mine is not. I want to scream,* she cried inwardly.

The lull in the conversation was broken by everyone suddenly starting to move about the room. Younger family members started to lay the table and carry dishes from the kitchen. Gladys appeared red-cheeked and with arms laden with dishes. *This family is generous and good,* thought Isabel, *but we're so different now.* Miriam and Isabel were so close at school, at least, until Isabel got more involved politically and into the voluntary work. When she reflected on it she remembered that they had seen little of each other out of school time from their mid-teens, when the Allende Government had come about. Isabel wondered if she was being mean in not telling them more about England. *I want to forget about London, England and Julian for a time and pretend I have always been here. I want to be fully Chilean again. The food preparations appearing on the table will help me. I can indulge myself in all these familiar dishes and pretend it is the old days.* She resolved she would try to tell them more of what they wanted to hear later but she found herself thinking that this was not the reunion she expected. *There's a great barrier between us because our worlds are far apart and we can't understand each other's truths.*

Suddenly the door burst open and in rushed two children of preschool age. They both started addressing their mother Miriam at once and then, as they become aware of an unknown person in the room, they simmered down their volume and their excited movements and shyly hid in Miriam's skirt. Their father followed them into the room and Isabel was introduced to them all. Jorge, Mirium's husband was warm and affectionate in greeting everyone in the room. He attended to the children and placed them at the table as everyone was invited to sit down. Isabel found herself next to Jorge and felt more relaxed in his company as he didn't immediately press her with questions.

The food was exceptionally good, as ever when Miriam's mother prepared it and just as Isabel remembered Chilean food. The *ceviche* of raw fish in its lemon juice dressing must have been prepared hours beforehand or last night thought Isabel. The *almejas* were enormous compared to European clams and they looked exquisite. Some were served raw and some were cooked under the grill with a wine dressing and grated cheese. The *locos,* one of the many Pacific shellfish Isabel had not tasted for twenty years, were a delight with their mayonnaise sauce. Gladys had laid out the slices of avocados in circles with tomatoes, peeled of course! Isabel recalled the amazement of British visitors to her home in England when her stepmother peeled the tomatoes. How much more trouble the Chileans were prepared to go to than the British in order to eat well. How much more time was spent preparing and eating food. That, she realised, was something she could tell the company about British culture and the hundreds of preprepared meals in the supermarkets and the takeaways on every corner, all of which invariably disappoint and are fattening, salty and not good for you.

"Most families don't have *nanas* in the home and two parents generally have to work, so the factories producing preprepared meals are meant to replace the servants but it doesn't work well. The more processed the foods are, the worse they are for you and the motivation of the makers is profit not good and nutritious meals. You don't see much of this yet in Chile but you wait a while - when the North Americans have had more time..." Isabel wondered if she'd gone too far again. Then to try to put things right she thought of another story she could tell, of which the spread had reminded her. When she and Julian had been at Staithes near Whitby, Julian had bought a pile of crabs on the quayside from a group of returning fishermen.

"Julian knew I loved shellfish and normally in Britain the price you have to pay for them is a lot and there isn't the variety we have here. We saw a small boat being tied up, on its return to the harbour and the group of fishermen were handing around the crabs they had caught between themselves. They appeared to have finished passing them out but there were more crabs in the bucket and Julian leaned over the quay and asked how much they might sell them for. He was told he could have all that were left for thirty bob and I had no idea what the man was talking about. But Julian handed over some cash and was very excited at what he called a bargain. Well! There were thirteen crabs in all, some huge and some not so big. They would have cost 20,000 *pesos* and we got them for about 1,500 *pesos*. We kept them alive in the hotel room's sink overnight and returned to London the next day to share them with friends, and family and put some in our freezer."

Miriam had wanted to know a lot more about Julian but that would have to wait till another opportunity, Isabel mumbled to her. Gladys began serving a casserole of fish stew - *caudillo de congrio,* a dish to which Pablo Neruda had written an Ode. It was too substantial a platter to call it a soup as it had large slices of the famous pacific fish as well as potatoes, tomato, green and red peppers, leeks, onion, garlic and the secret flavourings that Gladys was so skilled with. Isabel could only guess they included coriander, white wine, oregano and lemon. Miriam brought in the finely chopped lettuce, cut in strips half a centimetre wide and the runner beans which had been cooked earlier and were served cold with spring onion and a dressing. When Isabel was feeling suitably full, fillets of pork arrived together with *pebre,* a coriander and tomato sauce and vital accompaniment to meat. She told them how they regularly made *pebre* in England and all their British friends who visited loved it. Isabel translated for them into *pesos,* the high price of coriander in the famous supermarkets around where she lived and they were astonished. Isabel didn't think they believed her when she said how little quantity you get for your money as well, not like the massive bunches sold here for a few *pesos.* She told them how she'd got to know where the Indian shops were in her part of London and in these, large bunches of coriander could be bought at reasonable prices and these enabled her to make *pebre.*

"All the British who try *pebre* ask for the recipe," she said, but she hoped they were beginning to understand that it was very expensive living in England and that the exiles were not living in luxury. On leaving Miriam's family home, Isabel was overwhelmed by the warmth and affection they showed and their many insistences that she would be with them again very soon. Isabel planned a day with Miriam when the children would be at the *Jardin Infantil* and they could "really talk to each other" as Miriam felt was absolutely necessary.

-oOo-

At home that night Isabel began reflecting on the meeting with the family. *Perhaps I've come too soon after the plebiscite that said "No" to Pinochet. People have not yet woken up and Pinochet is still so powerful. I wonder if I was too quick to judge them? Do I resent those who lived under the dictatorship and who survived without being directly touched by its violent repression?* She knew well enough the fear and the pressure in trying to live unnoticed under an authoritarian regime where any petty official or soldier could weald his arbitrary power at any moment against you. She had lived through it for six years until she felt she could not stand it a moment longer. It was hard she thought, to imagine living with that repression for seventeen years.

Miriam and Isabel met up again a few days later. They had agreed to meet soon after Miriam would leave the children at the nursery so that they would have a full morning ahead of them to "properly talk and share their news," said Miriam.

"There are very big changes that have taken place and I don't like all that I see," said Isabel in response to Miriam's first enquiry. "I think we had something more beautiful before or at least we were trying to develop a caring concern for one another," she said, rather testing the water with Miriam. "I can see the developments now toward a consumer society and a materialist concern that we never had before. Showing off your wealth was never in evidence before, even by the better off. Now the middle class is learning 'to keep up with the Joneses as they say in England. It seems more popular now to make some show of your possessions." Isabel responded to Miriam but she added a question of her own. "Am I being a bit hard? But that is one of my first impressions since I have been back." Miriam actually agreed with her.

"There is more affluence now but there does seem to be a constant competition between some people about their latest tv or HiFi system. I hear the mothers talking at the nursery gate."

"I think all this undermines the collective concern for one another and the ambitions to eliminate poverty and poor housing that we used to have and these problems are still very much here, aren't they? It's obvious there is still a lack of decent quality housing. These were our aspirations before the coup."

"The poverty became more terrible than ever in the early years after the coup. Perhaps now there is a better standard of living for most people and they want to enjoy it and don't think of hiding it."

"There are more consumer goods, electrical especially. I remember the poverty, the things not available after to coup, the people struggling. The country's growth rate has been spectacular in recent years but the inequalities are clear to see. The concern we used to have for one another is definitely not the flavour now..."

"Do you remember how women felt they could not even wear trousers after the coup?" asked Mirium. "They said we might be in trouble if we did."

"Yes, women were arrested simply because they were wearing trousers! Trousers were too modern, too assertive and too threatening to the cowardly men who didn't want women to have equality. The Regime had the typical fascist attitudes toward women's place and role." Isabel pondered what great strides had been made, previous to the coup, in women's equality. How women had been participating politically and asserting their rights and their capacities in this very conservative and traditional society. But she didn't want to keep on too heavily with the theme with Mirium. She could see the consequences of this twenty-year setback and knew that the shadow of the military dictatorship still hung over everything. "The sad thing is," she said, "that progress to greater rights for women will not now continue from where we left off when the military coup interrupted everything. The setback has been huge and many rights and arguments have to be won all over again."

Mirium didn't seem to want to respond to this. She felt her life was busy enough and however much she might agree she couldn't see herself getting involved in such a campaign. "Jorge is very decent, you know, and says he wants equality of men and women. But he's not keen on my going back to work when the children are both at school and I want to start a whole new career. He feels it's his job to provide for me. So we shall see! Now, you promised to tell me all about Julian. Come on now."

Isabel wanted to say that she didn't know where she was with Julian or where she wanted to be. *Perhaps that has been the problem,* she thought. *Perhaps I haven't been committed, as Julian has said I haven't.*

"Come on. Has there been a problem which is why he's not with you on this trip to Chile?" Mirium asked with a kindly smile after waiting for a reply. "Tell me how you met."

"I met Julian at University when I finally got to go there at age 25. We met at the Politics Society meeting when they had a speaker from Amnesty International. I was impressed that a student of social work was interested in international affairs and then it turned out his first degree was in Politics and he was passionately committed politically and interested to know more about Chile and what we had tried to create under Allende. He'd been a volunteer for Shelter, a homeless charity and helped to furnish houses allocated for Chilean refugees. Well, I was smitten. He looked all right too, I mean I was deeply attracted to him. We did have some very happy times getting to know each other."

"Things have gone wrong since?"

"I was frightened of involvement with an English person. What about all my desperate longing to come home one day? I had said I would never get involved with a British guy or rather, with a non-Chilean. How would anyone not Chilean understand how I felt about what had happened here? I had to think long and hard but I really did mean it when I said I was prepared to stay in England forever. That was only right if I was going to make a commitment."

"Of course."

"Julian did seem to appreciate what we were trying to build here. He appeared happy to hear my Chilean songs all the time, as much as I did. I didn't even have to worry about imposing my music in a foreign language on him. He began learning Spanish through the songs and said he liked the music. He said the words had a political purpose and he valued that. They were not just superficial love songs like most pop music. Julian liked the sound of the music too and going to the concerts in London of the various Chilean groups in exile in France and Italy.

"But I don't think Julian could ever really understand how or why I had completely withdrawn from the world when we first arrived in England. I never told Julian how I hated everything I saw around me and most of all the cold, the eternal cold that bit into my bones. I hid, literally, under the blankets, but emotionally too under tight wraps to avoid knowing anything about Britain or developing the little English I had. I longed only to be able to come back home. Then I realised I was leaving everything to Mamadre and it must have been just as bad for her as for me. She fed me and comforted me and I don't know how she managed shopping and paying bills and dealing with the outside world. She made our home a little corner of Chile, that awful

29

cold, damp council flat, with rusting metal window frames. It was the only place where I existed for months on end, at the beginning."

"Then you decided to try to make something good of the opportunity of being there?"

"Well I didn't see it as an opportunity but Eugenio, my step-brother persuaded me to sign up for the English class he'd registered for and Mamadre was so supportive. She made it easy for me and I realised I had to push myself to get out of the depressed state I was in. Mamadre set about getting my school exams accepted in the UK and eventually I applied to go to University. I hadn't wanted to apply for a long time. I really believed I'd be coming home soon and I had no motivation to study there. But eventually, I gained a History of Art degree and I absolutely loved the experience and of course, I met Julian. It was all wonderful. Julian would take me to many parts of London I did not know and we talked endlessly of Chile and of British politics and world events. We were very happy and seemed to get on together so well. We had similar values and believed in what a government like Allende's could achieve. Julian was interested in art too and we went to many galleries together. When I had university work to do we would work at his flat with my Chilean music playing and he'd be studying Spanish whilst I was writing an essay. I studied as many Chilean artists and their works as I possibly could as well as of course, all the other painters and sculptors whose work I love."

"I should have loved that too. Maybe that gives me an idea of what I can do when the children are a bit older. I need to talk to you about that another time, but tell me now, could you get a job with that degree?"

"After the degree, I studied for a Documentary Film Making Certificate and then I got a job with an agency that produces such films. I'm hoping I can make a film here that the agency will help promote, though, of course, I had to resign my job to come here for a long stay but I have contacts and hopes of getting back in - if I go back."

"What do you mean, 'if you go back? What about Julian? You will go back to him won't you?"

"Honestly, I don't know right now. I just want to concentrate on being Chilean again. I mean I've never felt anything but Chilean but I want to become absorbed again in this country. The truth is right now I feel like an outsider here just as I felt like an outsider in England. I need to keep a critical awareness to try to analyse what is going on but I think that keeps me on the fringe looking in rather than letting me relax into enjoying being here. Perhaps I can't fit in as I felt I did before."

"I hope you can fit in again. You know you are very welcome at our house. *Mi casa es tu casa*. But tell me, are you writing to Julian and keeping in touch? You haven't told him it's all over, have you?"

"No, no I've not. That wasn't my intention and he tried to understand why I needed to come alone. Yes, I do want to go back to him but I have this overwhelming need to throw myself into being here again for a while at least. I don't feel comfortable with 'me' anywhere at present. Am I still looking for who I am? Do you know what I mean?"

"I'm trying to but maybe there will be quite a long while of adjustment. As you said, you've changed and Chile has changed. Take it slowly, little by little rather than rushing at a critique of the changes here, that clearly get you worked up."

"Yes, you are probably right. But many things have made me so angry. The blind man begging in the street, for example. How can that be? Why don't state benefits give him a dignified living? What we were trying to build before would have respected his need and his disability. We wanted to respect the sanctity of every person, knowing everyone deserved a decent minimum in housing, education, living and working conditions. This country's rich resources would be fairly distributed as they grew. Now this country reminds me of Thatcher's Britain where the gap between rich and poor has grown so great and the harshness of the inequality is so palpable if you care to look at the areas of poverty. I've seen first-hand the lives of people in old and inadequate housing in a place like Brixton, where I first lived in Britain. I've seen what it's like where Julian works, with the disadvantaged in Tower Hamlets. I've learned plenty from him. Chile seems to me now to have the same atmosphere of injustice and the hard-bitten, uncaring lack of concern in the midst of the first shoots of affluence for some and the flowering consumerism."

"There you go again, getting worked up when I think most people would say they are glad they are better off now than they used to be."

"The papers tell me that delinquency, crime, family breakdown and drug abuse are growing too. Actually of course it is worse here in Chile.

31

At least in Britain, there is the safety net of the Welfare State for all but the illegals - there's the minimum to avoid the greatest extremes of poverty. I've seen in the right-wing media talk of scroungers but they are ignorant of how humane and how civilised this minimum of a Welfare State makes a society. All the British should value the Welfare State as a fundamental characteristic of a decent culture. They are so proud of their country as "the best in the world" as they too often claim about everything. Being out of work or disabled or punished by a recession could happen to any one of us. Being underpaid, uneducated or homeless is what we should all see as "there but for the grace of God go I" as the Brits would say. They are stupid to be letting that safety net slip away under Tories. They are losing a sense of community and solidarity which Julian tells me was much greater before the Thatcher years. He regrets I've only lived in Britain in those Tory years when inequality has grown. But it has prepared me for what I can now see has happened here in Chile."

"There you go again analysing everything and getting emotional. Calm down and tell me more about what has gone wrong with Julian."

"Ok. Well, I was genuine about my commitment to him, even if it kept me in England and we began living together. It was loving and beautiful at first. I softened his rather 'male' flat with a feminine touch and some Chilean pictures and rugs. After a while, many issues became frictions. Something always seemed to crop up to cause a misunderstanding. There was always an issue we should discuss, a matter to deal with from our different viewpoints and somehow the communication just didn't happen or it went off with an exploding row. I know now I was angry but I couldn't admit it then and he said I was aggressive, verbally I mean." Isabel didn't want to say aloud the further thoughts she was thinking. She'd always felt the need to protect herself - from what, she couldn't quite say. She had withdrawn, she had disappeared or just didn't speak and that had provoked such anger in Julian. "I used to feel desperate pain when I separated myself off from him but eventually, I think I just did it too often, I didn't care what effect it had. Then I wanted all the more to escape or close myself off," Isabel couldn't admit to Mirium, but she thought to herself, *I pretended to be proud, even when I felt so bad at holding out, refusing to speak, as if to justify I was right.*

"Arrogant and stubborn he called me," said Isabel out loud. "My grandmother used to say the same, so he was probably right. Things seemed to get so difficult at times."

"Why didn't you go to a Latin country? I think it would have suited you better."

"And then I would never have met this 'nice Englishman' who made me want to tear my hair out at times. I'm sure you're right. England offered the first refugee route out to Mamadre. General Franco had not long died and the Spanish were working out a new constitution and their future was very uncertain, smeared as it was by an attempted *coup d'état*. So going to Spain didn't appear to be an option. Perhaps we should have waited for the chance to go to France or Italy. I didn't want to learn English. I didn't like it and I refused at first to go to classes."

Mirium suggested a walk around the park. She was keen to pin Isabel down to another meeting but Isabel made excuses though promising to see her again soon. It had been good to see Mirium and they'd been able to talk freely as they had as teenagers. However, Isabel explained she had plans in place to see other school friends and they shared some memories of their schoolmates before they left each other that morning. Also there were people Isabel had not kept in touch with but with whom she must try to make contact - the volunteers she had worked with, the families living in the *barrio* Manuel Rodriguez, and contacts her stepbrother had given her. There's another side to Chile I know, she thought: my closest friends, even people within my mother's church...I'll find them, those who made the old Chile flower...I'll find them again and I'll see what they are doing now.

-oOo-

That night in bed the conversation with Mirium went through her mind again. Had she been too outright in her comments about Chile, she wondered. Had it seemed rude to a woman with a comfortable existence, just trying to do what is best for her family? Isabel had wanted to say a great deal more. She had the distinct feeling that Chile was now like a kettle about to blow off its lid but some heavy weight of the past was holding it down, but only just. People were avoiding the truth, holding it back, frightened of the explosive consequences of taking off the lid. She knew the Truth and Reconciliation Commission had examined the crimes of the dictatorship and these could no longer be denied. Though its mandate had been limited, 95% of deaths investigated were attributed to the military. The current elected President had 'apologised' for the crimes and talked of reparations but no prosecutions had happened yet to any military person. Nor will they, thought Isabel, with Pinochet still Head of the Armed Forces and his sickening constitution. She knew he had it written into his new Constitution that no official of the national or any local government could be investigated for any action taken during the period of Pinochet's Presidency. It was so blatantly a total cover-up for any crime, corruption, killing or misdemeanour that it was hard to believe it could be included in a constitution, even one of a dictatorship.

*Julian used to talk about being transparent in our relationship as politicians have to be,* recalled Isabel. *If it was hard for me to be accountable and admit when I was wrong, how much less likely were the politicians, the executive puppets of the military and the military themselves, to ever admit anything with a constitution like that to protect them? The Truth Commission wasn't even allowed to name those they found guilty of crimes,* she thought, getting emotional again. Isabel also knew that many disappearances still hadn't been investigated and those that had survived, the imprisoned and tortured had not had the crimes against them acknowledged yet. It seemed to her also that many of the population didn't want to believe the revelations of the Commission anyway. They appeared to actually want a whitewash and to turn their backs on the suffering. *I fear my mother is one of them,* she thought and that pained her a great deal. Pinochet and the military leadership had just dismissed as untrue the report of the Commission and nothing had happened to them. *It's like you give the silent majority more evidence that they were wrong to support him and it pushes them further to defend him and repeat his propaganda of justification. At times I feel I'm more frustrated here even than in exile in England and I never expected to feel like this.*

*I must get this sense of frustration into the documentary I want to make. I need to show the propaganda of the regime and the extent it is believed, how the lies and the support manifest themselves and in some way I must suggest the fear that still exists. What a challenge! How do I show these abstract notions? It isn't going to be easy this task. I must show also that the Truth Commission has not dealt with any cases of the 'disappeared' so its job is very far from done. That would illustrate a painful source of frustration. I need to have persons in the video who can prove a disappearance, for which there has been no official recognition. That's true of my father's case and I want his case recognised.*

-oOo-

Esperanza was keen that her daughter should go with her to the *Fiestas Patrias* Independence Day celebrations at her church and she managed to convince Isabel that the events would remind her of her childhood in Chile and that it would be good for her to recall some happy memories and not just sad ones she seemed only to have indulged in so far. She had returned angry or upset from her visits and had been forced to share a little with her mother when clearly troubled on her return. This would be different, promised her mother and Isabel wanted to say that she didn't mind being reminded of sad matters - this was the reality she had to face and to grieve for. She had to re-live the memories and she and everyone must never forget, she wanted to demand. But she decided not to create another argument with her mother, knowing she wouldn't really understand and she agreed to go to the various church events with her.

Firstly, church members were to go to the local *hogar de ancianos* to sing and dance with the elderly residents. Six women of the church and six men were dressed in traditional costumes, the men with beautifully woven ponchos and the women in lacy layers and they danced the *Cueca,* a traditional Chilean dance, in the large living room of the old peoples' home with all the armchairs pushed back around the walls of the room. *Cueca* dancers always hold a handkerchief and flick and drag it through the air with the swaying and turning of their bodies. The lovely traditional sound certainly animated the residents and some of them were fit enough to gently dance the *cueca* too, taking up invitations from each of the dancers in traditional clothes. They had all made sure they had their handkerchiefs ready too as these were essential. The Padre was there joining in and two guitarists and an accordion player made the music for them. After the dancing, much singing and clapping took place as all the well-known traditional songs of the country were played and sung. Isabel thought they must have had the full repertoire before the evening was out and she had to admit it was a lovely experience of Chilean warmth. She was glad also to be reminded of all the songs she'd known from long ago and had almost forgotten about.

The next day was Independence Day 18th September, and a gathering of all the church members was to take place at the home of the parents of one of the more affluent members of the congregation. They lived on the edge of the city in a rural setting with a large garden - ideal for a gathering of more than 100 church members and all the extended family of the owners. Many members, including Esperanza, brought food for the shared *almuerzo.* A traditional drink was served called *mote con huesillo,* dried peaches cooked in sugar, water with cinnamon and mixed with husked wheat. The twelve dancers were there in their traditional dress, dancing the *cueca* with the guitarists and the accordion player accompanying them yet again. Others, including Isabel, joined in the dancing and another type of music was blasted out of a ghetto blaster - modern North American and European pop music that had become internationally famous.

Isabel asked the young man playing the music if he had any tapes of the famous Chilean groups of the *New Song Movement,* and she was told they hadn't much except a tape of *Los Jaivas.* If she had any he would be willing to play them. Isabel had brought a few tapes in the hope of them getting a hearing. Most people had nothing more sophisticated than cassette players to play music on in Chile at that time and she was right the ghetto blaster would do tapes. Isabel had brought her own little portable CD player from England but tapes were still on sale in Chile and she had a few for gatherings like this. She thought she'd better start with a very well-known group that they must have heard of. She offered an *Inti-Illimani* tape.

"The group had been on tour in Europe when the Coup happened and they weren't allowed back into the country," she ventured to say. The young man seemed interested. "The group were only allowed back into Chile after the 'No' vote."

"I helped with that a bit," said Felipe, introducing himself at the same time. He spoke quietly, "My parents didn't like it but we had to get a 'No' vote and get a change."

"Absolutely! I'm so glad to meet you. I'd like to hear more about your involvement. I wasn't in the country then. You know that one of *Inti-Illimani* songs was *Venceremos,* about winning and overcoming, had been the song taken up by the *Popular Unity* in their campaign to bring Allende to the Presidency. I was involved in that campaign way back then. I bet you had to be much more careful than we did then and it wasn't easy to campaign for 'No.'"

"No, it wasn't. Any large gatherings were broken up by the police. Any posters we put up - at night, secretly - were torn down. We had to be careful taking leaflets door to door but that was all we could do. No TV time was allowed us you know. But word did get around, especially among the younger people. We had our networks just like when we passed around the music of the exiled groups. We did listen to *Inti-Illimani* and *Los Jaivas* and others when we were teenagers. Some parents tried to stop it. Mine were not keen because they said it could be dangerous and so we had to play it quietly until we got ear speakers. Then we'd be together in a group of friends, all listening and laughing and signalling to each other but no one could hear us."

"Wow! That's so good. You kept our music alive. Do you know the origin of the name?" Felipe shook his head. "*Inti* is the Sun God of the Quechua people, descendants of the Incas and *Illimani* is the name of a Bolivian mountain in the Aymara language, another Andean language in the north of Chile but mostly spoken in Bolivia. This music was authentic Chilean culture and you and your friends kept it alive. That is so great to know." Felipe put on for Isabel one of the tapes she had but after a few songs into an album, the man whose house it was, turned it off. He said it was time to eat. Some family members clearly weren't happy with the music and later the pop music and the salsa was resumed and the much-acclaimed abroad *Inti-Illimani* was quietly forgotten.

*Perhaps the saddest thing of all,* Isabel was thinking late that night whilst playing her music on her CD player with earphones, *is the tremendous division in Chilean society. I do not believe the country was ever so divided in the past. Right and left will naturally disagree but now there is a massive chasm where each side cannot tolerate a thing of the other. Felipe told me there were people there today who could not bear any talk of the dictatorship and they deny anything terrible happened. They believe a strong man was needed to save the country from chaos and ruin. He wasn't surprised they found an excuse to turn my music off. On the other hand, there are the poorer people who really know what suffering the dictator and his regime caused and both sides are so angry with each other. I must represent this division in my film but how am I going to do that? When the Truth and Reconciliation Commission has found the regime guilty of causing deaths, who would speak in support of the regime? Can I show the hidden power they have in some way? They don't admit their support, they just enjoy their power silently. How can I get to talk to some of the businesses that have got rich? Maybe I could put a microphone under the nose of a chief executive entering his office. He'll refuse to speak but his actions will speak and my commentary will speak.*

*People have to take one side or the other, even if they were not directly affected. They may try to remain indifferent but morally they have to choose. There is no way the human rights abuses can be defended, no justification for the unaccountable government and the lack of democracy and if anyone doesn't accept that, then they are one with the abusers,* concluded Isabel in disgust. *I know I was aiming at portraying the subtleties but injustice has to be adamantly opposed or it triumphs. That is what has happened and I can't condone it in my video. I think I should take the themes of what is wrong with the constitution as a way of illustrating there can be no transition to democracy as they pretend without a new constitution.*

# Chapter 3

F inding herself in a *micro* bus again, which noisily rattled along the squared network of streets, Isabel was on her way to see if she could make contact with her step-brother's friend and some of those she had known when she had done voluntary work as a teenager. She wondered if the little corner shop that had been at the heart of the community in Manuel Rodriguez would still be there and she was heartened to find that it was. The *micro* stopped just outside and Isabel stood a moment, eyeing closely the individuals around the street and especially those entering the shop. She wasn't sure if she was just wishing she would recognise someone or just taking in the feel of this typical *barrio popular*. It looked so like a great many poorer areas all over Chile. Every city and every town had its workers' areas and Santiago had a great many of them but the degree to which they were so similar in all the length of Chile was remarkable. *It must be the tiny bungalow-style homes cheek by cheek, whether they are brick built or wooden, that is the key factor of this resemblance,* Isabel thought. *What an incredible similarity exists in these kinds of barrios, throughout a country that is so long with towns and cities thousands of kilometres apart, but at the same time, the people find themselves so monumentally divided and disunited.*

Isabel approached the corner shop and its window displayed only handwritten signs in white on the glass, offering the bargains available. These were clearly to tempt you past the dowdy exterior that had obviously not seen a tin of paint since Isabel's last time there. Inside the shop, the shelves of goods extended quite a long way back and it did appear to be well-stocked with a good variety of groceries as well as fresh fruits and vegetables, newly baked bread and a range of hams and salamis. What surprised Isabel was the large upright fridge full of colas and fizzy drinks and the shelves of plastic bottled drinks beyond. There was not a natural fruit juice to be found in the fridge - cold, just as she fancied it, but she did find on the shelves, an individual-sized container with a straw attached, of what was described as pineapple nectar, which had to do her. She began thinking, *all those sugared sodas that are so bad for you. Even this so-called nectar, with water and sugar added, is not pure juice. These sugary, fizzy drinks didn't use to be here in my time but how symbolic they are. All that suffering and loss of life, just to get things that are bad for you on the shelves to extend the markets of the North American companies!* Isabel despaired at the wickedness, yet again felt her anger rising and had to stop herself from screaming, not for the first time since her return to Chile.

Isabel made herself turn again to the task at hand and she wanted to see if she recognised the face of the shopkeeper, who had his back to her, cutting processed meat on a slicing machine. She didn't recognise him but then his wife came from the back store and her's was a face Isabel knew. Isabel began to explain who she was and gradually her face lit up with delight and surprise. Veronica rushed around the counter to give Isabel a big hug.

She said, "This is my husband Mateo." He had turned on hearing his wife's excitement, and he greeted Isabel. "My first husband was killed," she whispered in Isabel's ear. Veronica took Isabel to the back room and began making tea for them both. Very soon they were recalling people they could remember who had lived in the *barrio* in Isabel's time and she was getting all the news. Some had been taken in early morning raids by soldiers and never returned, some managed to get out and find work elsewhere, and a few still lived here. There were few remaining who had been children that Isabel could recall looking after, whose mothers were still around, according to Veronica. Most of the names she could remember had been teenagers in Isabel's time and not many of them were now in the neighbourhood but Veronica was able to tell Isabel where to find one or two. Everyone always knew everyone else in those poor, close-knit communities and Isabel was soon finding her way around the streets of the cramped little, single-storey homes, each with its own small front patio. At least the area had been 'adopted' and now there were pavements, street lights and electric cables strung across from poles to each house. Isabel recalled how this area had been only composed of small wooden homes and dirt streets on land taken by the rural poor but now as well as pavements and street lights almost every little house had an extension or two. These developments made almost all the houses touch one another but each one was of individual style.

Isabel remembered a big family in a corner house, where one of the sons had been very involved with the community activities she used to come to help with. He was a youth group leader in training with the volunteers who came to assist the local priest working with the children and teenagers. Recalling the mother, Patricia, Isabel smiled at the thought of such a warm and welcoming woman who had been delighted when Isabel offered to look after her younger children whilst she went to the women's literacy group. She had such an intelligent gleam in her eye and wasn't going to miss an opportunity like that. There hadn't been schools for all children when she was a child, not in the faraway villages. She'd had to help her mother milk the goats and grow maize and root vegetables. When a local boy had promised to take her to the city when they were married, it seemed a wonderful promise of escape. Life of course had been rather different from that dream, trying to survive in a city *toma* when one child after another arrived, but there had generally been work for her husband, insecure and low-paid though it was. There were joyful times too, cooking with other women in the communal kitchen to celebrate special days or any excuse for a get-together and a singsong.

Isabel eventually found Patricia, not in the same corner house but in a very little bungalow a few streets away. Now she was in her 60s, widowed because her husband, as well as two sons, had been taken away in an early morning raid by soldiers soon after the coup d'état. Patricia had been devastated and had had to go to work to keep her younger children fed.

"I had to travel an hour each way to a *barrio alto*, the only work available being as *una nana,*" she said as they reminisced about old times. "I had to do all the cleaning and cook *almuerzo* for a family of six, including grandma. I asked my neighbours to keep an eye on my children, but they were largely left to fend for themselves before and after school.

"I couldn't get home until about 4.00 pm," said Patricia, "and then I'd

41

have to start preparing *almuerzo* for us, which the children were desperate for by that time. School finishes at 2.00 pm so that the children can go home to have lunch and I always felt bad it was late for them but I couldn't help it. They took sandwiches for a mid-morning snack at school, which of course, I had to get the children preparing for the next morning after our meal was finally eaten and cleared up. There was always something one of them needed from the local shop and then there was food to think about for the next day, so I'd often send one or two children out to Veronica's shop with quite a list when I had the money. I never minded the children clamouring for what they wanted to eat because they helped to get their sandwiches ready. There was a lot of activity until all the jobs were done. The house always seemed full of life." Now Patricia was alone and in poor health and Isabel guessed her pension would be absolutely minimal. Her story was so like that of thousands of other women in Chile.

"Patricia, I know it is painful for you to talk about all that has happened to you and your family since the coup d'état but what do you think of the argument that the country needed a strong man and he saved the country from chaos?"

"I never expected you to say that."

"No, no I'm not agreeing with that point of view, it's just that I hear it put quite often and as a person who really suffered the consequences of the military coup, I wanted to give the opportunity to you to answer that."

"It's hard for me to remain calm to respond to that - but I have challenged this thinking whenever I have heard it said. It has to be corrected. Sometimes a politician comes into the area and talks this nonsense. I tell them the only chaos was created by the powerful who opposed *Popular Unity*. The lorry drivers' blockade brought shortages and massive holdups on the main roads and it was ordered by the owners of companies to cause chaos, shortages and fear amongst the people. The newspapers too were full of lies about the Allende government. They always vilify good people. Anyway, nothing justifies the seizing of innocent citizens and their imprisonment, torture and disappearance. Nothing."

Isabel put her arms out to hold Patricia's shoulders and then embraced her, their heads bowed against one another. Eventually, Isabel explained that she was making a film about the current situation in Chile and that she wanted to include commonly held attitudes and counteract them. "Would you be willing to talk on camera, just saying what you have told me, to answer that point of view?"

"I think you should ask our women's group to do that. All of us together would be more impressive than just me and many of them suffered as I did. That is why I like to meet with them because they know how I feel. Together the group would be powerful. It's not all unhappy talk either. We try to look after each other and make each other laugh and have good times."

Isabel thought the women's group was a wonderful opportunity and arranged when she could return with her video camera. With more contacts and leads from Patricia, Isabel went on to try to track down Eugenio's friend and others she thought might be helpful to her film project. Groups of children hung around her and asked her who she was as she walked the streets of the *barrio*. Isabel chatted and laughed with them and obtained some street names out of them, as various streets appeared to have lost their name boards or perhaps never had them. Finally, she arrived at the house she was seeking and she wondered what sort of reception she would get, not knowing these people before and recognising the fear in which many people still lived. That's one of the greatest damages the military dictatorship has done - the lack of trust amongst people, the caution that dampens their natural, spontaneous warmth. How can I represent that in the video? Perhaps I could ask the women's group if they thought it was true and to talk about that too. I could ask them as well about their employment opportunities and what they thought of their children's education and job chances.

She wondered, when knocking on the door of the family she was seeking, if she would be regarded with suspicion in a barrio like this. Police spies had come in many different forms in the past and the people had learned to trust no one. The first encounter went better than she could have hoped. Isabel explained she was Eugenio's half-sister and she'd come from England. She was welcomed in and a lot of catching up on news began around the table. Naturally, food soon began to appear and Beatrice insisted that she stay to eat with them. Miguel, her husband made an extra place at the table and their oldest child began bringing in various dishes. Eugenio's friend Miguel had been imprisoned for six years and had lived hand to mouth ever since, doing whatever insecure and unskilled work he could find. He had been on the point of going to University, like Eugenio, when the *golpe* came about. It had always been tough, to get into University from a working-class background after attending the local state school but he had worked very hard and the priest had got him some extra help. The *Popular Unity* government gave grants and more places with support to people like him. Isabel recalled that new universities were created to give working-class students the opportunities that only middle-class young people had had in the past. The necessary backups included additional tuition, subsidised canteens, health care and dentistry and grants for fees and accommodation.

"It's practically impossible, since the coup," said Miguel, "for students from an area like this to go into higher education. Pupils here are never up to standard compared with middle-class young people with the privileged private schools available to them, or even up to the level of the better-funded state schools in the middle-class areas. Things had begun to be fairer under Allende whose government had given more money to state schools. But all of that was reversed of course by the military regime."

Beatrice butted in on one of her trips from the kitchen, "In Allende's time primary schools became available for all children, even in the remotes parts and they gave the children milk to drink every day and free school meals for those who needed them. Now it is really hard for a student in a state school in a poor area to pass the University entrance exams. They just haven't had the preparation for the exams, however hard they work. In richer areas, the money the local authority has from the government can be added to through local taxes but in poorer areas, they don't have the resources to do this, so even the state schools vary in quality enormously. Even the buildings look different. In the popular *barrios,* the schools are more run down and not maintained, the classes are larger and the teachers are fewer."

"True," said Miguel. "And there are many schools still where the teachers have to work a second shift with a new class of pupils in the afternoon, having already worked nearly a full school day from 8.00 am to 1.00 pm with their first class. They have no time for preparation. *Almuerzo* is a rushed affair and then they have to begin the school day all over again. That happens in primary and secondary schools around here still nowadays." Miguel paused as if contemplating the enormity of what this meant for state school teachers' lives. "And they are not very well paid either. What chance then had I, on being released from prison, of getting the opportunity to study and go to university? There were no grants. I also discovered the military government had banned all courses of the type I had wanted to pursue. All the universities' social sciences departments were swept away by the regime. The dictatorship didn't want anyone studying dangerous subjects like politics, sociology and social work, which might lead them questioning the actions or inaction of their government or let them debate what might be the state's duty or its responsibility, not to mention the human rights of its citizens."

Isabel explained she was making a film about Chile in the transition to democracy. "Would you be willing on camera to explain exactly what you have told me about the ongoing lack of opportunities for working-class people?" Miguel looked at his wife, "Yes, both of you," she added quickly.

"It would have to be with the camera at an angle so we couldn't be recognised. I'm sorry but that's the only way to be safe. The outside world needs to know, but it would have to be anonymous," said Miguel.

"Absolutely, I understand,"

"I was very young, only 16, when I became a member of the MIR - the Revolutionary Left Movement. You know it's a Marxist/Leninist revolutionary party and we did not form part of the *Popular Unity* Government of Allende but we did support *Popular Unity's* success in gaining office. We continued our work to create popular power amongst local communities, demanding their rights, expressing their needs and developing local leadership. As a result, the MIR was especially targeted by the death squads after the coup and our members were particularly the subjects of extrajudicial executions and disappearances. I was 18 when the coup blew our world apart but at that age, I was not any kind of leading figure in our group, fortunately, so I guess that's how I survived when many people I knew did not."

"I can't imagine what going through six years of imprisonment in dire conditions, cruelty and torture must have been like."

"I learned a lot from the other prisoners in the concentration camp. It was a university of political education even though we had no books of any sort for learning such things and we had to be incredibly careful that our conversations were not overheard or understood by our guards. My political awareness grew a lot and my determination to work for a better society was strengthened. You know, of the books we were allowed, there

45

were many of Shakespeare's plays. With the guards too ignorant to realise how political such books were, we were able to produce a Shakespeare play amongst ourselves in the prison. We had in our group, university graduates and lecturers, teachers, actors, journalists, writers, the lot! I remember the courage and strength of so many of them and the devastation when a few were dragged out from time to time and never returned to our overcrowded cells. Their shouts and screams could be heard though, from not far away. One Christmas we were allowed to stage Hamlet for the other prisoners' entertainment. They understood the hidden messages, the critique of leaders, and the subtle hints at malpractice. There were good times - times when our humanity triumphed."

"What was it like when you were finally released?"

"Bea' was very patient with me. I lost my temper far too easily but the frustration was enormous. It was almost as much as when I was first locked up. I tried desperately to secure a reasonably creative and satisfying job rather than just the sort of manual work you have to do for other people. I did hard physical work to save money and then I travelled Chile to try to secure a decent job. Every professional job I applied for - like I tried to get into journalism and into law firms, but apart from my lack of qualifications and my unexplained six years, I am certain I am blacklisted. However modest the local paper or magazine and however obscure the backwater law firm I approached to be a junior apprentice, hundreds of kilometres from the capital, I never could get any acceptance.

"I didn't have a *pituto* - your family has to know the right people and be in the right social class. It was always the tradition here but now it's worse than ever. I travelled up and down the country looking for a chance to get started and always ended up returning home, here to Manuel Rodriguez to go back to painting or gardening or factory work just to survive and help my mother and then later Beatrice. I still dream of taking Bea and the family to a better future somewhere else but so far it's not worked out."

Isabel had much to write to Eugenio about and of course, she gave Miguel details so he could write. Isabel had one more question to ask before leaving.

"There was a semi-famous leading member of the MIR who was a cinematographer, Jorge Muller Silva. Did you ever know him?"

"I've heard of him but I didn't know him. He was one of the disappeared whose death had never been explained nor declared as a fact. He might have come from Concepción, as many of the creators of the MIR did. That's where it started amongst the student group there."

As Isabel was leaving, she planned with the couple when they could do some filming together. Miguel asked her quietly "Will you let me take you to meet a friend that would be a useful contact for your search for what is really going on in Chile. He knows a lot of people in Concepción. It's someone I'm sure you would be glad to know but I can't tell you any more about him at this stage. I have to ask him first."

-oOo-

A few days after filming the couple, the neighbourhood and the women's group, Isabel had a phone call to her mother's home and it was Miguel saying he'd set up the meeting that he knew would interest her. With no further information than she had the chance to travel to the south, she would have to go on trust or she would miss a valuable opportunity and Isabel agreed she wasn't about to do that. She was told to bring a little luggage, overnight essentials and a few changes of clothes. The first thing was to have a cover story for her mother. She would tell her that she'd arranged to see an old friend in Concepción and that she especially wanted to see the murals at the university there and in nearby Chillán.

"I wrote about both of them in my Uni exams," she told her mother. "They were donated by Mexico and executed by Mexican artists as part of the restoration and solidarity offered by Mexico to Chile after two different earthquakes - 1939 in Chillán and 1960 in Concepción. The murals are in the Diego Rivera tradition. They portray the high level of cultural development of the Aztecs and Mayas when the Spanish invaded and the cross and the sword are the symbols of Spanish cruelty."

"Now don't start blaming the church for everything again…" her mother interrupted.

"The murals represent the fusion of the Hispanic and American races." Isabel thought she'd better leave it there. Her mother had listened with growing impatience so Isabel decided definitely not to go on to tell her that one of the artists Siqueiros had been implicated in the failed attempt on the life of Leon Trotsky when he was at the house of Diego Rivera in Mexico. She decided just to mention the famous couple.

"*Mama,* Diego Rivera was married to Freda Kahlo, and did you know that they divorced after a tumultuous relationship of ten years and then remarried again a year later in 1940. Sounds a bit familiar," the words slipped from Isabel's mouth. It was the most she'd ever hinted at telling her mother about her relationship in England, which had felt so turbulent and on and off at times but couldn't be let go. Then she hurried herself to make plans for travelling and was relieved her mother seemed prepared to leave it at that. Esperanza actually thought that Isabel might be making a reference to her own marriage and her separation from her father when Isabel was only seven. She might be suggesting that links once made can't easily be dropped or shouldn't be, with children involved. Esperanza didn't want any discussion on that and besides, it was far too long ago, even to think about. She was content not to ask anymore. Isabel thought she must make a more conscious effort to improve her relationship with her mother when she came back from her trip.

"That's not much luggage to take for a couple of weeks", said her mother as Isabel prepared to go the next day.

"I've a few T-shirts, jeans and shorts, underwear and a toothbrush and my cameras - that's enough to be carrying around," replied Isabel trying to sound as casual as she could. "Yes," she assured her mother she'd jumpers and a jacket for the colder south. She had in fact got all she thought was essential for her journey into the unknown. She met Miguel at the central bus station of Santiago - a massive, sprawling, noisy place from which almost every journey to anywhere in that 4200 kilometres long country had to begin, now that the train lines were largely closed. Isabel saw Miguel as she approached the ticket office.

"Where are we going?" She was dying to know but Miguel said he wasn't going anywhere, only she was and he took her to a tiny café within the bus station, one of the hundreds of small businesses just managing to eke out a living from the travellers. They had coffees and then the middle-aged lady behind the counter gave a nod when Miguel looked at her. At this Miguel stood up and beckoned Isabel to follow. They went to the back of the shop, squeezing around the end of the counter and there was a door into a back room. Inside was a man in his 40s, waiting for them. He signalled for them to sit down at the small plastic table with four old wooden stools and then he began firing lots of questions at Isabel. What was she doing in Chile, why had she sought out Miguel, why had she asked about Jorge Muller Silva, how long was she to be in Chile, where was she going whilst in Chile, whom did she know in the UK amongst the refugees? It went on and on and then the questions centred on her political beliefs, values and what contacts could she offer them if they assisted her in her research into political movements in Chile.

Isabel was wondering who her questioner was and why all the secrecy. The Communist Party had just been made legal again in Chile and a woman Gladys Marín had been elected to the most senior post of that party. Isabel was hoping for a contact with the higher echelons of the Communist Party but thought that needn't have to be clandestinely. MIR members might act in this way or perhaps this interrogator was from the *Frente Patriotica Manuel Rodriguez*. She remembered this Popular Front had been formed in 1983 and Isabel knew they had made an almost successful attempt to kill Pinochet when he was still President in 1986. That wasn't knowledge that the government had wanted to escape from the country but it had been impossible to prevent that news from getting out. Pinochet had had to appear on television on the night of the attack to prove he had survived, as rumours ran riot all over the country. Five of his bodyguards were killed and eleven injured and Pinochet and his ten-year-old grandson travelling with him to his country house, survived, with only minor injuries thanks to his chauffeur driving his armour-plated Mercedes Benz car backwards along a mountain road at great speed and under fire. *What a very great pity that attack had failed*, thought Isabel taking a moment's indulgence. Then she decided to ask the man outright if he was one of the *Frente Patriotica Manuel Rodriguez*. It was time she knew something about him.

"No, not now but I was one of those who split with the Front after the failed attack on Pinochet. After the attack, many of us split and now that there is at least a partial return to democracy, I want a peaceful mass civil disobedience uprising of the people and not armed insurrection. Whatever the rights and wrongs of the armed struggle, violence is futile against a heavily armed enemy and the bloodshed would be so enormous and so wasteful." Isabel began thinking how many times she had debated with Julian the justification of violence if the state is oppressing its people by force, but she had to admit it would be suicide against the current army.

"The repression that followed the Pinochet attack was really terrible," continued Juan. "Hundreds of people more were detained, most of them completely innocent and there was then a new wave of disappeared persons. Twelve leading *Frentistas* were killed in a big military operation nine months after the attack, but hundreds were seized. On the day of the attack on Pinochet, the dictator's own security men had only managed to kill four *Frentistas*." Juan couldn't help smiling at the inefficiency of all those bodyguards and security soldiers. "Pinochet's convoy included a lorryload of army commandos and members of the Intelligence Organisation, the CNI but they only got four of our men."

The large sigh of relief that Isabel let out was noticed by Juan. She was nervous of getting too involved with a group that still aimed at the violent overthrow of the state. "The *FPMR* is right that the current President and other leading politicians were in part responsible for the coup d'état," she said. "They hadn't opposed the coup when they should have, thinking the military would rescue the government from *Popular Unity* which had triumphed in free elections."

"Yes, absolutely. They thought the government would quickly be put back into their hands and saw themselves as the rightful governing class in Chile. *Popular Unity* was trying to change things too radically for them and it was a temporary aberration that had to be corrected. They had proudly considered their democracy made Chile superior to all other South American countries because it had been stable for decades and they were the liberal elite who felt they had a right to always inherit the privilege of governing."

"And to make sure not too much changed, certainly not their privileges," said Miguel. "They never imagined the exceptionally harsh dictatorship that would not deliver power back into their hands for seventeen years."

"We must never forget it wasn't the liberal elite that achieved the 'No' vote against Pinochet," said Juan. "It was the major grassroots effort we all made working together and in the face of a powerful regime with full control of all the media, we won the plebiscite. Pinochet had been confident of victory and had hoped that vote would keep him as President for another eight years. He was so sure he couldn't lose, he even declared he had won soon after the vote closed, but as the vote was counted, eventually he had to concede defeat. Did you know too he was a superstitious fool? He thought the number five would bring him good luck, so he chose a date with a five in it, but he still lost!" Juan thumped his fist as if celebrating again the triumph. "Superstition is why he has five stars in his cap. The cap front has to bend backwards to get all the stars in a vertical row on the peak! He can strut around like this...". Juan made Isabel laugh at his nose-in-the-air face and the stamping of his boots, nazi style.

Juan continued, "We need to do a mass movement like that again, the masses must demand a new Constitution and greater equality in the place of Pinochet's Constitution with its strong bias in favour of the elite. That's what I want to see us achieve."

"But isn't that what a good majority wants?" Isabel asked. "Not the privileged classes of course, that this constitution serves, but most ordinary people."

"Not enough will stick their necks out for it yet or understand all the arguments yet. But we will get there. There has to be a mass rebellion against the elite or this injustice will just go on for years and years," Juan said. "Did you know that under the constitution the government is controlled by and subjected to a military council, which has to approve every decision that the government makes?"

"And Pinochet is of course still Head of the Army."

"There cannot be democracy whilst this is the case. This is what we have to oppose by civil disobedience and loss of our fear," said Juan. "I have to be very cautious when I'm out, especially in the capital, to try to avoid being recognised because they still follow those who have been in 'disruptive activities'. We are seen as subversive and we have to be repressed but there are hotbeds of support in Santiago and we are growing. Now I want to go south to Temuco and Concepción to support the contacts I have in those cities and rally more support. I thought you could see the grassroots activities going on and film them to show others what we are achieving and to bring in more people in that way." Isabel showed enthusiasm for this idea and for Juan's position. She liked the idea that a mass movement could be developed through community activities in every neighbourhood. "We need funding especially to set up health centres in all the poor *barrios* where access to health services just doesn't exist and where the doctors and state hospitals are many kilometres away. We try to offer support work with families. Opportunities for children and young people are essential to give us the chance to raise awareness and build the movement. That is why I asked you about your contacts in England, Trades Unions perhaps. Is there any chance of help with funding these sorts of actions?"

"I'll do all I can. I could try to make contacts through my and my partner's Trade Union. Chilean groups in England might be willing to fundraise."

"Do you know that we also need to counteract the Mormon Church's activities all over Chile? These are gaining greater influence through bringing North American money in to promote rightwing politicians, giving bribes to compliant voters." Isabel knew the falsehood and lies of the beliefs of this non-mainstream sect and she was horrified at what she had heard of its growth in South America.

"We need a film to be made of the work we are trying to achieve and our message," urged Juan and Isabel was certain she could help there. She wasn't going to miss the chance to ask Juan to contribute as well to her film for the exiles and others outside of Chile to know how far the country is from a democracy, how protesters are labelled as subversives and how repressive Chile still is. Juan did agree, keeping his identity anonymous but he also thought he could assist with illustrations of the repression. Isabel agreed to travel with Juan and knew she would be glad of the chance to meet like-minded people. Helping people to lose their fear and dare to go out on a demonstration or on strike would be a tough challenge. Who was she to tell them what to do? She hadn't been there in all their suffering for years. However, she too had deep and painful motivations and she felt she had no choice but to try to do what she could. She would see her friends in Concepción and near Temuco while she was in the south and she could genuinely tell her mother that she was going on from one city to the other and would be away for quite some time. Miguel went to get bus tickets for them and the cafe owner made sandwiches and thus Juan and Isabel set off for Concepción.

-oOo-

The six-hour bus ride began with a slow start in the traffic of the city as they were winding through the *barrios* and *poblaciones* with occasional stops but eventually, they were on their way and Isabel was pleased to see the Chilean countryside again. There were kilometres and kilometres of vineyards with backdrops of hills on the right and mountains on the left. The road followed the wide green valley south of the city and passed through several small towns and centres of horticulture. Isabel hadn't yet been in touch with her school friend whom she knew was now in Concepción and she wondered how she was going to explain her turning up in the city without contacting her beforehand. Hopefully, the timing would be convenient and she did already have an open invitation to stay with her. She thought it best to pretend she was ringing from Santiago and plan something for a few days hence. That would mean staying wherever Juan was planning to stay first and she knew that a contact of his would offer at least an alcove with a single mattress filling the space and a curtain offering a little privacy from the rest of the household. Well! That would do - for thousands it was normal, she told herself. She also was keen to see whom Juan was planning to meet and what he wanted to show her. She couldn't just disappear to do what she wanted and she'd have to be available when he was ready to move on as planned to Temuco. The public space of the bus didn't permit much talking and soon she began to fall asleep, the first stop being Curicó in at least a couple of hours.

It was early evening when they finally pulled into Concepción and Juan was quick to find a local bus to a *población* with which he was clearly familiar. Soon a family was welcoming them both and serving *onces,* served around 6.00 pm. When the youngsters in the family learned Isabel had been living in England, the usual questions began. Prepared this time, she asked, "Do you know why we call what we are having now *onces*?" They didn't know. "When the British came here to build mines and railways to take away our copper and other resources, they used to have a break from work mid-morning about eleven o'clock. They called it 'elevenses'. The Chileans took their word in Spanish but applied it to a little snack and a cup of tea in the late afternoon. They took the tea-drinking habit from the British traders too as coffee doesn't grow here. The English think it very funny to call five or six o'clock tea elevenses." They all laughed and everyone tucked into the mashed avocado, ham and soft bread rolls. After these came sweet, sticky buns but Isabel had not seen buns or any other cake in Chile served with fresh whipped cream.

"Wow, this is real cream like in England," she blurted.

"Well, you are in the south, we've cows and green fields here, you know," Isabel recalled the countryside she'd seen from the bus and it had looked like England, except there were snow-capped mountains in the distance.

"How great! I can't stand those artificial creams. They are so sweet. Thank you so much. What a treat."

The father of the family Nicolás saw this as a good opportunity to do some education with his young family and knew the visitors would back him up. The young people might especially listen to them, he thought. He began by saying to his children, "You know how important copper is to Chile, the country's wealth is dependent on it. Well, the Allende government nationalised copper and when the military government swept away the socialist measures of the *Popular Unity* and put all they could back into private hands again, they did not denationalise the copper industry. They recognised how valuable it was to the economy and wanted to keep control of it. They wrote into their new constitution that the copper industry was to pay 10% of its annual profits to the Armed Forces. That way they knew they could nicely finance the Army, Navy and Air Forces, no matter what expansion was demanded of them."

Isabel butted in, "the situation still remains the same. How they like socialism when it suits them,"

Juan recalled the outrage from the North Americans when Allende wanted to nationalise the copper industry. "The process of 'negotiated nationalisation' had already begun under the previous government because everyone knew massive profits were flowing out of the country, mostly to the USA and had done for years, so it had become a mainstream political demand to stop this bleeding of Chile's resources. It was not seen as an extreme left-wing move. Allende received a unanimous vote in Congress to fully nationalise at a stroke all the copper mines and the day the law was passed in Parliament with immediate effect, became *El Día de la Dignidad Nacional* - The Day of National Dignity - on 16th July 1971."

"The foreign investors never forgave Allende," continued Nicolás, "and of course, it was a major reason for the North American support of the coup d'état. Allende even paid compensation to the shareholders although they had already received 'excessive wealth' from their investments. The compensation levels, Allende announced to the United Nations, were going to be made according to the declared tax returns of the copper mining companies. He knew their declared profits were a fraction of their actual profits so the compensation was to be far less than they pretended their investments were worth. They couldn't argue for more, however, against the value they themselves had claimed for tax purposes."

"It made these greedy mine owners, and the USA government, even more incensed at the loss of their annual flow of profits," said Isabel.

"The North Americans had their cruel revenge on the country, however, only two years later," said Juan. The young people knew that he was referring to the coup. Juan wanted to hurry on to discuss what these activists had been doing recently so that Isabel could include them in her filming plans. A passport into communities like this was really valuable to Isabel, so she got out her pen and pad to take notes. In no time, it seemed, evening supper began to arrive. How generous people with very little resources are, she thought and soon she was shown where she would sleep. It was indeed a little alcove, the size of a single mattress, off a passageway, just as she'd expected. Hers was one of two, each with a curtain - one for her and one for Juan - the two bedrooms of the house needed of course for the couple and their children but the visitors caused the two oldest teenagers, who would normally sleep in the alcoves, to double up with the younger ones.

Over breakfast, the couple began to explain that they were in the middle of a typical Chilean *toma*, composed of wooden little bungalows that the residents had built for themselves. They knew Isabel was there to make a video and so she began to film the area. Nicolás narrated a commentary.

"New people are still arriving in the area but it takes years to get an area like this adopted. A scheme has recently come about, since Pinochet left the presidency, that government grants in kind will be given to families in need of homes if they meet certain criteria. They can apply for certain plots of land and they'll be granted a bathroom and a kitchen unit, with all the infrastructure necessary, when the government is adopting an area, and then the family is expected to build the remaining rooms of their home themselves around the basic necessities."

Nicolás' wife Julia added, "We're not saying they get a fully fitted kitchen, simply a prefabricated room with a kitchen sink with running water and a bathroom with a sink and loo and piping for where a shower could be added. No tiles, no doors, no shower cubicle, no kitchen cupboards - these have to be paid for by the family. The applicants have to show they have a stable job and an income so that they will be able to add the rooms they need to the granted units over time."

"Grants for kitchens and bathrooms are only available in areas recognised by the local authority and this area recently has been adopted." Nicolás continued. "But these kitchen and bathroom grants won't be available for those of us already here. And we struggled a long time to get these very basic facilities. What you need to know is that there are very few of these areas being adopted compared with the huge need for decent housing and the great number of *tomas* nationally. Did you know the system of *tomas* had been going on for most of the 20th Century but the process of adoption can take as long as a couple of decades? Barely a start has been made and clearly poor housing conditions and the lack of quality housing is a crucial political issue." Isabel too was just then thinking this was going to have to be a major theme in her own film, which she had decided she was calling *Chile Actual* or *Chile Today* in English.

"Housing was something the Allende government had been starting to address but I gather the military government did nothing except tear down some of the worst slums in tenement buildings in the cities. I suppose getting rid of the worst slums drove the tenants to search for housing further out of the city centres and they often had to create new *tomas,*" said Isabel.

"Yes, there were no houses given them in exchange for the loss of their tenement rooms. The city centre sites have been developed into more elegant and better quality private housing but the rents of these were far beyond the reach of the original occupants."

Julia then took Juan and Isabel to look further around the *barrio*. The wooden structure of the community hall that the residents had built themselves was an impressive, substantial building. It had a small veranda and the original unstripped trunks of the walls made it appear an attractive, large log cabin. Every community needed such a hall, first and foremost, when a member of the community died, it was a place to hold the candlelit vigil - as was considered essential. Family and neighbours must be given the opportunity to pay their respects to the deceased and they usually don't have a room in their little houses for this to take place. Fortunately, the community hall was put to other good uses. A pre-school nursery opportunity, run by volunteers, gave the youngest members a chance for early learning. However, the resources were poor, thought Isabel and this was clearly another theme for the video for Juan and an area where funds from outside were needed.

"We've always had a close link with the University here, through our political group. Many of our volunteers are students and we are hoping to start classes for adults with volunteer lecturers," said Juan, "for our people to learn history, economics and politics, to develop an awareness of the structures and international forces that determine their lives." Isabel knew this was a necessary approach to change but she was saddened by the idea of starting all over again. She said,

"When I was in my teens there was such a level of awareness politically and it seemed so many were enthused to build a just and more fair society - all of which the military has done its best to destroy."

"That was when Chile was a much more egalitarian country too than it is now," said Juan. "And before the most active people were removed and this terrible fear set in." They continued their tour and Isabel filmed the log cabin. Nicolás continued,

"The hall is used later in the day for an After School Club, where children are given opportunities to do their homework with student volunteers available to assist with any questions, and then they do some non-competitive games with them. In the evenings the young people come together to listen to music, usually from a ghetto blaster radio and one of our volunteers tries to promote activities and debates on current issues in their lives."

"Few areas have these sort of community facilities," Juan explained, "and this is an example we want to model to others in *poblaciones* throughout Chile and to local Universities and school teachers that could help. A film to inspire what can be achieved would aid that mission. Do you see how valuable your work could be? A people aware, for example, of what the Pinochet constitution means, will lead to them not tolerating it for much longer. Individuals too can be helped to gain more education and develop their own capacities and confidence. They will better fulfil their own lives but they will also want change at the political level and be able to articulate it." Isabel knew Juan was right but felt a great responsibility. She was inspired as well and felt a great sense of purpose. "This is what I am here for," she thought and she smiled thoughtfully at Juan.

After five days of filming, interviewing volunteers, both students and lecturers from Concepción University, residents, adults, children and teenagers, Isabel thought she had sufficient material. In fact, she had too much and knew the editing wouldn't be an easy task. How stimulating she had found the days and the discussions and debates so enjoyable. She also had a sense of having found "the real Chile" and it warmed her heart.

It had been agreed with Juan that Isabel should go on to see her friend in Concepción the next day and then go on to Temuco and Juan would meet up with her again in twelve days' time. Juan was to stay on to do some teaching and chase up some potential volunteer contacts at the University.

# Chapter 4

Isabel hugged herself inwardly, waiting for the bus to start as she anticipated seeing her school friend again and the amazing murals in Concepción and Chillán. It wasn't long before she was hugging Marita on the other side of the city and after dropping her bag at Marita's house, they went out to see the town.

"Let's go first to the University because it has some architecture worth seeing and of course the murals you want to see," suggested Marita. As they arrived at the entrance Isabel could see the impressive archway building called the Arc de Medicine with its Ancient Greek style freeze of figures. Entering under the arch they saw the large green lawn with the famous Clock Tower on the other side.

"The campus here is enormous," said Marita, "over a million square meters and it is full of museums, parks and sculptures. Only less than a quarter of the land has buildings on it"

"Wow, how lovely to have a lot of space to enjoy the outdoors and the architecture is impressive. I love looking at sculptures too," responded Isabel as they began their long walk around.

"This is the third oldest university in Chile and the first to be built in the south. It was started in 1919 and you know it is a private university but one with a very good reputation."

"Yes, you can't say that about all private universities, but this is a good one I know." Eventually, they came to the place where was the mural Isabel had wanted to see. "It was a gift of the Mexican Government after an earthquake and …," she gasped as they entered the room and saw the mural.

Eventually, Marita, who had been a student here and knew it well, finished Isabel's sentence for her.

"It represents the unity of all Latin American peoples and cultures. It was painted by Jorge González Camarena between 1964 and 1965." Isabel just stared and stared. "It's meant to emphasise the value of fraternity," continued Marita. Taking in every detail, thrilled at last to see the mural she'd only ever seen pictures of before, Isabel kept finding new details and kept pointing them out with excitement.

"Look this is from the native culture and this represents the syncretism of the Christian religion with the native beliefs of the indigenous inhabitants. And here is the dual use of American maize and European wheat that together sustained the development of this continent. Here is a Spanish soldier and a native woman who symbolise the riches of the continent. And this is the native flower of Mexico intertwined with the native flower of Chile, the *copihue*." Isabel fell silent again, stared and became completely enthralled. She was also thinking how the mural could be woven into her video. It could be in the introduction, she thought, the notion of brotherliness and integration after the original conquering violence and how we in Chile need to find that union again after the polarisation of the dictatorship. She began filming large sections and closeups of the 300-meter mural. At last, Marita was able to drag Isabel away and get her to agree to go and have some lunch in one of the student restaurants. Marita had been a student in the School of Veterinary Science and she told Isabel about her work over lunch.

"I mostly attend animals on farms all around Concepción but also I see house pets that people bring into our surgery in the town. A group of us set that up recently, we've three vets and a receptionist/secretary. We've been amazingly busy since it was set up and clearly, it was needed."

"This student lunch of *Pastel de Choclo* is very good and great for me to have this traditional dish again," said Isabel. "We've not seen each other since we were at school together, have we? Just after to coup, you told me your family were moving to Concepción and you gave me your address. Tell me all that happened to you since then."

"My parents decided it was best for us to get out of Santiago and go to my grandparents' house in Concepción. It was certainly quieter here, for us anyway and my grandparents had quite a big house in the countryside, just outside of the town. So I was able to do that last year at school we still had to do and then get on with university without much interruption. It was different for you I know. I am so glad I passed you my new address and we kept in touch with Christmas and birthday cards, with long catch-up letters included."

"Yes, I'm so glad we kept in touch. It was great to have your long letters of news. I didn't finish my school exams until two years later than I should have. Just too much happened in the first years after to coup. I spent all my time searching for or worrying about my Dad and Raúl. Do you remember him?"

"Yes, I do. I went out with his friend for a bit. I was sorry when I had to move away from him. We lost touch. Of course, it was nothing serious at that age but I did miss him and I was a bit angry with my parents over it. I gave him my address but he didn't bother to write."

"What a shame. I remember, his name was Gabriel but he didn't get arrested like Raúl."

"No, I never heard that he did. My dad was obsessed that I keep out of trouble and have nothing to do with the types we met through the voluntary work, like Raúl and Gabriel. I was a coward perhaps but once we were living here and curfew stopped us going out, I just got used to staying at home and getting on with my studying. Animals and nature became important to me. I'd go on endless walks in the countryside, sometimes with school friends. We had to make the most of the days because we couldn't meet at night, so birds and flowers and farm animals became essential to my life."

"Our lives went in very different directions."

"I don't know how you lived with the anxiety of not knowing where your father or Raúl were. You told me you went searching for them all the time. I felt guilty that I couldn't do anything. Did you ever find out what actually happened to them?"

"Of course you couldn't do anything and you weren't guilty in any way. You were a school girl out in the countryside, down here. We went endlessly to the morgues and all the hospitals and the police stations, over and over though it was pointless, but we were driven to keep trying. By 'we' I mean sometimes I went with my step-mother and sometimes I went with Raúl's mother. We went to talk to people in so many different *poblaciones* in the hopes of finding someone who would know what had happened to them.

Some people started to be released after two or three years and eventually, we found a couple of men who had known my father inside. They said he had not returned from an interrogation one time. Then Mamadre and I found a few more men who told us the same. The police never admitted his death nor where he was."

"How awful. How could this happen in our country in our time? I still can't accept it."

"I know. I don't know whether I should still be trying to find out where my father's body is, if it exists or just accept that would be an impossible waste of time. Sometimes I feel bad that is not my main mission here but I did try for six years and I think he would want me to be looking to the future and doing something to contribute to a better world."

"Yes, I think he would. I remember him, you know, when I stayed at your father's house once in Valparaíso."

"Oh yes, I remember. It was in the summer holidays. It must have been in 1972. Glorious, hopeful times. Now tell me, I know you haven't married, but there must be someone on the scene?"

"Well, sort of, but we only recently met. I thought I'd never meet the right person and anyway I was always busy with work or studying."

"So this new guy might be the right one, yes?"

"I don't know yet. I need to know him a great deal more than I do, but we'll see."

"Oh come on! You must have a feeling that it's something special, if it is."

"Yes, I think I do but I don't know if he has yet. We'll see."

"Tell me who he is at least."

"He works here at the University. He lectures in biochemistry."

"Oh, that's great. Let me know how it turns out. What's his name? Can I meet him?"

"Carlos. I could invite him for dinner tomorrow night if you like and we could go to the market tomorrow morning and get some spider crab or some shellfish. If you wouldn't mind, I would like to invite him. I had told him I'd be with you for five days."

"But that doesn't exclude him. Yes, definitely get him over."

"It means us going to Chillán the next day."

"That's fine. Let's do it."

In the afternoon they strolled around the town, visited the Plaza de las Armas in the centre and sat around in the squares and parks. Marita made her phone call. All was set for the next day. Down by the port they watched the few late fishing boats come in. Marita prepared a meal at home that evening and though they were tired from so much walking, they talked and talked about old friends and memories till late into the night.

The next day the friends made it quite early to the port and they saw large numbers of fishing boats delivering their catches. Isabel was always pleased to see the fishermen but she also thought about how they risked their lives in their tiny boats on the rough ocean sea. The waves on the shore along the Chilean coast were always large and a bit frightening and she wondered how dangerous it was to go out fishing. Isabel liked to see also the process of unloading the fish, the auction and sales of the fish and shellfish in the market and to listen to the shouting and general bustle. They bought reineta fish and spider crabs, the latter being a real treat for Isabel since she'd never seen one in England and they were her favourite shellfish of all. She felt them to have an even more exquisite flavour than normal crabs and better than lobster "any time," she claimed. Not that she'd had a lobster for a long time either and certainly not in England.

"You know when my Dad was a student at Valparaíso Catholic University, he lived in accommodation provided by the monks at a monastery in Cerro Barrón, just near the port there. The father of one of his fellow students was a fisherman and he used to bring the student group lobsters quite often. They had so many that they got to the point of saying 'oh no, not lobsters again!' My Dad liked to tell that story. You can't imagine how expensive lobsters are in England and so to have too many lobsters that you're fed up with them is beyond my wildest dreams."

In the fruit and veg market, they bought two heavy bags of various foods for salads and cooked vegetable mixtures and a mountain of fruit including chirimoyas. Isabel said she could never get enough of chirimoyas and she loved their delicate flavours. "You know the best of our fruits and vegetables never get to the market here, they all get sent for export, mainly of course to the United States," said Marita with a little anger and disgust in her voice. Isabel looked sad. "You have to pick very carefully what you are buying here. There are only a few of the best quality and loads of the 'not so good' fruits. Then they really charge for those that are the best quality. It seems so unfair and especially to the poorer people who only get the mass of the 'not so good' and this is happening in a country where we produce such excellent quality fruits." Marita had made Isabel think of a valuable lesson that should go into her film.

"I'd noticed some of the fruit wasn't top quality. We are only used to the very best 'granny smiths' in England, coming from Chile or grapes or any other Chilean fruits - they are always the best around. That is terrible if you can't enjoy the best products of your own country here. That is part of the whole economic picture of what is going on here." Isabel began to explain to Marita the film she was making for the UK and the European market.

After carrying the heavy shopping to the bus station to get tickets for the next day to Chillán, they took a collective taxi home to Marita's house. They made a quick lunch of *reineta* fish, fried in flour and seasoned coating and salad and saved the spider crab for their evening *cena* with Carlos. Marita had to do some visits to local farms that day and she had invited Isabel to go with her to view the surrounding countryside. They drove west of the city towards a peninsula where the rainforest finally meets the sea. Before that, however, a large area of the forest had been cleared and herds of cows and goats were being raised. Isabel stayed in the horticultural garden surrounding a farmhouse whilst Marita went with the farmer to the cowsheds. A little girl of eight or nine years started talking with Isabel and told her that she fed the chickens and collected the eggs every day and that she had been looking after a baby goat whose mother had died. The girl's name turned out to be Malena and she explained in detail how she'd been giving the goat kid a baby's bottle each day that week. Isabel thought it all a wonderful existence for a child until Malena talked of riding her bike along the rough track that Marita had just driven down, to catch the bus to school every day and she described how muddy it was in the winter. Isabel began to realise that this rural life was not so idyllic in every sense. She knew the winters were quite tough in the south of Chile with plenty of rain in those parts. When she couldn't cycle, it was a half an hour walk in her boots in the mud to the bus, Malena said.

On the way home Marita asked, "Did you know the Rock Group 'Los Tres' started at Concepción University?"

"No, I didn't know that. 'Los Tres' includes the son of Angel Parra. The father is my favourite singer. He's called Angel too and when I ask for Angel Parra disks they always think I'm asking for the son and 'Los Tres' and not the father but I'm not into Rock."

"They are very famous now in Chile, more than the father is nowadays of course. I like them very much. They are coming to play at the University again on Friday. Shall we go?"

"Oh wow. Yes of course if you'd like to. I need to know them and live music is always good."

The spider crab in the evening was exquisite and Isabel felt the evening was very enjoyable. She warmly nodded her approval of Carlos to Marita, when his back was turned to take the plates to the kitchen. He seemed to Isabel to be genuine, interesting and with awareness of the political reality and he talked of his support as a teenager for *Popular Unity*. Isabel couldn't resist testing his attitude toward the military regime.

"I can't believe there are people in Chile who still want to defend the coup d'état," she said. "Some of the neighbours around my mother's area, some of the people even at her church think of Pinochet as a saviour. How can there ever be any justification for the sweeping away of the democracy we had, by force? How can you justify concentration camps, torture, killings and disappearances?"

"They think Pinochet was saving them from Communism. They are always being told it was necessary," said Carlos.

"These are the lies they've absorbed. I thought it was the CIA that had the major responsibility for the coup and I know the evidence is indisputable that they were deeply involved, but now I see there were enough supporters here, not to mention ambitious politicians, military and businessmen, to enable it all to happen so easily. I had never met people like that. During my time here, it seemed we were all wanting to build a new society and share what we had so as to achieve justice and fairness, but it must just have been those I associated with. It wasn't nearly so many of us Chileans as I thought."

"We were very young and naive back then," said Carlos. "Everyone seemed involved and cooperating together. We were swept up in the excitement. I did some hard physical work helping to build wooden houses and it gave me such a sense of achievement. But my parents were a bit sceptical of the motivations of the students here in Concepción who got us involved."

"Really? I used to do voluntary work organised by Allende's party but I told my mother I was working in what the local priest was organising because we did work with the church volunteers too. Marita and I were mostly involved in the literacy scheme."

"Yes it was fun," said Marita. "But we were serious about what we were doing. It seemed so worthwhile and the volunteers would get together after the classes and we had a great time."

"Yes, we'd have a party nearly every night in the community hall or school," said Isabel. "All very innocent, just music and dancing but great for young people."

"How could anyone think it was so wrong and want to sweep it all away? Even more people voted for *Popular Unity* in the local elections, they were thought to be doing so well." Marita shook her head.

"I've done a lot of reading since then and I understand much more now. Before the coup, we believed the Right was a minority without much influence but they had all the real power and with U.S. backing they could do whatever they liked. In the United States's backyard, Chile would be the great experiment of the Chicago Boys, who liked the look of the 6% annual growth rate and didn't want to see it wasted on foolish "socialist" measures like housing and educating the people. They colluded with the traitors here, who were prepared to betray their own country and its people, to make a deal that would keep them in power and make them more money. But the politicians didn't anticipate the extent of the heavy hand Pinochet would impose. His was an iron fist with the power of an efficient nazi machine behind it."

"Yes. And only when the U.S. wouldn't back him any longer, and he couldn't overturn that vote in the Plebiscite, he was forced to step down," said Carlos.

"Do you know people have said to me 'wasn't he good to just go peacefully? I don't think he has either gone or given up the violence," said Isabel. "The Army is still the menace with which he can threaten both the elected government and the people. Why is everyone still so fearful? Because they know the repression could start again. I was at a small demonstration organised by the families of the "detained disappeared" in Santiago. It was entirely peaceful and round the corner came the vile armoured lorries and they turned on the water cannons and threw tear gas. What for? Why? There was no disturbance, very few people had gathered. There was no reason but to intimidate. How can they get away with that? Why can't the *Concertación,* the coalition government say it's not acceptable? Because they are all under the threat of violence by the Army again and Pinochet is still in charge of that!"

Isabel was getting worked up but she was glad she was with friends who understood. "You know the tear gas really stings and hurts not only your eyes but your nose and throat too... Have you ever seen the film Brave Heart? I cried and cried for Chile as I watched that film. Our history was a repetition of the Scottish story of the traitorous Scottish lords who did a deal with the foreign enemy to win power for themselves, ignoring the interests of the Scottish people."

"Chile has a long, long way to go to recover," said Marita finally. "The Truth Commission has to do its work in full, no coverups."

"Reconciliation can only be based on the truth, and the full truth is the only hope for an improvement in the vast divisions of this country. And people like my mother, my own mother, don't want the truth to be heard. The propaganda machine says you mustn't open up old wounds. Without the truth of where the disappeared are, where the bodies of the tortured and dead are, no kind of 'Togetherness' future can be worked on. I have had the feeling since I arrived here that there exists repressed seething anger but there is also this terrible fear that makes Chile want to sweep everything under the carpet. There is a self-imposed block to not think about the past, an unspoken rule that it is too painful to face, so we mustn't. It's painful for me but I want to face it, as no other way is healthy. I feel that there is a bubbling below the surface which is one day going to explode like a boiling pot despite the growing affluence and the consumer society."

"The economy is said to be booming. We are the jaguar of South America," said Carlos.

"Yes but in a neo-liberal consumer society the middle class get the goodies, the rich get richer from their assets and wealth doesn't spread down to the poorer half of society." Isabel thought she had better leave it there. She'd said enough and Carlos went to get some more wine from the fridge. He had brought several bottles. The conversation then became lighter and Carlos made them laugh. Isabel thought he would be good for Marita but wondered why he'd left it late, like Marita, to find a partner. Isabel liked what he had said. They resolved to go to bed not too late that evening but the conversation flowed like the Chardonnay and they ended up listening to some of Isabel's CDs of the Chilean groups now in exile.

Carlos had stayed over with Marita but was gone early the next morning. The friends made the bus but were rather quiet and both slept on the two-hour journey. They livened up on finding themselves in the central square of Chillán and looking at the modernist cathedral, built in 1941 after the earthquake of 1939 that had destroyed the old cathedral. The new building was composed of a series of half-oval earthquake-proof arches which were large and dramatic. They projected out beyond the infill of the roof and walls, which were also in a continuous curved flow from the centre of the roof to the floor. Isabel found the arches impressive on the inside of the cathedral too because the rows of windows that followed around each arch, gave rings of sunlight flooding into the internal space.

"The Cathedral is a memorial to the thousands of victims of the earthquake and particularly the 36-meter high cross next door," said Marita.

"That level of loss of life would never happen now in Chile," said Isabel, "because the Allende government made sure that earthquake-proof structures are required for all new buildings."

"Quakes are often worse here than in other countries but we can take even magnitude 8 in our stride. The biggest earthquake ever recorded anywhere on earth was in Chile, you know - in Valdivia in 1960 - 9.5 magnitude," said Marita. "It created a tsunami and that and the quake together killed over five and a half thousand people. Not only are buildings all required to be earthquake-proof now but there are strict drills and warning signals now in all the towns along the Chilean coast if a tsunami threatens. The people of the towns have to practice evacuations. Instructions and warning bells are everywhere."

The friends then moved on to see the town and decided to have some lunch before going to see the murals that Isabel was already getting excited about. She didn't want to be dragged away quickly from the murals because they were hungry, so they agreed that that visit should be saved for the afternoon. When they finally set off to see the murals, Isabel began. "You know we are going to an ordinary school in the town, not a private school, nor to an art gallery. The Mexican government donated a school to the town after the 1939 earthquake and Pablo Neruda asked two Mexican muralists, David Alfaro Siqueiros and Xavier Guerrero to come to decorate the school library and the stairwell."

"I didn't know Pablo Neruda was involved."

Isabel felt this time some of her knowledge from her Art History courses would come in useful and Marita wouldn't know all about these murals as she had in Concepción. "Siqueiros was adamant that art should not be locked away in galleries and museums but should be seen by all. Art should not be the privilege of the wealthier classes. It should be available without the need for entrance fees, he said. Also, he said art was not for the satisfaction of individual artists but for the sharing of ideas. I love that notion." Isabel was thinking that perhaps her video could finish with these murals and this concept of sharing. "Art inspires us to generate further ideas and create further artistic works. It was entirely appropriate for Siqueiros to go to decorate the new school. He was often in difficulties with his government. He was head secretary of the Mexican Communist Party at one time and after spells in jail, he had to flee into exile, when he was accused of instigating riots. What he was actually doing was defending the working conditions of workers."

"So he was in exile in Chile?"

"He first went to the United States and then came to Chile in the 1940s. Pablo Neruda actually negotiated as an alternative to a prison sentence, that he come to Chile to paint the proposed murals in Chillán. The Mexican authorities didn't seem to mind if he was exiled, so long as they got rid of a communist, which was great for us because he was an amazing artist. He is considered one of the three top Mexican muralists, you know, along with José Clemente Orozco and Diego Rivera." And then she gasped on entering the school library and she fell silent for a very long time. She felt Siqueiros' work, covering the walls and ceiling of this large room, to be intensely emotional. He depicted the effect of the Spanish invasion upon the Aztec civilization. Could she use this to illustrate the military assault of the Chilean fascists upon the free, unarmed people of the country? She would video all she could and was sure she could use it.

-oOo-

The bus journey back to Concepción was another welcome opportunity for a sleep before the concert that night which wasn't due to start till 10.00 pm. They had time for *cena* and then met up with Carlos who was happy to hear their enthusiastic comments on the murals, which were familiar to him.

"Los Tres became four when Angel Parra Jr. joined the original three," said Carlos as they walked into the University entrance. "He certainly helped propel them forward and they are now considered the leading Chilean Rock Band."

"I can't believe the first concert I'm going to in Chile is with a Rock Band when I am so used to seeing our famous folkloric groups in Europe," said Isabel.

"They are coming back. There are a few concerts planned for the summer. You'll be able to see them here very soon, I'm sure."

"In my time in Chile we thought Rock was the music of the imperialists and our unique music with native instruments was the authentic music of the people."

"But the groups were soon combining the two and that gained them real popular appeal. Los Jaivas I think was the first to bring hard-rock technology to the indigenous instruments. It was what made them really take off in popularity and it was very clever."

"Well yes, I guess you're right. It added excitement. Perhaps I'll enjoy this concert more than I thought I would. Perhaps it won't be so far off the mark for me."

"Let's hope," said Marita. "Wait and see. I think they are great."

In the event, Isabel was surprisingly impressed, though the sounds were harsher than she enjoyed. It was after 1.30 in the morning they all returned to Marita's house and indulged in another bottle of Chardonnay.

Isabel was not sleepy when she went to bed and she knew that she was missing Julian. She would have liked to have shared the day with him. He was fond of art and would have loved to see the murals. The Rock he would have enjoyed too, though he professed great affection for the music of the groups that Isabel admired, he would have found it exciting and vigorous and loved the mood of the crowd, as she had. Perhaps it was Marita being together with Carlos that was making her miss Julian, but she felt a deep desire for him. That depth of feeling was what had always brought them together again after whatever disrupting difference had caused a temporary schism. Why had she thought of these upsets as nails in a coffin that were being added to, one by one? She resolved she would ring him the next day. "What a hassle I can't just ring here and now. Oh no, he won't be up yet."

In the morning Carlos was gone soon after the three had breakfast together. Isabel was keen to make time to go to a call centre to phone Julian prior to her bus in the afternoon to Temuco.

"I'm glad you are going to ring. It is the first time since you've been here. Why have you hesitated or why now, is anything different?" asked Marita.

"I thought a lot about him last night. I don't know how it is that when we are together, the slightest friction seems to become a questioning of the whole relationship. We don't seem right for each other and then we are drawn back to each other. I should like it to work. Somehow we have to do better."

"Do you think he feels the same?"

"Yes, I think he does. He keeps asking when am I going back. I suppose the answer is when I've enough material for my video and I don't know when that will be."

"I think you should not leave it too long. It can't work if you are not together."

"I want to gain a full picture of Chile, not only for the exiles but for general awareness of what is going on here. I want to bust the myth that Chile presents as a democracy when it clearly isn't with this constitution."

"I know all that but Julian is feeling an emptiness and you might regret things if you leave it too long. Don't you think it could become irreparable?"

"Hm, I suppose it could."

"Could he not come here?"

"He has talked about the possibility of unpaid leave but he wants to improve his Spanish first to make best use of his time here."

"How can he practice without you there to help?"

"Well, we don't try to talk in Spanish. It's all too slow and boring. But what I do is listen to him reading and then correct his pronunciation. I think

71

his accent is not so bad as some students of Spanish because of that practice he has had with me."

"You're too impatient to be waiting for someone to recall a word in a foreign language. How did you get started with English? Did you know Julian then?"

"I did have some fluency before I knew him but he has helped with lots of meanings, and pronunciations and..."

"And frustrations, I bet," said Marita. Isabel had to agree.

"I was going to say continual practice with another person, speaking and listening help the most. I never mind being corrected. That is exactly what I want. It was hard trying to practice with Eugenio. We could never keep it up or we would end up in fits of laughter when one of us stumbled over a phrase. We'd make silly noises with our mouths, the other would join in and we'd end up shouting Chilean swear words at each other and then fall about laughing. Do you know it all seemed so unreal. It didn't feel like true conversation - it was just a game that would soon be over. It didn't feel real to me. Maybe that was part of the problem. I don't know if I can explain but speaking in English even to Julian had an unreality about it. It didn't feel like deep down it was me."

"But you talked seriously about yourselves, your feelings didn't you?"

"Yes, and I meant all I said but when I think about it now, my using English just didn't feel right. Something was missing."

"So your identity is totally tied up with your first language?"

"That's crazy isn't it, but I think you may be right. I think I wanted to come back here alone to be me, the Chilean who spoke Spanish with Chileanisms and never having to think in English. I wanted a break from all the effort of that unreality. I wanted to turn the clock back too unconsciously. I see that now and I know that was not reality. Things are very different here in Chile now and that's been a shock."

"Our lives have gone in very different directions too but I'm glad our lives have touched each other's again and I hope you will come again, with Julian preferably."

"Thank you, Marita, you have been so good. I thought I would be less imposing on old friends if I came to Chile alone but I know you would receive Julian well. It was just an excuse to not have him here. Now I'm going on to

Silvia in Temuco. You remember she was very involved in the voluntary work we did. We talked about her and other friends. It has been so good for me to look back with you but I think you've helped me look forward again as well."

"I hope so. Let's get to the call centre in good time and when you've phoned Julian we'll still have time for a coffee and another chat before your bus."

Isabel approached Marita from the call centre with a big smile which she could not have stopped herself from forming if she wanted to. "Julian is fine and understands what I need to do here. He's started a part-time Spanish degree so he's busy with essays and says he has to practice in the language lab for one of his courses."

"Well, it wasn't quite the romantic excitement I was hoping for, but I guess it all sounds ok," responded Marita.

"It was that too. Don't worry."

# Chapter 5

One of Isabel's closest school friends Silvia had greatly surprised Isabel when she had written to her in England that she was going to become a nun. They hadn't kept in frequent contact since Isabel had gone into exile. International telephone calls were expensive but occasional long letters and frequent cards had been their custom. The girls had been very close at school. Silvia and her family had always been more closely involved with the church than Isabel, but news of her becoming a nun was unbelievably dramatic to Isabel. She had immediately written back on receiving what she saw as this very disturbing news. It meant her reply would arrive nearly four weeks after the news was first posted to her from Chile and she worried that it might be too late to make Silvia at least hesitate and think again. Silvia was in any case determined and had committed herself after many months of thought. She was impervious to Isabel's pleading to consider the matter further. Isabel had not wanted to sound scornful of her friend's heart-searching decision, she admired Silvia's commitment to others that her future work would entail. *But why did she have to deny herself a normal life to give herself to the service of others? She could have been a social worker – wouldn't that have done?* Isabel thought, until she remembered that the military junta had swept away the social work departments in the Universities and local authorities. Social work remained almost only possible through the Catholic Church.

Silvia was another victim of the dictatorship, whose life had been interfered with and distorted, Isabel was convinced. She was giving up her own life in a way that she might not have done, had there been another route to work in the service of other people. She had been a fun-loving and adorable, generous friend as a teenager. She'd been serious, aware of the world, and deeply committed to the voluntary work they used to do together, but also she had been a leading and lively member of their crowd of girls and boys that went around together, enjoying a fun social life. Marita had also been part of that group but Isabel and Silvia had hardly gone anywhere with their friends without them both being present. Silvia loved music and dancing and Isabel could not bear to think of her friend 'imprisoned', as she saw it, in the monastic life or in a nun's habit.

Distraught for weeks, Isabel had awaited a return letter from Silvia after she had gently tried to challenge her thinking and begged her to reconsider. After eight weeks a reply had at last arrived, assuring Isabel that Silvia had considered her comments for a month before writing in reply. She also had been pondering this decision for more than two years and, in a sense, most of her life. She had wanted to fill a missing element in her life and didn't believe she would find it in the teaching she was currently doing. Isabel had been desperate ever since to talk with this rational, clever woman who, in Isabel's eyes, had been incredibly irrational. Isabel was equally surprised later to learn that Silvia, as a nun, was living in a wooden house in the Mapuche town of Melipeuco, an overnight bus ride south of Santiago, near Pablo Neruda's home town of Temuco. Silvia was doing community work with Mapuche women and living in an ordinary house in a pleasant residential *barrio* of the town. A visit to Silvia was a definite on Isabel's agenda when she returned to Chile and at last, the time had come.

Isabel would not even allow her passing thoughts about the stupidity of the closing of the railway line to Temuco from Santiago, to disturb her happy imaginings. Temuco had been a major railway junction and locomotive repair yard, throughout the majority of the twentieth century. *The closure of all long-distance railway lines was yet another destruction wrought by Pinochet's military regime*, she thought. Isabel's contentment, however, could not be shaken this day. She knew that her hero and favourite poet Pablo Neruda had spent some of his childhood in the Temuco locomotive yard. His father had been a train driver and had taken those magnificent steam engines on their route to Santiago. Isabel tried to imagine the excitement and fascination the engines must have held for the boy, privileged to indulge in every schoolboy's dream in that age of steam. Pablo Neruda must have been proud of his father and perhaps allowed himself to boast a little to his friends by taking them along with him to the locomotive yard. Isabel could picture too his father revelling in the affectionate admiration of his son. She then recalled the mutual approbation sadly wasn't maintained into the boy's teenage years when Pablo was seen by his father as 'wasting his time' writing poems. His father's condemnation was so great that the boy had had to invent the *nom de plume* - that of Pablo Neruda - to secretly publish his first works of poetry.

Soon Silvia and Isabel would be hugging each other and talking non-stop, she was sure, just like the old days. And so it was, when she had managed to find Silvia in the crowd, now wearing glasses and with shoulder-length bobbed hair. Isabel had first glanced round for a nun in a habit but Silvia was in ordinary clothes and she was there watching Isabel and holding out her arms, as Isabel descended from the bus. Silvia did look different from the rather more glamorous teenager she had been, but still attractive, slim and with a beaming smile, just as Isabel remembered her. Isabel soon became aware of a calming presence in Silvia's company and she seemed to have cultivated a very gentle way to speak. What impressed the most was the almost continual smile Silvia wore, with all the sincerity and warmth that was possible for a person to have. She seemed totally contented.

They had so much to tell each other and conversation flowed easily and naturally as Silvia drove out of the grid of crisscross streets of the town and across the lush, rich green countryside to Melipeuco. Initially, the countryside reminded Isabel of England but eventually, the dramatic Andean mountains in the distance began to add a very different feel to the scenery and snow-covered, volcanic peaks began to dominate the views. As they neared the town of Melipeuco, Silvia explained the snowy peaks were called Nevados de Sollipulli and that in those volcanic mountains there were hot springs and geysers spraying water between 40 and 70 degrees of temperature in the middle of glaciers. Silvia promised a trip another day to the Conguillío National Park with its *araucarias* monkey puzzle trees and to see the volcano Llaima, one of the most active in Chile.

Melipeuco, Isabel learned, was a very rural, conservative, agricultural town, where the native Mapuche population was in the majority. Silvia continued, "The Mapuches fought the expanding Inca Empire before they had to defend their lands against the Spanish Conquistadors. They struggled for three hundred and fifty years to defend their rights and lands and finally lost against the independent state of Chile. The Treaties they made with the Spanish Kings were continually broken and independent Chile treated them even worse."

"Really? In what way worse? That's hard to imagine after warring with them for so long."

"They renegotiated the Treaties, pushing the Mapuche Peoples into greatly reduced areas until finally, the Mapuches could no longer support themselves in their traditional ways, living from the forests."

"Did they gather fruit and nuts? I think I've heard they were vegetarian."

"They did gather fruit, nuts but some forest animals too and herbs were very important to them. They were part of their religious beliefs and their medicine."

"I've every sympathy with the Mapuches defending their entitlements to their land. But did European development not bring some advantages to them?" Isabel asked.

"They have been horribly discriminated against. Schools and health centres, developed for other communities in the 20th Century, were not developed for them. Driving railways through their land might have been putting relatively small amounts of land to good use, but vast terrains that were taken from the Mapuches, were never made productive nor were they conserved respectfully, they were just privately owned by Chilean landlords, just for the sake of owning land. Then the Mapuches would be shot at if they entered the forests. To the Mapuches land can never be privately owned – land is sacred, to be held in common and their lands are collectively their birthright."

Silvia drove alongside the town's central *plaza* with its large open green spaces and lush shrubbery and then approached a residential area, in which the houses, it appeared to Isabel, were luxury, detached, wooden log homes, each with its own beautifully tended garden. The houses were all of individual design, mostly two-storey, and all of dramatic modern architectural designs – straight out of Scandinavia, imagined Isabel.

"Wow, the houses with their steep pointed roofs and walls of glass are a very long way from the little traditional Chilean wooden houses I've seen before," said Isabel. They were very different too from the more modest and conventional-looking houses of two or three bedrooms of standard construction, which were closer to what Isabel had expected to be the home of her friend.

"Well, you know that in the forest areas of southern Chile, it's normal to live in wooden houses and these are the modern versions. Beautiful aren't they?"

"These are luxury versions and they are very impressive. Pablo Neruda, you know, lived in a wooden house as a child, in the forest. I'm sure it wasn't like these houses. He always retained his fear of fire, because fire burned his home more than once during his childhood. His fear of forest fires comes out in his poems from time to time." Isabel's mind wandered while thinking of Neruda's poetry. She remembered also that he wrote about insects, flowers and leaf forms and he had trained his eye in the minutiae of nature in the forest, which he explored as a child.

"The monkey puzzle trees, *araucaria araucana,* of the region give an especially hard and robust wood, ideal for the tall, steep angled roof structure of these houses," said Silvia as she parked in front of one of them. Shocked and amazed, Isabel entered the elegant home of striking modern design of her friend and she tried to take in the beauty of the tan-coloured, highly varnished wood of the beams and tree trunk walls and the polished floors. She liked the seductive curve of the wooden staircase and gazed at the mystery of the darker roof timbers, high up in the apex of the roof above the living room.

"It's absolutely lovely," declared Isabel and she then tried to take in the warm, comfortable feeling Silvia had given the house with her very modest furnishings. The church had rented this house for Silvia and another nun to use while allocated to tasks in Melipeuco. The house companion was away for a month. Isabel was soon to learn that the house was in fact, an average house for the better-off areas of the town. The bedroom and bathroom, to which Isabel was shown, were simple but comfortable, with adequate modern plumbing and they were closer to the basic, functional living that Isabel had anticipated likely for a nun. Delighted to unpack, Isabel was pleased to put her few belongings in a familiar, old-fashioned oak chest of drawers and hurry to join her friend again.

"Did you choose to come here or were you sent?" Isabel was dying to know.

"I was allocated this placement but I had indicated an interest in working with the Mapuches. I wanted to come to a rural part and I was fascinated to know more about Mapuche religious beliefs. Also, I hated the injustices they have suffered and thought it would be a particular challenge to win them round." Silvia looked thoughtful.

"Win them by evangelising with your religion?" Isabel asked in a playfully provocative manner, a little worried.

"No, no," responded Silvia immediately, smiling warmly at the teasing, "win them round to just cooperate with outsiders, so they can get a share of the modern society, like health services and education. We run women's groups to broaden thinking and knowledge on a range of issues, literacy classes and adult education classes. Also within the community of women that I work with, they breed ducks and they make duck down and feather quilts, which are sold in several European countries. That gives them an income and some economic independence. We have a house as a centre and we grow vegetables and herbs in the garden there too. Will you come with me to a women's group tomorrow? This afternoon I thought we could visit a Mapuche family that lives in an isolated valley, close to the Argentinean border. I need to see them for my work, I'm a little worried about how this mother is coping, so I call regularly, but how they live will be interesting for you to see."

Isabel went armed with her cameras for the afternoon trip. The steep-sided valley led on to numerous green fur tree slopes which huddled one behind the other, rather as a child might draw many more hills than are normally encapsulated in one view but here the many hills were the reality. Finally, these green hills lead to a line of snow-capped mountains, which formed the border with Argentina. It was a 'must take' photo opportunity for Isabel as one of the most unspoiled, remote and beautiful wildernesses she felt she had ever seen. Carrying her weighty video camera was undoubtedly worthwhile for spectacular scenery like this. Somehow she would work it into the largely urban story of post-Pinochet Chile. Isabel had decided to ask the permission of the Mapuche women's group to film them in their activities and discussions and she would ask for individual interviews too. The more she was learning from Silvia about the Mapuches' history, the more she saw as vital to include in her film, reference to the long repression of the Mapuche culture and to emphasise that this was still going on. Valuing cultural diversity, she had to admit, wasn't a notion we were very conscious about in my time in the 'old' Chile.

"In Europe, it's a fairly recent item on the political agenda, and I could develop that theme in this context," Isabel told Silvia and she felt pleased as she pondered her new bright idea for her documentary. "We used to like to think that our culture was inclusive and welcoming of other races and not discriminatory," Isabel said. "'*Negrita*' was a term of endearment when we used it in Chile, we used to say. But if Chile had had a lot of black immigrants I don't think we'd have done any better than the British or the Brazilians or many other countries in our attitudes towards them. It was only because black people were very few here, something of a novelty, we could tell ourselves we weren't racist."

"Yes, our minorities were the Mapuches and the Aymara y Quechua Peoples in the north and a few other minority groups." Silvia agreed. "We are as guilty of racism as much as any other country in the way we have treated our minorities. For Chile, the Mapuches are the largest significant group and we pretended for decades that they didn't exist. Chile made sure a great many of them didn't exist in the numbers they had done previously. The population fell to about one-tenth of what it had been after Chile fought its last war against them in the 19th century and that was when Chile tore up the land treaties that the Mapuches had made with the Spanish. The warrior race was left in a state of near-starvation after that war."

"It is shocking and I never heard it talked about in my time."

"Independent Chile revised the system of *reducciones,* the 16th Century efforts to collect the indigenous people together in small areas to convert them religiously and dominate them culturally. As well as their land, they even took their silver jewellery to fill the state coffers and the Mapuches have lived in extreme poverty since then."

"I didn't know that. I thought the Mapuches were especially skilled at silver jewellery work."

"They were, but much of their silver jewellery and their artefacts were stolen from them. And it was just at that time their vastly reduced land could no longer support them. So they were forced to work on the big landlord estates. Then in the 20th century, many of them joined the economic migration to the cities. They went to the shanty towns and became part of the urban poor. There is a large group on the outskirts of Santiago."

"Will you let me film you Silvi please on these issues? You're very knowledgeable and can articulate the Mapuches' position in modern Chile. You're passionate – that's what I need." Silvia was persuaded and Isabel was excited at including a neglected area in her documentary. After all that planning and preparation, the unexpected held the fascination of a refreshingly new idea.

"It was only last year a law was finally passed," said Silvia, "that recognised the Mapuche people and other ethnic groups in Chile and their languages. Did you know we now have Mapudungun, their language, on the curriculum of primary schools in this area?" Isabel was suitably impressed and confessed she had had no idea.

"Until last year Mapundungun was prohibited and very few Mapuches are literate in their own language. Less than a quarter are literate in Spanish and many, many of them are very poor, so there's a long way to go for them to gain any sort of equality."

Isabel felt ashamed that she'd not thought before of including this aspect of the Chilean reality into her filming ambitions. *But I was living in another reality. I've been away too long. How could I be aware of what's going on? I don't want to be away for so long ever again. Maybe I don't want to be away at all again.* All the implications of such a plan flashed through her mind – Julian, work, family in England, housing…the list was overwhelming. *I've so much to do here. It's going to take time.* "I must look at the position of the Quechua y Aymara when I'm in the north of Chile. Of course, all the minority groups in Chile should have their say and their rights," she declared emphatically to Silvia.

"You know there are a lot of Peruvians coming to Chile now to find work in our economic boom and I know priests and nuns who are working with the Peruvians in Santiago. They have to look for housing and work permits as well as jobs. The immigrants receive some very harsh attitudes even though the economy seems to need them. That's another 'racism' problem we have here." Silvia left the thought hanging. "What's the purpose of your film then? Where will it be shown?"

Isabel answered modestly, as she hadn't yet the confidence she could achieve all she dreamt of, though she said she had contacts and real hopes of a commission in England. She felt she couldn't explain the second film and its political purpose which she was endeavouring to achieve and show within Chile. She explained to Silvia that she hoped to interest a film company that makes documentaries for television and then a lot of possibilities would open up for her. "I've been working with various producers and documentary filmmakers as a research assistant and I hope to achieve my own production during this visit to Chile. It will be my first big test. I'm hoping for a news documentary filming job when I go back and I need a good portfolio. I think you are right about including the issue of the Peruvian immigrants and how they are treated in Chile today." *That is of course if I go back to England,* she thought, which she was far from sure about.

"You told me in a letter you studied Art History, didn't you? I'd like to take you to meet a Mapuche artist one day while you're here. I think you'll be impressed with his work. Here we are now at Ayelén's smallholding." Life on the isolated and tiny Mapuche farm was truly a lesson in living in a previous epoch. A teenage girl greeted them and she was keen to show Isabel around outside, taking in the goats, sheep, chickens, a cow and a donkey. The blossom of the cherry trees added a special beauty to the stunning mountainous countryside all around them. The girl chatted about the animals calling each by a name, then she momentarily disappeared and returned with a baby's feeding bottle to give one of the lambs some milk. The lamb was not that young now and seemed to have done well on this feeding regime. Isabel asked the girl to speak to her camera and she was happy to oblige. Her name was Suyai and she translated this into Spanish as meaning 'hope'. Yes, it was a long way to go to school, seven kilometres down a stony country lane but she loved being here with all the animals. When she left school she wanted to help her mother at home. Her father was working away in Argentina at present and only came home once a month, so she was responsible for the animals. Her mother had four other children, younger than her, including a new baby.

They went inside to see the rest of the family and Isabel was introduced to two boys of ten and seven, Huenu whose name meant 'sky' and Maiten meaning tree, a small girl called Pire, 'snow' and the baby boy Manque, meaning 'condor'. Mother's name was translated as 'smile' and this she did broadly for Isabel. Ayelén's features were very typically Mapuche, her face seeming wider than it was long and her unblemished skin appeared to be made of the most exquisitely delicate leather. It was hard to see her eyes as the puffy upper lids made them into narrow horizontal openings, especially so, the more she smiled. Ayelén didn't get up as she was holding the baby but she indicated Isabel should sit on one of the wooden tree trunk seats, and then she sat motionless again, not attending to the baby nor her visitors but just staring. Silvia took the baby in her arms to take a close look at her. Ayelén was monosyllabic in response to Silvia's questions. To Isabel, Ayelén seemed lethargic or depressed. Suyai raked the fire in the upright wood-burning stove that appeared to be a cooker as well. *Who wouldn't be depressed, thought Isabel, no electricity, no gas, just domestic work to survive...* Then Ayelén began to put out several plates of food she had prepared earlier. She peered into pots on top of the log-burning stove and spooned their contents onto plates, passing them to the children who quickly gathered around. Silvia and Isabel were then invited to try some food too.

To Isabel's delight, she saw that Ayelén was serving *humitas* which are well known all over Chile.

"These are traditional Mapuche food," said Suyai.

"I didn't know that," said Isabel. "They are lovely but a lot of work. I even tried making them once in London. After cooking the sweet corn, you scrape the grains from the cob and mix them with basil, parsley, spring onions and garlic. Then you make parcels with the mixture wrapped in the leaves. Is that how you make them?"

"Yes, but you add cream to the mixture first, or we do. Our cow gives us cream. We tie little parcels with string and we cook them in boiling water so the flavour of the leaves is absorbed into them."

"Lovely," said Isabel in great appreciation. In another of the several pots on the stove were potatoes and stewed with them were some seeds of the Araucaria tree, which Isabel learned, the Mapuches regard as sacred. The seeds had come from the trees in their garden and in the traditional way Ayelén had made them and the potatoes into a puree.

Then Ayelén began to dish out a chicken and mushroom casserole and Silvia explained that the traditional diet of the Mapuches was entirely vegetarian but, as Isabel had seen, this family kept animals. Ayelén also explained that the casserole had *triwe,* Mapundungun for bay leaves, which were supposed to cure many afflictions from headaches and colds to more serious illnesses. Silvia added that *triwe* was a good source of calcium so the Mapuches use it a lot. Isabel was thinking that Ayelén couldn't be very depressed if she found the energy to cook all these dishes this morning! Then a plate of *sopaipillas,* pumpkin bread rolls appeared. Isabel knew these as a favourite also all over Chile but she hadn't known they were a Mapuche tradition either. After the meal an infusion of *foye,* cinnamon was brought to Isabel by Suyai and she told Isabel that *foye* was another sacred tree of the Mapuche and that it was used in religious ceremonies to offer healing to people.

"You clean a cut to your skin with the bark of this tree and it never goes bad," Suyai added. "And this is for my mother, for her cold. We call this *diuka lawen* or *fira fira* and mother must take it three times a day." Isabel could see a lot of flowers in hot water in the cup for Ayelén and Silvia explained it was a decongestant. Later when they were leaving, Suyai insisted on showing Isabel and Silvia all the sacred trees in their garden.

-oOo -

The meeting the next day with the Mapuche women was just as engaging as the visit to the family had been. It was all that Isabel had hoped for her filming too and Silvia gave Isabel lots of well-summarised footage to begin. She started with the name the Spanish conquistadors had given to the Mapuches, that of Araucanians, after the monkey puzzle trees of their lands and she explained it had become eventually a term of abuse. Silvia described the militarized police abuse of their rights and she gave examples of poor educational opportunities and illiteracy and the racism that was still leading some Mapuches to feel they had to change their names to Spanish names to try to avoid the discrimination they encountered when migrating to the cities for work. Several of the women gave examples of their own experiences and the stories passed down to them, from their grandparents' silver being stolen to how they were forced to go to live and work for a landowner, whom the Mapuches knew had stolen and enclosed their own land by force. The army and police had supported the new landowners and terrorised the native people and this included rape and torture and this was still going on, they claimed. One woman, pregnant by rape, believed that her child had been stolen from her because she was told she was too poor to keep the child who would have a better life adopted abroad. She had felt pressured to sign papers she could not read and she had always regretted what had happened. Other women talked of their dreams and hopes, mostly for their children to have a better life than they.

The women were very proud of their literacy achievements and their work of quilt making. It was clear Silvia was encouraging not only individual esteem but pride in their culture and their group. She had had some opposition to her work with the women from some of the Mapuche men who said they couldn't see what was the point of their women learning to read and least of all to read Mapundungun. Spanish would be more useful for getting work the men said. When Silvia and the priest and a translator had called a meeting to hear their grievances, it emerged they felt it should be the men themselves that should be getting help to read or improve their Spanish. Following this, Silvia's companion nun had started Spanish literacy classes with the men.

"It was the Jesuit missionaries in the 17th and 18th Centuries that first started to write down the Mapuche language and of course, they made translations of the Bible and created dictionaries," Silvia informed Isabel. "They used Latin letters of course but there are four different dialects of Mapundungun, so they still haven't agreed on a final version of the alphabet. There are very few books around in their language but I have managed to get hold of a Spanish/Mapundungun dictionary and I've typed some words out for the women to learn to read and write and I have made a copy of the alphabet of the language used in this area. Now the women are making books for their children. They write a word or two on a page and draw a picture or cut out pictures from magazines and then they teach their children to read the words. They are very excited about all this. Naturally, I've talked about child development and the value of early stimulation and young children's ability to recognise letters and words. I think their men just look on in amazement.

We are getting ready now to start learning to read Spanish and then we'll see what the men make of that!"

In the video, Silvia pleaded for funding for a full-scale literacy campaign amongst the Mapuches. Isabel thought of the literacy campaign she and Silvia were part of in the old days in Santiago, when they used to go into the shanty towns and help the teachers, by giving individual help to adult students or by caring for the children whilst their mothers were in class. Silvia knew what could be achieved in literacy campaigns and had not lost her old values. This thought Isabel, is the "real" Chile and her film could refer back to those literacy campaigns and how they are still needed amongst those discriminated against today. Isabel, satisfied and delighted with the day's work, had to agree it was more than justified to take a day off the next day when Silvia proposed a day out in the surrounding countryside.

"Most Mapuches call themselves Christian by the way," declared Silvia the next day as she drove towards Parque Nacional Conguillio. "But I'm interested to learn from those that try to maintain their own religion and ritualistic traditions. There's a small group in this area and I go regularly now to their ceremonies. They worship always out of doors – it's a central tenet of their religion to be in and relating to nature and I feel it is perfectly consistent with my religion and the concept of God the creator. Occasionally other Mapuches jeer at those trying to keep their religion alive."

Suddenly the volcano Llaima came into view and the beauty of the scene overwhelmed any other thoughts for Silvia and Isabel. After they stopped, Isabel began to think of the camera work she would want to do but then tried to make herself fully appreciate the nature of the wilderness around her before putting a lens between herself and the panorama. She wanted to feel part of this nature and suggested they walk a little into the forest before she tried filming. "It doesn't seem difficult to relate to nature. Being in it seems to give a good feeling," she said and tried to concentrate on the emotion. Then she wondered how she was going to portray the immensity of the open view and the detail of these extraordinary araucarias in a video shot or two.

"The local people call them *paraguas*, umbrella trees" Silvia interrupted her thoughts. "Let's drive further on to what we call El Valle de La Luna. It's not famous like the Valle de la Luna in the Atacama Desert but this one is pretty spectacular. It's covered in cooled lava which flowed from the volcano

Llaima when it erupted 50 years ago leaving this barren track as lifeless as any desert, cutting through the lush forest." Isabel had never seen anything like this in her life before. The track of black, rounded, smooth-surfaced rocks was very wide like a huge, black, solid, river winding its way through a variety of rich green colours. *Could this be symbolic of the ugly destruction of the military regime into the blossoming beauty of Chile as it was?* Isabel took some film. Trees and other vegetation were starting to cover the edges of the lava rocks. *It's a terribly slow process,* she thought, *and this is fifty years on. We can't wait that long to recover the beauty.* The lava flow gave the forest a primaeval appearance in contrast to the moonscape of the desert in the north, thought Isabel as she recalled her trip to the Atacama Desert in her childhood.

On the next stage of their journey in Silvia's car, Isabel managed to take some moving shots of the sun sparkling between the *araucarias* with the volcano in the background. She was very satisfied with these and then Lake Conguillío come into the foreground and Silvia parked the car. Flowers from surrounding bushes and blue sky were reflected in the lake adding their colours to the many shades of green from the trees and bushes to the darker depths of water. The titillating lake, like a canvass of a million brush strokes, also reflected amongst its mottled colours the snow-capped, purply-blue volcano in the distance and the wildflowers close by. The intensity of all the colours in the view left Isabel speechless at its very great beauty.

"Now I realise why it is that people in Chile paint their houses such intense colours outside. It is because they are used to such intense colours in nature. Houses in Britain are white, or beiges and pastel shades and I've got used to those now and I thought they were rather more sophisticated in taste than the brightly painted houses here in Chile. But in fact, people here are used to strong colours in nature and it isn't surprising they reflect these colours in their houses. This scene with the lake is like a wonderful impressionist painting with a multitude of vivid colours merging in the sunlight."

Isabel took close-up shots of many different flowers in a range of yellows, oranges and blues as well as pinks and purples and then their gently moving reflections in the lake. The young women walked together at the edge of the forest finding a number of different trees and not just the dominant *araucarias.* The branches of some of the monkey puzzle trees had another weird aspect. They had wispy, dependent climber plants that smothered the magnificent fur trees in their fine lacy white gauze, all covered with yellow flowers.

Isabel and Silvia picnicked by the lake on goat's cheese and mashed avocados - mixed with chopped, hard-boiled egg. Silvia had put just the right amount of dressing to make it moist and tasty. She then produced both red and green apples and a couple of the juiciest pears Isabel thought she had ever tasted. As they relaxed in the warm sunshine after eating, Silvia asked Isabel to tell her about Julian. She claimed that Isabel had said very little in her letters from England.

"I never quite knew what to say," began Isabel, after a big sigh of contemplation. "I really thought he was the love of my life but I have often doubted it since. I didn't want to bore you when I was swept up in romantic love and I didn't want to tell you when the atmosphere at our house wasn't so good and I was in pain. You know that when I was a teenager, a fortune teller, here in Chile, said I would fall in love with an Englishman and I thought she was crazy. Before the coup, the idea of meeting an Englishman or going to live in England would have seemed as unlikely as going to the moon from this *el ultimo rincón del mundo,* the last corner of the world, as we call Chile. It was the last thing in the whole world that was likely to happen to me if I had ever thought about going to Europe at all, which I hardly ever had.

"I met Julian at the university and I thought we had so much in common. Julian is a social worker and he became very interested in Chile when Allende won the election. He helped Shelter get second-hand furniture to furnish houses allocated by the local authority for Chilean refugees. Most of the British young people I met in England didn't even know where Chile is on the map! Julian was different. He knew a bit about Chile. When I first lent him tapes and disks of Chilean music, he appeared enthusiastic about my music. The first one I lent was Victor Jara's *Manifesto.* Julian wanted to learn more and said that one day he wanted to visit Chile."

Isabel paused. "Once we lived together I think there were a lot of cultural misunderstandings in our relationship, a lot of differing expectations. At first, I couldn't understand what was happening and why he couldn't understand me. I know now I was hurting and still angry and I repressed these feelings.

Julian always wanted to talk about the differences, or what had been said or not said, to examine the problem between us but I didn't want to keep going over things, agonising over issues that I thought he should just have realised. It was like starting from square one every time, spelling out the basics when we should have been moving forward. I preferred to cut myself off and I refused to 'analyse the problem' as he wanted."

"What were you frightened of?"

"Was I frightened? I suppose I wanted to avoid being challenged. Was I frightened to look at myself? I refused to even speak sometimes. I know my silences were hard for Julian but they were safer for me. I felt less vulnerable, I felt tougher and more impregnable. I realise now I was impatient and difficult and I didn't want to change or be questioned. Eventually, I used to avoid going home to our house when I could and should have done. When I was there I ignored him which he hated the most. He called it sulking, and said that I was arrogant and stubborn - but I didn't think he could understand a fraction of the pain I was going through. Perhaps I wanted to test him. I went to *Mamadre's* house and passed time with her. She kept telling me I should go to Julian and not make it worse by staying away, but I couldn't face his telling me how it felt for him and his wanting 'us to agree on standards to which we should be accountable,' as he would say or 'hammer out our differences until we reach an agreement.' He always claimed he was looking for what he called the 'ethical' thing to do and I felt he ended up lecturing me."

"What did you mean you wanted to test him. Were you insecure? Insecure about his affection or insecure about your own identity?"

"I don't know. I've not thought about that. I was a bit arrogant and said to myself I'm not going to do what he wants just to fulfil his expectations of me. I suppose he was looking for a way to avoid our misunderstandings." Isabel thought for a while. "Perhaps I was not fully committed so I doubted that he could be. I have thought about this quite a lot. I didn't want to trust him completely because it would mean my giving myself to him completely."

"Isn't that what love is? That felt too vulnerable?"

She nodded slowly. "I think so. Was I afraid of commitment? Or frightened to be there all my life? What happened was that the more I ignored him the more mad he got. I know it's true I was angry but my anger was silent, smouldering. His anger was expressed. His anger was noisy. He began to shout and I absolutely hated any confrontation. I couldn't stand it. I just wanted to get away. I see now that the more I tried to look indifferent or to run away, the more I began to not know if I wanted in or out. I began again to look for a way to get back to Chile, like in my first years in exile when I believed that it would be possible very soon to return. I was only waiting for that."

"Have you forgiven him for his anger?" Isabel realised she could take these direct challenges from Silvia in a way she couldn't from others, including Julian. She wondered why had she never accepted any questioning of her own behaviour from Julian. She didn't know if she could answer this latest question.

"When thoughts of returning to Chile came to me again, it didn't help our relationship. We had some good times together, especially when we resolved to 'try again' several times but I think we were mostly drifting further apart. And here I am now in Chile and I knew I wanted to come alone although Julian begged me to let him come with me."

Eventually, Silvia said also, "Have you forgiven him for disappointing your hopes, which is probably as much your fault as his?" Isabel didn't want to answer that either but she knew it was valid. "He couldn't alone make up for all your pain of loss and exile." Isabel knew that was true but tried to reflect if that was unconsciously what she'd been seeking. After another long pause, Silvia asked, "Do you love him?"

"I can't answer that from where I am now. Julian has said that I have never told him that I love him since we lived together. It never felt quite appropriate. I was always waiting for the right moment and it never came. I wanted to say it at times. Anyway, the words mean nothing to me in English. My emotional language is Spanish."

"Julian must have learned enough Spanish for you to tell him in Spanish."

"Yes, I know, I know, but...I couldn't...Later I'll have to face it all and make a decision. I know I'm still putting off what I have put off many times in England. But I'm in Chile now and I want to concentrate on what it means to be here again and how this country is going to get healed after the dictatorship has divided the people so much. I see other families divided like mine. I wouldn't have believed in exile that my family's experience of bitter division is the common experience of families, even when all the members still live here in Chile. I thought my mother was especially strange to be so willing to take on board the propaganda of a dictatorship, but there seem to be so many who think like her - here in my country where I thought we were so aware and with such a strong sense of our values."

"You find it hard to talk to your mother? Would you like to feel you can communicate with her?"

"Yes, very much but she says things I can't tolerate."

"Have you tried asking her what she means when she says something you disagree with? Instead of answering, have you tried asking why she said that, just gently asking her to open up?"

"No, I suppose not," said Isabel thoughtfully.

"It would mean really listening to her point of view instead of disagreeing with her immediately. It might give you some understanding."

"She's been subject to this propaganda for more than twenty years. It has to have had its influence and she didn't have much of a critique before."

"Isn't that a judgement, rather than an understanding?"

"Ok, yes, I know what you are saying. I'll try."

"Do you remember we use to talk about the medium is the message? It may be not so much what you say but how you say it that gets heard."

"Yeh. I guess I close down the conversation when I rush in to argue. It's funny, I think I do the opposite with Julian. We are different, with different people, aren't we? I'd snap at something, he'd rush in to argue but then I'd refuse to speak. I guess we had both closed down the conversation already. I had when I made my point and nothing was going to shift my position. I thought it was better than a fight. He would then get more angry because I wouldn't talk. He was the one immediately going for the counter-argument but perhaps if I hadn't closed things down, like slamming the door shut on any hopes of resolution, I might have understood him better. I suppose right at the beginning I blocked the understanding you are talking about." After a pause, Isabel added, "It had its emotional toll too."

They sat in silence for a while. Isabel listened to the birds singing. Silvia thought a walk would do them good and suggested they clamber over a fence and walk further around the lake. It was several hours later when they returned to Silvia's car, tired but very satisfied with their exertion and their experience of nature. *Most of us live in cities and rarely have this experience,* thought Isabel. She had tried to pretend on the walk that she was Domo, the first Mapuche woman in their mythology, whom Silvia had told her about. Domo was made from a star and the flowers and grass were created so that Domo could walk on softer ground. Isabel had taken long elegant steps, lifting one knee high and then the other and pointing her toes like a ballet dancer as she proceeded along the country path. Her thoughts kept returning to what Silvia had asked her. Silvia was helping her to discover herself as she had never done before. She thought she should write down Silvia's questions that she had not answered because she recognised them as important and needing to be faced again. She pulled her notepad out of her bag. Had she lacked self-knowledge that would enable her to better handle the challenges in her relationships? *We have to examine our actions if we are going to discover our own personalities. Was that what Julian was asking when he wanted to scrutinise our conflicts to learn better ways to handle differences? It's a tough thing to do.*

"What are you writing?" asked Silvia.

"Just another thought about the video."

As they returned home in the car, Silvia said, "Do you know that the Mapuches now have one and a half per cent of the land they had when the Spanish conquest took place?" Isabel confessed she didn't. "The last Mapuche Treaty with the Spanish gave them all the land south of the BioBio Valley, a bit north of here. There are political demands now by some Mapuches that all the land south of BioBio River should be returned to them.

"That's a huge part of Chile and would be a very controversial political demand. It's difficult to know what would be right and what would be wrong. Perhaps unproductive land could be compulsorily made communal again for any persons to enter freely. We'd have to find a way in a new constitution to right the wrongs of the past."

"We must. Their religion is very ancient" continued Silvia, "Did you know the *machi* or shaman, is usually a woman, an older woman. She will have served a long apprenticeship learning all the healing properties of all the herbs and plants they use and the *machi* hold healing ceremonies as well as ceremonies for rain and to ward off evil. The *machi* is the only person able to eliminate the giant snakes, the *peuchen* that can suck the blood from animals and people. The Mapuche use the same word for vampire bats, but of course, their religious significance is that evil has to be opposed and stopped. Colo Colo is another serpent..."

"Like the name of the football team?" interrupted Isabel.

"Yes, named like the Chilean football team, but I'm sure the team is named after the Mapuche leader called Colo Colo at the time of the early wars against the Conquistadors. Another evil spirit is Gualichu and everything that goes wrong is blamed on him. He doesn't have a form and is merely a spirit but he's supposed to live underground. His name has become the verb we use for casting a spell on someone - *engualichar.*"

"I never knew that's where that word comes from. The Mapuches have had a lot more influence on our culture than most of us have ever realised. There are so many people in Chile who claim to know about various herbs that are good for you or can cure things wrong with the body. I bet most of the beliefs come from the Mapuches."

"I'm sure they do."

-o0o-

The next day Silvia said she had some visits to make and needed to prepare a literacy class, but she suggested that in the afternoon they go to find the artist she had spoken of. Isabel was glad of some thinking time that morning and to review the filming she had so far. She hoped the artist would also talk to the camera and permit her to show a little of his work but in addition, she wanted to plan how she could encourage him to fill the gaps in her film on the extent of the discrimination against the Mapuche people.

Isabel had lunch made when Silvia returned. She'd made a *Pastel de Choclo,* having found some minced beef in the freezer which she could put with the cooked chicken leftover from the previous day. Isabel had it in the oven to cook and brown the maize topping when Silvia returned. She'd also made a tomato and avocado salad to serve with the dish. Silvia did seem delighted with the results of Isabel's busy morning and they both needed a bit of a rest before setting off again. They were to meet the Mapuche artist at 4.00 pm and Silvia filled Isabel in a little on their short journey to his house.

"His name is Antiman, which in Mapuche means 'condor of the sun,' " said Silvia. She also told Isabel that the word Mapuche literally means 'people of the earth,' *Mapu* means earth and *Che* means people."

"No wonder they fought the Spanish with such determination and for so long," Isabel remarked. "It was quintessential to their very existence to hold onto their land if they saw themselves as people of the land."

Antiman was a very warm and friendly man in his mid-thirties, Isabel guessed. His studio was a typically messy place like artists the world over, but he did have a little exhibition of his work so that viewings and purchases of his paintings could be made. Mapuche traditional artwork, Antiman explained, had been primarily centred on metalwork and this developed into silver work when the Spanish had arrived with their silver coins. For centuries they have also traditionally made woven woollen cloths, blankets, carpets and ponchos which are so thick and tightly woven they are waterproof. "I try to include representations of these traditional crafts in my paintings, even if they are quite abstract. I like to try to tell the history of struggle too. Did you know the city of Valdivia and the town of Villarrica and others that the Spanish had established, were destroyed at one time by the Mapuches and abandoned by the Spanish for a time, during the 350 years of war?" Antiman took her into his little gallery.

"Some of my paintings include the plants and trees that the Mapuches use for medicines and I include some of the religious symbols and their drums," continued Antiman as they proceeded around the artworks on display. Isabel liked his impressionist-type representations of the natural world with the light playing on plants and trees and the landscape views. She decided she would buy one as a present for her mother but first, she persuaded Antiman to agree to her filming him describing some of his paintings and talking a little about the history of the Mapuches. Isabel was especially satisfied when Antiman talked to the camera about current discrimination against his people and he had a useful lesson to share.

"In the Mapudungun language, the words for Liberty are *Kudu ngunewun* but this literally means to make yourself the owner of yourself. This is a positive definition whereas the usual western idea of *libertad* normally means the absence from being captive or from being denied your rights," he declared. "You need assertiveness and personal responsibility whenever your rights are denied. You need to have a positive state of mind to cope even when in captivity or when you are denied a share of your birthright. I own myself," Antiman stated commandingly to the camera. "This way of thinking has helped the Mapuches survive in the face of injustice. Police atrocities, torture and rape, are still going on and we are still demanding our rights. We are calling for all the land south of the BioBio River to be granted back to us again, as was agreed in pre-independence treaties. The Bio Bio river for more than 300 years, marked the border between the Spanish colony and the territories of the unconquered Mapuche peoples to the south," said Antiman. *It is powerful stuff. He has spoken provocatively for my film, and this issue must be debated*, thought Isabel.

# Chapter 6

T he time had come when Isabel was due to meet up with Juan again, this time in Temuco and Silvia insisted that she would take Isabel to Temuco in her car and they would have time to do a little sightseeing before she met her friend. Isabel managed to avoid saying too much about who her friend was, only that they were doing some work together and Juan wanted her to do some filming for him.

"Where are you going to stay overnight?" Silvia wanted to know and she wasn't satisfied when Isabel sounded so vague and uncertain herself. "You know you can always come back here, though it's a bit of a way. You mustn't be stuck, nor your friend." Isabel was relieved when Silvia was prepared to leave it at that when Isabel promised she would return if necessary. "You know we have a new Art Gallery in Temuco, only built in 1981. We could go there if you'd like to. There is also a forested hill in the centre of Temuco with several hiking paths up to the top where you can get a great view of the city. It's called *Cerro Ñielol* and it is covered in original forest, just like the whole area used to be. It includes an area particularly sacred to the Mapuches too, where there are their traditional wooden carved statues. There are many *copihues,* our national flower, growing in the forest too." Isabel agreed it was a lovely idea to go there.

"You should see the new cathedral too, only completed a few years ago after the 1960 earthquake destroyed the old one." And so it was arranged that they wouldn't meet with Juan until 5.00 pm and the girls would enjoy a day in Temuco together. On the journey, Silvia had more to tell Isabel. "The word Temuco comes from the Mapudungun language and means *water tree.*

*Temu* is a tree, common in the forest on the hill *Ñielol*. It has orange-red bark and fruits that the Mapuches use for medicinal purposes. *Co* means water in their language and the tree often grows near water.

"And did you know that both Pablo Neruda and Gabriela Mistral both lived in Temuco for a while? Mistral became headmistress of a girls' school in Temuco and Pablo Neruda used to take his poems to her for advice when he was 15 years old."

"I had heard that but I didn't realise, it was in Temuco, but of course, it had to be here, where his father was a railwayman. Neruda would have been living at home at that age. He would also need to share his poems with someone who was keen to encourage him too when his father was so against him writing poetry."

"What we haven't talked about is going to the railway museum at the station where Pablo Neruda's father used to work. It's an amazing collection of old steam engines, even a turntable. You'll want to see that won't you?" Silvia sounded enthusiastic.

"Yes of course. I've always loved steam trains. Do you know I had a toy electric train set as a child - in those days considered a boy's toy? Perhaps it was because my cousins were all boys that I got interested." They decided the train museum should be their first stop when they arrived in the city. The large collection of engines was impressive and Isabel was thrilled to think about Pablo Neruda visiting that very place as a boy. The friends climbed onto some of the engines, entered beautifully preserved carriages and restaurant cars and saw the turntable in action.

They drove into the town centre and walked to *Aníbel Pinto* Square. "This is supposed to be the only city centre square in Chile without a fountain," said Silvia. "It does, however, have lots of trees of many varieties, some native and some imported, like the many palm trees." After a pause, when they were looking all around them, she asked if Isabel had seen the cathedral on one side of the square. Isabel had to admit that she hadn't seen it and Silvia pointed it out.

"That can't be the cathedral" responded Isabel, looking at what she thought was a modern office block. It was a tall, glass-covered, narrow building squeezed between similar other edifices that appeared to be office buildings.

"Yes, it is! Come and see the roof." Silvia steered the way through the trees so the roof could be seen by Isabel. That was a traditional pointed ridge roof and was the only concession towards a traditional cathedral, but it was way up high behind the very high tower of glass. As they moved to be near the tower, Isabel could see the large cross on the sidewall and on entering the cathedral itself, she was struck by the beauty of natural lighting coming from the large, tinted windows all along the side.

"It's stunningly beautiful!"

The friends went to find a restaurant for lunch and there was a great variety to choose from, of many different traditions from around the world. Silvia then explained how there were in Temuco, a high percentage of people whose origins were from many different parts of Europe, not just Spain. "The largest group of Spanish that came were Basques but the town is only 100 years old and throughout the 20th Century, immigrants also came from the Netherlands and Portugal right across Europe to Greece and Jews came from Eastern Europe and Russia. Arabs came as well from Lebanon, Syria and Palestine."

"What a great mix," remarked Isabel whilst concerned that the task of winning commitment to united political action might be that much harder, but she kept her thoughts to herself. They settled on a Lebanese restaurant and were delighted with the new surprises. The walk through the hill forest in the afternoon equally delighted them and the views from the top were magnificent. Isabel most enjoyed seeing the different coloured *copihue* flowers. From 10 to 20 centimetres long, their bell shapes in blue and pink and white were all over the forest. Isabel never had remembered seeing so many at once.

-oOo-

In the evening Juan took Isabel to the University in Temuco, which had only been founded in 1981. It was called the University of the Frontier which seemed appropriate, she thought. Juan had some student and staff contacts there and was hoping to set up volunteer groups that would offer literacy and education groups and child care creches, to less well-off workers of the town. There was a good turnout at the meeting and both Juan and Isabel spoke of the examples of such work that was going on in other parts of Chile.

Isabel asked permission to video a part of the meeting. She included in her presentation the work she had seen taking place with Mapuche families and the discrimination she had learned about. All agreed they were many Mapuches within the influx of poor rural people who had moved into Temuco and who were in need of help. Juan talked of the support politically that such work achieves, valuable when rights were having to be defended or political demands were to be made. A meeting was arranged with a group of key volunteers for the different areas of work and they agreed to meet with Juan and Isabel the next day to get further into detailed plans.

Juan had arranged they stay the night at the home of an ex-political prisoner and his family and again they were met with such warmth and generosity, Isabel was near to tears, she was so overwhelmed. She felt she had found the "real" Chile again, as she remembered it. She did admit to herself that her view of the "real" Chile was somewhat idealised but she treasured the thought nonetheless. She so valued people like this family who were welcoming her into their modest home. She was thrilled to know such a lovely family, all of whom wanted to try to make a difference and help others obtain justice. Even the teenagers were articulate and aware and the oldest son had been at the meeting at the University, as he was a first-year Agronomy and Forestry student. A beautiful time was passed late into the night, with another very typical Chilean dish being served for supper - *Churrasco* - thinly cut beef steak cooked on a griddle and served in *pan amasado* - doughy soft bread with *completo* as they called all the extras: avocado, tomato, onion and mayonnaise. A huge plate of chips to share came with all of this. Isabel was grateful Juan had thought to buy some wine and some fruit juice, which appeared from his rucksack.

There were to be meetings the next day at the University at 12 noon and at 5.00 pm and then there was just time to have a meal and catch the overnight bus back to Santiago. Isabel asked the meetings to permit a little filming as illustrations of the work planned in Temuco. Her mind wandered as she heard the debate on the content of the political awareness classes and supplementary classes to bring disadvantaged students up to university entrance standards, all of which were being planned. These were young people and academics who were willing to give their time to improving the lives of others and they were the essence of all that Isabel admired. She knew these were the sort of people with whom she wanted to share her time and effort. She was grateful to them for her new self-awareness. She felt she could trust their insights and their knowledge would be valuable for others to grow in understanding of the context of their lives. They will also help others to gain qualifications that would give them opportunities in life. The work would be backed by families like the one she had stayed with the night before who will support individuals in their localities and the students and teachers doing the work. Promoting this sort of work had to be her purpose and this video-making was an important part. It would have a useful role - to inspire what was possible for individuals, for communities and in making the nation a better homeland.

Isabel smiled and gave herself a little hug of satisfaction as she slid down under the blankets of her *cama* bus seat that turned into almost a bed on the luxury bus that was to take them back through the night to Santiago. *The long-distance buses in Chile now are truly comfortable to cover these long rides, not like in the old days,* she thought. The bus had three seats only across the width of the coach, making the seats spacious and their generous padding made them as comfortable as a mattress when they were tipped sufficiently far back and the leg support raised. Thank goodness you can lie down, she thought, then you can sleep fine.

Isabel was utterly contented, anticipating a good night's sleep but she couldn't stop thinking of the difficult conversation with Silvia. *Don't I want a future with Julian? Are there not many more opportunities in Britain to do fulfilling and creative things which I have been looking forward to? Do I not want to try to put right everything with Julian?* She had determined she mustn't dismiss the strategies Silvia was pointing her towards but try to make use of them. She knew in the heat of a moment's conflict with Julian or her mother, she found it difficult to not get angry. Could she do something about her anger first so that it didn't jump out when she least expected it? *Should I have tried writing about my anger and my feelings? Should I have expressed my feelings on paper and examined them so I could perhaps be more in control of them? Would I be able to find the fears that I always felt I needed to protect myself against? What are they really? I should look at the triggers that set me off like a gun and shut down any understanding of the other person. Have I lots of stuff bottled up still even though I thought*

*I had dealt with the trauma of all that has happened? Julian always said I was like a simmering pot ready to boil over. With my mother I am like a gun firing off without hesitation.*

Isabel had talked of all that had happened to her to the counsellors of Amnesty International not long after arriving in Britain. She felt she had dealt with that trauma. That was therapeutic for her but primarily it was to record the abuses of a dictatorship. *Do I need further therapy? How can I go forward in the best way?* She knew the anger was still there and ought to be allowed out constructively.

Before arriving in the capital the next day, coffee and sandwiches were served in the morning on the bus as they approached Santiago and Isabel groped to find her shoes and her toothbrush and paste for a trip to the *baño* on the bus, very like an aeroplane loo. Juan wanted to talk about their next trip and insisted the only safe place was their usual café in the bus station. The owner serving in the café smiled a broad smile to see them again and ushered them into the back room. She was never indiscreet, nor pressed them with questions, she was just supportive and kind and Isabel gave her a big hug on seeing her again. Juan wanted Isabel to go with him next to La Serena and then on to the cities of the north, right up to Arica. They had talked about the filming that she was doing but Isabel wanted Juan to see some of the results so that they could adjust the approach or emphasis as Juan might feel appropriate. Juan was encouraging and was sure it was all going all right and very worthwhile but he agreed to be in touch with her by ringing her mother's phone number when he had been able to make arrangements and a plan regarding their trip to the north. Before they left they would have a video session to help plan future filming. In the meantime, Isabel was to do some editing of her material and have a few weeks' break before she could expect his call.

-oOo-

The editing of both of the videos was going quite well, Isabel thought, though she expected she'd have to be even more ruthless in discarding much material if there was to be plenty more to be added from the trip to the north. She'd not heard from Juan but only a week had passed, when she noticed an article in *La Tercera,* a national newspaper, that there was to be an eclipse of the sun on 3rd November 1994 and it would be a total eclipse in the most northerly part of Chile, in Putre. A total eclipse was something Isabel had long wanted very much to see. She had, for as long as she could remember, had an interest in astronomy and she remembered the many stargazing sessions with her father all through her childhood. He had taught her the constellations of the southern sky and those that came and went from south to north. They were the ones she best recognised in the northern hemisphere. She used to get books from the library about the solar system, the stars and the origins of the universe. She knew that Chile's northern desert, with the lowest rainfall in the world, had some of the clearest skies in the world and for that reason, many of the world's most important telescopes had always been sited in Chile. Had she stayed in Chile, she might well have chosen astrophysics at University. Why had she neglected her interest in astronomy when in England? She loved those evenings with her father when her brother was in bed and she had his undivided attention. They would look at the sky at length, the Milky Way was usually clearly visible and very vivid. Then they'd go on to talk of many things. Isabel had longed to visit one of these giant telescopes her father had told her about but that was just another loss imposed on her life. The chance to see a total eclipse was also a dream and one she could definitely not miss now. If Juan had wanted her to go to the north in November anyway, it made a double imperative.

Planning for the event began to develop in her head. She knew she hadn't any time to delay. *The distances between major towns are so huge in Chile that you can't just pop on a bus and be where you want to be in half a day,* she said to herself. *It would be thirty hours at least directly to Arica, which is grim without an overnight stop on route and then Putre is well above that - on the Peruvian border.* She wondered if she could afford to fly. It could mean an overnight stay to pay for even if you fly. As Isabel thought it through it all looked too daunting, but she never gave up an idea easily. All would depend on getting hold of Juan and asking if they could meet in Arica and that they do their visits to the various northern cities in reverse, rather than starting as far south as La Serena and working their way up the country. One way on such a journey really had to be a flight, given the distances, she justified to herself.

When her mother was out she would ring Juan. She didn't want any discussion about with whom she was trying to plan a trip to the north. However, she regretted a day was lost when she tried several times to get Juan without success. Perhaps he was working in the daytime, to help replenish his funds to keep going. He had mentioned doing construction work and the dangerous conditions that workers sometimes had to work in. She would try in the evening. In the meantime, she'd go to an airline office and explore possible flights and prices. Isabel also went to a camera shop for advice about filming a total eclipse. She'd need to buy solar filters to cover the lens and protect herself and the camera. The filters, she learned have to be removed at the beginning of 'totality' and replaced at the end to cope with the changes of light. This is not simple if you want a continuous video and that is why amateurs often take a time-lapse video. Three to five-second clips were recommended to her every five minutes during the partial eclipse before and after totality. In the end, Isabel had to admit she didn't have the focal length on her camera that would be enough to give the coronal details and she had to recognise filming eclipses was best left to the professionals with expensive equipment. She would have to concentrate on the changing light levels and their effects on animals and people, but even that wouldn't be easy with the focusing issues involved. At best she could try to give the sensation of the experience but to be absorbed just by this natural phenomenon without the camera, was probably her best option and the greatest appreciation she could give to it.

A nagging feeling kept returning to Isabel, that the darkening sky of an eclipse could be used as a metaphor for the dark period of military dictatorship that Chile had been through and more importantly how it had not yet emerged into the full light of the sun with human rights fully respected. Some filming could be useful - she would see what she could do. For now, it was a matter of getting to Putre within a week. She got hold of Juan in the evening and he agreed that he had only arranged La Serena so far and that could be postponed. He had been in touch with other contacts in Arica and Calama but had not promised arrival dates yet. He was willing to start in the north and that they work their way down the country. He would meet her in Arica but it could not be earlier than 6th November. Juan said he'd like to go to Antofagasta to see a friend and break the bus journey on his way up the country and he would lay some groundwork for their visit there on their way south. Isabel was very happy he was so accommodating and suggested they meet up in the few days before her departure, to look at the edited film she had prepared so far. That was agreed to be a couple of days hence and Juan suggested they meet at the bus station café.

"You'll have to come to the editing suite I use. I don't have a projector here and I have to go to the suite with my film cassettes," she informed him. So Juan took down the details. Isabel was glad to have an intervening day to work further on the narrative she wanted to add to her video but that couldn't be finalised until all the material was assembled.

Her mother did want to know all that she was planning next, as soon as she put the phone down and when she announced she was going to Putre to see the total eclipse, her mother declared her crazy. However, she did have a very helpful suggestion to make. Esperanza had a school friend who was now in Arica and she was sure Isabel could stay with her and her family. That would be a wonderful help, Isabel had to agree and her mother was a little reassured she would be looked after for part of her mad trip at least. Esperanza rang her friend Magdalena and all was arranged for Isabel to arrive on 1st November. It was All Saints Day so the family would be on holiday and could meet her whenever she arrived and she could join the traditions and celebrations with them. Magdalena asked why didn't Esperanza come as well and wouldn't take "no" for an answer. Isabel tried hard…. to make it very clear she would be going to Putre the next day and she would be working after 6th November. She couldn't fly back with her mother. Magdalena was insistent she would look after Esperanza and would love to see her again. How many years had it been? And there were places she love to take her. Yes of course she would take her to the airport to return. Isabel couldn't get a further word in edgeways. All was decided and there could be no going back.

Esperanza couldn't quite believe it was possible to do the journey to Arica in two and a half hours or so. She had never flown in her life but she had done the long bus ride to the north more than once. She was excited by her new adventure and Isabel was glad to spend some extra time with her and was determined to try her new approach to any difficult areas, should they arise. She wondered what would be the political stance of her mother's friend and her sons and daughters. There were issues she'd like to ask about when in the north, about the people who were still searching in the desert for the remains of their loved ones, victims of the military regime that had been buried in shallow graves in the Atacama desert. She also wondered if the family would know anything about the telescopes that could be visited in the north. She might have time for such a visit while waiting for Juan to arrive. She tried desperately to work on her script for the video for Juan but her mother constantly interrupted her with questions about what clothes she should take and how did this or that look.

"It's the city of the eternal spring, *Mama*. All the year-round it's over 20 degrees usually. You don't need jumpers unless you are planning to go into the mountains." And that throwaway line suddenly prompted Isabel herself to think about a warm coat. She might well go into the mountains and even Putre is 3500 meters up. She'd been told it was only 10 or 11 degrees at that height in summer and she hadn't yet done anything about getting a winter coat. She was wishing she'd bought a Mapuche poncho in the south. She had been tempted but then she didn't think she would need it or wear it much. She said to her mother that after her meeting in the morning she would have to do a shopping trip. Esperanza, however, reminded her that they were meeting the family of a school friend of hers with whom Esperanza had always kept in touch. They were neighbours in a nearby street and they had invited mother and daughter for lunch. Isabel promised faithfully she would be back in time from her morning meeting but regretted she'd need to go out again in the afternoon for the shopping trip. With summer coming she wasn't sure it would be very worthwhile to be looking for a winter coat but there was the chance of something in the sales.

This came up in the lunch conversation the next day and a younger sister of her school friend said she could lend Isabel a really warm coat. Ximena insisted they go to her bedroom for Isabel to try it on. The coat was heavy, thick and warm and it was also blue, Isabel's favourite colour. It was waterproof too with a hood. It was in fact ideal. After many reassurances it would not be needed in Santiago with the summer coming, Isabel agreed to take it and was very grateful. How very Chilean, she thought to lend me a coat when she hardly knows me.

-oOo-

Magdalena and her husband met them at the airport on the north side of Arica and the welcome was very warm and bubbling with excitement. The two older women were counting the years since they'd last met and giggling in the back of the car about incidents in common they could recall. Isabel was glad to be in the front with Jesús even though he was pressing her with questions. When they arrived at the family's home, they entered a tall gate into a large courtyard with single-storey buildings on three sides. Isabel and her mother were shown to a room off the courtyard and it was clear all the family bedrooms and the living rooms too lead directly from this open space. *The benefits of the eternal spring in Arica,* thought Isabel. *No need to worry about cold or rain, you could always easily pass from one room to another via the outside.* The large courtyard was where the family normally ate at an enormous table and there was a food preparation area outside with a sink and running water too, as well as a full kitchen off the courtyard. The outside area was full of trees, giving shade and many seats and benches were scattered around. Isabel thought it a lovely arrangement for family life. She soon got to meet the rest of the family, Sofía and Paula and Javier and Jorge. Sofía and Paula had husbands and children in tow and Javier a girlfriend. Jorge the youngest still lived at home and the others were visiting for the *día feriado.* The women had been to the cemetery earlier and the main meal had been eaten but Esperanza and Isabel were soon offered an abundance of food and drink.

When Jorge heard that Isabel was off to Putre the next day, he begged her that he could go with her and Isabel thought it would be good to have his company. He too was interested in astronomy but he also had a good knowledge of the area and places to visit in the mountains. He suggested that after Putre, they make their way to the highest lake in Chile *Lago Chungará* and the second highest in the *Altiplano.*

"Lake Chungará is part of the Lauca National Park, which if you haven't seen it, is really worth seeing and you are going to be so close. It's a good idea to do an overnight at Putre when you visit there because a stay at Putre gives your body a chance to acclimatise itself to the altitude. Lake *Chungará* is over 4500 meters high but it is so beautiful. If you are in Putre you must go on to see it." Delighted, Isabel began thanking Jorge but he rushed off to talk to his father. A few moments later he was back to say they could go in his father's car. He was also able to reassure her that the car had an oxygen supply cylinder in the boot, just in case there were any problems with the altitude. "All the buses have them for going above 4000 meters, so it's a good idea," smiled Jorge. "I'll book some accommodation because Putre is going to be popular tomorrow."

Nothing could have pleased Isabel more than the plans they had made to see the total eclipse but the family party, with a lot of friends of the young people calling in, did make for a very enjoyable occasion too, she felt. It had not been easy for Jorge to book two rooms in the small town of Putre but finally, he was content. He had had to accept two rooms in a private house, through the tourist agency, but that sounded more preferable to Isabel than an overpriced hotel or a rough hostel.

They were waved off the next morning by Esperanza and Magdalena, everyone else having returned to their own homes or gone off early to work. Amid entreaties to not take any risks and repeated words of *"cuidate"* they finally pulled away in the luxurious four-by-four. The road followed the green valley of the *Rio Lluta* which Jorge said was the only river that starts in the high Andes in that area and reaches right to the pacific ocean. Jorge suggested a break just where the road turned away from the river and Isabel thought the views were breathtaking. The contrast between the green, lush valley and the totally barren desert hills surrounding the valley seemed incredible. She had seen this before where an oasis occurs in the desert because an underground river comes up to the surface and lush vegetation grows in the middle of a totally dry and arid desert all around. However, Isabel felt she was seeing it all anew, like a foreigner and had to pinch herself that this was her own extraordinary country.

The greenery on the next part of their journey disappeared altogether and it seemed the mountainous land was a desolate waste. Jorge said he had seen that area covered in colour when the desert gets one of its rare downfalls of rain. "This only occurs every five to seven years and of course not in all parts of the desert at once, but vast areas become covered in blooms," he said. Isabel hoped that she could see that phenomenon one day. Suddenly, it seemed the landscape had changed again. Out of this barren brown rock and dust, candelabra cactus began to appear. Their thick branches were all at the top of a central trunk, hence their name.

"We are over 2000 meters up now and we have to be at least 1700 meters to find these cacti," Jorge informed Isabel. "Some of these cactus are over 800 years old." Isabel couldn't believe it and Jorge stopped for them to walk close to one. Over three meters high, its fat branches were intertwined with one another and they were brown and green and without any spikes. The trunk of more than two meters had a furry hairy appearance but on a closer look, the "hairs" were sharp, long spikes, some 30 centimetres long. Jorge spotted a fruit on the cactus and what had been a flower attached to it, now a dark and shrivelled little arm. The fruit had a skin like a pineapple and though Jorge said all fruits of cactuses were edible, it didn't look appetising and they couldn't imagine it would taste very great. There was apparently no other vegetation around at all and no creatures that the cactus might have been protecting itself from with those sharp thorns on its trunk. They spotted a "young" cactus, Jorge said probably 80 years old and it was just a single trunk about a meter high, covered in spikes.

"Eighty years to make a meter," marvelled Isabel as she gazed out at the inhospitable reddy brown rocks. Soon, however, as they rose up further, Isabel spotted a lizard and yellowy grass started to appear between the rocks.

"The more rounded tufts aren't grass, you know, they are cactus spines. It's like they camouflage themselves among the grass and because their spines are so thin, they can be mistaken for grass." Jorge really knew his desert. Then a few wiry bushes, well-spaced out, started to appear. Gradually more variety of bushes of succulents and fern-like plants made their appearance and then a ground cover of green succulents. Finally, the slopes became largely green again and with the snow-capped volcanic peaks coming closer and closer, it seemed like they had entered yet another strange world. Isabel was told to look out for a rabbit-like creature, though not actually related to a rabbit, called a *viscacha*.

"It's related to the chinchilla," said Jorge. Soon there were llamas to be seen as well and Isabel was again informed, they were *guanacos* and *vicuñas* - other camelids of the Andes. "Only llamas and alpacas have been domesticated, llamas for their meat and alpacas mostly for their coats, but *vicuñas* produce the finest wool. It is very soft and fur-like but even nowadays this wool has to be taken from wild animals and they can only be shorn once every three years. Obviously then, this makes the wool very expensive. The Incas used to protect these wild creatures with laws, as we do now but in between times they have been so much hunted that they nearly became endangered but now their numbers are recovering. Did you know llama meat is nought per cent cholesterol? It has a good taste to eat too."

The landscape was becoming green all around and they were soon to enter the town of Putre. The single-storey houses were typical of traditional houses of Chile, built of *adobe* - sun-dried clay brick and a few very old houses had thatched roofs. One such building in the town centre was the tourist office and Jorge was soon getting the information about where they were to stay. In the northeast corner of this little town of 3000 people, they found the address of an elderly widow, who welcomed them as if she hadn't found anyone to talk to for a fortnight and though it was hard to stop her from talking, her welcome was warm and friendly. Their rooms were simple but clean and pleasant and from the back of the house could be seen the snow-covered mountains. As soon as they could tear themselves away from the landlady they went into the town to find a place to have *almuerzo*. It soon became clear that Jorge was looking for somewhere for Isabel to try llama for the first time. She enjoyed it and they sat in a little courtyard at the back of a simple restaurant, under the branches of a mature tree. Jorge told Isabel about the research that was going on concerning *adobe*. He was a civil engineering student at the University of Tarapacá in Arica and he knew about the comparisons that had been made between traditional materials and modern concrete. The latter could be built with earthquake-proof structures but concrete buildings had proved themselves much poorer than *adobe* at insulation, keeping out the heat when necessary and keeping the warmth in when required, especially important at altitudes like Putre's. "Work was going on," Jorge said, "to find a way to make *adobe* construction resistant to the earthquakes."

Late in the afternoon, they enjoyed a walk around the picturesque town to see the shops with *artesanía* but they soon discovered there was an abundance of street stalls of art and craftwork at this time of many visitors. Beautiful woven patterns of cloths that had come from Inca times were much in evidence and Isabel had always loved these designs. She treated herself to a scarf that she thought she would make good use of in London as well as in the mountains right away.

The town was becoming full of bustle and very busy, as the keen observers of the total eclipse arrived in greater and greater numbers. Languages from around the world began to be heard, Japanese, German, Swedish and different accents of English from Australian to North American. These were added to the Quechua, the language of the Incas and Aymara, the local people's language with their links to Bolivia, both of which Jorge and Isabel had become quite familiar with by then. They met up with some Chilean astrophysics students in the evening and enjoyed an evening of eating and drinking around an outdoor fire with them. They also took advice from them about a good viewpoint to see the eclipse the next day.

Isabel had decided to put her video camera on a tripod and leave it running during totality and a little before and afterwards, hoping that a llama or two would be captured and possibly some human 'whoos' and 'aharrs' would be recorded. She would not attend to the camera but indulge herself entirely in the natural experience. Soon after the sky began to darken in the morning, Isabel went to reserve her chosen spot but at 9.00 am she was already late for the ideal place. She did find a position close by with which she was content, looking over green farmland to the volcanos beyond. As the sky darkened further with the partial eclipse, the mountains took on wonderful shades of blue and purple and she felt she had to capture them with her camera. The whole sweeping panorama was before her and she covered it all slowly. When the light was only about 20% of normal sunlight, Isabel heard birds fluttering and squawking and saw a huge vulture spread its wings and swoop away. Animals began to make low howling noises but some alpacas just seemed to close their eyes as if thinking it was time to sleep.

The sun was now just a crescent and the snow of the mountains turned orange and yellow and red. Then suddenly the moon, looking sinister and totally black, blotted out the gold of the sun. Total darkness ensued and with it a strange coldness, which affected Isabel more than she had expected. She ripped off her eye protection and starred. The silver ring around the moon seemed to give up hope of life in its struggle with the moon and the corona's spiky efforts were weak and dying in their attempts to give the world light. Stars came out and Venus lit up. Totality lasted nearly three minutes and then suddenly a ray of sunlight and the diamond ring effect was seen. Tears welled up in Isabel's eyes and she heard a Chilean declare *"¡Que lindo!"* Isabel wanted to keep staring but she knew she had to put on her protective eclipse glasses again very soon. She and Jorge hugged each other and people began to cheer. The animals started to move after being so still and silent and a horse neighed.

-oOo-

Jorge and Isabel set off early the next morning to go to *Lake Chungará.* The landscape became very barren again until they came to the lake in which the River Lauca starts. The beautiful snow-capped volcanos were always in view and after another hour along a dry and desolate valley, llamas and their wild cousins appeared again amongst the grasses around the lake. The land around Lake Chungará appeared like marshland with huge smooth stones lying amongst the pools of water. Some of these were covered with lush, thick mosses.

"*Chunka,* in the Aymara language, means moss and *ra* means covered by," said Jorge, "but now people usually only talk of the other meaning that *Chungará* has been given. That is 'bearded' - referring to the myth that a bearded man came to these parts and destroyed a community by fire. I think it might refer to the lava flow from the Parinacota volcano that blocked the river and made the lake form. Hardly any water escapes from this lake." As well as the mosses, Jorge was keen to point out the beautiful y*areta* plants. "These massive hemispherical plants are evergreen and can grow up to six meters in diameter." Isabel thought them really lovely. "They only grow above 3,200 meters and up to more than 5000 meters and they grow 1.5 centimetres in a year."

"So that means these huge rounds of several meters must be very old."

"They can be up to 3000 years old," said Jorge.

"Wow! There really are some amazing things in this country," but then Isabel wondered, "How can people live at these altitudes?" but it was clear that a few do.

"They have their arts and crafts work to show to the visitors, and they hope for a good number of sales on a busy day like this, when visitors have come for the eclipse."

"But the rest of the year, caring for their animals, exchanging their meat or skins for some vegetables and fruit from other parts, coping with the low oxygen levels…what else?" worried Isabel.

"They have their *papas chuños*," said Jorge. "They dry potatoes on the roofs of their houses and when they want to eat them they soak them overnight before they cook them. They say they are delicious." Jorge smiled at Isabel's sceptical face.

The reflection of the snow-covered Parinacota volcano was perfect, clear and still in the blue waters of the lake. With the green mosses and the *yareta,* it was, Isabel thought, an absolutely lovely palette of colours. The huge expanse of wilderness surrounding that view of the volcano and its reflection, seemed to stretch to infinity. They walked a little along the shore of the lake and were grateful for the stall selling hot chocolate drinks, on their return.

Jorge and Isabel returned to Putre that night and the next day they were back at Jorge's parents' house and Magdalena and Esperanza were greeting them with calls to come to supper. Later that night, when mother and daughter were alone, Isabel wanted to ask her mother how she had got on with Magdalena and she wanted to find out the position of her friend towards the military regime. She knew she couldn't ask outright and perhaps was stepping into difficult territory with her mother but armed with her new approach, she thought she would test how well she could have such a conversation with her mother. She also wanted to make an opportunity to improve her relationship with her mother and her mother's understanding of her.

"How did you get on with Magdelena, *Mama?*" Isabel asked.

"Fine, of course, why should you ask? We were very close friends, you know."

"Yes, but people drift apart and their lives go in very different directions. But you could still get on well with her?"

"It was just like old times. It was amazing like it was no more than a week since we last met. And she's been so kind and taken me everywhere to see the town. I'm so glad I came."

"Do you think you see the world and all that has happened in the last twenty years in a similar way?"

"I don't know what you are trying to get at or why you think that matters. We can be good friends even if we disagree on some matters."

"Yes, that is exactly what I want us to be - good friends, even though we've disagreed on many issues in the past."

"I'm glad to hear you say that," said Esperanza and she lowered her head. "I've been so upset when we seem to be at loggerheads."

"I'm sorry *Mama*. I do want to try to understand how you feel." Isabel went towards her mother who was half undressed and preparing for bed. They hugged each other like they had not before, except perhaps the day Isabel arrived back from exile after many years.

"As it happens Magda and I have a similar view on the military government. We did talk about it a little. We agreed it must now be put behind us because there were some terrible things done, but we can't keep going over those so-called atrocities, we have to go forward together not divided by bringing them up all the time." There were several words there that Isabel would normally have flared up to oppose. "Can't keep going over" when the truth hasn't been established and "so-called" as if the atrocities weren't real. She managed this time to say nothing.

"You're worried about this country being so divided as I am?" she said.

"Yes. I've seen the awful divide between family members too often and when you were away there was quite an emotional disagreement between Magda and one of her daughters. Paula said that her friend had lent her a book on the disappeared, the second book by the journalist Patricia Verdugo. She started to talk about the cases and said the book showed proofs of their disappearances and Magda got quite mad with her and said it was wrong to keep bringing up these matters and repeating them over and over. She said, and I agree with her, that it stops us going forward and we have to heal the divisions, not keep making them worse."

"You think hearing of real cases makes things worse?"

"We all know dreadful things happened but the country has to put it behind and make a new future."

"I still want to know what happened to my father. Don't you care about that?"

Esperanza just looked at Isabel. She shook her head and then began to cry. She could not answer. Isabel was relieved she had not shouted before they reached this point and she went to put her arms around her mother again. She knew Esperanza had reached the contradiction as Isabel would have wished.

"Tell me what this work is you are going to from tomorrow. Who are you working with? You are not going to try to find out what happened to your father again, are you? It's so pointless and hopeless now. Please don't waste your life on that. You did all you could."

"No, no. I'm not searching for him. We know more or less what happened although I'd like a government apology. I'm trying to make a better future for Chile. I'm doing my little part, looking forward. We need a future of justice and freedom."

"There you are off again, banging the same drum," and Esperanza began to cry again."

"I'd like your support in trying to build a better future, *Mama,*" said Isabel, who was not sure she could keep the calmness up much longer.

"Yes, yes, yes of course but I'd like to know more about what you plan to do. For one thing, how can you do much here when your life is in England. What about Julian? You will go back to him, won't you? He needs you. You need him and you have a good life there haven't you? How can you think of staying here?"

"*Mama,* I making a film about where this country is now in the return to democracy and I want to return to England and get it accepted by commissioning agencies, for the world to know what is the truth about Chile and for the refugees from here to be aware of the situation if they are thinking of coming back."

"That's a bit ambitious! Do you think you can really do that? Will my daughter be a famous filmmaker?

"No, no, but I've some contacts and hopes to reach some people."

"The BBC? Wow! But why do you never tell me anything about Julian? Why isn't he with you now? Well, I suppose he has a job to do but are you going to be with him soon and make a good future with him and grandchildren for me?"

"We'll see, we'll see. I have to get my film back to England soon, in two or three months and then we'll see where we are. Julian is a very good guy. I think you would like him but he needs to get more Spanish before you can talk with him and get to know him. You'll have the chance, don't worry."

"Ok. Well, you don't throw away a good guy. Mind you don't. Let's get some sleep please."

-oOo-

Just as in the south, Juan had some wonderful contacts in the northern towns they visited. Isabel stayed, as before in very ordinary little family homes and in the company of so many generous, intelligent, aware and committed persons, who impressed her again as part of the 'real' Chile. She made video film of women's groups created to support single parents made single by the injustices of the military or women abandoned and without financial security for their families. She recorded youth groups debating direct action, non-violent action and the risks. They were making plans to ensure that their voices were heard. She interviewed on film a nurse who had set up a health centre with volunteer help at the edge of a city, where official medical services were remote. She talked with teachers, lecturers and volunteers from a variety of backgrounds. She filmed unemployed men who had been taught the techniques of self-built wooden homes and videoed the impressive constructions they had achieved.

"These are the ways our organisation can help the people," said Juan. What greater social problem does Chile have than inadequate housing? If we only had more funds for purchasing the wood, we could do more. But a lot is being achieved and I am more than satisfied that your video has all the material we could wish and will be an excellent promotional video for our political purposes."

"I think it will be inspiring to others. It is to me. All that I have seen."

"There is just one other topic that I want to spread the word about, but I know it is a risk to put it on film," said Juan. Isabel looked curious. "I should like to make a training video of how people can take direct action, how they can peacefully carry out civil disobedience protests, how to react if arrested, and so on. What their legal rights are and what is not legal on the protesters' part and on the policemen's part. Also what is the most effective way to react when they start with the tear gas and the water cannons, how to regroup and go in again."

"Wow! I should like to do a training course with you like that. Isn't that what we should be preparing groups to take on? We could make such a film anonymous. I could talk with my brother about the legal bits."

"Good, yes. This is what I have been talking to the most active volunteers about but I think it could be more systematic, more inspiring, more organised and comprehensive with a film. Then I would like to see people like you and me, and there are a few others capable, putting this training into practice with these groups we have around the country. Also, separately from the video, I think they need more education about the history of this continent and the way it has been exploited, not just by the Spanish conquest but economically by the British and then the North Americans. With a clear understanding of the context of their lives, activists' motivation will be strengthened. Their determination will be reinforced from a clear vision of what and why they have to keep demanding change."

"Yes, I agree completely that the educational element can reinforce motivation. I will think carefully about what you have said. I feel I must return to the UK to try to get my video on Chile currently, into the film circuits or even on TV. I can attempt some fundraising too for you. I promise I will consider this further role you would want of me. Do you want to work on the training video for direct action before I go? Are we going to go down the Martin Luther King non-violent route, which could include strikes and sit-ins and descending on government buildings or are we going to follow the suffragettes and include window breaking, some damage to property or worse? Both are non-violent to persons but a choice of principle has to be made. Either way, people can become liable to arrest. Martin Luther King was absolutely non-violent but went to prison several times. We've always stuck to the non-violent path in our meetings with activists. But violence towards property is still not violence to people."

"These are big issues. I think we have to think much harder about our future tactics. But it is interesting the examples you choose. Those movements achieved a lot but they weren't carrying out simple marches with banners which don't seem ever to have accomplished change."

"'There comes a time when silence becomes dishonesty,' said Frantz Fanon. I'm not suggesting that violence is right, as Fanon eventually turned to but we do have to train our people in non-violent resistance as a minimum."

"Well, we will see. I have much to discuss with party colleagues. Martin Luther King could arouse large numbers of people. Gandhi as well took thousands on his marches with him. The time had come for their ideas. We've got to get far more people mobilized and violence to property can alienate them."

"Look, my plan at present has to be to work on editing your video first in January. I have some interviews lined up in December to complete the filming I want to do for my video. I expect to get that edited later in January and into February and then go to the UK, definitely before the end of February. If you feel you are ready with the training video in February, I could do that too. But that doesn't mean I'm not interested in what you have said. I will think very carefully about what you propose - the history sessions and direct action training."

They hurried back to Santiago after a month's intensive work in the north. Much of the material for Juan's film could be appropriately used in her own and she would review it all for useful illustrations for her own film. She had been able to capture views and expertise on issues of health, pensions, education, and housing.

Isabel felt there was no let-up for her on her return to the capital, in that she must get her remaining interviews in Santiago and Valparaíso done before Christmas as the summer holidays were approaching. However, she was well advanced and Juan was to give her a final interview in early January. That would also be useful to complete the picture of Chile currently and she knew she could steer Juan to fill any gaps and emphasise key themes. She also had useful interviews that illustrated all that made impossible the transition to democracy under the Pinochet constitution.

She felt a need to get finished now and she kept recalling her mother's words, "You don't throw away a good guy." She knew her mother was right and she knew she was missing Julian. She thought long and hard about her future and she and Julian had some prolonged telephone conversations once she was back at her mother's house. She invited him to write to her or phone her there as she was not planning to move on again. She resumed frequent letter writing to him and sent many picture postcards of Chilean views and places of interest. She told Julian she would complete the editing of the two videos in the New Year so she could return to the UK in February after spending a bit of time with her family.

Much affection and the desire to be together were expressed between the couple, both in their phone calls and in their writing. Though Isabel's usual tendency was to avoid firm dates and promises until the last minute, she had made a clear decision she should return by the end of February. This time she felt she was determined to stick to this commitment and finally assured

Julian that she would fix her return flight accordingly. She would have a brief summer holiday with her brother and family, having been invited to join them at the coastal town of Quintero and she would spend some time with her mother and then go home to Julian.

# PART 2

# Chapter 7

*I*t is an unnerving feeling when all you possess, all you have in the world *available to you, all you are going to survive with, in the coming months, is that which is contained in one large rucksack and a small bag,* Julian was thinking as he first took his seat in a bus at Santiago Bus station. It was over a year since Isabel had returned to Chile for a second time and six months since he'd heard a word from her. His flat in London he'd rented out, his car he'd just sold, his job from which he'd succeeded in taking a year of unpaid leave, were all another reality seeming so very far away now. He was going to meet people he'd never met before and try to live and work with them, struggling as he still was with their language but he hoped he could contribute something. The essential condition of his leave from his Social Services Department was to do voluntary work in the developing world. Though he knew Chile was not nearly as poor as many countries, it had large sections of poverty and it qualified in the 1990s to get him his leave, whilst keeping his job for him on his return.

Julian's thoughts, as he sat on the bus to Quillota, soon turned to Isabel, as they did every day. *Where is she? Will I ever see her again? Is she hurt or detained? Why did her letters and phone calls stop completely a few months ago?* The letters had only been arriving every three or four weeks and were non-specific as to where she was, though full of enthusiastic details about the work she was doing. There had been regular phone calls too. But then all communication stopped. Nothing. It had quickly dawned on Julian that it was more weeks than normal without a letter and the longed-for phone calls had not come. She was never at her mother's house when he tried to ring her there. Isabel could rarely give him a phone number or an address of where she was because she said she was always moving on, from one city to another in the north of Chile. He waited and waited, but still nothing and he was deeply frustrated and a little worried, given her talk of the need for direct action and civil disobedience or nothing can be achieved, she kept saying.

Isabel had returned to the UK with all her video material after her first visit to Chile, to attempt to get her film about Chile in transition, accepted by programme commissioners and film distributors. She had succeeded in getting it released on the private film club circuit. At least the Chilean exiles were getting to see something of what was going on in their homeland and a small film club audience was seeing the truth of Chile's so-called democracy. She had also been able to get it circulating in the US and in various countries of Europe. Isabel had done some further freelance work for a year, with success and she had appeared fulfilled and to be enjoying her work in England again. Julian thought Isabel had a new calmness as if she had resolved some issues by her first visit to Chile - issues of loss and separation, he imagined. The aggressive edge had mellowed and they had both made an effort to be patient and tolerant. They had both been keen to give and reciprocate affection and their mutually loving relationship appeared to have been restored. Julian thought they communicated better and there were fewer periods of sulky silences on her part. There was much less of a feeling of living their lives in parallel and separately and he thought they were sharing their thoughts and feelings better than they had. They had talked of having a child, which Julian desperately wanted to happen but so far that had not come about. They had agreed that regular trips to Chile would have to be part of their future together, which he understood as visits together within work holidays rather than lengthy visits by her alone. Though both of them were very pressured with their work and he additionally with his Spanish studies, they had made time for each other and Julian had felt the happiness of their early years together had returned. They'd been to several concerts of Chilean touring groups in London and Isabel had gone to talk to the groups backstage, about her film. She seemed contented to be in England and very keen to regularly meet up with Constanza and her stepbrother, whom Julian delighted in seeing too.

They had recently enjoyed the usual big party at New Year to see in

1996 with the Chilean exiles and all had seemed like old times. Weeks later Isabel had said she was planning to return to Chile and quite suddenly it seemed, she was gone. Julian could hardly believe she had done it again. At the very last minute, she had mentioned her plan so he hardly had time to get used to the idea, let alone decide what he wanted to do as a consequence or make any plans of his own. *Why did she always do this 'last minuting'? We have discussed it so many times before.* This time he felt it was a bigger 'last minute' blow than normal. *It is always as if she hasn't the courage to say sooner when she is wanting to do something independently. She must have been planning and arranging her trip for weeks and could have been open and honest much earlier. Why was no opportunity given to planning for me to go to Chile with her?* Then he realised he should have expected this news when she bought a laptop. She had said how she missed the desktop they had at their home, when she was last in Chile and how very expensive electronics were then in Chile. Isabel couldn't say how long she'd be away, or where she would be and she refused to answer any questions. The only intention she revealed was that she wanted to do the political history and economics classes that Juan had asked of her, that she had been doing some reading and now she felt ready. *What about me being ready for another long separation,* thought Julian.

Julian had tried to accept the situation calmly and lovingly but he was hurt and furious too. Isabel's letters and phone calls continued intermittently through most of the following year, including news of her planning to look for a teaching job to help finance herself for the following year, just when Julian was hoping there would be news of her return. Soon after that and for the last six months, there had been not a word. Isabel had said she could teach art and the history of art and was applying to public and private schools but she never told him the results of her job search. It was obvious that she wanted to remain in Chile a good while longer and so Julian instigated the first steps to get leave to do voluntary work in a developing country. That needed several months' notice to get agreed and find a temporary replacement for his post.

In her travels around the northern cities, Isabel had told Julian about the voluntary teaching she was doing on the recent history of Chile and the economic and political realities affecting the working people. These, together with her classes on the undemocratic nature of the constitution, had been about raising awareness to encourage political direct action. She had also been promoting the need for civil disobedience, which she said, world history tells us, is the only pathway to major change. She had also carried out such demonstrations and got herself arrested on one occasion. She had been released within a week and had not suffered any injury of lasting impact, only bruises, she thought. Julian had been desperately worried when he heard about this after the event, especially about what might happen to her in the future. That was not long before she told him she was thinking of seeking a salaried teaching post and then the total silence had begun.

Julian had tried ringing her mother but she said she didn't know where Isabel was. He wasn't sure whether to believe her or if she was saying what she had been told to say and if that signified Isabel really didn't want any further contact with him. The language barrier with her mother didn't help him understand the nuances. If Esperanza really didn't know where she was then it was worrying that something might have happened to her. Surely she would not have her mother worrying whether she was all right or not. Had Esperanza looked for her? He'd not been able to get an answer to that question from her. *Perhaps she knew something that she wasn't telling me. Was it another example of Isabel being so strong-willed that even her mother didn't like to interfere? Has she made a complete break with me?* He tormented himself again and again with all the same repeated questions and he constantly was rehearsing the same memories of their relationship with the eternal searching "if only" he'd done this or that differently. Was it the cultural differences that had made their relationship so stormy? It appeared riddled with misunderstandings, but Isabel never seemed willing to want to clarify. Always she seemed to keep secrets to herself so Julian never quite knew what she was thinking or couldn't get an issue sorted out to their mutual agreement.

*Has Constanza in London not been telling me something that she knew?* Of course, he'd asked her more than once if she had heard from Isabel and though her answers were vague, Constanza always reassured him that she thought that Isabel was safe and not to worry. There must be something Constanza was not telling him and just like her mother, Isabel wouldn't leave her anxious about her safety. But Julian could not accept that their relationship was all over without a final word directly from Isabel. If only this mysterious and seductive woman didn't have such a hold over him. Isabel had done disappearances before, kept apart, made herself difficult to contact, driven him to distraction and then returned, almost as though nothing had happened. She always wanted to remain unaccountable and he knew it wasn't appropriate to not have examined these behaviours. To not have been honest with each other about the causes and effects so that together they could try to establish a better way forward, he knew was foolish. But Isabel would never do this and her silence and absenteeism remained clouds hanging over their relationship, unexamined and destined to be repeated.

It had felt too fragile to risk spoiling the happier year they had had on her return from Chile. She always said it wasn't words but actions that mattered and he'd tried to act lovingly and avoid too much discussion during that year. The action he had wanted from her was to agree that they must both be accountable for their actions. He thought perhaps he had pressed her too hard in the past when he had only been met with a refusal to speak. There always seemed to be a threat to the future of the relationship coming from her and Julian didn't want to risk that again either. *Was I a coward because I feared losing her? I know I have been. She refused to read my efforts in writing, analysing what I thought was happening in the way we related.* At least he could stay calmer with this approach and it was therapeutic to get his feelings out on paper, but she was not interested to read his words. He had never felt he could just give up, the pull of the relationship had been so intense and commitments made can't just be abandoned, he believed. The post-Chile year had been one of much less conflict, but he knew he'd avoided the risky areas.

Now at last he was in Chile, but he had a job to do and he couldn't just go off searching for Isabel. He would have to wait again before starting to make contact with her family and with people in her old haunts that she had talked about. In part, he had told himself he wanted to go to Chile to complete an unfinished episode of his life, as they had always talked of going to Chile. He knew as well when he was thoroughly honest about why he had come to Chile that he was here to make a desperate search for her. The voluntary work gave him a purpose and kept his job available to him on his return.

*At the first opportunity, I will go to see Esperanza but for now, I have to settle for a wealth of new experiences through the voluntary work I am here to do and to these, I am genuinely looking forward. Stepping into the unknown always has its challenges but is exciting too,* he thought. Julian couldn't wait for the two-hour bus ride to be over and to arrive at Quillota. He knew they were expecting him at Quillota where Padre Pablo, the Catholic Priest had said he could do voluntary work in his parish and had supplied the required letter of acceptance to Julian's work. The padre had rung that morning to ask if Julian would be in time for lunch. Julian had informed the padre when he first arrived in the country and had given his friends' telephone number three days before.

Julian had been met at the airport by Chilean friends he knew from England and he had his first look at Santiago with them. He had met Rodolfo y Antonia in London when Rodolfo was doing a year's academic visit to the City University of London, an institution closely linked with the City and the financial world, which the Chilean government was keen to learn from and supported the visiting lecturer's exchange programme. Though with very different values from Julian, the couple had been very warm and supportive as the friendship developed between them. They had met quite by accident at the Tate Gallery and Julian had been keen to talk to them when he knew they were from Chile. He told them he was starting to make the necessary plans to go to Chile himself. Over the months before his departure they had met up in each other's houses several times and Rodolfo and Antonia insisted that they would meet Julian when he arrived at Santiago.

So it was that Julian's first view of Chile was from a Santiago house in a *barrio alto*. The family had an amazing view of the *cordillera* from their house and garden. The snow-capped mountains of the Andes made a magnificent backdrop to the city and for Julian, it was wonderful to see those impressive mountains at last. He felt he'd been waiting ten years to see them but he was sad it was not with Isabel that he had first encountered the white, dramatic peeks, the second highest in the world. He had waited to see a lot of other things as well and if it could not be with her, it would be despite her. He just had to be here. The *nana* brought Julian a drink on their arrival at the house. It was a large glass of chirimoya juice. He'd come across the fruit in Spain but Isabel had always said the fruits were much bigger in Chile, up to a kilo each in size. Well, Julian was to go to stay in the centre of the chirimoya growing area of the country and he liked them so much he was determined to eat them as much as possible, *the bigger the better,* he thought.

Rodolfo took Julian for his first look at the city of Santiago the next day and they went first to the Plaza de la Constitución where the president's palace stands - the *Moneda*. Along one the side of the square was the Hotel Carrera, which Rodolfo pointed out.

"That was the hotel from where journalists filmed the now-famous footage of the bombing of the *Moneda* in the Coup d'Etat on 11th September 1973." Julian could see some holes still visible in the walls of the building, though he knew the main damage had been from bombs dropped from aircraft above. Julian was moved and just wanted to pause and think a while, though Rodolfo seemed keen to walk on. Julian wanted to recall a few of the words of Allende's final broadcast to the people from the *Moneda*, which Julian had read and heard more than once: "I am certain that my sacrifice will not be in vain, I am certain that, at the very least, it will be a moral lesson that will punish felony, cowardice, and treason." Julian knew that the realisation of this deserved punishment had yet to come.

Rodolfo was waving to Julian from across the square and he was taken next to the building that had been the Parliament in the past before the coup. He was told that the president before Allende, Eduardo Frei was still held in quite high esteem and had a government like his remained in power, history might have been very different and the coup would not have happened. Julian thought that was because Frei wasn't seeking to change very much - the poverty, the housing, the education, the profits flowing out of the country to American owners of the mineral mines - but he decided not to say anything but just listen.

"The son of Frei is now the current president," continued Rodolfo, "but I don't have a high opinion of the son. He is a technician rather than a politician but he is honest and I think the tradition we had in the past, of politicians in Chile not being corrupt, has been restored again." *That's leaving aside the corruption of the military and Pinochet himself with his fortune safely stashed abroad,* thought Julian but again he didn't want to say anything. There has been more information in the international press than was available here to the Chileans, Julian knew, but Rodolfo wouldn't have been looking for such news when he was abroad. Antonia had assured Julian that morning that the police could be depended on if he needed to seek help. They would regard it as a very grave insult if money was offered to them. Accepting bribes is not their tradition, she had assured him. Julian didn't like the look of their logo, however. It was a shield with two crossed rifles. *What kind of a symbol was that for a police force?* But he said nothing.

The next stop on the tour of Santiago was the *Plaza de Armas* where many people *pasean* on Sundays as this day was. "It's become a tradition now to walk around in this square to pass the time and enjoy the city, that is to say, the working-class people," said Rodolfo. "During the week, the square is full of business executives, bankers and government figures but on Sundays, it is very different. The square is full of workers and immigrants from Peru are plentiful nowadays. Many of them are illegal immigrants because the success of the Chilean economy is attracting others from outside, especially from Peru where Fujimori is not making much of a success of the economy." Julian listened and looked. He enjoyed the little craftwork stalls in the square, the painters and the copper art workers selling their accomplishments. Julian loved capital cities and enjoyed the atmosphere when he was pounding the pavements in the central areas. He had done it in many of the cities of Europe with Isabel. He wished so much she was the one showing him her country. He remembered they had agreed that it felt so vital to walk the streets of a city and they couldn't imagine seeing a foreign city from a bus window. It would be like only seeing the place on a film, they agreed and not the real thing.

Rodolfo and Julian finally arrived at the Central Market, famous not only for its fruit and vegetables but for its fish and shellfish too. The variety and the size of the fish and shellfish were impressive. Isabel had always told him that the Pacific fish were huge compared to what we were used to in Europe. A plaice could be a meter long not a mere thirty centimetres, she had said. Everything was bigger, and by implication better, here in Chile, Isabel had always claimed. It wasn't that Julian didn't believe her but he was amazed and surprised to see giant celery bunches, twice the width and twice the length of a European one, the huge lettuces and most impressive of all were the pumpkins. They were so enormous that they had to be sold in slices, each of which was still a large portion to take away. Then there were fruits he'd not heard of and the giant chirimoyas, their white flesh, delicate and beautiful. Julian insisted on buying some chirimoyas immediately.

They met up with Antonia and the couple's young daughter and went to eat in one of the many market restaurants. These are not elegant places to dine but they have a reputation for authenticity and excellent food. Rodolfo recommended Julian try *picoroco,* a shellfish that comes to the plate in its shell with beak-like shapes sticking out of the openings of the heavy white stone shell. "Their name translates as 'beak in the rock'. Pull the beaks," he was instructed and an indistinguishable blob of pale 'body' appeared which could then just be popped into your mouth once you'd squeezed on the Chilean essential - lemon juice.

"Exquisite," declared Julian finding it tasted rather like crab and very much to his liking. He didn't remember Isabel having mentioned *picoroco.* Rodolfo said, "They are only found along the Chilean and Peruvian coasts. They are very special. Glad you like them."

-oOo-

The bus pulled up very close to the church in the main square of Quillota and in no time Julian found himself in the office by the main church entrance and being introduced by the secretary Claudia to a number of active members. There was Mario the mini-bus driver and his friend Martín, a priest in training, currently on placement with Padre Pablo, a nun who had just called in and a mother with two young children. They were all very friendly in their welcome and the women all gave cheek-to-cheek hugs. Julian had the impression the church was a very lively place with much going on. Padre Pablo arrived from his quarters and he was very welcoming and warm with a long, firm handshake. Padre Pablo took Julian into the modern church building whose architecture gave Julian the impression it was built in the 1950s but Pablo said it was erected in 1970. It looked a bit deteriorated and old-fashioned for a 1970s building, Julian thought and it needed a coat of paint. On the staircase, he noticed some asbestos panels. These were likely dumped on the developing world when they were banned in Europe, he thought to himself.

Julian was taken upstairs to an enormous living room with a large circular dining table looking rather lost in one corner of the room's spacious, hexagonal shape. Julian was told that there were bedrooms off from this central area, comprising the Padre's quarters and bedrooms for the priest in training, the Padre's sister, the bedroom where Julian was to be and another visitors' room. The Padre suggested Julian put his bag in the corridor to his area and that he would first like to take Julian to the kitchen, where he would meet the woman who had prepared his room. The kitchen was a large room off another of the sides of the hexagon. He was introduced to the *nana* - Emilia who came each day to clean and prepare lunch for the assembled company. The lunchtime gatherings varied, he was told, but there were usually a number of key workers in attendance. That day there was to be the nun Julian had met, called Patricia, and the head of the Old People's Home run by the church, joining those who lived in. Her name was Gabriela. There was an older woman helping in the kitchen too and she was introduced as Ximena, an older sister of Padre Pablo who had come to live in the household as she was getting too elderly to live alone. Ximena had a lively personality and appeared full of vigour despite her age. She was very warm in her welcome and it was she who explained that there was usually a group of people who gathered for the lunch, the *paracaidistas* she called them, those who regularly "parachuted in" she said with a smile. Ximena seemed good fun.

Emilia served hot dishes to add to the salads already on the table and everyone gathered to sit down. Mario joined the group this day too. Padre Pablo said grace, which for Julian was a nice surprise as it evoked memories for him. He'd not heard anyone say grace since his childhood when his father and mother had kept up that tradition. The company told Julian about many of the activities of the church and some were cultural rather than religious, classes of guitar for example. Padre Pablo said it would be helpful to many people if Julian was prepared to do English classes for those interested because English would help many people in their job opportunities and education. It was essential nowadays for the young people particularly to have English.

"Those interested would be people who couldn't afford to pay for private English classes. Their school opportunities have been limited too."

"Yes, of course, if that would help," Julian said, thinking to himself he had not come prepared for English teaching and knowing he would have to do some very thoughtful preparation. "Would there be any materials in the local library?" he asked.

"You are unlikely to find any resources in the town library."

"Not to worry. I've done a great many training courses in my work and studied books on adult education. I think I'll be able to use the principles well enough and bring some variety to the sessions."

After lunch, Julian helped others clear the table and made his way to the kitchen to assist there. However, as it was his first day, everyone agreed Emilia should show him to his room and help him settle in. Gabriela went with Emilia and they hurriedly made the bed for Julian. He was surprised and delighted to have his own bathroom off the corridor leading to his room, very basic though it appeared with its rather ugly, unhidden pipework. The bedroom was modest in size, plain in decor but adequate enough with an old wooden wardrobe, some wall shelves and a desk and he thought he would soon be able to make it his home. He took out his portable CD player and asked if there was a shop to buy disks in the town. Yes, they assured him.

"I love the Chilean folk music, groups like *Los Jaivas, Illapu* and *Quilapayún* and my favourite singer is Angel Parra. I like the voice of his sister too, *Isabel*. I wasn't able to carry many disks from England and much of the Chilean music we listened to there was on cassette tapes, so I'm hoping to replace these with the newest technology."

"Do you know that Angel and Isabel Parra were the children of Violeta Parra who is regarded as the mother of the *New Chilean Song Movement?*" asked Gabriela.

"Yes I did know that but I don't know much about her except she was famous and did international tours."

"Yes she did but when she was younger, Violeta Parra travelled all over Chile, even to remote parts, collecting the traditional folk songs of the people. She met singers and songwriters who were still composing and performing at local musical gatherings. She wrote out the music and words so they could be known around the country and performed many of them herself. She was also a poet and Pablo Neruda spoke well of her poetry, you know. She began setting some of her own poems to music and performing these together with the traditional folk songs she had learned on her travels. This was the authentic culture of Chile, she said."

"She wanted the people to know this tradition in contrast to the unrelenting diet of imported North American pop, isn't that right?"

"Absolutely. Violeta Parra became internationally known and especially wrote songs with themes of social concern. Her children carried on her work. Both are now in exile and Angel suffered imprisonment under the dictatorship. Some of their children are famous musicians now too." Julian was glad to know there were people like Gabriela who still valued this music and these artists. Then Gabriela had to be off.

"We'll meet again soon at the Old People's Home because Padre Pablo is planning to bring you over on his next visit." Julian was left to unpack and for an hour or so after lunch, the house became very quiet and still and Julian was to learn this was the usual routine of the day.

The offices downstairs became alive again mid-afternoon and upstairs the kitchen became a busy meeting hub by tea time when *onces* were brought in by someone. Regular visitors took it in turns. This day avocado was being mashed with chopped hardboiled eggs and Patricia came in with soft bread rolls and Ximena was making tea. Padre Pablo arrived and talked to everyone privately in turn before sitting down to have tea and a roll. He said to Julian that he was going that evening to take mass at a village church out of town and he invited Julian to go along. Mario was waiting for them when they went downstairs after tea and so was Fabio with his guitar. Fabio would often play for Padre Pablo at formal services and informal meetings and Julian was to come to admire the extent of this man's devotion and the time he gave to help the work of the Padre and the church. Mario saw them into the mini-bus that he'd parked on the pavement just outside. The town was busy and it took a while to get through the traffic.

Julian was amazed at the number of electrical appliance shops they passed, all competing with each other with modern pop blasting out from large speakers in the doorways. There were plenty of TVs on show and Pablo said TVs were now part of every home. There were men in smart suits and white shirts with ties at the doorways, ready to entice any passerby they could into their shop for the latest stereo music systems or latest TV models. The prioritising of these entertainment machines was very obvious but where were the white goods? Julian wondered if there were fridges and freezers and automatic washing machines at affordable prices to make lighter the load for the women. None were to be seen from the outside of these numerous electrical shops. He learned later they were available inside.

When they were out on the open road they soon turned into a narrow country road without asphalt and the quality of the surface began to get worse and worse until they were bumping along quite violently towards their village destination. In the chapel there awaited about twenty people and they all wished *Bienvenido* to Julian and each gave him *un abrazo*. Padre Pablo asked them all to gather around the altar and Fabio began to play guitar. They all joined in, to a subdued and serious-sounding hymn. It was all very beautiful and Julian began to think how much his father would have appreciated the whole approach and atmosphere. He was a protestant church minister and he would have liked the way the Padre gathered the people all together around the altar, not setting himself in a hierarchical position and distant from anyone else. Throughout the proceedings, Padre Pablo invited them all to say a few words about themselves and their lives. Julian introduced himself as a social worker in London and said he had been brought up in a family very committed to their Christian faith and very active in the church. The people of the countryside are poor people said Padre Pablo on the way home when Julian remarked how especially warm and friendly they were, not only to him but to each other. "That's because *Dios* has a preference for the poor," said the Padre.

When they reached the town again, Mario took Padre Pablo and Julian to the hostel for homeless men. The Padre went around greeting everyone there and stopping to talk to all those who wanted a word with him. A worker came to talk to Julian and told him that the men did not pay anything for one night's stay and for the meal they received that night. This was another church initiative thanks to Padre Pablo. The day-to-day running was financed on the same basis as the Old People's Home, to which Padre Pablo took Julian the next day. The Padre had managed to get money out of the church for the capital expenditure on these buildings but his local church had to find the running costs. Padre Pablo said he had a number of donations regularly throughout the year from interested supporters, some of them overseas contacts, mostly exiles from the Pinochet regime who lived in Sweden and Switzerland. Also, some parishioners from previous places he had worked sent money and a few local better-off church members gave regularly. In addition to these, local horticulturalists and farmers brought food to the Home and the hostel and local people gave fruit and vegetables from their gardens and shops. Amazingly there was always enough. "We never know where it's coming from or when it's coming but it comes! We just exist on faith," declared the Padre. "The money will arrive" he would say and it did.

The Old People's Home was another hive of activity. There was no question of the residents just sitting about doing nothing, which Julian had so often seen in the UK elderly care homes. Some of the residents were a bit more able perhaps than the average person in a care home in Britain, but primarily, he thought it was the enthusiasm of Gabriela and Padre Pablo that ensured the place had a warm, caring and active atmosphere. Julian met three residents sitting at a table in the kitchen helping the staff prepare the lunch. They had been cooking all their lives, they told Julian and they saw no reason to stop now. Gabriela thanked them for their much-needed help. Then Julian met two men in the garden weeding a vegetable plot and tending some flowers. They explained that a new extension to the home was under construction and that was why the garden didn't look as neat and tidy as normal but they were planning a new garden between the extension and the main lounge. The heavy digging was being done by the volunteer gardener but Julian was impressed that the residents were keeping themselves active and they were proud of their participation in the gardening activities.

Julian was shown one of the bedrooms for two residents with their own furniture and pictures on the walls. There were a variety of armchairs and sofas in the large living room, arranged in three cosy areas and there were armchairs in a wide hall with tables between each pair, so people could sit to play a game of cards or a game of chess or have a little privacy for a one to one chat. The armchairs and sofas looked like they had been donated by families when they were no longer needed, which, though not smart, gave the Home a comfortable resemblance to a normal home and not an institution. There were books on the bookshelves along with ornaments and religious icons and one resident was dusting all of these with loving care. Julian agreed he would do regular visits to the Home, just to ensure all residents had a visitor and someone to talk to. He saw that as a relatively easy task as he knew old people like to talk about the past and their families and he was happy to let them do so. He was relieved it wouldn't be very taxing on his Spanish but great practice.

Now Padre Pablo had another major project in the planning and that would be financed in its day-to-day running by the same method, *"el dinero llegará"*. That was 100 place nursery, which Julian found hard to believe could be done on the basis that "the money will arrive". However, he was already impressed with what this semi-famous Padre had already achieved. Ximena explained to Julian after lunch that day that the church, in the person of the Archbishop of Valparaíso, insisted that when the new church was built in the poorest *población* of the city, it was to be a very large building, constructed for many decades of expected future growth of the congregation. By any standards, Julian thought that over-optimistic when he saw the enormous size of this barn of a building. Padre Pablo had argued that it did not appear ethical to place a huge church at enormous cost in the centre of this poorest *barrio*. The Padre lost the argument with his archbishop except that his plea to build in addition to the church, a *guardería* for neighbourhood children won the day. Again the agreement was that the church would pay for the building but the running costs would not be paid. The children's nursery had not yet materialised.

That afternoon Padre Pablo emerged from his rooms after his quiet time and joined Ximena and Julian still sitting chatting at the dining table. He said to Julian that perhaps the greatest social problem of the area of San Rafael, where the new church had been built, was that there were a great many children of poor families left unattended while parents had to go out to work. In that area, there were a very great proportion of abandoned mothers and with no state benefits, the single parents had no choice but to leave the children and go to work to survive. Hence the need for a nursery with breakfast and after-school facilities. Theoretically, neighbours or grandparents were usually asked to take care of the children or to keep an eye out for the school children when they arrived home ahead of the mothers but the real level of care for some was dubious and offered little stimulation or loving nurturing. Padre Pablo, in the absence as yet of his dreamed-of nursery, wanted Julian to go into the area and gather children around him who were hanging around the streets and do educational activities with them so that they were safely occupied and stimulated for a few hours each day before their parents arrived home.

Julian immediately began planning activities that he could do and gathering materials from local grocers, stationers and a book shop. He bought different shaped pasta and dried beans for collages, paper and paints, brushes and crayons, coloured cards, glue and stickers and he was shocked at the paucity of children's books available. He was even more shocked when he went to the town's library. It consisted of one average living-room-sized space with a single large table in the middle and some books on the shelves of the four walls around the table. Little room existed to pass between the table and the shelves. A few "students" were sitting at the table and Julian had difficulty bending down in the area where he was told he'd find the children's books. There were in fact, on the very bottom level, only a few very old-fashioned and ancient-looking storybooks. They had a Dickensian appearance to them, both in their condition and their illustrations and he wondered, *what century are we living in*. Julian didn't believe that these would be typical of the materials available to middle-class children, but there had not been many children's books in the book shop either. Consumerism hadn't extended to children's books on a big scale yet. Clearly, the burghers of the town had no sense of valuing childhood and the importance of learning, let alone a sense of encouraging children into the habit of going to a library.

Julian did, however, manage to find a book of the stories of Robin Hood and this would prove to be invaluable in the weeks to come. The children were quick to gather around him when he stood on a corner of a street where Padre Pablo had taken him and he started to take out some materials and his Robin Hood book. Julian read one story and suggested the children might like to paint it afterwards and there was much enthusiasm for this. One child offered to get water for the brushes from his house and another brought a little bench from their patio.

"The wonderful thing is," Julian later told the Padre "I've ended up with a pile of paintings of Robin Hood and every one has Chilean mountains in the background." Including the mountains was as normal for the children, he soon realised, and as natural as a young child in Britain who would paint a little box house and put in a door and windows, so these children painted what they were daily conscious of - the Andes mountains, looming constantly high above them.

"Let's have an exhibition of the children's work," said Padre Pablo, "in the Church entrance hall at Christmas."

The number of children grew each time Julian went back and that was every weekday. Soon neighbours were offering their little front patios for the children to gather in, more wooden benches were supplied and a grandmother brought water with orange juice in a jug and plastic cups. Padre Pablo christened the work *biblioteca de la calle*. Julian asked the church workers to save yoghurt pots, boxes and jars and the imaginative models grew. They played some cooperative games, fortunately, Julian had a book of such games in England and had been able to remember some of them. He would get them to sing some of their own traditional songs and enabled them to make primitive instruments with boxes, rubber bands and bits of metal he had acquired. Sometimes they would walk a little out of town as the countryside was very close and they would sit under a tree to do their activities. He felt like the Pied Piper of Hamelin when a crowd of them followed him down the road.

Julian was surprised how respectful the children were of the resources he bought for them to work with, like paper and paints and these lasted longer than he'd expected. It was likely that the children couldn't imagine having these things for themselves and so they felt them to be precious. When Julian tried to buy a large pack of paper for drawing, just normal printing paper, nothing specially meant for art, he was asked how many individual sheets did he want to buy? This would be how paper was normally sold, not in reams or whole packs, as he'd anticipated from his own culture.

Julian also found the children affectionate, friendly and polite and he could imagine them being as tender and warm as their parents when they were older. There were occasional conflicts between the children but these were rare, fortunately, and he could identify the children with relationship problems. Amongst the older children who arrived after school time, was Paloma, who was a precocious 11-year-old but very small for her years and she was often getting into fights with other children, which she usually started, physically at least. She always wanted to sit herself next to Julian and he was frustrated with his language ability to give her all the warmth and guidance he wanted to give. He did his best repeatedly to calm her and try to encourage tenderness and tolerance and he did feel there had been, over time, a reduction in the incidents of conflict. Julian learned Paloma was from the family that the nun Patricia had told him about. The mother had abandoned the family and the grandmother with whom the children now lived, wouldn't allow them to speak or move during mealtimes and they had to eat everything on their plates. The grandmother was one of those who allowed the children's group to use her front patio at times. There was also an aunt in this family with a mental disability and Julian appreciated the difficulties Paloma was growing up with. After a few months, an art student Mauricio started to help with the activities when he was home from college and their work started to expand. They also did sessions in a neighbouring village and Mauricio brought his artistic ideas and he was able to encourage Chilean traditions of singing and games. Julian valued the friendship that grew between them.

Mauricio enabled Julian to get to know the town, suggesting first that they go to a cafe after finishing a session with the children. Julian learned that Quillota had originally been planned as the capital of Chile after the Spanish conquest as it was the oldest town and situated on a fertile valley but since its founding, several earthquakes had destroyed many of the buildings and the plans never developed.

"All the investment went to Santiago and its port, Valparaíso and as they grew in importance, Quillota declined," Mauricio said. "The town council is inclined to the Left but it has few resources from the central government." Julian realised he had been quick to judge them when he saw the state of the library. "They have very little money to work with. Richer areas of Santiago add local taxes to their spending to be able to offer better schools, libraries and nurseries. Quillota can't do this very much. It means that areas of Chile are very different, very unequal." In the central square Plaza de Armas, they went to see the monument erected by the town council for the *desaparecidos*. "Not all towns would acknowledge what happened under the Pinochet Regime and remember those that disappeared in this way," Mauricio assured him.

-oOo-

After a few months of work at Quillota, Julian could not hold back any longer from carrying out the plan he had been developing in his head for a while. He had to go to see Isabel's mother, face to face. He had decided against telephoning her or giving any warning he wanted to visit, in case that was refused or a plan was hatched by the family to say nothing to him. He felt he should tell Ximena what he would be doing because she would otherwise worry about his disappearance all day or possibly all weekend. She would also reassure others and silence any questions with her insistence that he was having a weekend off, starting Friday morning.

In Santiago, Julian travelled on the metro, which he found surprisingly quiet as well as modern. He knew the carriages ran on rubber tyres, modelled on the Paris Metro stock and he was impressed how this lowered the noise level and smoothed the ride. He travelled to San Miguel and quickly found Esperanza's house, but decided to pop into a corner shop to take a drink and compose himself a little before approaching the door. It was 12.00 noon and he calculated that if Esperanza had gone food shopping that morning, she would probably be home and starting to prepare lunch. He was right, the oak door was opened by an elderly woman in an apron and as soon as he asked if it was Esperanza, the lady turned away and shouted into the house. By the time Esperanza came, Julian had told the first lady that he was the partner of Isabel and she had permitted him to step inside. He was relieved at this as he didn't want to find himself not even allowed in and the door shut on him. Esperanza just listened to who he said he was and how he was hoping to be in contact with Isabel. She didn't answer his plea for help but she did say she was glad to meet him and suggested he had better come in and have some lunch and then there would be time to talk. What a relief! The first woman Julian had seen was Matilda, the *nana* that had been with the family since Isabel was born. She lived with her now-adult daughter Mercedes in a wooden house at the end of the garden. Julian was introduced to Mercedes who was preparing food in the kitchen along with her mother. Matilda began to explain how enormously fond she was of Isabel and how she missed her when she had gone to live with her stepmother after her father had disappeared, something she said she never felt was right. When Esperanza was out of the room for a moment, Matilda whispered that Isabel and her mother used to have huge rows about the Allende government.

"As soon as Isabel was 16, she said she was leaving to go to live at her father's in Valparaíso, but in the end, she only stayed for the school holidays and had to come back and stay at the same school here. But later she went to her stepmother's and I did miss her then," said Matilda. "That was an awful year before she went. Isabel was as stubborn as a mule when she wanted to be."

"I know what you mean."

"She'd be moody and refuse to speak to her mother and she would walk out often and then when she returned she'd take some food from the kitchen, and she'd go straight to her room. She knew I would leave something ready for her," said Matilda. "She was out every afternoon after school on that voluntary work she was doing." Esperanza came back to help with lunch preparations and then Matilda started to reminisce about Isabel being her first baby to care for, and how much she loved her and played with her for hours.

Lunch did not start until they were joined by Isabel's younger brother Carlos who had come as normal from his work not far away to eat *almuerzo* with his mother. He was surprised to find Julian there but he was warm and welcoming. They shared a lot about their lives over lunch and when the table was being cleared and the washing up started by the women, Julian seized the opportunity to tell Carlos he was desperately looking for Isabel and could Carlos help him. Before he left to return to work, Carlos slipped a paper with his phone number into Julian's hand. Clearly not much could be said in front of his mother although Carlos had assured Julian that she was alive and well.

Julian went to help wipe the dishes in the kitchen but soon Esperanza pulled him away into the living room to talk with him. Yes, Isabel had stayed with her a few weeks when she came back to Chile last time. "That's a year and a half ago. I've not seen much of her since then." Esperanza became a little tearful, "It's because we so disagreed and didn't get on well, but things were improving and all that happened in the past doesn't mean I don't care about her or need to know that she is all right. She didn't phone often from England but that I understood, as it was very expensive to call and at least I knew she was all right there. She seemed very happy when she knew you and she told me about you. Why didn't you have children? Was there a problem? She'll be too old soon if she isn't already. I hoped she would settle down in England and she could visit sometimes with grandchildren. When she was here I knew she was going to her old haunts and you know there have been awful problems in some *poblaciones*, violence and clashes with the police and arrests are still happening when it all should have stopped long ago and we should now all be getting over all *that*. I told her when she was here to stop all this political action, that was going to get her nowhere and I knew she'd go and get herself involved with the wrong sort again..." Esperanza didn't stop for an answer to any questions nor to ask Julian's point of view or anything about him. She was distraught in her own grief and Julian could hardly get a word in edgeways. Finally, he got to ask if she knew Isabel was all right - he didn't want to say 'alive' for fear of upsetting her more. She said that Carlos keeps saying she's ok and she can look after herself and not to worry "but he doesn't really know and doesn't worry like a mother does."

Eventually, Julian elicited that Isabel had visited the last Christmas and she had talked of travelling around the north again, so Isabel couldn't say where she would be exactly but in a phone call she had said she was going to see a friend in La Serena. "I can't see how she can stay with friends for months on end and she won't tell me where she is when she phones, she just keeps saying 'I'm fine, don't worry and the more I demand to know where she is the more she is *terca.*" That's obstinate and stubborn, thought Julian. He remembered looking up that word when he lived with Isabel. He knew exactly what she meant.

"Can you tell me where it was in Santiago that Isabel used to do the voluntary work when she was a schoolgirl?" It was clear that Esperanza didn't want to talk about this and was very disapproving.

"It wasn't voluntary work, it was propaganda for the party that brought about so much trouble in the end. I told her not to get involved but *terca, terca!*" Julian ventured that she did some babysitting whilst mothers went to literacy classes but Esperanza dismissed this. "They used her and that boyfriend led her astray."

"Do you know where the boyfriend lived," Julian pressed her but Esperanza waved her hand in dismissal of him.

"He disappeared like her father. She went completely off the rails when she spent more time with her *Papa.*"

Finally, however, when Julian kept bringing her back to his question, Esperanza let out that she had used to go to *población* Manuel Rodriguez and that she talked about an Alexander who lived there. Concerning Isabel's local friends when she lived with her mother, some parents might still be neighbours but their children had moved away and she was very reluctant that Julian try to contact these people. She gave him one name but she didn't think it would help him at all now, it was all too long ago. When he thought he'd obtained all the information he was likely to get, he decided he should extract himself before getting involved in *onces* and small talk. He had great hopes pinned on Carlos giving him more news. He also knew the name of the friend of Isabel's stepbrother Eugenio from England, which was Miguel and he knew his address was still in the area that Esperanza had mentioned.

"*Gracias, muchisimas gracias por todo.* I promise to see you again." and they hoped he'd come with news. "If Isabel rings, please tell her of my visit and how much I want to see her." They all wished him well.

# Chapter 8

I t had all gone rather better than he might have expected although Julian hadn't learned a lot. He was desperate to ring Carlos and he found a phone box and tried the number. Carlos's wife Mariana answered and said Carlos was not back from work yet. Julian had hoped he'd been given a work number and could have met Carlos as he left the office. He explained to Mariana that he would like to talk with Carlos and told her who he was. She immediately suggested he come to their house and Carlos would be home in about an hour. Julian would have to get a couple of underground trains to Vitacura where they lived. He was given directions from there and was told it would take close to an hour to get there so he would make it around the time Carlos would be home. He hoped Carlos wouldn't mind too much having to see him again so soon. Mariana was clearly curious and Julian didn't want to delay. As it turned out, Carlos was home before he arrived, Mariana having rung him to make sure he'd leave his lawyers' office on time that day. The couple had two children, two-year-old Liliana and five-year-old Antonio who both came bouncing up to greet Julian. *Onces* were soon served and when Mariana took the children to get ready for bed, Julian had the chance to talk to Carlos. He told Carlos what his mother had said and asked if he knew any more. Carlos confirmed Isabel had taken a teaching job in La Serena now but previously he knew she had also gone further north and had been in Antofagasta, Iquique and Arica, several months at a time in each city.

"She put herself in some danger and got herself arrested in Iquique," said Carlos "And I had to go and act for her - you know I'm a lawyer? After that, she assumed a false name on the advice of a political friend who knew people who could make a false Identity Card for her. She decided then to base herself in La Serena where she had never demonstrated or been known to the police. She couldn't tell her mother her false name or if questioned she felt her mother couldn't be trusted to not give it out."

"Do you know what it is?"

"Yes, I do and it is the only possible way you could find her if you insist on going to La Serena. She is teaching Art and Art History in a top high school there." Carlos said. "Her new name is Helena, which is her second name in fact and her chosen first *apellido* is García. That was a very common surname so she could be lost in the crowd. A more unusual name would be less anonymous, she said to me. I didn't approve of any of this. She said she'd chosen the name because she thought highly of García Lorca, but I never knew what she had chosen as her second *apellido*. It could be Bolívar," said Carlos laughing but then he hurriedly added, "No, no, I'm joking. It's not that. That would be too obvious. The great Liberator who travelled through various Latin American countries trying to win people to his cause of freedom from Spanish rule. It's not so different from what Isabel thinks she's up to, going from place to place seeking supporters for her 'freedom' cause. It's all well and good and I can't say I disagree with her so long as she stays away from civil disobedience. That's what will get her into trouble and if she gets arrested again, the consequences will be worse." Julian looked very anxious.

"Don't worry. I think she is more settled now. She did well to get the teaching job in such a prestigious school and she likes it. She has to be on her best behaviour to keep that job."

"So the school know her only by her false name?"

"Yes. And that is why she wants to keep us at a distance. So she won't give us a phone number. She rings her mother and me from time to time and that is all she allows. And when it is the school summer holidays I believe she is going to travel to the north again." Carlos could give him no further information about Isabel's whereabouts in La Serena nor the school friend she claimed she'd gone to see originally. Julian pressed him then about any names or addresses he knew of contacts in Manuel Rodriguez, but Carlos had only been 11 when Isabel started to get involved with the community outreach of *Popular Unity*. He was able to give a couple more names of her friends' families in San Miguel though Isabel's generation was largely not living there now. Carlos insisted Julian stay overnight as he doubted he would make the last bus to Valparaíso and he needed to eat supper with them and tell them more about himself and their life in Britain. "Right from how you met, I want to know it all," demanded Carlos and a long evening of talk and good food and wine ensued.

-oOo-

The next morning was Saturday and Julian thought that to visit Manuel Rodriguez on that day, he was more likely to find Alexander and Miguel or anyone else who knew Isabel, at home than during the week, so he decided he must go there before returning to Valparaíso. After breakfast with the family, he said his goodbyes and gave his assurances to meet again and followed Carlos' instructions to get to the poorer *población* on the other side of the city. It was so like Quillota's poorest *barrio* in the appearance of its housing that he felt quite at home. He had left the bus where the bus driver said was the main stop for Manuel Rodriguez and the nearest to the centre of the *población*. Where else to start but with the general store immediately ahead of him. A man was cutting cold meats at a machine and a woman nodded to him and said *hola* as she continued to empty newly baked bread rolls into their container. He found a Peach Nectar and made his way to the counter and rather hesitatingly he asked if the woman knew Isabela (she liked the more Spanish form of her name) Henríquez. The woman stopped smiling and looked at Julian firmly without blinking.

"Who wants to know," she said finally. Julian hurriedly explained he was Isabela's husband (he thought that would sound more acceptable than 'partner') from London and he mentioned he was also looking for Miguel, her step-brother Eugenio's friend. He thought that would prove some local knowledge and connection with Isabel. Veronica softened and invited him into the room behind the shop. She wanted some more questions answered.

"Why are you looking for Isabela? Why don't you know where she is?"

"We were in touch when Isabel first came to Chile and for a year after her second visit but recently I haven't heard from her. I'm worried about her of course and I've come to look for her." Veronica had to agree it was

145

concerning and surprising that Isabel hadn't kept in touch or said something definite to him.

"I've not seen Isabel for a long time," said Veronica. "I can tell you where to find Miguel and also the mother of a family Isabel had been much involved with, Patricia." What luck! Julian was delighted and again promised to return with news when he could.

He made his way to Miguel's house and children ran to him to ask him who he was and giggled at his accent. When he reached the small brick-built single-storey house which buffered up close to the neighbouring house in the usual way, he received no reply at the door. Children around informed him that Miguel had gone shopping with their mother and they'd be back later. Julian decided then it would do no harm to see Patricia if possible, though he didn't think she'd be able to help him forward. She was in and after hearing his explanation, invited him in. She was delighted to hear something of Isabel but she said,

"I haven't seen her for three years now. Please tell me about Isabel's life in England. Did she have any success with the video she was making?"

"I thought there was something familiar about your face. Of course, you are on the video with the women's group. You all spoke so well, although it was so terribly sad what had happened to your families. Please don't say anything to anyone about my trying to find Isabel, in case it is harmful to her in any way or any contact of hers." Patricia fully understood.

"I don't know if Isabela has had any contact with any of my children, the ones that survived the repression that is. The ones who Isabela had been most friendly with, did not survive. They were the most active ones. My oldest son Alexander and the next one Pedro were taken, along with my husband in an early morning raid. They were violently pulled from their beds at 5.00 in the morning. I remember it like it was yesterday," said Patricia apologising for being tearful after all this time. Julian understood it was something she would never get over.

"You'll never be able to forget it. You'll always going to miss them but I hope you can find some joy in life and happy moments."

"Yes, I can. I know." They thanked each other and hugged.

"Isabela talked to me about you and your sons and how hard Alexander worked for a better world. She was very fond of you, Patricia. I hope we will all be together one day when I find her. We will come to visit, I'm sure," he said and he left to go and seek out Miguel.

Miguel and his wife Beatrice were back and Julian began explaining again who he was, but Miguel interrupted him and they welcomed him into their house. Miguel had written to Eugenio after seeing Isabel and he had received a few letters back, so Miguel was very clear about who Julian was. "Eugenio told me that you were coming to Chile." Miguel hesitated before continuing, "He wasn't sure if his stepsister wanted to cut the relationship or if she was in hiding and Eugenio didn't know how much danger that meant she might be in. Chile is opening up now and has had elections of course, but Isabela wanted to make more political demands and Eugenio has no way of judging the situation or the risks from outside. He recognised that and said that to me in his last letter."

Beatrice said, and Miguel agreed, "If she wanted to finish the relationship, she should have made that clear to you and not left you living with uncertainty. I don't think she would willingly do that. People were still being arrested and detained, though nothing like in the same numbers as before but whenever there is a demonstration there are people picked up and some very nasty stories of their treatment have come out. I don't want to worry you but you need to know the reality."

"They take every chance to frighten and intimidate," said Miguel, "apart from all the *lacrimógena* they throw. You really have to move fast when they start with the tear gas, not only because it hurts your eyes and stings your nose and your throat but because they then start rounding people up." Beatrice looked warily at her husband, believing he'd got himself too involved at times, in her opinion.

"So far he has had only close escapes, but one day, if he isn't very careful… And having been in trouble before, they could do anything with him." Beatrice disappeared to the kitchen to prepare lunch and Julian began to press Miguel for any contact he had who might know where Isabel was.

I can't give a name nor an address, because I don't have them but I will try to contact the person Isabel first went south with and see if he will meet you. The problem is how can we be in touch? I don't have a phone, do you?" Julian confirmed he didn't. He was reluctant to give the church office number, not wanting to trouble the church staff nor Miguel having to ring

147

him. "I know," said Miguel. "Veronica at the corner shop has a telephone and we could communicate through her." Julian thought that a good idea. Miguel could easily see Veronica and not have to make an additional call. Julian agreed to see Veronica when he went for the bus and Miguel would leave her a message as soon as he could.

The following week seemed to Julian to pass very slowly as he awaited news. He told himself he must be patient and he made efforts to arrange and prepare all the materials and plans he would need for his commitments in advance so that he could take some time out if he was asked to go to see Miguel's contact. He wondered if he should go to La Serena anyway and thought someone could tell him which were the best high schools. However, La Serena was an overnight bus ride away so a visit there would entail a few days away. He didn't want to have to waste a lot of time in what might be a futile search when he had so little information and he had commitments to fulfil.

-oOo-

Padre Pablo took Julian and Ximena and Martín out in his car the next Sunday afternoon. They took the main road north to La Calera which Pablo explained was the name of the town but it also meant quarry and there was, he said, a very large quarry there. It had become the resource for an enormous cement works, which was the main employment of the town but Pablo worried for the health of the people in the town, where the dust from the cement works appeared ever-present. Padre Pablo also said that he knew from the priest in La Calera that drugs were a serious issue in the town as it was situated on the crossroads of the main route going south and the road going to Argentina, which were principal highways for drug transportation. The padre there had talked of school children left unattended when their parents had to work, getting into drugs and being used as runners. Pablo felt Julian's work with the children was so important as the problem was spreading to Quillota. It was affecting the young people even more and the Padre wanted Julian to also get involved with the youth group Martín was building up in the same *población*. Julian was pleased about that as he had had some experience of youth work at his father's church and had done group work with teenagers, both in his voluntary work and with young people who were "in care" in his professional life. He felt he could relate well to young people and he liked to listen to them. They seemed to open up to him.

The Sunday trippers travelled through some impressive countryside of steep-sided green hills to reach the sea at Holcón. At last, Julian felt he was seeing the sea of Pablo Neruda! To see the Pacific Ocean from Chile's coast was like a dream come true. He took a photograph of Padre Pablo dodging the waves as he jumped from bolder to bolder, rather as Pablo Neruda used to do with his dog on the beach near his home in Isla Negra. Julian remembered the now famous black and white film of Neruda and his dog and talked with Pablo about it.

"You'll have to visit Isla Negra," said Pablo "It's along the coast further south from here. Neruda's house has just opened as a memorial to the poet, after being left wrecked by soldiers and then boarded up and left to deteriorate in the dictatorship years."

"He had a house in Valparaíso too, didn't he?"

"Yes, and one in Santiago. You should see them as well. They are all interesting and make you feel you are meeting the man in person. The library in the house in Santiago is impressive. You know he spoke several languages and he had collections of books in all the different languages he spoke. He also was a big collector of various artefacts from shells to boat figureheads and his collections are worth seeing."

Walking further along the beach they came to a number of small fishing boats lined up on the shore. They seemed incredibly small to Julian to face going out into that wild-looking Pacific Ocean. The sea looked decidedly powerful as quite large waves crashed into the shore, and this is a calm sunny day, he thought. *The open boats aren't much bigger than rowing boats and they look extremely dangerous,* thought Julian. The party had a cup of tea in a simple cafe on the beach and soon they had to get back for Padre Pablo's usual duties on a Sunday. Julian had so appreciated the trip and said so on the return journey. He planned with Martín when he would be meeting up with him and the group of young people and apart from that there was little conversation. Ximena seemed tired from the walk and Julian was glad to sit quietly with his thoughts. Without having ever known Isabel, he might not have known much about Pablo Neruda, though he was famous enough as the greatest poet in the Spanish language of the twentieth century. Certainly, without

Isabel, he wouldn't have started learning Spanish and become committed to a part-time, undergraduate degree course in Hispanic studies, which he was so enjoying. Without Isabel, he wouldn't have been having these experiences he was loving here in Chile. *But...where is she? Why were we not doing these things together? When am I going to get the chance to track down this contact who might know her whereabouts?* It burned inside him somewhere he couldn't quite define. He thought it might be in his soul.

As soon as they arrived back Julian wanted to look again at Neruda's *Twenty Love Poems and a Song of Despair*. He had brought his copy with him to Chile. It was one of the first presents that Isabel had given him and it was the first publication of poems that Neruda achieved as a very young man. Julian's copy was in Spanish with an English translation on each opposing page. Isabel had told him that the poetry collection was quite often a gift that young people gave in their early romantic encounters in all parts of Latin America, even nowadays. It was first published in 1924 and is so expressive of tender emotions, eroticism and the agony of love lost, that Julian could quite believe it was still popular. He recalled a poem about the sea and the rocks just as they had seen that day. *"...the solitude of the sea. Headlong, violent, stretched towards the sky. You woman, what were you there, what ray, what vane of that immense fan? You were as far as you are now."* When he arrived at the church house, Julian went straight to his room and looked up *The Song of Despair*. A few lines stood out for him:

*In you, the wars and the flights accumulated.*
*From you, the wings of the song birds rose.*
*You swallowed everything, like distance.*
*Like the sea, like time. In you, everything sank!*
*Oh flesh, my own flesh, woman whom I loved and lost,*
*I summon you in the moist hour, I raise my song to you.*
*Like a jar, you housed the infinite tenderness,*
*And the infinite oblivion shattered you like a jar.*

Julian recalled that so many of the poems were about absence, both the writer portraying absence from the subject or the subject herself seeming absent and elusive from the writer. Julian recalled one of the poems set to music, of which he was very fond and he remembered the crackly tape recording he and Isabel had often played. It was about a girl in a grey beret. It personified the absent lover, just as he felt Isabel absent and he was recalling her presence with pain. Neruda had expressed that pain at his memory of the *la boina gris.*

Julian had learned through his literature studies at the university that Neruda had become a spokesperson of the free love movement that was emerging in student and artistic circles in the 1920s and he remembered Isabel, although wanting to reject bourgeois conventions, had declared the poems as male chauvinist thinking with their references to sex and abandonment. But of course, she knew they had far more depth than that, more subtlety, abstraction and emotion. Julian recalled the poet speaks of love and loss through memories but he obliges the reader, who isn't directly spoken to and seemingly is absent, to seek to recreate the emotional experiences of his/her own life, just as Julian was doing right now. *No wonder with all that emotion they are still popular and had so much influence on later poets.*

One discussion of the poems with Isabel had led to Julian mentioning the notion of 'open marriage' which was in circulation in the UK at the time. Julian certainly didn't mean that in 'open marriages' couples should accept adulterous relationships by either one. He considered 'open' to be about relationships needing to be honest, and each of the couple being free from being owned or controlled, but making conscious efforts to strive for equality and reduce power imbalances, which couples were so often engaged in, including, he thought, their own relationship. Isabel didn't get it though. She was blinded by the belief that 'open marriage' could and only does mean seeking other sexual partners. Perhaps she was right. That does seem to be all that it has come to mean but he was talking about transforming traditional men v. women partnerships into something richer, more satisfying and giving of the whole self. Looking back, it seemed another nail in the coffin of their being together. Of course, he wasn't talking about inflicting the pain and hurt that having other sexual partners inevitably brings. That didn't sound at all like the equality and accountability he was wanting to convey. Another complete misunderstanding, which brought more lack of trust and disbelief in himself, he felt.

*Getting lost in Neruda's poems would be preferable to be thinking about now rather than sad memories,* Julian told himself and he continued his reflections. The remoteness of the loved one couldn't be better represented than in the twentieth poem *Puedo escribir los versos más tristes esta noche:*

*Tonight I can write the saddest lines.*
*Write for example, "The night is starry*
*And the stars are blue and shiver in the distance."*
*The night wind revolves in the sky and sings.*
*Tonight I can write the saddest lines.*
*I loved her and sometimes she loved me too.*

And later:

*Love is so short, forgetting is so long.*
*Because through nights like this one I held her in my arms*
*my soul is not satisfied that it has lost her.*

Julian revelled in his memories for a while. *Neruda makes you recreate your own emotional experiences - what an indulgence!*

-oOo-

There were 75,000 people at the concert in Santiago which Julian had been determined to attend from the moment he heard about it. The occasion was the thirtieth anniversary of the death of Ché Guevara and performers were to include singers he knew from the *New Chilean Song Movement* such as Ángel Parra and Patricio Manns. The Cuban singer Silvio Rodriguez was to be there and Chilean groups that were new to Julian like *Sol y Lluvia* and *Los Miserables.* The concert was to take place in the infamous National Stadium where thousands of political detainees had been imprisoned and many killed when the military Junta turned the stadium into a concentration camp. The military regime had done the same with another sports stadium in Santiago, the Chile Stadium and that was where Victor Jara had been imprisoned from the first day of the coup and where he suffered torture and death.

Julian invited one of the more politically aware and older members of the youth group with whom he had now formed a particular friendship - Eduardo - to accompany him to Santiago and from Eduardo, Julian learned a lot. They visited the *Universidad de Chile* and Julian bought a couple of new CDs: Ángel Parra and his daughter singing the poems of Nobel Prize winner Gabriela Mistral. The other new disk he bought was by *Los Jaivas*.

"Do you know the origin of the name *Los Jaivas?*" asked Eduardo.

"Isabel told me about that. The group had wanted to call themselves, in English, High Bass but the pronunciation of High Bass sounds exactly like the pronunciation of *jaivas* in Spanish. You muddle up the way you say your 'v's and 'b's. So everyone thought they were saying the word for crabs. The musicians finally accepted they couldn't hold back the tide and that *Los Jaivas* was their name. I don't know anything about *Sol y Lluvia*. Do you know them?"

"*Sol y Lluvia* was formed in Chile in the 1980s and they didn't go into exile," said Eduardo. "But they made clear their opposition to General Pinochet and somehow they survived. One of their most famous songs is *Adios General* but that was first publicly played by the group in a concert in 1990 when General Pinochet had already had to step down after the Plebiscite. *Sol y Lluvia* combines modern instruments like electric guitar and saxophone with traditional Andean instruments like the *charango*."

"I know that instrument - it's like a very small guitar."

"Yes, with twelve strings. Did you know that a *charango* was originally made from a shell of an armadillo? But now that is illegal because armadillos are an endangered species, so they are made of wood. *Sol y Lluvia* also use *zampoñas*."

"Yes, I know the *zampoñas*," said Julian, "I love their sound. I've seen and heard Chilean groups using these pipes in concerts in London and the pipes come in all different sizes." This was to be Julian's first concert in Chile and it was of greater excitement to him than he dared to admit and the emotional context of the stadium, where it was to be held, moved him a great deal. "Do you know *Los Miserables?*"

"It's a punk rock band. They've participated in human rights events and done voluntary work in poorer communities. They are definitely anti-establishment," so Julian thought he would be glad to see them too, though he would have to tolerate what was not his usual taste in music.

They did both enjoy all of the concert and the atmosphere was tremendously enthusiastic, and Julian thought that the other Chile Isabel had been searching for, still existed and the dictatorship had been unable to crush it. *Sol y Lluvia* sang *Adios General* to massive applause and another of their songs was *Nunca Más,* referring to the dictatorship. It was impressive how many young people seemed to know all the words of the songs, even by artists famous from before the coup, so that still their music lived on despite the years of repression. When Ángel Parra sang of *La Libertad,* he really knew what freedom and imprisonment were. He had first been held in that very Stadium and then he was sent to the Concentration Camp at *Chacabuco.*

"Ángel Parra was arrested because he was very much associated with the *Popular Unity* government of Allende," said Eduardo on the way home. "Incredibly, he was only held for less than a year. His wife had some influence with a famous lawyer, Jaime Guzmán Errázuriz who became a right-wing senator. This man took part in the writing of the new Constitution for Pinochet. He also founded the notoriously rightwing UDI party (*Union Demócrata Independiente).*" Julian was staggered at the contradictions that such a society can throw up.

"Supposedly he had known who Ángel Parra was?"

"Yes, he must have. Ángel had been on television before the coup. He was involved in the beginnings of Chilean TV in stage management. Later he was an assistant director and he performed as an artist. His mother Violeta Parra had been famous enough even for someone on the Right to have heard of her. Ángel had done some European tours with his mother and his sister Isabel in the 1960s but it is still amazing that Guzmán was involved in his release from being a political prisoner. Ángel's wife must have been clever. It's 'who' you know that counts. He was held long enough to suffer a lot of interrogation and torture, like many others, I'm sure because this happens mostly in the first months."

"There's a disk, called *Chacabuco,"* Julian said, "I know it well. Isabel told me that just before he was released, Ángel sang to the other prisoners in *Chacabuco* and someone had managed to record his songs. With some editing, it was released, outside of Chile, as just *Chacabuco.* We had a crackly old cassette tape of it."

Julian resolved right then to try writing to Isabel again, at her mother's address. He didn't have any other address for her but he longed to tell her about the concert and more about the work he was doing. He thought Isabel might well go to her mother's house at Christmas and it would be a good idea if there were letters there waiting for her when she arrived. This was surely the "old Chile" that Isabel had been looking for and it was clearly vibrant. She would be thrilled to see and hear so many people wanting a new and changed Chile. Perhaps Isabel was even at the concert. Who knows? But he must give her the words of encouragement that he could from what he had experienced. This time he thought he would write in Spanish. Rodolfo had praised his written Spanish last time he had written to him, so he thought he could do a good enough job. If Isabel's mother opened the letter, she would be able to understand it too and if she had not already passed a message to Isabel that he was in the country and looking for her, then the letter might prompt her to do so if Isabel was in contact with her mother.

-oOo-

Reconciled to the waiting game again, Julian tried to fully focus on the work he was doing. He did enjoy the time he spent with the young people's group and especially the democratic style of leadership of Eduardo within the group. If Eduardo was persuaded of something, he could bring the others with him and facilitate their contributions and their creativity and he never appeared to be pushing onto them anything they did not want to do themselves. Martín had suggested they might like to prepare some entertainment for the residents at the Old People's Home and with Eduardo's encouragement, they were throwing themselves into this. Two guitarists and a drummer in the group were practising hard and four girls were rehearsing singing together. Others were making little prizes for a lucky dip for the elderly residents. Several were involved in producing a one-act play and all the rest were helping to paint the scenery and erect it on a frame. The lad directing this was quite an artist and Julian nervously watched him throw a whole bucket of house paint over a large canvas spread out on the floor in one of the church rooms. He then began to brush the paint out to the edges with a floor mop. In the end, he had made a good backdrop of a distant landscape of forest and snowcapped mountains and an interior of a farm building. He brought in others of the group to participate in the painting in broad swaths of colour whilst he concentrated on the details.

The group had done some fundraising to enable all this activity to go ahead. One Saturday they had made hot dogs and sold them on the street. They called them *completos.* This being Chile, they had made some delicious sauces to enhance the sausages: mashed avocados with lemon juice, tomatoes peeled and finely chopped with dressing, mayonnaise and mustard sauce. In addition, the young people ran a raffle in which the prize was the head of a pig which they had persuaded a local butcher to donate. This apparently was quite a tradition and there was a serious take-up of raffle tickets to win the pig's head. They carried it around the *población* on a plate, knocking on doors to interest neighbours in buying tickets. In the end, the day was quite profitable for the youth group and certainly, they declared it a success.

Whilst keeping up the several commitments that he had, Julian had the chance of a number of new experiences, one of which moved him greatly. He was taken by Padre Pablo to an *Hogar de Cristo,* a children's home run by the church. A deeply shocking sight awaited him and Julian thought he would never be able to get it out of his head. He was taken to an institution where he was told, 86 children were housed and there were only three members of staff on duty at any one time. There were only six staff in total, all nuns. The children ranged from four to fourteen years. Of course with practically no individual attention, the children were desperate for affection and they were led to crave attention from anyone who entered. A number of children clung to Julian almost as soon as he and Padre Pablo walked in. Everything Julian could see around him was the complete opposite of all that was considered essential in the literature on modern child care and child development. He could not believe what he was seeing and could not believe that no one in the church had sufficient knowledge to have ended a practice like this many decades before. All he had learned about children's needs for affection, attention, bonding and parenting and all he had read about the damage of institutionalisation was flooding into his head and he was absolutely despairing.

Forcing himself to turn his attention to the children and to answer their questions about where he was from, he thought it might be useful to recall a Robin Hood story and the Major Oak in Sherwood Forest. He tried to be affectionate and responsive with the children that came to him and it was extremely difficult to extricate himself from the clinging and eventually to say goodbye. Padre Pablo couldn't say much to Julian's criticisms of how that situation could ever be allowed. Why were there not many more staff, surely there were enough nuns that could give permanent care to a small, family-sized group of children and form parental-type, loving relationships with them? Padre Pablo knew Julian was right but explained that these were not children who were available for adoption.

"It doesn't matter that they are not available for adoption. They still need to form a bond with one adult carer, for a few months and certainly for a few years."

"Parents have given the children up in situations of family tragedy, poverty or conflict," said Pablo, "and there was supposed to be the intention of reclaiming them again." However, he had to admit that some had waited years for this to happen.

"Imagine the emotional damage it would do to be waiting and not knowing for how long this would go on. And all this on top of the harms of separation and loss and broken bonds already suffered. Not forming a close relationship with one adult in all those months and years of waiting would likely stop a child from forming healthy relationships in their adulthood. Any emotional nurturing was non-existent! Nothing was offered to heal some of the damage of the loss of their parents?" Julian was beside himself with rage and could not get over his anger and his feelings of pity and empathy for the children. Unable to stop thinking about the children's home, he talked to all the church workers who came to *onces* that afternoon and he talked to Padre Pablo about fostering in the UK and small family size group homes in much of Europe. Martín thought it would be a good idea that the Youth Group took the entertainment they were preparing to the children's home and Claudia thought the Youth Group could spend a whole day with them playing games and doing activities.

"These efforts are not the answer and they might make their sense of deprivation even worse!" Julian said, but finally, he was persuaded to go along with such a plan with one condition. "It must be part of a commitment that there will be regular visiting. It can't just be a one-off and then dropped, to leave the children again with a feeling of being let-down, abandoned," he insisted and all agreed. In the event, the first occasion was considered a good experience for all. It was undeniably a happy day and Julian was incredibly impressed with the way the young people reacted to the children. They were warm and affectionate and unpatronising. They threw themselves into the activities, games and dancing with enthusiasm and without shyness and they promised to go again the next month. Julian wrote another letter to Isabel describing how angry he was with the set-up of the children's home and all that they had tried to do in response. How he wished that Isabel and he together could create a fostering scheme although he was aware of the lack of legal structure and social workers to implement such a project. The "old Chile" would emanate and the caring, loving goodness of so many people would triumph. *What a dream! How pleased Isabel would be to achieve such a major social measure. But I know I can't write proposing a madness such as this but I must write about the effect this has had on me,* he thought. He knew again it was unlikely she would receive the missive for a long while but it felt therapeutic for him to tell her all about it. Sooner or later, when she visited her mother again, his letters would be waiting for her.

-oOo-

In mid-October, Julian experienced his first earthquake. He had just gone to bed and was reading and listening to music with his earphones and the whole building started to tremble. *It's all right, it will stop soon,* he said to himself as the shaking grew more intense. *This is a bit much, it's going on and on...* He decided he should get out of bed and stand in the frame of the doorway and there he stood with his portable CD player grasped in both hands, wondering when the trembling was going to stop. It did finally but, he learned in the morning, that it had been one of the most prolonged earthquakes, lasting two and a half minutes. It had seemed to Julian like five minutes at least. Everyone was talking about it the next day and the epicentre had been close to Ovalle in the Coquimbo Region of Chile, north of the Valparaíso Region. In Ovalle, there had been a great deal of destruction because it was an old town, dating from 1830. Padre Pablo heard also about a nearby village called Punitaquí where a family of five had all lost their lives and 80% of the village had been destroyed because they were mostly living in old adobe mud-brick houses. The Padre felt these people had been somewhat forgotten in the concern about the many victims in the town. He launched a campaign of help for the people of Punitaquí and presents of food, clothing and bedding kept arriving in impressive quantities at the church. Some donors thought of plates, cups, kettles and pans. Others thought of toys for the children.

Finally, it was the day to get the donations into the minibus and very early the next morning, while it was still dark, Mario the driver, Fabio with his guitar and Julian set off for Punitaquí. The journey took six hours, the minibus not being able to travel very fast with all the weight it was carrying. Fabio took a share of the driving and Julian offered but they didn't need him to take a turn. The people of the village were really appreciative. They had been given tents and one water tap for the whole village had been installed. Some temporary loos of wooden seats over a trench had been set up with canvas cubicles around them. A few children took Julian to see what was left of their houses of adobe. As ever, the people were exceptionally warm and friendly and made some lunch for the visitors from the food that they had brought, insisting that the travellers must eat with them before returning home.

What struck Julian about the area around Punitaquí, which they had journeyed through, was the wealth that was evident in the perfectly tendered vineyards they saw for mile after mile. The vines were green and lush and perfectly weeded and their value must have been huge. Were the vineyard owners fairly taxed to provide health services and education for the poor labourers that worked for them and their families, Julian wondered. Were those living in the mud-brick houses that fell on their occupants or their belongings, paid decent wages? He also wanted to know what rates of pay were paid to those who worked in the local nationalised copper mines, as many of the men did from Punitaqui. No one around him was able to answer these questions. *Aren't these questions relevant to the awareness-raising teaching that Isabel has been doing? People need to know the context of their lives and those working to improve their lives need the facts to press for change. If only I could get hold of Isabel and we could work on these sorts of matters together. We used to discuss matters like this in the UK in the past and get informed. We used to both feel close when we were working on social issues together. We had a purpose and it enriched our relationship. Would that it could be like that again. Ojalá,* he said to himself.

159

# Chapter 9

A t last, a phone call to Veronica brought forth a message from Miguel. Julian was to go the following Saturday to meet Miguel at Santiago's main bus station when he would take him to meet his friend. Miguel would be calling on Veronica for confirmation on Thursday that week if Julian could go or not.

"I'll be there, for sure," said Julian excitedly, "Twelve noon, as Miguel suggests. Tell him definitely, Yes, please." The long-awaited visit to Santiago again finally came round and Julian found himself sitting on a bus once more to the capital. Miguel was at the station although the bus pulled in before their meeting time. Julian began immediately to be concerned that the other person he was to meet was not there. However, Miguel was reassuring and asked him to follow him.

"I'm taking you, just as I did Isabela," Miguel said as they jostled with the crowds towards another part of the huge station. "We're going to the same place to meet Juan." Julian was duly led into the small café and the lady behind the counter nodded acknowledgement and Miguel pressed on to the back of the shop. He took Julian into the small room and assured him Juan would not be long. The woman in the shop came in with coffees and Juan arrived. He began to talk as if speaking to a political rally, though in soft tones, and made a long list of the social and political problems of the country: the pension system, the health service, the educational inequalities, the need for a new constitution and more. Julian said he was keen to learn more about all these issues but right then he was desperate to know if this man could lead him to where Isabel was. When he finally got a word in edgeways he asked directly,

"Do you know where she is?"

"I mention all these issues because they are what Isabel has been teaching to create greater awareness and to get people demonstrating to demand change. It is really important what she has been doing and I want you to understand."

"I know Isabel's passionate interest in these matters," Julian confirmed, "but when did you last hear from her and where is she?"

"She spent several months in many of the cities of the north: Antafogasta, Calama, Tocopilla, Iquique, Arica getting alongside working people and she had been involved in a number of demonstrations and strikes for better working conditions and after getting arrested in Iquique where they held her for seven days and she was threatened and beaten, she felt she had to be less open in her activities. For a time at least, she thought she should get away from the towns where she might be easily traced." Julian looked horrified.

Juan said, "The police take individuals to intimidate the people, even when there are no actual charges and they have to let them go soon. They break up communal kitchens to spread fear in the neighbourhood to keep the opposition under control. And at an open demonstration or strike picket, they shoot rubber bullets and teargas." Julian was getting desperate to know if Juan knew where Isabel had gone and when he last heard from her.

"She was still in La Serena when she rang me a couple of months ago. She had a false name which she didn't tell me, quite rightly, and she said she was teaching there to try to build up a little money to survive. I think that's where she wants to stay."

"Do you have an address?"

"No."

"Do you have a phone number?"

"Yes, but it is not hers and it's only to be used if absolutely essential. I thought I should leave her in peace and not ask any more of her until she is ready to come to me again. She has done a lot. She had one piece of filming destroyed - fortunately, it wasn't all of her material. She has already given me some useful video apart from all the teaching and demonstrations she has promoted."

"If it's not her phone, how do you know who to ask for if you ring?" said Julian.

"She said I should ask for Helena. That's all I know."

"Do you think she is still there in La Serena?" Julian had a mass of questions still to ask.

"I suppose so as we are in the middle of a school term. For the next school year, she might decide to move on if she could get a job elsewhere. But I think she felt fairly safe there and was liking it."

"Are you going to give me the phone number you have?" Julian felt he was pressing his luck in the face of the reluctance he could sense.

"I think I should ask her first, so I will try to ring."

"Can you do that now, please? It's a long way for me to come to Santiago again, it's two hours on the bus. *Porfa, porfa,* as the Chileans say." Juan agreed and said Julian should wait for him where he was.

"Do you want to give me a message?"

"Tell her I want to see her and I will travel to wherever she is or is going. And that I'd like her phone number. Oh, and give her this church office number for her to ring me," he added, handing on a piece of paper he'd prepared in advance.

It seemed a very long 20 minutes that Juan was gone. Julian's heart sank however when Juan returned with the message that Isabel was going to be away from La Serena for the coming three weeks with a big commitment for the school. After that she would be busy returning to her visits to the northern cities before the election in December. She says she promises to ring you when she is more available again in La Serena and then you could be in touch. She'll give you her number then. She is going to the communities she had been working with before, to try to strengthen commitment for action and to support them," added Juan as if to justify everything.

"And she'll take risks again," said Julian.

"No, no, she knows to be very careful now. The meetings are just to make plans with key people. The elections are an important time."

Sitting on the bus back to Valparaíso Julian felt so frustrated like a slippery eel had just slid through his fingers. He'd have to wait - again - get on with life but wait! He tried to stop himself from speculating about where he might be able to meet with Isabel in the north. He wanted to see the towns where she was going at some stage of his stay in Chile.

-oOo-

The opportunity for another concert was coming up and Julian decided this time to invite not only Eduardo but Alicia from the Youth Group and Ana, the daughter of a very active family within the church. The very famous music group called *Quilapayun* was to be at the Quinta Vergara in Viña del Mar and it was another absolute "must" for Julian. On a visit to the Old People's Home, Julian learned from Gabriela that *Quilapayun* had been formed in 1965 and their name meant Three bearded Men in the Mapuche language.

"There are seven of them now and all of them are competent in many different instruments which they swop and change throughout a performance. It's great to see… and hear them."

"I've only ever heard them on disk."

"At their first performances at the Universidad de Chile, Ángel Parra was their musical director. Soon they were winning prizes for their Andean folkloric music and Victor Jara became their musical director. They were ambassadors for the Popular Unity government. Fortunately, they were on an international tour when the military coup happened, but at least they were safe. If only Victor Jara had gone with them. The dictatorship banned and destroyed the record label they recorded with and they were forced to remain in exile in France."

"You know all about these groups and singers, you must love to hear them when you can. Do you want to come with us?"

"That would be great but with this job and young children, I haven't been to a concert for years. Well, these sorts of concerts are only just coming back, of course. I'll have to talk with my husband. I might be able to take you all in my car. I will try. The Quinta Vergara Amphitheatre is an enormous outdoor circular theatre with a huge stage. They have the International Song Festival there every year. It is due to be pulled down and rebuilt very soon. At present, it is constructed of wood and the new concrete one is going to be even bigger than the 15,000 seats it has now. The theatre is in a lovely setting too. The Quinta Vergara is a park and the original house is an art gallery."

Gabriela was able to take them and all agreed the concert was inspiring and rousing. Gabriela and Julian were especially encouraged to see thousands of young people who knew and loved the music and the words of the songs. They knew also the political message that *Quilapayun* stood for. A discussion developed between the young people on the way home.

Eduardo said "I'm not going to vote in the election because I have no respect for any of the current politicians. There are no politicians who reflect my opinions."

"In Chile, people are legally required to vote," questioned Julian, "so aren't you taking quite a risk to protest in this way?" Eduardo shook his shoulders.

"I keep hearing this argument," said Alicia, "and I think a lot of young people will abstain from voting this time."

"Yes, many young people are taking this stand," said Eduardo. "The politicians keep on claiming its apathy but it's not. We would vote if there was a party who truly represented the working class and will improve their lot."

"But why not vote for the alliance of the Left?" said Ana. "A large vote for them would give a much-needed shock to the political system, even if it didn't win a majority. It could be a step to a win next time."

"The alliance isn't truly of the Left," said Alicia. It's part of the political class that thinks it has the right to govern and they wouldn't change anything in favour of the workers or the people that are struggling to make ends meet."

When the group parted and had said their thanks to Gabriela, Alicia said to Julian, "I've never been to a concert before and it was great. Thank you." Julian was so glad he had invited her. This evening is something else I must write to Isabel about, he thought.

-oOo-

On the 24th November 1997, it was Pinochet's birthday and the General announced that he was going to retire himself from being Head of the Army but that he was going to enter the Senate as a life peer. Julian received a phone call, Emilia knocked on his door very early, to tell him, and the call was from Alvaro, one of his students of English.

"Have you heard the news?" Alvaro asked. "There is to be a demonstration in Valparaíso against this outrage. I'm going to go and I thought you might want to as well."

"Yes, absolutely." They arranged to meet outside the church in half an hour.

In the *colectivo,* Alvaro asked what Julian thought of Pinochet's justification that they have life peers in the Upper House of Parliament in Great Britain.

"There are not any ex-dictators in the House of Lords and no one can self-appoint themselves, they have to be appointed by the Prime Minister and I don't think Chile's President would freely agree to this."

"No, I think not, but under pressure from the military..."

"But the unelected principle of the House of Lords had always concerned me as it's not democratic although ex-politicians and people who have made good achievements, do make a useful contribution in the House of Lords."

"The Chilean Upper House has 19 appointed Senators and 38 are directly elected, which is deliberately designed to ensure the House majority would always be to the Right of the political spectrum. The appointed senators, like the elected ones, serve for eight years, half changing every four years. The notion of life appointments is completely new to the constitution and yet somehow Pinochet thinks he can adapt the constitution to suit himself. There have long been demands for a new constitution but it has always been considered impossible to get a new constitution through an always conservative Senate. Yet this adjustment to create a life peer can somehow be made with impunity."

Sadly, there were only a handful of people gathered in the *Plaza Victoria* from where they were due to march. Everyone was saying the people are still very fearful but Julian and Alvaro began to make their way with the few others, along the main road *Pedro Montt* towards the Parliament. When coming close to the huge, dominating, arched building of the Parliament, they passed the Catholic University. Julian had hoped to go that day to the English Department of the University if there was time and not much else could be achieved, but the friends found they could not enter the University and neither could the students get out. The rector had locked the gates to prevent the students from going out to demonstrate outside the Parliament. The students were now protesting not only that Pinochet would be entering the Senate but protesting this sudden lockdown as well. They were shouting from the windows and painting on walls inside the gates *garabatos* against

Pinochet. A few students on the outside said that "negotiations" had been going on for hours and a crowd began to gather outside in support of the locked-in students during the lunchtime break. The supporters began to disperse when it was time to return to work, amongst the cheers and thanks, there was suddenly a metal and wooden chair which came flying out of one of the University windows. There was much banging and shouting from inside. The crowd outside rapidly dispersed and Alvaro and Julian decided to move on. Alvero heard talk of a big demonstration when Pinochet actually entered the Senate in March. Julian was sure he was going to have to be there and imagined Isabel would not want to miss that either.

He was also certain that Isabel would be incensed about this latest development. She had not yet rung him but she had said she would be very busy during November and prior to the elections. This news of Pinochet entering the Senate would, Julian thought, make Isabel busier than ever. She'll be wanting to demonstrate and might take risks again. *If only I could talk with her. I'll have to write again, knowing there can be no early response. Should I carry on with this? Am I utterly foolish?* Julian was very quiet on the return journey but he was grateful that Alvaro said he would arrange with his M.P. a visit to Parliament and he would take Julian with him.

Congressional and Senate (partial) elections followed soon on 11th December which were interesting for Julian to observe. He found the atmosphere very different from the elections he was used to. Election Day was one of quiet, sombre mood and the few people in the streets seemed to feel they needed to whisper to one another. The shops were closed and there were soldiers on the streets with guns. The back of a voter's hand was stamped with an ink mark that wouldn't easily rub off the same day, as proof they had voted, so they could not vote again. The amount of propaganda time on the TV for each party was determined by what they could afford and not proportionate to their last vote nor subject to any limit on what they could spend. Only the minority Socialist party appeared to criticise Pinochet going into the Senate as undemocratic. During the campaigning time Pinochet made a patronising joke, that he was going to vote for Gladys Marín's party - the newly legal communist party - presumably to help them out as their vote was going to be so small. When reporters asked Gladys Marín what she thought of the joke, she said she didn't want to talk about the joke, she wanted to know where were the disappeared persons. Little else was said about this subject, the most serious legacy of the dictatorship.

Julian wondered where on earth Isabel would be watching the election results that evening on the TV. He presumed she would have been able to register to vote. The Minister of the Interior announced that they had counted all the votes by 11.30 pm, that over six million voting papers had been delivered to the ballot boxes but only 5,200,000 were valid and over 800,000 were *nulos*. These *nulos* had been deliberately spoiled or they were *blancos*. These figures spoke of the huge dissatisfaction that existed with the current government but this transitional coalition of the centre triumphed again - the *Concertación*. Analysis showed that if only one-quarter of those who voted *nulo,* had voted for a party like *Popular Unity* had it existed, then it could have been an impressive possibility for change next time around. What particularly stood out to Julian in the TV coverage, was the complete lack of enthusiasm for any candidate. Reflecting on the quiet day, there was no sense of celebration even when a win was announced. The politicians interviewed seemed to have to pretend there was something to celebrate but it was as if they were play-acting a role. There was a lack of authenticity and absolutely no cheering for anyone or even applause after a speech. President Frei declared the *Concertation* would not change course, that more democracy and more equality were needed, that education had to be improved and the society had to become more open, with more *solidaridad* and more opportunities for young people and better health services. There wasn't even a clap or a shout of support for this. The President's sister didn't want to accept the *nulos* and the non-registered voters were votes of protest. Together these would total more than a million. An interesting day and Padre Pablo gave his wry smile to Julian as they watched the TV together but he said very little.

-oOo-

Julian had a letter of introduction to a contact in the English Department of the Catholic University in Valparaíso from his professor at University College London. He was hoping this would give him the opportunities he sought in connection with the part-time Spanish Degree that he was pursuing with UCL. He had started evening classes in Spanish at UCL when Isabel went to Chile in 1994 and he had needed to fill the hole in his life. He had asked if he could register for a part-time Degree course in Hispanic Studies. This they had been willing to accommodate and he committed himself to three modules a semester. Full-time students would have to do six modules, so it was going to take time to complete but Julian thought he would love the courses in literature, history, culture and politics of Spanish-speaking countries. He also felt his work could accommodate flexible hours and enable him to go to one or two lectures or tutorials in a day in term time and make up the work time after 5.00 pm. Fortunately, his boss was agreeable and understanding, though reluctant to make anything officially agreed in writing. However, Julian had told him honestly and with his nodding agreement, that was enough.

Julian returned to Valparaíso to go to the English Department of *La Católica,* as the University was known, to meet Dr Renata Muñoz. She introduced him to all the teachers gathered in the English Department staff room and Julian offered his services voluntarily in any way they thought would be helpful. It was soon agreed that they would like him to do a number of classes for the students to practice comprehension after which they would ask questions and have to write up what he had said. Other classes, in which he should talk on any subject he wished, would be for simultaneous translation practice. They thought it would also be helpful if Julian also could read and correct some dissertations written in English and prepare postgraduate students for oral presentations. At the end of the discussions, Renata said,

"He looks so typically English doesn't he?" Julian could only smile but he guessed she was referring to his mid-brown hair and those indefinable features that together seem to make a typical face. He knew what she meant but couldn't think of a reply.

In return for all the classes he would offer students, they were sure that the Departments of Literature and of Social Work would be willing for him to attend some classes and he was introduced to staff at these departments the same day. It was agreed that he would attend classes in 19th and 20th Century Latin American Literature and the Epistemology of Social Work and the Sociology of Development. As he sat on the bus returning to Quillota he contemplated with great pleasure all that he had achieved that day. He realised he was going to be busy and he still had to seek out the voluntary social work he was to do in Valparaíso. The university term would begin in mid-March after the summer holidays and he hoped desperately that he would have met up with Isabel by then. He longed to share his news with her. He must write to her again about this and the election.

Julian began to think of subjects he could talk to the University students about: the British unwritten constitution, the UK economy, the monarchy - they always want to know about that and common assumptions need putting into perspective. He thought he could use some materials from his Spanish University modules and he had with him a CD with copies of paintings one of his professors had used in a course entitled *'The 19th-century view of women in Spanish literature and paintings'*. He thought that much of modern misogyny was still influenced by the attitudes of the 19th Century and before. Julian had used the paintings in training courses with family care workers in the project he had initiated. They were intervening in families where children were abused or neglected and domestic violence, sexism and misogyny were common. The mothers had been themselves abused and undermined as children and as adults and they were victims of oppressive attitudes dating back into history. These were rarely challenged and certainly not by the men in their lives. Julian felt he had learned so much relevant to social work from his study of literature. That gave him another idea. He would have to talk about racism in Britain and he could use some ideas from his social work training to look at the media portrayal of black and ethnic minority people and the general discrimination they suffer. He could talk about the economic and political situation of the UK as he'd studied these in his first degree in Politics and these subjects had remained of interest to him. There were plenty of ideas, it wouldn't be a problem, but they would need some preparation and he'd have to make time for this in the summer holidays.

-oOo-

All the usual activities in Julian's schedule continued up until the time of the Christmas celebrations. He got the *bibliotheca de la calle* children making Christmas decorations for their houses, chains and Father Christmases from loo roll centres and red crepe paper and cotton wool and with paper plates with red crepe paper hats. They made party hats for themselves like those found in British Christmas crackers and he helped them make presents in the form of crackers for their mums or grandmas with little trinkets he found in the market and more hats, made by the children and folded up, for them to use at home at Christmas. They also made Nativity scenes from painted paper cones and beads, pieces of material Julian had gathered over weeks from others, with pipe cleaners or plasticine animals and angels of gold paper and glitter. Matchboxes were useful for the cribs with matchstick legs and the children gathered branches and twigs to make the stables. Julian learned that in Chile the baby Jesus is not put in the manger until his birth during the night of Christmas Eve so that he appears for the first time on Christmas Day. In his English classes, Julian taught, in advance, the vocabulary of all the cracker jokes he could think of and he made crackers for them to pull at their Christmas party night together. When they'd pulled their crackers the students were able to read and understand their jokes and they put on their paper hats. They also learned a couple of English carols and sang them, with lots of Spanish Christmas hymns, on a class visit to the Old People's Home.

A Christmas pudding arrived from England from Julian's mother to his great surprise and the Padre's household seemed to enjoy the pudding when Christmas came. Julian also set out to get some good champagne for the house for Christmas too, only to discover that Chilean champagne costs no more than an average bottle of wine and you really could not pay any more. He found it was as good as the single opportunity he'd ever had before to drink champagne in England. He remembered that Isabel had explained that Chile was the only country in the world that was allowed to call fizzy white wine *"Champagne"* like that made in the Champagne area of France. In the 19th Century, wines over a large part of France and in parts of other countries of Europe had suffered a terrible epidemic of phylloxera which wiped out their vines. Chile had all of the French vines, brought originally from France to establish the wine growing of the early settlers. Chile was able to resupply all the vines that France asked for and in exchange for this assistance, Chile was granted the concession of being able to call their own sparkling white wines with the name *Champagne*. They were not, however, allowed to export it, which was a pity thought Julian, given the price. There was one vine that was not resupplied to France and no longer exists there and that was *Carménere,* which Julian had come to like as his most favoured Chilean red wine.

# Chapter 10

"**A**nd so, that is how Ana Cortés, now 102 years old, the first female professor at the University of Chile and ex-pupil of this very school, La Serena High School, became an internationally known artist," stated Isabel, concluding her lesson on the Chilean painter. She was especially glad to give examples of famous female achievements in the hope of inspiring the girls to imagine all things are possible for them as much as for the boys. As the teenagers poured out of her art room in noisy and lively chat, Isabel pondered again the setback in women's rights that the military dictatorship had caused. *We were so well on the way to full acceptance of equal rights and recognition of the capabilities of women and the need for equal opportunities, before the coup, it's tragic the setback that has occurred and the attitudes, especially of some parents that I've come across in this job,* she thought. *Perhaps Ana Cortés felt she had to repeat the same arguments all of her long life, right through the 20th Century, through advances and setbacks.* Isabel gathered up the copies of a few of the post-impressionist paintings of Ana Cortés that she had shown the class. She'd been one of the few women in the *Group Montparnasse,* the group of the leading artists that were working in the Montparnasse Quarter of Paris in the 1920s, together with Picasso and Cézanne. With these influences, they changed the Chilean tradition of painting and created a new world of art in Chile. *That can't have happened without a struggle, ridicule and setbacks. Change doesn't come without a fight,* she said to herself as if to revitalize within herself the determination that she must never give up striving.

Isabel made her way to the staff room where a discussion was taking

171

place involving the whole staff group that was there. "We could organise a bus, one class at a time, rather than a convoy of buses," said one teacher. "It would be a very long day out," said another, "couldn't we arrange an overnight." "That would be expensive for some parents and much more hassle for us," said another. Isabel looked puzzled and her friend the young maths teacher whispered in her ear *"el desierto florecido."*

"We don't need to go so far that it needs an overnight," said the biology teacher, taking command of the discussion. "I want the children to see this amazing phenomenon and I plan to tie my lessons to this flowering of the desert. This time it has been six years of total dryness and now parts of the desert, relatively near to us, are blooming again. It's even happening south of La Serena and Coquimbo but along the coast to the north, there are thousands of square kilometres of carpets of yellow of different species of plants. There are huge carpets of blue covering the plains around here too, I've read. Tourists will be coming here to stay to see the desert flowering and there aren't many places to accommodate lots of people further north until you are beyond the area where the rains have come this time. So the tourists will be coming here to La Serena and travelling from here on day trips. The best show will be in October, so we've time to organise and fit other work around a day out for every pupil. This flowering hasn't happened since 1991 and it is so spectacular. If you've never seen it, then it's hard to imagine but I hope we'll all be behind the idea of every child having a day out to see this incredible delight and help organise the timetables to accommodate the trips. I'll do some planning and I'll go and see the Head and come back to you."

"I want to be one of the teachers that accompanies the children," said Isabel to Mateo, the biology teacher as they were leaving the staff room together. I've never seen this incredible occurrence though, of course, I've heard about it."

"They'll be thousands of visitors from Santiago I expect, as this time it is happening here rather than in the far north, and it's not so far for the visitors from Santiago to have to travel this time. We'll have to plan carefully where to stop with the children and where they can get water, use loos etc. Do you want to help me? We might need to explore the area with an advanced trip. I know you are fairly new to the school but where were you in 1991?"

"I was at University," replied Isabel, not wanting to say she was in exile, but she thought she'd better say something about going rather later to University than is the norm. "I pursued an art and film career and then realised I needed to go to University first for a mountain of reasons. Well, obviously... I'd love to help you organise the flowering desert trips, if I can be of use, I'd be very glad to."

Mateo and Isabel set out the following weekend in his car. Isabel had made a picnic and bought a cool box to take it in. Also, she had a large five litre bottle of water and smaller bottles to fit in the icebox but she'd put in some fruit juice and a bottle of wine too. Mateo handed her a map and said that they should head for *El Totoral* about an hour and a quarter away. They followed the coast initially until the mountains went right up to the coast, steeply rising from the sea so that the road turned inland and rose up a valley between sweeping high slopes. The road then began to rise even more steeply with U bend turns to climb up and out of the valley. At the top, the most magnificent sight appeared before them - yellow flowers in all directions for kilometre after kilometre. Mateo stopped the car and they jumped out. Isabel could only gasp and tears of wonder came to her eyes. Mateo was soon walking amongst them and looking closely at some of the plants.

"Senecios" he called them and then, "Viola, yes yellow viola," he added when Isabel looked surprised. He named a few other species and they agreed that this would be the first stop with the children. They had only been travelling 40 minutes in the car, say an hour in a bus, not too far for a first look at the wonders of the flowering desert. They moved on and the hillsides to the wide valley had broad swathes of blue. "Cristaria," declared Mateo. "There are 20 to 30 species native to South America, he continued. They turned off the main road a little further on, to approach the coast again and towards the small town they were heading for. Following a valley again with steeply rising hills on both sides and crossing over a dry riverbed, they soon came to yet another coastal plain. Covering almost completely the plains as far as the eye could see, were millions of blue flowers like upturned bells. "Let's stop," said Mateo pulling over. "These are Nolana, also called Chilean Bell Flower, though they are native to Chile and Peru." Isabel could only stand and gaze in amazement.

"Let's have some coffee," she said finally, turning to the car but Mateo was walking amongst the bells.

"We'll have to tell the children not to pick any flowers but some will be tempted. I'm tempted to dig up one or two by the roots, but if every visitor did that, it could be an ecological disaster."

"Well, you do know how to look after the plants and will respect them. You even know what they all are. I can't see one expert taking a few plants in these millions will matter," replied Isabel bringing him a cup of coffee.

"The Chilean National Parks haven't yet taken all these areas into their care and if they had it would be illegal here to take any plants. National Parks have concentrated on the south of Chile mostly and the very obvious places in the Norte Grande, like the Lauca National Park and Parinacota. But this area, the Norte Chico, they've ignored until very recently when they instigated the Llanos de Challe National Park, just north of Vallenar, mainly to protect the varieties of cactus there."

"But there is a long-established National Park near Coquimbo Bosque de Fray Jorge," said Isabel.

"That's true and that one was one of the first National Parks ever, dating from the 1940s and then they seemed to forget about this region until very lately. They haven't really taken on board the need to preserve the desert flowering, just because it only happens once every five to seven years. There are 1900 species of plants in the Atacama Desert. What I should like to show you most of all are the huge blooms of the *Garra de León*. They are literally the size of a lion's paw and bright red and each is made up of perhaps 20 red cups with dark centres. I have seen them in the area north of Vallenar in the Llanos de Challe but thousands of them were cut in the past and sent for export, mostly to the United States, of course. They've become quite rare today but they were perhaps the most important reason the National Park was set up for that region two or three years ago, apart from the cactus. The *Garra de León* plants you definitely cannot take legally now. Isabel offered Mateo an egg mayonnaise roll. It was gratefully received as mid-morning was the usual tradition for a "proper" breakfast. They then had a banana each and another coffee.

"Let's go into El Totoral and see if there is somewhere we might arrange for a busload of children to arrive every day for three weeks or so and we can have some lunch too. We can always have the rest of the picnic later or save it for when we really need it if we are in an isolated spot and there's nowhere else to go."

"That's what the picnic is for really - just in case," Isabel had to agree. "Lunch and a beer would be nice." In the little mining town, they did find a restaurant ideally suited to visitors to the flowering plains. Near to the town football field, which gave an open view of the plains towards the sea, a quite large but unpretentious restaurant with a lot of outdoor tables under trees, looked definitely worth exploring. Mateo went in to talk to the owner. He was gone quite a while but Isabel was glad to have the opportunity to take some more photos of the surrounding yellow flowering plains. She explored the town a little. Just a small distance further along the road, she found a street called 'Los Copihues' which made her think of her time in Temuco with Silvia. Turning along that road she came to one of many large, green, cultivated slopes which quite clearly showed a rich agricultural area. *Where on earth do they get enough water for all this greenery?* she wondered. *It can't be the Camanchaca fog that causes low cloud to come inland. That only gives a mist but it's not proper rain and it seems to keep the cacti in the desert going but it wouldn't be enough for agricultural crops. How would there be enough water from the mountains here to store and irrigate their crops? Some riverbeds have been dry for thousands of years, I have read but there must be some water getting here somehow. Mateo would know.*

She hurried back to ask him various questions over lunch but he had lots to tell her about what he had arranged for the school visits. The restaurant had another good size hall used for weddings and such gatherings which they could make available to the children and not interfere with the tourists they were anticipating. So long as the school provided a firm contract with notice, the restaurant would arrange everything for them to have lunch, drinks, etc. for three weeks of daily buses. Bathrooms were available. Mateo could hardly believe his luck in these remote parts. It made the whole plan viable. He thought he could persuade the Head to agree the children only pay a little more than their usual payment for school lunch and the school would make up the difference.

Mateo and Isabel began to relax and talk about other things over lunch and to know each other a little more. Isabel asked if he had been to the Lauca National Park and Parinacota. Mateo had not but he knew the south better.

He'd been hiking in the Torres del Paine National Park, which was still on Isabel's to-do list. They made a plan for the afternoon.

"Let's head north for Vallenar. There are supposed to be spectacular flowerings along the hillsides to there and beyond. Let's see how far we can reasonably take the busloads of children. Vallenar isn't more than two and half hours for the return journey to La Serena, so it could be a final stop of the day, *onces, baños* and then the buses would drive non-stop back."

"Are you suggesting we do the same plan for ourselves this afternoon?"

"I'd like to suggest something different for us. How about looking for somewhere to stay overnight in Vallenar and then we could go north of there tomorrow to try to find the *garras de leones?*

"Don't you have someone waiting at home for you?" asked Isabel and when the answer was negative, she confirmed that she didn't either. She smiled and agreed to the plan.

As they pressed north inland to Vallenar, swathes of yellow on the plains, gave way to lavender-coloured hills and some white flowering areas. Mateo pointed out that what we call plains are really plateaus this high up in the mountains. He thought they were presently about 1000 meters up. They stopped to look more closely at the white bell-like flowers with yellow centres that adorned whole hillsides and at the pale purple flowers that were poppy-like in form and covering hundreds of square metres. They also found as they walked about, some primrose-like flowers amongst some larger rocks, in pale pink and in yellow. They spotted some orange flowering cacti too. Isabel especially liked the small daffodil-shaped flowers that had yellow trumpets but their outer petals were mauve. They dropped down into the valley of the Huasco River and huge areas of green cultivated crops were all around them between the high barren brown hills they were leaving behind. Mateo confirmed it was the mostly underground rivers flowing from the mountains that fed these areas and enabled the people to irrigate the area to grow crops.

As they entered the town Isabel spotted a small hotel called *Garra de León* and suggested that with that name it was surely as good a place as any to stay. They were able to book a couple of rooms and Mateo was soon in conversation with the owner about where they might find the lion's paw flowers. He thought they ought to know and he was able to gather some useful tips. He also wanted one or two suggestions about where a busload of children might be able to take *onces* and the owner's wife had a suggestion. Her son ran a good size Breakfast and Lunch restaurant, near the centre of town but a special arrangement could be made to open it to accommodate 40 or so school children and accompanying adults in the afternoons for a few weeks in October. She herself could help if her son needed extra help. The restaurant was named after her after all, she said. "It's called *Los Sabores de la Abuela*." She rang her son and they were invited to go and see the place. With all arranged, the very self-satisfied teachers were then free to find a place for a drink for themselves and explore the town.

Sitting near Park Square in the town centre, Mateo mentioned that the Member of Congress for the area was the same as for many small towns south of Coquimbo, Isabel Allende. "It's a huge rural area to cover. You know she is the daughter of President Allende. She was the last member of her family to see Allende alive in the *Moneda*. Allende ordered all women to leave when the bombing of the palace began and his daughter was one of them. She was in exile in Mexico until Pinochet lost the Referendum."

"She's promoting a divorce law," responded Isabel. "I can't believe this country still hasn't made divorce a legal possibility for all. Of course, if you had money you could always get an annulment. It's very hard on a lot of women who end up as abandoned single parents and they've no right of some settlement for child maintenance or financial protection, let alone the freedom to marry again. The church can't stop marriages from breaking down, they just make it harder on the single parents who are left with the children. It makes this country seem so far behind the western world."

"It's not the only way we are far behind," said Mateo and it soon became clear that he was interested in politics and he had voted for the Socialist Party for which Isabel Allende was a *diputada*. Isabel decided eventually to answer his earlier question more fully.

"I didn't want to say much before, but the reason I went to University late, was that I was in exile in Britain and had to get the language and the entrance exams done in England before I could go. I didn't go into exile until I was 23 years old and my English was pretty poor then. We were waiting and hoping for news of my father who was one of the 'disappeared.' " Mateo put an empathetic hand onto hers. He'd friends in exile and an uncle who 'disappeared', he said. They continued to share details of their lives that evening. Mateo was waiting for the divorce law to be passed to resolve a difficult personal mess he'd found himself in. Isabel confessed to the difficult decision she had to make. She'd lived with Julian for seven years before first coming back to Chile. She'd been back for a year but felt she had to return to Chile and she said she had written to Julian quite often at first, but this year she had not been in touch. She knew that Julian was now in Chile doing voluntary work in Quillota and he had visited her mother and her brother. "It was a big decision to make a commitment to Julian in the first place and I thought I was prepared for staying forever in England, but now I'm here in this reality, I don't think I want to return. I can't pick up the relationship again unless I'm sure I could say honestly I would live in England again long term and I don't think I can say that. I gather he is looking for me."

"You should not be pressured into anything and not feel guilty or obliged to him. He'll get a great deal out of the experience of being here and he'll conquer the language, so you don't owe him anything you don't want to do." Isabel knew Mateo was right but what she didn't want to tell him was the enormous, passionate and sexual draw the relationship had for her or it would never have lasted as long as it had with all the tumult it had brought.

"He's been able to message me through a friend and I have said I'm not available for three weeks with a big commitment with the school that takes me away from La Serena and then I will be busy catching up after that, so I've promised nothing."

"Catching up? What do you mean by catching up? Is there going to be so much school work to do because of these visits to the desert?"

"No, no, catching up with my voluntary work. I'll tell you about it another time. Let's go to eat now, as you suggested."

-oOo-

Without troubling with an early start the next day, they asked if *Los Sabores de la Abuela* was open on a Sunday morning and on learning it was, they decided to try a mid-morning breakfast there. They met up with Fernando again, the son of the hotel owner and a lavish cooked breakfast was brought to them, compliments of the house. Well satisfied with what Isabel called a brunch and promising to see them again next month and throughout October, they left their new friends behind. They'd been advised to take a walk along some of the newly created pathways cutting through a large green expanse by the river, very near the town centre. This was a recently developed leisure area for the town and clearly, a great deal of development work was going on in Vallenar. They agreed the town architects had vision in their creation of a 3000-metre green corridor along the river for the townspeople and visitors to enjoy and for the biodiversity it brought. The river water was being used primarily for agriculture but here was a lovely feature of the town just for pleasure and exercise. The trees, bushes and grasses were a lush, rich green and an idyllic rural haven was being created very near the town centre. It was hard to believe the town was in the driest desert in the world.

"It's hard to believe we are in Chile," said Isabel. "Parks, recreation grounds and country footpaths are common in or near British towns but it's rare here in Chile for town councils to create areas for leisure and enjoyment. There is a real lack of that sort of development and to achieve it so well in the middle of a desert is quite remarkable. Land in Chile on the edge of urban areas is often left wild and untouched but in private ownership so that local people can't even access the land or just go for a walk in the countryside. That is one of the things about England that I really like. There are footpaths in the countryside all over the country."

"Sounds like you're trying to talk yourself into going back," provoked Mateo.

"Well, not everything was all wrong... just most of it! No... it was mostly my problem. There was always this vast longing to be somewhere else..."

"I'm sorry. I shouldn't be flippant."

About an hour further on and after they had turned towards the coast, Mateo thought he'd found the tall, spiky cacti that the hotel owner had spoken of, opposite a faintly marked side track branching off the road. Near the rocks ahead, he parked the car as instructed and they got out to explore the area. On dropping down the other side of the summit of a small hill, protruding from behind a large rock, there was a long brown stem with single leaves all along its length and at the end a magnificent bright red flower the diameter of a human hand. Each individual bell, making up the large spherical head, had red stamens and green seed pods and they narrowed into a dark velvet-looking centre. Isabel didn't think she had ever seen a flower quite so beautiful.

"This is *Leontochir ovallei* - Lion's Paw - a species native to Chile, only found in the area of the Llanos de Challe National Park. It's in danger of extinction. There are yellow ones too but they are even rarer," Mateo said. "Of course, they only appear when *El Niño* brings rain to the desert."

"Look, I've found several over here!" Isabel shouted from behind some further rocks and she was busy with her camera, between gasps of delight. As they wandered the area they found a few more and quite a variety of other flowering plants amongst a lot of green foliage and cacti. As they climbed a slope they suddenly had a view of the coastline. It was utterly unspoiled and natural and with not a house or any sign of civilisation in sight.

"Shall we have some picnic lunch here in this lovely wilderness?" Isabel suggested. They walked back to the car and found a place sheltered from the wind. She mashed a couple of avocados, cut tomatoes and put out the little bottle of dressing she had made. She had Roquefort cheese to offer too. The bread rolls were still soft and thank goodness she'd brought the avocados uncut, she thought, or the flesh would have been dark brown by today. She'd apples and pears to serve too and fruit juice. "We are in the middle of nowhere and it is so beautiful."

"Perfect you brought the food," Mateo stared long and hard at her and their eyes met. "*Gracias,*" he said and their eyes remained engaged. Isabel smiled and looked away.

"I'm glad you brought me. It has been beautiful to see these areas." Mateo continued to look at her intently as she diverted her gaze and then he turned his attention to studying the map and suggested they go on towards the coast after lunch and then turn south along the coast to Huasco.

"We'll have to come back from the coast then, to return to Vallenar. There's no road further south along the coast. It means we're about four hours driving from home now. What a pity we can't bring the children this far, but we can't."

"There's no rush for us and it's not late yet. I am so glad I have seen the *garras de leones*. And those vast sheathes of coloured hills. It really is an amazing phenomenon. I want to give you a very big thank you."

"I am enjoying this weekend enormously." Mateo attempted to engage her eyes again but without success. "I hope you will come on all the day trips with the children?"

"I'm willing to but I don't see how I'm going to cover any of my classes if I am out every day," said Isabel.

"The staff have agreed to do classes for us & we can give lesson plans with a big emphasis on practical or individual work. I imagine that's easier with art than with many subjects. It's going to be a nightmare with the timetables, but the science teachers are going to cover most of my classes."

"It's great that the teachers seem behind you," reassured Isabel. "We are going to be busy with a lot of preparation before the trips start." Mateo put his arm reassuringly around Isabel's shoulders as they returned to the car. She did not attempt to avoid his touch and they smiled at one another.

Reluctantly, they left the beauty of the wilderness around them. Isabel took some further video of the panorama. When they were on the move again in the car she said, "Looking at the map, I suggest we don't stop in Vallenar on the way back but if we want a break after a couple of hours of travelling, we could stop about halfway home from Vallenar in the village of Incahausi. I thought Incahuasi was a volcano."

"You're right. It is. The volcano and the village take their name from the Quechua word meaning Inca house. Could be another good place to check out in case we have to stop again with the children on the return."

Sipping a juice outside a little café cum corner shop in the village of Incahausi, Mateo had a suggestion to make. "Let's not stop for food here, even if we could find somewhere in this tiny place. Let's have dinner together in La Serena when we are back. I want to invite you." Isabel smiled and looking him straight in the face, she agreed.

When they arrived in La Serena, Mateo drove his car to the house where Isabel had a room. She was keen to change out of yesterday's clothes covered with the dust of the desert, but he insisted on waiting for her. She showed him to her room. It was a kind of studio, a large bedroom/living room but she was fortunate enough to have her own small kitchen and a bathroom to herself on the same floor. She offered drinks and nibbles of nuts and disappeared into the bathroom. Mateo dipped into some of her books while she was away.

"You have a good collection of art books," he remarked when she returned.

"Most of them I've bought at second-hand bookstalls in Santiago or Valparaiso. I brought a few back from England last time I was there. They have charity shops all over Britain and there are wonderful bargains to be had, not only in books but in pictures too. You can often pick up a print of a famous artist and a lovely pricey frame for very little. The Sunday morning antique fairs here are good too. I do the reframing myself where necessary. Look at this great tool I brought from England," said Isabel pulling out a belted contraption from the bottom drawer of her desk. "It holds the four corners of the frame in place whilst the glue dries and you tighten them with this handle." Suitably impressed, Mateo didn't think he'd ever seen one of those on sale in Chile.

"Another good reason to go back," he said, fishing.

"There are lots of good reasons but I'm not sure anyone can really feel and be themselves in a different country from where their roots are and where their heart is."

"That's the key, surely - where your heart is. Exile isn't like going voluntarily to another country and if you are always longing to return, it's like a small heartbreak every day, isn't it?" Isabel felt there was some real understanding of her by Mateo. She put her hand on his arm in an unconscious gesture to thank him. Their eyes met. She sensed he wanted to kiss her but she pulled back and declared herself ready to go out.

They called briefly at Mateo's apartment and then took a *colectivo* and were soon sipping wine in an Italian restaurant and wishing s*alud* to each other and clinking their glasses. When the question was posed after the meal, would she come back to his apartment, Isabel knew that she wanted to. She felt excited that this handsome, perceptive Chilean, with his attractive mop of thick black hair, was making her feel an intense passion like she had not experienced in a long time. The dilemma for her was how was she going to reveal to Mateo all the political work she was trying to achieve and the time that would involve her being away for long weekends from La Serena, which weren't going to be conducive to a new relationship. Then there was the matter of her false name. She felt she knew she could trust him enough to tell him about the work and that he would be sympathetic with the cause, but giving only fleeting time to him might not be acceptable. She decided that's how it had to be, take it or leave it and she would tell him at his apartment. Isabel was unusually quiet in the *colectivo* on the return journey and when he asked her why she said she had something to tell him.

When they were back in the apartment, Isabel began explaining her commitments in the northern cities of Chile and that she would have to go the next weekend, the last in September, from Thursday night to Monday morning, if they were to have three weeks in the flowering desert in October with the children. During these weeks she wasn't going to have Fridays off as usual and she would have to go off for long weekends away again as soon as the desert visits were all over. Mateo just listened. When she stopped talking he leaned over and kissed her. He held her tightly and she put her arms around him and hugged him.

"I want to help you," he eventually gasped and kissed her again.

"You'd be risking your job, your career." But he silenced her with further kisses. "I want to be honest with you, I'm going to be busy. I want to build on all the work I did last year. I can't drop it..." the kisses were going down her neck and her blouse was being undone.

-oOo-

A couple of evenings later Mateo was cooking up a supper for Isabel and himself. They had had *almuerzo* at the school but Mateo knew that Isabel liked a cooked evening meal and he wanted to have the long talk they had agreed on, for him to know exactly what she was planning to do on all these weekends away, of which she had spoken. She had given him quite a grilling on their return from the desert about his political affiliations and his views on the central issues she'd been demonstrating about for nearly two years now. She thought him genuinely wanting to help and willing to do something more radical because he could see change was so slow in coming. His main area of concern was an *educación sin lucro,* for education to be without the profit motive, without the private schools and private universities run as businesses and privileging only the fortunate. Mateo was very committed to the need for change and became emotional over the injustices and inequalities of the education system and the profits being made by some schools and universities, most of which were of dubious quality.

"Worst of all," he said, "the public universities have to charge large fees because they don't get enough funding from the government, grants are almost non-existent now and families without resources just cannot afford to send their children to the state universities. Furthermore, the quality of the secondary education a pupil receives and whether they can get into university is very much dependent on where they grew up - how rich or poor the local authority was and if parents could pay for the privilege."

"I agree with you. The system is very unequal which makes it very unfair."

"Now tell me about all these weekends away that you tell me you have to do. What are they all about?"

"Throughout 1996 I was doing voluntary teaching classes on the history of Latin America, Chilean politics and economics," said Isabel, "but I was also working with various groups on planning protests and how to carry out non-violent direct action. Just marching doesn't ultimately achieve very much. What gets attention and publicity is direct action and civil disobedience and I'm afraid we have to resort to these methods to get anything accomplished. A lot of my teaching was based on Galeano's book *Las Venas Abiertas de América Latina*. That book was one of the few possessions that Isabel Allende took into exile with her, by the way. Brilliant book! Both adults and teenagers in the poorest *barrios* really related to the historical details I took from that book. They knew they were living the consequences of that history. One example is the case of tin from Bolivia. The English owners became multimillionaires, in the 19th Century and in the first half of the 20th Century. One of the ten richest men in the world was an English tin mine owner, at a time when sixty per cent of Bolivians were illiterate, half the children never went to school and the tin miners died with putrid lungs. Another example and Galeano had researched all the details of these matters, was where industrial activities were beginning in Latin America, as in Chile, but Britain supplied grand quantities of ceramics, glass, wood and metal articles and textiles to aid its own industries at home and it imposed the harshest protectionist laws of Europe to prevent the import to Britain of such articles made here. Do you know they even made ponchos, yes, ponchos in England to export here! All the railway development was to take out the minerals and the food products but the trains were also used also to deliver here the manufactured goods of Britain. And it is still going on. They take out the natural products and export the manufactured products to maintain our economic dependency. The poverty wages here finance the high salaries of the United States and Europe. Look at the price of electronics here now.

I couldn't buy a laptop here I had to get one when I returned to England."
Mateo nodded and pulled a resigned face.

"Another example is Haiti and the revolution of the slaves which, incredibly for that time, led to the independence of Haiti but it was a country born in ruins because of the bloodbath that was the uprising. Haiti has never recovered because it had to pay European and Wall Street traders and bankers vast sums of money in reparations to former slave owners and it was threatened by gunboats just off the coast. It is now still the poorest country in Latin America. I used to encourage the class to read Carpentier's novel set at the time of that revolution at the end of the 18th century."

"He is an excellent Chilean writer."

"Yes, he paints wonderful pictures. The language of Galeano is so graphic too, creating dramatic drawings that capture the imagination. He talks about the railway lines that formed a decisive part of "the iron cage of dependency," for example. You can stir your audience with pictures like that and I enjoyed using them.

"What is the most tragic, says Galeano, and without ethical justification, are the number of coups d'état and military regimes that have occurred to maintain the interests of the imperialists and the compromised native upper class that are complicit with them. Galeano's book was first published in 1971, before the coup in Chile and then a military dictatorship came to us as well, the so-called most stable democracy in Latin America. Any real change of power could not be tolerated. Later editions of the book include Chile through the 1970s and Galeano details how 12 million dollars from the US were distributed amongst the enemies of our legally elected government to sustain a strike by the lorry owners to paralyse the economy and put around fear of shortages and create chaos, which led to the coup. And then there was the money given directly to Pinochet - 290 million dollars - to sustain his military regime. Videla in Argentina equally received US money." Isabel was getting angry and emotional by now but she wasn't done. Galeano says torture wouldn't exist in Latin America if it wasn't efficient for the purpose, like when the 'formal' democracy cannot guarantee that the economy won't escape from the control of the existing owners of power."

"They lost that control in Cuba and they were determined it wouldn't happen again," responded Mateo. "I'm not defending some aspects of the

Cuban regime but there's no denying they have the best statistics in Latin America for levels of health, life expectancy, infant mortality and educational achievement, everything."

"Yes, you are absolutely right. All from the profits of sugar. Do you know they have a longer life expectancy in Cuba than in the United Kingdom by three or four years? And they did all that, as you know, with a US boycott and US efforts to spoil their harvests, going on for decades. Galeano gives all those details too. Think how well off the peoples of all Latin American countries would be now, if the profits of their natural resources had gone to the people and not to the greedy accumulation of wealth by the few and to foreign investors."

"Haven't you found people very fearful still to come out to demonstrate?"

"Students are becoming more aware and I've met working-class people who are very knowledgeable and very willing to take action. *Educacion sin lucro* is certainly one of our key themes. Our education system is profoundly unequal. Also, there is the pension scheme, the *AFP,* which the young people know they will soon be forced to pay into, costing more than they will ever get out and which gives pensions that people can't even live on. So much goes on profits for the companies. Then there is the high cost of medicine and the unequal access to health care and there is the desperate need to change the military government's constitution."

"But what do you do on these visits to cities in the north? I realise they know you from working with them before, by why keep visiting them?" asked Mateo, wondering if it was really necessary.

"I want to be sure the grassroots groups have their banners and posters prepared on all these topics and their plans in place, before the election coming in December. I want the groups I have helped to build in various cities in the north, to be highly organised and confident in themselves when they demonstrate because they are sure they have planned every detail well. I want to be sure they have thought and prepared how they will give support to any persons arrested, contacting the family and getting legal help. I want to be sure every demo has its authorisation from the Regional Government where we can get it, and a decision on what we are going to do if we can't have permission or if they are going to exceed the permission by some form of civil disobedience. Either way, we need a clear plan of action and they have to arrange the logistics, transport, water to drink and sanitation. I have to check they have made their demonstrators feel cared for and that they all are as composed as they can be. I want to know if they have had a good number of people to prepare their banners and placards in advance and worked to get a good turnout, done leafleting, for example."

"Impressive," said Mateo, "You really have thought of everything."

"I've had time to, including my time under arrest," replied Isabel. "Two years ago at a demo on the 11ᵗʰ September anniversary of the military coup, there were the usual demos in different parts of the country. I was in Iquique - they held me for nearly a week. It was frightening because you don't know what is going to happen next, if you are going to be knocked around again, have your hair pulled or worse and you don't know for how long they are going to keep you. When help has not been planned in advance, you don't know if any of your family knows where you are, nor if there's any chance of some legal help. I've been trying to get contacts and support from the law schools in the universities to voluntarily assist in these situations. My brother is a lawyer and I eventually had his help, when he knew."

"That's good you had him and he must have been a big help to you. But how long was it before he knew you'd been arrested and how did he know?"

A friend where I was staying, Amalia, who tried to get information from the police without success, decided to look in my bag and found my mother's telephone number. It would have been better if we'd planned she should ring my brother, rather than involve my mother, who of course went mad about it and phoned Carlos. Now I know we must plan these things in advance for everyone taking part.

"They couldn't pin any illegal act on me nor the destruction of property but you never know if false accusations will be brought. Some demonstrators had lit bonfires that time, you know the usual thing every 11ᵗʰ September. Because they cut the city lights to make things difficult for anyone out and about demonstrating, the light of the bonfire is the only light you have, so you have to stay near. They put up barricades to provoke confrontations and you can't get away even if you want to. They kettle you - that's what it is called. We only went to light candles in memory of the disappeared and in homage to the thousands tortured."

"How did you get arrested? Don't they usually break these things up with water cannon and tear gas?"

"Yes, they do. I've had some soakings and the tear gas is nasty but on this occasion, I wouldn't give up. I ran away with everyone else, you've no choice with the water canon and the tear gas and then I returned with a good crowd which was reassembling and then we had to run again and fewer of us returned and then the same again. The numbers got less and less each time but I suggested we all sat down in front of the *Intendencia* government offices. We still had placards showing what we were about and we were entirely peaceful. We were soon carried away of course and into police vans.

"I have to be careful now because Carlos says if they hold me again it is bound to be for longer and they will be harsher. For that reason, I decided to base myself away from the northern cities where I was getting known and I thought that from La Serena I could visit the north but not be too available if they decide to check on me or if they want to blame some incident that occurs onto me, without proof but just because they have to blame someone. I also was running out of money and needed to earn some if I could. And so I came to be at the High School here. I couldn't believe my luck to get the job and I have really enjoyed the teaching."

"Well, I'm very glad you came to teach here and settle down a bit."

"It really is important to keep demanding change. We can't go on with this undemocratic constitution. I couldn't do anything this year on 11th September because I had classes and couldn't get to a northern city or to Santiago for the evening. I was so angry though and sickened because of the usual military celebrations that day - a disgusting affront to the people who suffered at their hands - but this year it was Pinochet's last "11th" as head of the army and a special salute was given him by 300 right-wing politicians, members of the army high command and ex-ministers of the military regime. I can't accept these criminals still have so much power and the right to strut about celebrating! Celebrating death and disappearances," quietly screamed Isabel in tears now.

"I know. I know. I saw the photos in the paper but next to the picture of the parade for Pinochet was a photo of the widow of Allende at a mass in the chapel at the Moneda for the memory of the fallen. Families of the victims were there too. At least there was some attempt to give the other point of view in the press."

"They couldn't really do much else if they were reporting what went on that day but I bet the majority of the press, who are right-wing, didn't attempt to balance the military celebrations with that news."

"A lot is going to happen this year I'm sure," said Mateo. "People like you won't let them ever forget and Isabel Allende, our M.P. remember...last month was declared as a witness before a Spanish judge who is investigating the disappearance of Spanish citizens during the regime of Pinochet. She detailed what happened when the assault started in the *golpe del estado* on the Moneda Palace and she said that the crimes of the dictatorship have to be clarified. She wished such an investigation was happening in Chile but in the so-called "transition," it hasn't yet been allowed by the military. But the people need to know."

"Just like the Spanish people were informed after their dictatorship," replied Isabel sarcastically. "Not a soul has been prosecuted in Spain in their own total cover-up."

"Yes, you're right. But this Spanish judge has instructed a process for genocide against the Chilean dictatorship. That's quite something! Let's hope something comes of that. Come on, let's eat now and relax a little and then we can plan your next weekend visit to the north."

Later, when they were clearing the table Mateo said, "You can't possibly do three cities so far apart in one weekend and two overnight buses, it's too much. You know the distances involved and you'll be knackered," he insisted. "Look, you go overnight on Thursday as you insist, to Antofagasta and spend Friday with your people doing the preparations and all you've described. I'll come Friday afternoon by plane because I only have classes in the morning and we will do the demo in Antofagasta on the Saturday as you planned. Saturday evening we can go to Tocopilla by bus or taxi and you can see your people Sunday morning and in two hours we can be in Calama, so you can see the people there too in the afternoon and we'll fly back Sunday evening. There are a good number of flights from Calama. You can't work Monday after another night on a bus."

"I've done it before."

"Oh, have you! I don't know what the Head would think of that!"

"I can't afford to fly and the people I work with would be horrified. It wouldn't occur to them in all their lives that they would be able to just jump on a plane."

"I know. I am going to pay because you want to get so much done in one weekend because you're helping me through October and you can't travel then as you might have done. I insist. And we don't have to let your people know we are flying. We go off, apparently to get the overnight bus and we go to the airport instead. No problem." Isabel had grave doubts that this was right but it was a plan that made the three cities a feasible possibility in one weekend. But she had another problem to discuss with Mateo. She decided to come straight out with it.

"They know me in the north by another name. Isabel." She had never told Mateo that her real name was not Helena García and she recognised she was compounding her lie further.

"What?"

"I use the name Isabel in the places I go to in the north. You will have to use that name if you come with me." Mateo looked aghast but tried to think how it might not be unreasonable but safer to have a false name. He didn't like it however and was quiet for a while.

"Do I really know who you are?" Mateo asked after a while.

"Do I really know who you are?" she replied.

They watched the news together but were not as passionate as their last evening had been.

"I really appreciate your help," Isabel said as Mateo was seeing her into a *colectivo*. She said she would prefer to start her school day from her own home the next morning.

"What are your surnames in the north?" he asked. She stared at him. "I need them to book hotels as we've agreed."

"No, you don't. We are Señor and Señora Mateo Martinez. Is that your real name or...?"

Mateo looked exasperated. "You'll have to show your ID at the hotel." Isabel thought he was fishing.

"I've got my ID as normal. Helena Isabel García Sepúlveda. What's the prob...?" She couldn't finish her words for the kisses that were stopping her speak. The collective taxi whisked her away.

# Chapter 11

T he following weekend, for which Mateo had made bookings for Isabel's journeying in the north, all went to plan and Isabel had to confess it was great to have someone looking after her and arranging the practicalities. Mateo booked the flights and a couple of hotels for Friday night in Antofagasta and Saturday night in Tocopilla. Friends with whom she'd stayed before seemed a little dubious of her new friend taking her away from them but they appeared to understand well enough. In Antofagasta, the people she had done history and politics classes with before, seemed exceptionally delighted to see her but they had some rather depressing news for her. Since they had last seen Isabel they assured her that they had been working hard in their *barrios* and workplaces but they were not confident of a good turnout for the pre-election rally in the main square. Despite their efforts, many people had refused to register to vote and many who were registered had insisted that their best course of action was to spoil their ballot paper or just place the paper in the ballot box *en blanco* - without choosing an option. They assured Isabel it was not apathy. It was a deliberate form of rebellion and a political vote in itself. She could see there was good reason to feel disillusioned with the "transition" to democracy and she knew there could be no democracy with the current constitution, but it went against all her instincts to agree that you don't vote or you ruin your ballot paper. The debates were long and hard over this issue.

The key activists had organised a couple of speakers for the rally but they were candidates who did not see themselves as having any chance of election. They were willing to articulate their critical contempt for the present parliament and the constitution. They had liaised with some student contacts and found that the student speakers had pulled out and the general message from the young was not to vote at all. This was a rebellion that could be significant if it happened throughout the country. Isabel rang two law students who'd promised help and to advise if needed following any arrests. They were still committed to assisting if there were arrests but they weren't prepared to be at the rally and agreed with the 'no vote' policy. Isabel joined in the preparation of the communal lunch cooked in the Community Hall but the atmosphere was not as usual. It was a little sad and depressing. Isabel loved the feeling of warmth and common purpose such days normally brought, but this was very different. When Mateo arrived in the early evening, she introduced him to everyone making posters in the community hall and Mateo was soon deep in conversation with a group of young people who'd come in after school. Finally, at the end of the day, very sad she threw herself on the bed in the room Mateo had booked. She was glad to be indulged in all his affection and in the comfortable surroundings his support had provided but she was devastated that things were not as she had expected.

"It's like we are at the beginning again, with everyone so fearful they don't want to be active in any sense."

"No, it's not like that. This is a definite movement and the politicians cannot ignore it. The young people especially don't feel they have any other choice. These are the most aware people that are not voting. And they are willing to take a risk to make their rebellion. They have a legal obligation to register and to vote, you know of course. They don't know if there will be consequences."

Next evening on arrival in Tocopilla they reviewed the day. The turnout had not been great but the banners were impressive. Their slogans had highlighted the issues and reflected all that the speakers had to say. There had been no trouble and the occasion had been seen by the regional authorities and the police as a legitimate pre-election event. Mateo was pleased that *educación sin lucro* was well flagged.

"I hope some people are going to support these minority candidates we've been promoting," said Isabel. "It's sad we don't have a strong national party in opposition to the *Concertación* and the Right. So many people are likely to spoil their ballot papers or not vote at all but if all the discontent could be channelled it would present a real opposition."

"I know. You are right. But I think we flagged up the issues and asked people to think of all that needs to change, whether they vote or not."

Similar discussions on the best tactics for the Parliamentary elections were debated at their meetings in Tocopilla and Calama. The lack of registration to vote and the rebellious mood for the election was widespread. Finally, they came round to agreeing on a plan of action for rallies and marches in November. Isabel drew out of the groups all the preparations they needed to make by clever prompting rather than lecturing them on what to do and she seemed to inject some new enthusiasm into the disillusioned activists. Mateo thought she'd done it well and told her so. She tried to thank him but wanted to apologise for the weekend not having been all she had hoped. She was worried he had found it a waste of time and money and he assured her he didn't think that at all. She had given her encouragement and support, which was the purpose of the trip. He knew Isabel would never have been satisfied if she had not tried her best. Isabel was very glad of the quick flight back to La Serena, instead of a night-long bus ride and her own bed to sleep in after a supper visit to Mateo's.

Throughout October the children's visits to the flowering desert went very much as planned and everyone seemed supportive of the effort, even if there were frustrations with the timetables on occasions. Isabel did five days a week with Mateo on the school trips and she had to work on Fridays through November to make up some classes she owed. She was so glad they had travelled to the north early to make plans for November demos and the December elections. Mateo had done some teaching on the bus rides about the seeds that lie dormant until the rains come. He had photocopied material to hand out and got the children to draw and label the parts of plants. No marks would be deducted for untidy work when writing on the bus, he promised them. He had quite a lot of the curriculum to make up however and was doing extra classes throughout November.

-oOo-

Isabel had increasingly the feeling that the parliamentary elections were of little significance and her contacts were confirming all that they had learned on their recent trip to the north. There was increasing talk in the press about the lack of responsibility of the young people who hadn't signed up to vote. Mateo wanted to suggest a plan. They should return to the north when the school had broken up for Christmas and the summer holidays. They could travel around to all the places Isabel had contacts without the need to rush from place to place and they could have a few holiday days, to see interesting places in the desert between meetings and attending political demos. Isabel thought the plan a good idea but she would have to see if her contacts agreed and that not too many key people would be on holiday.

On the 24th November 1997, when it was Pinochet's birthday and Isabel heard the news that the General was going to retire himself from being Head of the Army and enter the Senate as a life peer, she was incensed. "I've absolutely got to be out with the people demonstrating against this further affront to democracy," she said to Mateo.

"You know you hardly have any time before the end of term and everything has been set up for the election demos. You don't need to rush off, give yourself a chance."

"I ought to be out there doing something. We can only put our bodies to swell the numbers and show how we feel. What else do we have and what else can we do? Look, in the news today there was an authorised march in Santiago yesterday by the juvenile wings of the parties of the *Concertación,* which they called "an act of repudiation of the figure of Pinochet and his future presence in the Senate." I should be with the activists in the north and we ought to be out there too, showing our disapproval. As it happens the Santiago march led to a journalist being seriously hit in the leg by a tear gas canister. As usual, the police blamed the marchers for trying to remove barricades but the police were accused of aggression by a foreign journalist who was seized by the police along with a blind and mute person who was in no way taking part in the demonstrations but became caught up in them."

"Well, that just shows how nasty things are likely to get. People on both sides are going to get angry and blame each other. You'll have to be very careful and you especially mustn't get arrested."

"The key issue now is to demonstrate about Pinochet, not the coming elections. How do we stop him from entering the Senate? As you can see in the papers, others have clearly concluded the same. The response from the State, however, does seem to be getting nastier and nastier. This issue should be the main theme of the election demos. I must be in touch with my contacts. I should go to visit again. It's a bit much to ask them at this stage to do new posters but they must put the emphasis on Pinochet never being allowed to enter the Senate. There must be one large poster at least on that theme. There must."

"You can't just dash up to the north again now. There will be plenty of time to ensure that is the main theme of future demos from Christmas to March."

"But it's not right just to leave it now. It should overshadow the elections but it won't if we allow it to be just accepted as normal. And it's so difficult in the summer after Christmas to get people out to do much. They see it as holiday time. Why don't the people serge out in big numbers immediately against this outrage? What's happened to this country? I could scream."

Mateo attempted to calm her down but Isabel wasn't sure he really understood how significant this was and how important for the people to oppose it. Why wasn't he enraged like her? There had been something else in the paper too that day that caught Isabel's attention but which she didn't mention to Mateo. There was a report of a discovery of 58 coffins in an old cemetery associated with the nitrate industry and its workers' villages, along the main road from Calama to Antofagasta. The suspicion was, however, that the coffins were from clandestine burials of detained people who had disappeared during the military regime and this scepticism arose from the fact that the coffins were of the same size and characteristics as those found in Pampa Blanca, only seven kilometres from the ex-detention centre of Chacabuco. The news article said the Vice-President of the Republic claimed the preliminary findings of the Criminal Court and the laboratory findings of the Police technical investigations, were that the coffins were 100-year-old cemetery remains from the nitrate industry days. The Vice President, however, said he was awaiting confirmation of this. Similarly, the Organisation of the Families of the Detained Disappeared were also awaiting confirmation but they announced that they had been able to find out that some bodies had the remains of clothing and some were wrapped in blankets, which added to their suspicions and their hopes of identifying the cadavers.

Isabel recalled a woman she had met in Calama who went into the desert almost every day to try to discover some evidence of the burials which were known to have taken place there, of disappeared prisoners of the regime. Her husband she believed was one of them and twenty years later she was still searching for clues of where his body might be. It was known that soldiers buried bodies of prisoners in desert locations. This woman raked through the rubble on the surface of the desert for tiny pieces of clothing, a button or any possession that might have been dropped. She was working systematically and had covered a huge area but in the immensity of the desert, it seemed a pitiful effort. However, it was something she felt compelled to do. Isabel cried for this woman yet again.

Finally, Isabel was persuaded to telephone her main contact in each town and suggest a giant poster for each election demo: "No dictator in the Senate" and they agreed the opportunity to make this point shouldn't be lost. They hoped it would increase the interest in their manifestations. In the event, it hardly appeared to be an issue amongst most candidates but the low turnout for them possibly reflected the discontent with the whole of the system. The election came and went with very little change to the party makeup of the Congress but, adding together the one million who had not registered, the abstentions and the *nulos* and the *blancos*, over thirty-one per cent of Chileans who could vote, did not vote. This was a huge rise from previous post-dictatorship elections.

"Listen to this," said Isabel and she read to Mateo from the paper, with cynicism in her voice. "'The Presidential seat La Moneda is said to find the results incomprehensible and to be in a "state of reflection." This more liberal paper does recognise that the large number who have not voted or spoiled their opportunity, "could not be attributed to error or to ignorance or apathy but to a firm rejection of the government or the system."'"

"Well, I guess that is something."

"But I looked at the papers in the library today and most of the mainstream press are stating there was a high increase in the apathy vote."

Three weeks after the news of the discovery of the coffins, Isabel received a phone call. An activist contact in Antofagasta wanted to see her most urgently but could not say what it was about over the telephone. Isabel trusted her friend and colleague but baulked at the thought of travelling there and back in two overnight buses for a reason about which she had been given no idea. Her friend did not think it ought to wait until after the Christmas break. Isabel decided not to tell Mateo immediately but to travel on a Thursday evening overnight and then she could return Saturday overnight and still have Sunday to relax and recover. When she arrived at Mateo's apartment with a rucksack and a ticket and said she would be getting the overnight bus that evening, he was a bit taken aback. Why on earth it couldn't wait till they had planned to go together to the north in January, Mateo couldn't understand. Miffed he wasn't going to see her till Sunday, he declared he would be meeting her off the bus Sunday morning and she was to have breakfast with him. Grateful, Isabel asked him not to say she was away or where she was going, to anyone. "I don't know why, I just have a feeling. Don't say a word." And he promised he wouldn't.

On Friday morning, as Isabel arrived in Antofagasta, she reluctantly dragged herself out of the *semi-cama* seat of the bus and turned towards the sea and the port. She knew that Daniela, her friend would be at work at this time and she would have to wait until lunchtime to see her. Finding a café with a sea view to have breakfast, she went to the bathroom first and then ordered a large coffee and a croissant. She decided she would pass the morning in the University library and there she searched the local newspapers for further news about the finding of the coffins not far from where she was at present. Again, Isabel had a feeling any news might be relevant to her trip although Daniela had not given anything away in her phone call. All Isabel could find in the local papers was repeated denial that the coffins were any more modern than from the nitrate industry times but that investigations were still in progress. While at the library, Isabel thought it might be useful to learn more about the nitrate industry itself and she found some historical information. There had been a number of nitrate extraction works in the desert, founded when the north of Chile was part of Peru but most had become uneconomic even before the Great Depression finished many of them off and before fertiliser could be made from a synthesis of ammonia on an industrial scale. Most nitrate works had thus closed a hundred years before, like Chacabuco, although one famous one, Humberstone, now a ghost town, had survived till the 1950s with a new method of production. The old buildings of Chacabuco nitrate works had been used by the military regime as a concentration camp but this was not common, the reference book claimed. *Or was it,* wondered Isabel. *Ideal, old barn-like buildings in remote desert locations...?*

It was time to make her way to Daniela's house and of course, Daniela was preparing lunch for Isabel and the family. With the children around, Daniela didn't want to say more about why she had asked Isabel to come so urgently. Finally, the children were fed and went out to play and Daniela, with occasional glances at her husband as if seeking courage and reassurance, began to explain how a woman had come to them with some evidence that she thought would demonstrate that the coffins found in the desert recently, were ordered by the military during the dictatorship years. Isabel smiled inwardly. She'd had the feeling this secrecy would concern the coffins and real evidence would be so valuable. "The woman," said Daniela "was terrified of the consequences for her if it was known that she had helped bring this information to light but she felt it had to be revealed." Isabel couldn't agree more.

"What is the evidence she has?"

"The woman was in the Army Women's Auxiliary Service. That was created during the military regime to bring women into the Chilean Army," added Daniela not knowing if Isabel would be aware of that as she had been away.

"Yes, I did know they created a women's section. The majority were given only administrative jobs to do but it released more men for military duties. However, some women became involved in intelligence and a few even participated in torture sessions." Isabel had read.

Daniela continued, "The woman's father is an Army Officer and she said how she had had absolutely no knowledge of the crimes that were taking place by the armed forces after the coup d'état. She had been only three years old in the year of the coup and naturally, she had grown up totally believing the propaganda of the armed forces and the government. The military government she thought was all for the best, just as her father had told her. At 18 she joined the Army Women's Auxiliary Service, before the referendum on Pinochet remaining as president and only then did she begin to hear another viewpoint about what had been going on in this country. At first, she was in total denial and still does not believe her father would knowingly be part of any kind of abuse of power. Gradually, however, she said she learned more of the illegal torture and killings and she sought out news without telling her family. She kept a very low profile at her work as if she was as ignorant herself, as she now found to be the other women and men in the Army that she came across. She decided, whenever she had the chance, that she would look through the old files in the offices where she was based, in case there was any evidence of any abuse or illegal act by anyone stationed there. She didn't want to tell us even where that was, she was so frightened. But she said she had to tell someone that she had come across an order for coffins made in 1973. She took the paper, doubting it would ever be missed and that is what she is offering to us. She has kept the paper and has not yet even told me her name. Of course, she is desperate the paper's disappearance is not traced to her. She wants to be sure this evidence will not be hidden again but gets into the hands of someone who can use it to show the practices of the army. Why else would a military barracks need coffins in "peacetime" other than if they had detained persons that had been killed?"

Isabel said she thought that most victims of illicit killings had not had coffins but were just thrown into mass graves. "In 1990 they found 20 bodies in a mass grave in Pisagua and which had been a detention centre under Pinochet in the past and that was not the only mass grave found. I'll come back to that. For now, I want to say that the bodies they found had not decomposed because of the minerals in the very dry desert. The flesh was still preserved and bullet holes were visible. Clothes were also preserved by the desert and some still had blindfolds and tied hands. They had not, however, had coffins."

Daniela responded that she had actually asked the woman why on earth would they have put political prisoners in coffins. "She seemed unaware that they might not use them. Perhaps they thought coffins were necessary but later the number of bodies to be disposed of became too many. She thought that it might have looked less suspicious if the coffins looked like they were from the old cemetery of the nitrate town and if they were discovered they would be ignored as nothing to do with the military in modern times."

"It would be a way of covering up what had been done. That makes some sense."

"The woman is convinced they were used for the *detenidos desaparecidos* prisoners. She wants her paper to go abroad, like to Amnesty International or somewhere so that the evidence can't be denied. I told her about you and she agreed to see you. I've asked her to come tomorrow when I knew you'd be here." Isabel's mind began to whirl. Whoever holds on to the original paper will be in danger, she thought, but this woman primarily is in danger.

"But we'd have to think carefully about giving up the original paper. If only a copy is sent abroad, journalists or others will want it authenticated. If the original was put back in the file, if that were possible without a huge risk, it could be destroyed when investigators want to start to search it out. How much can we trust the Court apparatus and the police experts that are supposed to be investigating? They seem to be a long time dating or tracing the origin of the coffins found. The safest hands to get it to might be the Spanish judge who is attempting to prosecute the deaths of Spaniards in Chile.

"There is a lot to think about before we decide what to do. For now, let me finish what I was going to tell you before. Did you know that Pinochet himself was Camp Commander at Pisagua when he was an Army Captain in 1948? The government then had turned the old nitrate port of Pisagua into a concentration camp for Socialists, Communists and Anarchists. Pinochet thought the camp was a true Marxist-Leninist University! He said he feared they would all become agitators if released. It has been confirmed that one of the torturers at the camp was a Walter Rauff - an SS Commander from Nazi Germany who escaped to South America after the war. He'd been responsible for creating mobile gassing vans in Germany. He became an adviser to the DINA Secret Police in the Pinochet Regime."

The whole sad issue was put aside for the rest of the day. Daniela's husband went back to work for the afternoon/evening hours and the two women talked of 'No Dictator in the Senate' demonstrations they would have to hold before Christmas, as afterwards, there would be few people around. They also agreed on leafleting Daniela's neighbourhood and others and Isabel said she would find some funds for that. They got down to designing a handout immediately. "They can be given out on the day of the demo too," she said. They went to visit the likely volunteers to help put these leaflets out and were warmly welcomed by familiar faces. Isabel did love to be with these passionate, committed, courageous women of the *barrio*. The nagging thought about how to handle what was being asked of her kept returning and kept her awake a while that night. She wished she could discuss it with Mateo but that was impossible over the phone. She had a strong feeling that the person she really wanted to discuss it with was Julian and that made sleep even more elusive.

In the morning Isabel made a couple of phone calls and secured an agreement on the funding she was hoping for. She walked to an ATM to be able to leave some money with Daniela from her own account. Meanwhile, Daniela agreed with an artistic neighbour friend of hers, that she would add some illustrations to their leaflet and she saw a young woman who would do the typing of the leaflet and get it photocopied in one of the shops near the University. "They always have the keenest prices. There are so many photocopying shops near the Uni, all in competition with each other," Daniela told Isabel. The leaflet would be black and white but quite eye-catching, she promised.

After lunch, which they prepared together, the woman who was to see Isabel arrived. They went to the couple's bedroom to be alone, each with a cup of tea.

"I will have to know at which Army barracks you are stationed and where the paper from the old file was found." The document certainly looked authentic. It was just an invoice from a supplier but specified the goods clearly and was dated. They agreed on the false name for her of Sofia, which would be synonymous in both languages and would be a familiar name to the English ear, for any international recognition.

"Of course, I promise absolute discretion and anonymity for you but I have to know your real full name and ID number."

"Oh no, please, isn't this enough? I can't risk being found out. My whole world would fall apart and my family would be at risk. I can't let that happen."

"Look I have to have that because you are the only proof this is a genuine document. I promise I will keep it on paper in a hidden place and separate from your document. No one will be able to contact you without my writing to you that you must ring me. I would never put your details on an electronic document, but I do have to show that this is authentic to the authorities looking into the truth." Finally, Sofía agreed and Isabel took a few photos of the document with her 35 mm camera, which would be hand developed by a trustworthy contact of Isabel's.

"I will take them myself and might be able to develop them by myself but in any case, I will never be parted from them and I can remain in the developing room. The man at the photoshop is a good friend now and lets me help in the developing."

Sofía nodded. "We now have to decide to whom the photos should go."

"I feel it is too dangerous for you to retain the original."

"Yes, yes. I agree you should keep it so that you can produce it when necessary."

They agreed that initially photos only should be sent to the Spanish judge and also to the organisation of the Families of the Detained Disappeared and the original to the Catholic Church's human rights organisation - the *Vicaría de la Solidaridad*. Sofía knew nothing of this organisation but Isabel explained,

"They were the only human rights organisation working in Chile from the beginning of the military regime and they have supported families of the persecuted. Their collected evidence of human rights violations is now maintained by the Archive Foundation of the Vicariate, the original Vicariate having closed," said Isabel, "but I'm sure that still there are persons working for the Foundation who are familiar with the processes of their legal department. They defended people and denounced atrocities and they will know the way forward with your document. Their files are being used to attempt to prosecute cases and the Foundation has an international reputation for the quality of its organised recording of cases and evidence gathering. I hope you can feel reassured, Sofía and not be too anxious if I go to them with your paper."

When Isabel climbed aboard the overnight bus that evening she felt as though others were looking at her, as if she had a guilty secret, even though of course she was trying not to behave any differently from normal and no one was likely to be interested enough to take any notice of her. Poor Sofía, she felt, having to return to her family, feeling far more emotional and anxious than Isabel was experiencing and likely to be much more under scrutiny from persons who knew her well, who would sense if there was the slightest agitation. Isabel knew it was likely to be much worse for Sofia than anything Isabel herself had to face.

On the other hand, Isabel didn't find it as easy as usual to fall asleep on the bus that night. She could not decide what she was going to say to Mateo. She suddenly realised that she didn't know him all that well. He had been very supportive of her political efforts and appeared to agree with her aims but if it came to something a little dangerous or illegal, however legitimate ethically, what would his stand be? He'd kept his head down throughout the military regime. His middle-class life had gone on smoothly as if nothing terrible was happening in the country. Then she remembered he had said that he had lost an uncle in the dictatorship years. He had, however, been able to study just what he wanted to study - the biological sciences. The regime hadn't felt threatened by the university science departments and they had been left to carry on as before, unlike the social sciences. Mateo had never talked of being in any sort of trouble nor participating in any activity as a student. Why would he be committed now to action, she wondered? Was he very close with his uncle? Isabel had not given any thought to a long-term future with Mateo, she'd just been enjoying his company and his support after a long time of feeling very alone. Things had seemed smoother somehow, than with Julian and she had to recognise she had just gone along with the opportunity of a relationship with an attractive man. Did it have the same intensity of emotional involvement? That might explain why it seemed an easier ride or perhaps it was that the cultural differences were not tripping them up and the unconscious assumptions weren't leading to misunderstandings in the same way as they had with Julian. Or maybe it was just early days yet.

Isabel brought herself back to the more immediate issue of how she was going to explain her trip. She could just say very little though she could see that the lack of trust wouldn't be much appreciated and could be damaging if there was to be a longer term. She was sure though that she didn't want to talk of all that had happened that weekend until she had put the original document from Sophia in a safe place. This paper, she had decided, was to be in a hidden place in her old room in her mother's house. She had planned to go to see her mother at Christmas and she hoped that she could go to the Vicariate in Santiago on the same trip. She would ask Mateo to be patient, that she couldn't explain any more for the present but she would promise to tell him as soon as she could. He knew the matter wasn't something that could openly be spoken of. He would have to accept that.

Isabel received a warm welcome on arrival at the bus station. She looked tired and that gave her an excuse to be rather quiet. Mateo had the table laid for breakfast when they arrived at his flat and he was soon serving up scrambled egg with onion and smoked salmon. When she had finished the meal and he had served a second coffee, he said one word whilst spreading out his arms. "Well?"

"I can't tell you much. I've promised absolute secrecy," and as Mateo shook his head, she fumbled. "I'm sorry, I can't say much until I have done something that will put the matter in someone else's hands."

"So you don't trust me."

"Oh, come on, don't be unfair. I have to think of other people in danger. And it's safer for you not to know anything."

"Are you in danger then?" came the quick response from Mateo. He really did sound concerned.

"Not like others but I must protect them. Please accept that I will tell you as soon as I can. Something is going to happen that will take it all away from me."

"You hope! And is that putting another person at risk? Should you do that?"

"An organisation with protection, status…it's different. Look, I wanted to talk to you about Christmas. I feel I ought to go to see my mother and my brother's family. That is if you have family you can go to. Do you? In Santiago, I can deal with this matter and then I can talk more. Please give me the time I need. Now tell me about your family. Do you normally go to them for Christmas?" Mateo seemed willing to leave it at that but she found it difficult to know what he was really thinking. She hadn't had that kind of experience with him before. It was as if he determined to meet her silence with his own silence. But his was a sulky, resentful silence. She recalled what Pablo Neruda had said about the Chileans' capacity for an emotive silence. It was highly charged and uncomfortable and she had never felt that from Mateo before. She knew she had done it on occasions to Julian herself. Mateo cleared the table, forbade her to go to help in the kitchen and he stayed there to do all the clearing up. The only sound was clattering pots. He didn't even put on music as he usually would.

-oOo-

Within a few days, Isabel was on her way to spend Christmas with her family. She felt it would be good to see her mother again and Carlos. He was coming for lunch, as usual, she was told as soon as she arrived home from the overnight bus. The first priority for Isabel was to hide the coffins invoice in a little box of some childhood papers that included her swimming certificates, junior school certificates and a few childish artworks of hers. She thought the precious document could best be hidden with other papers and hopefully would be missed amongst the unimportant if anyone ever cared to look. She could not of course inform her mother of what she had hidden there and she hoped it would only be for days. She replaced the box in the bottom of her wardrobe and then she noticed a small pile of unopened letters on her dressing table. She knew the writing immediately and looked at the postmarks to check if the bottom one was the first to have arrived. She was desperate for a shower after the journey and to unpack but she couldn't resist opening the first of the letters. It moved her to see it was written in Spanish. There were several pages and she flipped to the last page where declarations of love and concern for her were poured out, bringing tears to her eyes. She turned to the beginning and began to read of Julian's visit to the children's home and the highly emotional condemnation that it elicited from him. She noted the plea that they could do something together to give publicity to this to encourage urgent change to come about. *"¡Dios mio!"* thought Isabel. There are so many things that need our action. And what am I going to do about Julian? I promised to ring when I was more free to do so and I haven't yet. What do I say? What do I want? I have a commitment now to go to the north this summer with Mateo but Julian is here in my country and why I am I not with him? What a mess I have made. What am I going to do?

After showering and dressing, Isabel wanted to look at another of the letters and she tore open the envelope of the next in date order. She was moved by the description of the concert in Santiago and wished she had been there. She cried at the professions of love and noted that Julian was hoping to move to Valparaíso in the new year and wanted desperately to see her there or Santiago or La Serena or any other city she named. Isabel's mother was shouting to her that she had been a long time and what was she doing. Isabel thought she must find time that day or Christmas Eve to ring the church

205

office at Quillota. After lunch with Carlos and all the talk of Christmas celebrations planned, she thought she had better ring Julian without delay or the church office might not be open for the holidays, but first, she wanted to read all his letters. It seemed only right to give them the attention they deserved.

The next letter described the concert at the Quinta Vergara and how costly and difficult it was going to be for Ana's parents to pay for her to go to the Catholic University of Valparaíso. Julian spelt out the cost of £600 a month for the fees and that she would have to do two hours travelling each day because there was no question of paying for residential accommodation for her. Julian stressed how bright Ana was and how hard she'd worked to get a place and how wrong it would be if she could not take advantage of the place. *There are thousands like her,* thought Isabel. *He writes as if I don't know it but Julian's feelings about it all are affecting me, I have to confess. We could be a good team,* she thought. *He really is finding out about my country. But which reality do I want, Chile or England? It is so hard.* Isabel wiped the tears from her eyes after reading the further professions of affection and opened another letter.

The next letter talked of the attempted demonstration on Pinochet's birthday and how the students were locked in to prevent them from attending. *Yet another proof that there is no democracy, as he says.* Julian listed what he was going to do at the University next term. *He is very lucky to have that experience,* thought Isabel. *There's many a Chilean who is denied that. He's right in his summary of the election. It was a farce and totally uninspiring. This man has insight and cares about my country. What can I say to him on the telephone? I'm committed to a trip to the north with Mateo.* There were, in the letter, all the usual professions of love.

Tearfully, Isabel opened the last of the letters awaiting her. This time Julian talked of his proposed move to Valparaíso after New Year. He said he had passed a day house hunting and exploring Valparaíso but he couldn't stand to be in a property with a view dominated by rusted corrugated iron on the walls or rooves and there seemed to be so much of it around Valparaíso. It was for him so ugly and a symbol of poverty but he didn't want anything too pretentious either and he was certain he didn't want a modern flat in affluent Viña del Mar. Valparaíso had an authenticity about it and he felt he should be

206

able to find a modest but respectable place within his means. *There's much more zinc in Valparaíso than Viña, what he calls corrugated iron,* thought Isabel. *It's an essential protection from the winter rains.*

*I'm glad Constanza, my Mamadre, could help him with some contacts and her friend Elisa took him out,* she thought. Julian talked in the letter about the huge contrast between the wealthy, luxury apartments he had seen along the coast to the north of Viña del Mar and the modest homes he had been inside, in Quillota where the winter rains had left their marks and the people used hardboard to line their walls. Julian then recalled the picturesque European places with traditional housing, that they had visited together, like Saint-Jean-de-Luz, in France, Llafranc in Cataluña and villages in Andalucía. Isabel had said they reminded her of Chile, with their little single-storey houses with orange tiled roofs. Chile was now developing and changing so fast and the inequality was growing even faster, Julian commented. The modern developments were very different from those picturesque places of the past in Chile. Memories of the holidays in Europe came flooding back to her. She loved those places and had enjoyed that time with Julian so much. Then she recalled when she had stubbornly refused to speak when they were in Greece. She could not remember now why. *On a ferry boat under a deep blue Aegean sky, we sat on different sides of the vessel, tortured with pain. I felt his eyes keep looking at me and I adamantly would not return his gaze nor respond to his repeated efforts to approach me to heal our differences. Why did he never realise I needed more time, I was aching and I just wanted to be left alone? Did I not have that right? I can see now I wanted more time than was fair, especially when a holiday is such a limited, fleeting break from real life and I was wasting it. Why have I been so stubborn and difficult at times? I could never admit that I was these things. They did seem the only option I had at the time.*

*Julian was right I was stubborn and uncompromising but I had said I wasn't easy to live with before we embarked on living together. Not that I ever explained what I meant by that. I tried to be honest but I guess he had a shock. My anger burned inside of me so often, Julian said I was like a saucepan about to boil and throw off its lid. It was better I said nothing than to say what I would regret. So I simmered with the lid on tight and I wasn't going to lift it, despite having no release for the steam. I remember that we went to visit a Chilean*

Margaret H. Townley

contact in Coventry once and she was a poet. She said I wore my pain on my sleeve. I didn't realise anyone could see it like that, but the poet saw it within a few hours. I rarely did explode but I have to recognise I was constantly simmering just below boiling point and that made life uncomfortable and unpredictable for Julian. Julian also was no angel. He tried to look reasonable but became as angry as me and he did the exploding. I couldn't stand the shouting but worse was the continual "rational" analysing, begging me to talk when I didn't feel like it and when I knew it wouldn't be constructive. All those sickening efforts to "understand" had an air of patronising superiority about them. All his long written letters of what he called "analysis" of what was happening between us. They were rationalisations and I couldn't bear to read them and I soon gave up, though his efforts kept coming.

What am I going to do? Can I risk going back to that? It wasn't like that in our last year together, after my first visit to Chile. Perhaps that visit was the release I needed. The year was mostly a very lovely interweaving of our lives, now I come to think about it. We had some good times together, like at the beginning and he is so delicious in bed. Why did I feel it was so essential to return to Chile, again on my own? Alone was the only way I could do a lengthy stay here and I remember feeling I needed that so much again. I also felt it was the only way to get on with the political commitment that I must have with my country. I can't do anything for Chile thousands of miles away in England. I had to come and try to achieve something. Does that mean I should stay here and not return to England? Surely things have got to change here soon. I can't spend my whole life being away from the person I want to be with. What if he was willing to come here long-term? That's a lot to ask and wouldn't be easy financially. Apart from that, I can't ask a foreigner to come and live in this non-democracy while I go on risking arrest and getting treated badly. An arrested person isn't even allowed a lawyer for a week here. There are so many things wrong... but I feel at home. I love the atmosphere of being here. I love my homeland. What am I going to do?

Perhaps this summer holiday with Mateo will help me make a firm decision. It will decide things one way or the other. I know they should be separate decisions but I don't seem to be able to separate them. I know I should decide now and tell each of them clearly my decision, but I can't decide. On the other hand, men often seem able to have two relationships going on and regard it *almost as normal or part of them being men. It's not of course. I prefer ethical people who play fair. What else is loving? So why am I being so unfair and so unethical? But men often think they can just carry off the deception like it's macho and adds a thrill to their lives. They don't feel they have to make themselves accountable to anyone, not even to themselves. How do they think and how do they justify what they are doing? How do they live with themselves? I guess they never try to face themselves. They avoid moral self-honesty and never answer to their conscience. So why can't I do it? Why can't I be free to love two people? What is so wrong with that? Am I really trying to decide? In my case it won't be two at once, it will be one now - then make a decision - and then possibly the other. Why not? Why do I feel so absolutely guilty and awful even thinking like this? Why cannot Julian just be a good close friend who I telephone from time to time and then we'll see where we are?* Isabel's mother was calling her again. She wanted help decorating the Christmas tree. *I'll have to appear downstairs again and then try and ring Julian around onces time. He should be at the church house then.*

There were butterflies in Isabel's stomach when she heard Julian's voice on the telephone. She began apologising that she really couldn't ring earlier, she had been so busy with her travels in the north and then the news of the dictator entering the Senate, which made them try to do a quick change of approach for the election material, then the election itself and then an emergency which took her back to Antofagasta, which she couldn't tell him over the phone but she would tell him about when she could.

"Look, stop, just tell me you are ok and that this emergency isn't anything to do with you, your health or your being in trouble. That's all I want to know. And where are you?"

"Julian, I'm fine. I'm ok. The emergency isn't about me but I've got to do something time-consuming to ensure someone else is safe and that the truth gets out. I'm saying no more now."

"So you mean you are as busy as ever, with no time to spare at present. It's Christmas, aren't you going to stop for a couple of days?"

"Yes, yes, I'm at my mother's but I'll have to attend to this other matter immediately after Christmas Day - the next day, the day you call Boxing Day."

"Will that take you away from Santiago?"

209

"No, it's here in Santiago but it may take me two or three days. But tell me about you. Have you got everything arranged for your move to Valparaíso?"

"You read my letters then?"

"Yes, I have. Thank you very much for all of them. Your written Spanish is getting good. I was very moved by so many things you said. We have to talk about a lot of things."

"When can we do that? Can I come to Santiago when you've done your special work? Does it involve any more video, by the way?"

"No, it doesn't. And I have to go back as soon as I've sorted out this issue. I've promised friends I'll go with them to the north because I need to go but it will be a bit of a holiday too. It will be great not to have to rush around but to be able to visit some of the historic places I've never had a chance to see before."

"I'd love to see those places in the north. I've missed the flowering desert this year. I felt I had too many commitments here to just go away."

"It was wonderful but don't worry, there'll be another opportunity. In the New Year you have to arrange your move and you'll busy with your new voluntary work, won't you? Have you got a place yet?"

"Yes, I have thanks to Ximena and her friend of a friend. You know how it works. The flat is modern but in a very small block and it's in Cerro Barón."

"Oh, that's where my Dad used to be when he was at university."

"You will come to see me there, won't you?"

"I will and we can be in touch again when I'm back from the north."

"When is that then?" said Julian, not expecting a date because that wouldn't be true to form.

"Mid to end of February. Do you have the address of your new flat?" Julian was able to give her that.

"I had better warn you now the living room is painted pink, which is awful but apart from that, the flat is ideal. It sounds like a long time till I'll be able to see you. I want to be with you, you know. Isn't there a chance before you go away?"

"Not really, I'm sorry. I can't see how and you will have a lot to do to get settled in at Cerro Barón. I must go. I will see you soon."

*"Te amo,"*

*"Gracias. Feliz Navidad."*

*"Feliz Navidad. Chao."*

# Chapter 12

On the day following the Christmas celebrations, Isabel thought the studio with the photo-developing darkroom would be open and went to see. She had managed to complete the roll of film and another one, taking shots of the family over Christmas time. She had developed quite a friendship with the owner of the photoshop in recent times and believed him sympathetic to what she had tried to do in the past. She had assisted him in developing her film with him before, so she hoped she'd be able to casually offer to do these rolls for herself. She arrived in the area called Santa Lucía and the shop was open but the developing room was occupied. She agreed with the assistant that she should return in the afternoon if she really wanted to do the pictures herself. She was of course invited to leave the rolls, but she declined, sounding enthusiastic to do it herself or at least to help again, if possible.

Isabel thought it couldn't be much more than half an hour's walk to the Santiago house of Pablo Neruda, *La Chascona.* She decided to visit and took a *colectivo* most of the way. She learned from the visitors' information that *Chascona* was a Quechua word meaning dishevelled and Neruda had given the house that name in reference to the wild red hair of Matilda Urrutia, his lover when he bought the house. He bought it as a love nest for them and Matilda lived there for two years before Neruda left his wife and joined her. He later married Matilda. The military destroyed much of the interior and flooded it soon after the coup d'état but when the banned public funeral of Neruda took place and those hundreds of thousands marched through the streets with his casket in defiance of the regime, Matilda had held the funeral reception at the damaged house. She wanted the world to see what the soldiers had done. Matilda restored the house eventually and restored the theme of the sea that Neruda so fondly had created. She also managed to restore his library with its impressive range of books in several European languages, all of which he had spoken. Isabel wondered how many of those books had been just thrown to the ground by the ignorant soldiers and maybe many of the original ones had not survived the flooding. *What a heartbreak the damaging and flooding of your home must be, but to go through that on top of your husband having just died and a military coup, must have been soul-destroying.* Isabel knew there was even a suspicion that Neruda might have been poisoned as the regime would certainly have seen him as a threat, a figure that an opposition might gather around.

A little sad, but very glad she had visited *La Chascona,* Isabel waved to a *colectivo* to take her back to Santa Lucía. She just had time for an *empanada de pino* in the artisan fair at Santa Lucía. Though she preferred pasties of seafood, she did find the minced beef, hard-boiled eggs and olives pastie very good. Then it was time to return to the photoshop. Her friend welcomed her and was happy to leave things to her in the developing room when he'd just reminded her of the process and prepared the right mixture of developing fluid and fixer. She was excited to see her brother's family gradually appearing on the wet, glossy paper. She was happy too that the invoice document photos had come out well and clear. How impatient she was for them to dry but then at last she was set. She showed a few pictures of her niece and nephew to her friend and tried to sound quite relaxed and jolly in thanking him. She paid for the photo development and made her way to the Archive Foundation of the Vicariate in the La Reina district of Santiago. She should have guessed. It was only open in the mornings from 9.00 am to 2.00 pm. She had wondered if she should go there earlier, but without the photos, she thought she would not be taken seriously, with nothing to show. As the San Miguel station drew close she began to ready herself to sound lively and cheerful without a care in the world on arrival at her mother's. She needed to sound delighted with her visit to the poet's house and had some great photos to show her mother and Matilda. Matilda was very fond of Carlos, whom she had largely brought up like Isabel and she thought she would give Matilda a few photos of her brother and family and one of her with her brother.

The next morning, with the photos of the document in her rucksack,

Isabel returned to the centre of Santiago. By Metro, the journey meant two changes but she thought that was the safest way to get to the Foundation, rather than walking part of the way in the streets with her precious cargo. She asked to speak to the Director and when asked what it was about, she said she had some important written information to give him. It seemed enough to get her request accepted and a few minutes later she was introducing herself to the Director. Isabel explained what she had brought and how she had obtained the document, photographed and developed it herself and gave him a copy.

"I know that you are not making investigations of cases nowadays nor acting to assist victims but I think this document is important evidence and I beg you to get the photo to someone who would know how to use it effectively in the current investigation of the coffins discovered in the old nitrate cemetery. Any action taken will have to be, for certain, without the police or the courts being able to block its revelation." The elderly and kindly-looking Director seemed deep in thought and it was a long time before he began to speak.

"You will have to leave it with me and I will make a few phone calls. The Foundation's current role is to respond to lawyers, historians or other professionals engaged in establishing the truth about abuses that occurred during the years of the military regime."

"I felt I didn't have anywhere else to take this matter and I know I can trust you and the Foundation but of course, I am concerned that the document helps to establish the truth and avoids the whistleblower being revealed."

"I will not describe what the document contains over the phone but try to find the right hands to place it in."

"Thank you. May I return at the same time tomorrow? I would prefer that, to leaving my mother's phone number. May I also bring the original invoice to the Archive for safekeeping tomorrow, because obviously, it poses a threat for an ordinary person to be holding it, particularly the original person who came upon the invoice? That is why I was willing to take it from her."

"Yes, of course, it can be safely placed in our charge. You can come tomorrow, a little later to give me time, if I don't reach the right person today."

"What proactive measures can be taken to get to the truth about these coffins, do you think?"

"I can promise nothing at the moment. It depends on the advice of the person in whose hands I finally deliver this document."

Isabel thanked him for seeing her and left. A little disappointed with not knowing what might happen, she returned home on the Metro but walked the short walk between Line 3 and Line 2, instead of using Line 1 as she had done earlier. This walk took her past some of the University of Chile buildings (she thought about Ana Cortéz, the painter) and past the Palace of *La Moneda*. This would give her a bit to talk about, like *La Chascona* had given her the previous day, to explain where she had been when she got home.

The next morning Isabel set off again and took the Metro all the way to the Vicariate, feeling more vulnerable than even the day before, if she should walk the streets. She had the original document safely in an envelope tucked amongst papers and two books in her Bolivian woven rucksack. At the Vicariate she had to wait a while on this occasion and a man, who arrived after her was shown in before her. When she was called into the Director's office, she was introduced to the man that had gone in ahead. He was a famous human rights lawyer and he explained how he had journalistic contacts who would leave their sources anonymous. She was also told that this lawyer had worked with the active Vicariate over many years and was now working through two organisations continuing their work with detained persons and relatives of the executed or disappeared.

"My friend here," said the Director, patting the lawyer on the shoulder, "has also been working much of this year with the Rettig Report - the official enquiry into the abuses of the military regime, the National Commission of Reparation and Reconciliation."

Isabel recognised the lawyer's name from the newspapers and felt most fortunate to have met him. "I am sure you will be able to advance whatever can be achieved with the document I have presented," said Isabel as she gave him the original document and the paper, handwritten by the woman in Antofagasta with her name and details. "I read about your recent interpretation of a Supreme Court ruling that the Amnesty Law could not be applied to 200 cases of disappeared persons," Isabel continued. "The Defence Ministry tried to apply the Amnesty Law and they are still trying to maintain another interpretation of the ruling is possible, aren't they?" The lawyer smiled and raised his eyebrows.

214

"The claimants and the representatives of the military world all want an interpretation favourable to their own interests but we are winning gradually. There will be prosecutions eventually. We will use the evidence you have brought to good effect as well, don't worry."

"Can I mention my father's case whilst I am here in front of you? He is one of the disappeared." Isabel then went on to give all the details she could. The lawyer said one of his team dealing with the Valparaíso region would be asked to get all the information he can.

Isabel's head reeled as she came away, satisfied that this was even better than she had expected. To meet this famous lawyer was quite a privilege. Isabel was desperate to tell someone but felt she couldn't just pour that out when she got to her mother's house. She decided to ring her brother who would know the name of the person she had just met. Of course, she couldn't say what was the reason the meeting had come about. Carlos was suitably impressed and insisted when they next met she would tell him all. She hoped by then it would all be out in the news and she told him that she had mentioned their father's case.

"If we can find out more that would be good but it is prosecutions that we need and none have happened yet, but I'm glad to know he confirms they will come eventually." The usual bantering and jokes between them then followed and Isabel found it hard to say goodbye, as she was leaving for La Serena the next day. After a big sigh and wishing that she had not had to be away from Carlos so much of their lives, she then had to find something else quickly to fill her head with and to talk about upon arriving at her mother's house.

She decided to go to the new Pre-Colombian Art Museum, which she had not seen before but which had been opened near the National Fine Arts Museum which she knew very well from her old days in Chile. Isabel didn't find it easy to get her head around the mythology and religious ideas of ancient civilisations with her head full of other things but she did her best. She especially liked the god of agriculture and vegetation - the life-death-rebirth Aztec god Xipe Totec. Most of all she loved the woven materials of the Tiwanaku peoples with their repeated geometric patterns of many bright colours and especially in their later period, 800 - 1000 AD, their four-cornered hats. She saw that the geometric patterns had been clearly passed on to the Chimu peoples of the Andean coast, who added complex tapestry art

215

to the patterns. They created ceremonial tunics, loincloths and turbans and Isabel smiled at their three-dimensional tapestries representing vegetables and human figures. Their ceremonies primarily concerned agricultural fertility, which isn't surprising, thought Isabel, in an arid desert but she was particularly interested to see the tapestries also showed the worship of the mummies of their ancestors. She knew that she and Mateo were planning to see soon the Chinchorro mummies in the north. The museum information here assumed that the worship of the Chimu was performed by a social elite or class of priests. *How sad* Isabel thought, *that a tiered society had replaced the single strata societies of the Chinchorros who had begun mummification, but that was thousands of years before.*

-oOo-

In order to celebrate New Year with Mateo, Isabel went back to La Serena and a couple of weeks later they flew to the most northerly city in Chile, Arica. During these two weeks, they were both busy with finishing off work from the previous term, marking and beginning preparations for the next term. Isabel had said little of her trip to Santiago and he had not pressed her, but as soon as there was time to relax and talk again, he was clearly waiting for a full account. On their first day in Arica, they went to relax on the beach known as the Chinchorro Beach, named after the ancient peoples whose mummies had been found nearby. The beach was largely deserted, perhaps because it was subject to a lot of wind and no facilities had been developed along its long sandy stretch. Well away from the possibility of being overheard, Mateo wanted to hear her news in full. Isabel told him all that had happened concerning the coffins' invoices, the Vicariate and he said nothing until she was fully done.

"I still think you should have trusted me and told me what was happening because it is horrible to be on the outside."

"I know, perhaps you are right but I was very anxious with that document in my possession and I didn't want to put you at risk."

"If I am associated with you and you are questioned about anything, I will be at risk too. You should have trusted me."

"But what you didn't know, you couldn't tell."

"That would not help if I was questioned because they wouldn't believe that I wouldn't know. What hurts is that you thought I would tell and couldn't hold a secret for you."

"Do any of us know what might happen under such severe pressure? Of course, we are very determined we won't speak to incriminate someone else, but who knows...?"

"You think I might hurt you like that?"

"No, of course not, not deliberately, I know you wouldn't. But someone else you've never met? I couldn't just say look here's her name and ID number and I'm going to hide it in a place you would be fully aware of. How could I?" Isabel lay down to try to take the sun. A silence ensued. After a while, she added, "You might even have tried to save me by revealing where that paper was because you were put in the awful position of choosing between an unknown woman or me. Well, it could happen and I couldn't risk the poor woman."

"You talk as if we are still in a military dictatorship," responded Mateo.

"Well, we are if it comes to the police or the military needing some information or their reputation is being threatened or to prevent their lies being revealed. They knock you about if they get to arrest you, they interrogate for information very heavy-handedly, they shoot with rubber bullets and they hurt people, even taking eyes out, they shoot water canons and tear gas and people get injured. They may not go as far as they did under the dictatorship, but it's bad enough."

Silence fell between them again. Isabel went for a swim and when she returned Mateo held a towel to put on her shoulders and hugged her tightly as he wrapped it around her.

"Let's go and have some lunch and go in search of the Chinchorro mummies this afternoon," he said.

A *colectivo* took them a little way along the Azapa Valley to the Archaeological Museum 'San Miguel de Azapa,' part of the University of Tarapacá, where Chinchorro mummies were to be seen in glass cases. They learned that there were many more mummies in store that the museum had not yet had the money to display, because of the special conditions that they need to prevent their deterioration. In the storeroom, they were kept in the dark and their ventilation was strictly controlled. Mateo and Isabel also learned that the earliest dated artificial, that is, humanly modified mummy found so far, was dated 5050 BC and it was a child.

"I've read a paper by Dr Bernardo Arriaza, an anthropologist involved in the investigation and preservation of the mummies here," said Isabel. "He has posed that the loss of a child is so grievous for a parent, that attempts to preserve that child in some form, was a strong motivation for the beginning of the practice of mummification. As many child mummies as adult mummies have been found and even mummified foetuses. Also, it is likely that the infant death rate was quite high due to the high levels of naturally occurring arsenic in the water of this region and arsenic causes frequent death in childhood and miscarriages."

"Yes, you can imagine that tragic human loss is a motivator for mummification," said Mateo shaking his head sadly. I've just read over there that even older, naturally mummified bodies have been found in the exceptionally dry desert, which has a high concentration of nitrates and these prevent the bacterial deterioration of the body. The desert dryness evaporates the body fluids. The Chinchorros would have discovered this natural conservation of bodies and it could have led them to have ideas of improving on the preservation or better sending a body to an afterlife. They did major modifications to the bodies."

"What I like is that all the mummies found were not of an elite but the process was carried out widely across the non-hierarchical, hunter-gatherer society. Nor did the mummification favour one gender above the other. Look at these tools buried with the mummies showing the work or the role of the person. Clearly, the men hunted and dived for seafood with harpoons and the women worked with sharp-edged stones to cut, filet and cook the fish. They thus had the skills to take out the organs of the body in mummification."

"These people began experimenting with artificial or human mummification 2500 years before the Egyptians began," said Mateo. "Most of the mummies date from 5000 BC to 2000 BC. It had all finished by 1800 BC."

"Look it says here, 'It is known that the Chinchorros maintained their mummies for several months or even a few years before actually burying them. They might have kept them for ceremonial worship or perhaps parents kept their mummified children in their homes with them. A stick to support the body enabled it to be displayed sitting up, and when the organs were removed, the body was stuffed with reeds of the kind growing in the Azapa Valley by the river, and then the skin was replaced.' "

"In later periods they were bound in bandages or covered with mud or a layer of white ash. And later they even removed the brain and fixed the skull back onto the body."

"Here it says a mask was added with features that resembled the original person," said Isabel. "They've done bone surveys that suggest the facial shapes and the masks match. That's amazing. That is artwork."

"Yes, and they were very sophisticated creations. Look at these with wigs of natural hair."

Mateo and Isabel came away utterly fascinated and glad to know that further displays of more mummies were planned for the area as well as at the museum.

Whilst looking around the city for a restaurant that evening, they discovered an artist and her workshop, where she was selling paintings and hand-printed materials with Chinchorro mummy masks and patterns of the Tiwanaku geometric traditions. They stopped to talk with her. Isabel was pleased to find a book illustrating this artist's work that she could use with her school classes.

"To give the children more pride in their culture, its traditions and achievements, is always good and especially an example of a woman artist. Perfect," she said.

"Thanks."

The next day Isabel had made appointments to meet up with some of her activist contacts in the afternoon and the couple spent the morning looking around Arica market which was very large and seemed to contain absolutely everything. Isabel liked the woven artisan cloths and rugs and the knitted alpaca wool ponchos. In the food area, they found fresh llama meat and Isabel suggested Mateo should try it when they ate that day, as he had never tasted it. She herself was more inclined to have fish, preferably shellfish and the market restaurants were offering both fish and alpaca dishes for *almuerzo*. Well satisfied, they took a walk afterwards along the coastal path around the Morro - the very high projection of rock and compressed sand like a barren desert hill that overhangs and dominates the port of Arica and reaches to the edge of the sea. Isabel loved to watch the sea lashing against the rocks as they walked around the narrow coastal path, in part through caves like porticos and then to see the sea rolling in on the little beach they came to beyond the Morro.

Isabel seemed to Mateo particularly quiet and thoughtful that afternoon. She was thinking about what she was going to do about Julian and the lie she had made to him. She wondered why had she done that. What, or rather who did she really want? She hadn't even told Mateo yet that her real name was not Helena García. That lie had become even more difficult to explain since the big fuss that was made of her keeping the secret of the coffin invoice from him. What had happened to her? How could she be weaving this web of lies about herself? She had a right, she had said, to justify herself, to handle whatever she needs to handle in her way, a right to be trusted and not be pushed for information she didn't choose to give, a right to live her life without the emotional pressure of silent sulking. When Mateo interrupted her thoughts, she said she'd been thinking about a Chilean exile she had met in London who had been the youngest mayor in the country when he was voted mayor of Arica in Allende's time.

"He and his party supporting *Unidad Popular* did a great deal to bring employment and economic development to the city. They even had a fledgling car manufacturing plant under licence, which they felt had a serious economic future. Chile had until then had to import all its vehicles from outside. The development was swept away of course by the military. The mayor and his colleagues spent several years in prison under the regime."

"We just have time to climb up the Morro before your meetings. The view they say is great. There is a military museum at the top but I'm not bothered about seeing that unless you want to."

"No thank you very much," replied Isabel emphatically. I don't want to be reminded of Chile taking Arica and the nitrate industry from Bolivia, leaving Bolivia landlocked, without its seaport. And Chile took the guano fertiliser from Peru."

"They were provoked by Bolivia imposing an export tax on the nitrate firms."

"But that wasn't a reason to eliminate the whole of the Bolivian army and take their coastal town. All three countries were as bad as each other. The oligarchies that ruled these countries didn't want to pay taxes. I think it's one of the more shameful aspects of Chilean history but typical of what elites do."

"So you would rather that the town we are in now was not Chilean?" demanded Mateo.

"Yes, we could still visit if we wanted and Bolivia would have its necessary port."

"Actually Arica is a free port for Bolivia now." The couple left the matter at that and were silent as they climbed the hill to the top of the Morro.

The meeting with Isabel's friends and contacts went well though Isabel would have liked to have arranged an earlier rally against Pinochet entering the Senate, before the day he was actually due to enter. Others argued that it was the holiday season and it wasn't worth risking further clampdowns and possible arrests before the big day. They assured Isabel they would definitely be demonstrating and they were anticipating many others would be out with them too. They had that day well planned, as Isabel went through all the considerations with them. What she did manage to get them to accept, was a leafletting scheme before the day, which might encourage more people to come out and it was a chance to mention "free quality education, decent pensions, free health care and constitutional change." A couple of enthusiasts started immediately on the leaflet design when the meeting broke up for tea. Isabel quietly left some money with the leaflet designers to get them printed.

"The bus is at 9.00 am tomorrow to Iquique," said Mateo on the journey back to their hotel.

"I'd like to stop at Pisagua on the way," Isabel said.

"Oh no, it's remote and there's not much there and there won't be many buses that will stop there. In fact, you have to go off the main road and wind down quite a long way to the port. There's only one way in and out."

"I know but I really want to visit there. It's one of the few concentration camps now open to the public. I need to see it. Perhaps the bus will let us off on the main road and we can get a taxi to the town. Surely taxis will meet the buses when they are due."

"Do you want to go to the bus station now and find out?" said Mateo with sarcasm and an expectation the answer would be 'no'.

"No, there won't be much information available at this time. The offices will be closed. Let's hope we can arrange something in the morning."

The next day there was a bus to Pisagua at 12.00 noon and that seemed a safer option than begging the bus driver to let them off, which he might not have been prepared to do as it would be against the rules. No one had a Pisagua taxi number in Arica. Mateo was none too pleased with the change of plan, expressed by a cold silence rather than an open expression of an opinion.

"That gives us time to go along the coast to the Cuevas de Anzota," declared Isabel. "If you want to?" Somewhat moodily Mateo put their luggage in a left luggage deposit and they took a taxi. There were no buses or *colectivos* and the taxis had a monopoly but as promised, it was worth the trip. The sea birds and the wild, strong ocean waves crashing on the black rocks were worth seeing and one of the caves had a pre-historic drawing of an alpaca. Alpaca skins were traded from the port in ancient times and even earlier than that, these caves must have been explored by the Chinchorros. That was thrilling to Isabel to imagine and it moved her more than the Chinchorro connection with the Morro, in the foothills of which many mummies were first found.

Mateo was hungry when they arrived at Pisagua and he wanted to go to a restaurant before anything else as it was gone 2.00 pm. He worried they wouldn't be open much longer and there were only a couple to chose from in this little town centre. Isabel agreed it was a good idea to eat first but didn't like the rather gruff way Mateo had insisted. She thought she might get too upset to want to eat if they went to the concentration camp first, but she was concerned about when and if the camp might open in the afternoon. She learned it would be open from 4.00 pm to 6.00 pm and she contentedly rejoined Mateo for lunch. Mateo did not want to go with her on her visit to the concentration camp and she was glad to be alone to concentrate on picturing her father's suffering in such a place. The buildings were those of the old nitrate port, grim and untouched from the time of the dictatorship. Almost certainly they were untouched from the days of the nitrate exports, she thought. No one would have cleaned and painted the place for it to be a concentration camp. Just the dirt and the risk that creates, causing infections to injuries, was bad enough to think about, let alone the waterboarding, electric shock treatments and beatings. Isabel had tried to think of what her father went through many times but she felt very close to him as she went through this building, imagining his suffering all over again in that reality. She somehow needed to be just quiet and sad again, as if it was the least she owed him.

"Why did you not want to go to the camp?" she asked Mateo eventually, after sitting quietly at the table when she came out.

"Do you want me to really say what I think?"

"Yes, of course."

"Well, I think it's a bit self-indulgent. You can't keep going over it again and again. Defence mechanisms will water it down and eventually, it will become a self-pity exercise." Isabel was quite shocked and had never thought of her memories of her father and of her grieving like that.

"Oh, you're quite the psychologist! It might be more healthy than repressing it and pushing it away so that you never really face the pain and the grief and yet those things are there inside you and they can burst out in unexpected ways and destroy current good things." She was thinking of what she had learned about some of her own behaviours with Julian, her seething anger and her moods. "Were you not close to your uncle who disappeared?"

"Yes, he was my favourite uncle and a big part of my life…" the words couldn't come out further. Mateo had a tear in his eye. They sat in silence. After quite a while, Isabel squeezed his hand and went to find out when there was a bus to Iquique, to ring her friend there and to order *onces*. She reckoned if Mateo didn't want to eat now, he would be glad of something to take on the bus.

When she returned to Mateo, Isabel asked him again, "There is an element of love in recalling a lost person. It's a loving act and I want to keep that up. Tell me about your uncle. What did you use to do together?"

After a pause came the reply, "He would come most Sundays to our house. He was my mother's younger brother. The only brother that was not married. We would go out and kick a ball around together or we would go down to the sea and run along the beach with the waves just lapping at our feet or we'd go to see the penguins and sea lions at Coquimbo. He used to take me too to the botanical gardens and he gave me my love of botany. He could name all the plants and all the parts of a plant."

"He sounds a lovely uncle. When someone disappears you don't know when to start grieving for their death."

"You've already grieved and worried and hoped desperately for their return, throughout all their loss. But when do you have to actually accept they are not coming back? You've no funeral, no news, nothing to tell you now is the time to grieve properly, after keeping it on hold for so long. You are so much in the habit of trying to keep hoping they are alive and so used to pushing away thoughts of the worst, you go on hoping and you never come to terms with it. But you know all this..."

"You never will fully get over it," said Isabel. "Your mother and grandma must have been in a terrible state. Did you ever talk with them about the ongoing feelings you had of not knowing when to give up hope and grieve properly?"

Mateo just shook his head and continued looking down. They sat quietly for a while.

-oOo-

In Iquique, the couple was able to stay with one of Isabel's friends, Amalia who had insisted that she could accommodate them both and would like to. They were warmly welcomed, though their time of arrival had not been confirmed until late that afternoon. A late supper was spread before them and the plans that had been made so far with the group of activists were explained to Isabel. The activists would definitely be out in force on the day the ex-dictator entered the Senate but they doubted any demo was worthwhile before then. There had been meetings in the universities up until Christmas and last-minute planning meetings were arranged for early March as the students begin to return to college. They had distributed a lot of leaflets before Christmas and were planning street leafleting and posters to remind people just before the 11th March. They had large banners and posters from demonstrating the previous October and November and they planned to go to key high streets of the various *poblaciones* of Iquique as well as to the various university sites around the city. Isabel didn't feel there was much she could suggest but she said she'd like to see some of the supporters and her friends if she could. A meeting was to be arranged in a couple of days' time.

Free to explore the region thus the next day, Isabel and Mateo set out on a tour. The first stop was Humberstone which had been an important nitrate production town but was now a ghost town. More highly developed than most such towns, Humberstone, started by the Englishman James Thomas Humberstone in 1872 had a cinema-cum-theatre as well as a large church, a school and a library. Visitors were able to go into the English-style, little houses of the workers, into the school classrooms and climb onto the locomotive that would drag the saltpetre trucks away. The economic model of most nitrate mines collapsed in the Great Depression but a modernisation made the Humberstone works productive again in the 1940s until the late 1950s. Isabel felt for the workers who must have been laid off and lost their homes as well as their jobs in the inactive years after the Great Depression. "When are we going to have a world where people are not just cast aside but are given some compensation and opportunities to retrain or take further education?" she expressed to Mateo. She was thinking of what had happened to many coal miners in the UK too when she had first gone into exile.

"And paid fairly when they are working," Mateo responded, thinking of the massacre of the workers in Iquique. "We must go to the museum in Iquique while we are here. The Santa Maria School Massacre in 1907 was about desperately poor nitrate workers striking for better wages and conditions. I expect some of them were from here and their women and children went with them."

The tour then took them on to the extraordinary town of the Oasis of Pica whose name comes from the Aymara *picai*. It has long been inhabited despite its remoteness, far from the coastal towns and deep into the barren desert. Habitation is possible, they learned, because at Pica the natural underground rivers and volcanic thermal springs of the desert come to the surface and produce a rich oasis. Their tour guide told them that the local people grow an abundance of fruit including mangos, guavas, oranges and their own special variety of lemons which are famous for their intense flavour.

"In Pica too there are natural large pools of water called the *Termas de Pica* - hypothermal waters which reach a temperature of 33 degrees, heated by the volcanic rock and they are now popular swimming pools," said the guide. When they arrived in the main square, they found it rich with trees and vegetation. "The tour will leave you here to enjoy this town for the rest of the day and will collect you from here tomorrow morning at 11.00." Isabel liked the pre-Colombian houses that lined the streets and was delighted that their overnight accommodation was in one of them. They entered what appeared a modest single-storey house from the street, to find a large courtyard and many rooms leading from it.

They explored the town and in the evening they went to a restaurant with a large courtyard with a log fire burning in a sunken, circular, fire pit. The pit was big, so many people could sit around the fire and a guitarist played. They all joined in singing traditional Chilean songs.

The next day they visited a remote lagoon which appeared to the couple strangely unbelievable and like a mirage, in a vast open expanse before the distant mountains. Surrounded by arid desert, the large lake was amidst green fields of vegetation, where local people from the occasional, isolated cottages kept their alpacas and vicuñas. Beautiful as it all was and a place of perfect peace, Isabel wondered how people could live in such isolation but Mateo thought he would be perfectly willing to do so. He enjoyed the idea of the challenge of the hard practicality of life in such a situation and was proud that he thought he had the practical skills and the psychological strengths required. Isabel felt she would not be able to bear that isolation, as much as she might admire those who can but she felt, for those who did live here, life was full of surviving and would never give much time for creating.

Their mini-bus driver then took them to the famous village of La Tirana, which annually in July has one of the biggest pagan and Christian syncretism festivals in Chile, *La Fiesta de la Virgen del Carmen.* The guide described frightening devil headdresses he had seen which were made to represent the nitrate in all its horror, which Isabel thought sounded highly appropriate. The guide added that some of the elaborately costumed dancing groups can be seen in other northern cities throughout the year and Isabel recalled that she had seen them in the streets of Arica many years before.

After lunch in La Tirana, they were taken to see the *geoglíficos* called Cerros Pintados in the National Reserve Pampa del Tamarugal. Hundreds of large figures cover the hillside, human-like figures, animals, fish and geometric symbols, all created by scraping away the top desert surface of black stones, revealing a lighter-coloured surface below. Some were left like that, the contrast quite distinct and some figures were outlined with dark-coloured rocks. Were they for ritual or just art for its own sake, the guide posed or were they guides in the desert for the llama caravans that were known to cross the desert to the sea for hundreds of years before the

Spanish conquest? Archaeologists, can't be sure of their purpose but Isabel appreciated them as works of art.

"Imagine having this vast desert as your canvas and contemplating what image you were going to draw. Doesn't that stir you and cause you to wonder," Isabel said, slipping her hand into Mateo's but he didn't seem much perturbed.

"I love plants too much to appreciate these brown hills when they are not flowering. They are vast expanses of brown and barren rock." Isabel couldn't help thinking he'd missed something somewhere but didn't quite know what to say.

"But there is a grandeur and a drama to these desert hills, no?"

The small group then moved on to the Atacama Giant which was the most impressive of all the geoglyphs, a huge, squared, two-legged figure created on another desert hill 30 miles to the north. Archaeologists believe this 86-meter geoglyphic figure dates from 100 BC to 700 AD but are again unsure of its meaning. The Atacama has more than 500 geoglyphs, the guide told them on their return to the mini-bus and he made clear the difference between a geoglyph and a petroglyph. The latter is a carving in the rock, of which Chile also has very many too, he said.

The couple had time to go to the Iquique museum the next day, where they were given a detailed reminder of the massacre of the nitrate workers and many wives and children on 21st December 1907. Workers and their families had gathered from all over the north and had camped in the grounds of the *Santa Maria* School for a week, trying to negotiate improvements in their conditions and pay. Their living conditions were described as *la miseria*. They were paid in tokens which could only be spent at the mine owner's shop. The workers asked the government to intervene on their behalf, with the British owners of the nitrate companies. Instead, President Pedro Montt sent two more regiments to join the two already in place in the north. Early photographs showed the terrible events that ensued when the order was given to disperse the people by shooting at them. Documents portrayed evidence of the official suppression of any knowledge of what the Chilean Army had done until it was brought to light under the Allende government. There were a few academic books detailing what had happened from the 1950s onwards but most of the population knew nothing of the massacre. Estimates of the number of victims were uncertain but were thought to be over 2000. Far from the government defending the people against the exploitative British owners, Government Minister of the Interior, Rafael Sotomayor Gaete ordered the army to crush the strike. Not only was the strike broken but very repressive measures followed, crushing the fledgling trade union movements of the industrial north for many years.

Silent and stunned, although they thought they had known about the massacre before, Isabel and Mateo then took a lengthy walk along the long sandy beach almost without speaking.

As they neared the centre again, Isabel said, "We talked about it earlier but seeing the evidence laid out like that in the museum had a big impact. It was very moving."

"Yes, I was very moved. I've read about it recently before we came on this trip."

"But you knew about it before?" Isabel said, "Quilapayun made the massacre famous through their cantata *La Cantata de Santa Maria de Iquique,* in the early 1970s."

"Quilapayun's version I don't know." Isabel was very shocked to find that Mateo did not know the story through these words and songs.

"But what were you doing during the Allende government period?" asked Isabel, shocked with disbelief. Didn't you hear about the Santa Maria massacre then and the *Cantata?"*

"Well don't sound so amazed. I was a teenager getting on with studying and life and I lived well away from the capital, remember. I liked pop and jazz." Isabel realised they had grown up in very different worlds although Mateo was Chilean. *Of course, he's not had chance to hear the music since the military coup. I have heard it often abroad but no wonder I have doubted his commitment to my world, to my values. How much does he understand? Can I blame him if he is just learning now? It's good he seems to want to learn. It's all been denied to him for all these years. Why did he not learn more from the uncle that disappeared? He must have had a political involvement at some level.* Isabel resolved she must find out more about the uncle and about Mateo. That's what this trip is about, she reminded herself.

-oOo-

Isabel was especially fond of Iquique of all the northern cities and despite that it was where she was arrested, she found parts of the town very attractive and she loved the long ocean coastline that bordered the city. She also had very happy memories of staying in the spare room of her friend Amalia for several months whilst teaching there. Also, she was very fond of the students she had taught in her politics and history classes. They were adults who had been denied opportunities in the past but were intelligent and determined, they were very committed to a better future for themselves and others. She recalled one of them who was particularly able to contribute to the class discussions, Ivan. He always said something intelligent and thoughtful, but she had had to do individual sessions with him to correct the spelling and grammar of his written work. He'd just not had that kind of assistance before. Somehow he'd got through school without really getting to grips with these basics. He left with no qualifications and his writing just could not reflect how intelligent he was, it was clear to Isabel.

Isabel wanted to just relax and enjoy being in that town again with friends like Ivan but she could not get out of her head that she needed to understand Mateo better and not judge him unfairly. He did after all seem to be a good person with an attractive personality. Did she want to settle down in La Serena with him and be a teacher and that is what her life would be about? *I can't keep on forever with all this activism, which ought to achieve something soon, but then what? What if enough people are not as incensed as I am and there is no change soon? Would it take an uprising? Would Chile ever allow that? What would I do if things got violent? Where would I stand then? What if we can't bring about change soon by peaceful methods? Could I stay and just settle down to be a wife and teacher in La Serena? Is that what I want for my life? Would I want to have children with Mateo?* She didn't find herself rushing to say 'yes'. *I couldn't fault him, I'm sure. I like how he is with the school children and with the young people we've met in these activist groups. He would doubtless be a lovely dad. But I can't get enthusiastic about the idea. Should I be, if that is the right thing for me?*

*How long can I keep going with this activism hat on?* Isabel thought she should face this question. *Even being here in this town, I feel a little anxious in case I should be recognised by a policeman. I'm just another tourist in the crowd at present, but I am a little wary of being spotted and don't want to be here too long. What a pity that is, because I want to be with the friends I have here. How can I keep being the agitator and live with the fear of being recognised? Will it have an effect on me long term? I have to hope not because I know why I have to do it and I've no choice in a sense. But how long can I keep it up without results? And how long can I combine that activist role with teaching? One may affect the other sooner or later. What do I like the most? I love teaching art history but I think I enjoyed most of all the political history teaching I did here and elsewhere with the purpose of inspiring activism. That added its own excitement and motivation. Would I rather go back to that than continue teaching in the school in La Serena?* Yes, she felt was her unhesitating reply to that. *I guess it's having that additional purpose. School teaching has an ethical purpose and is valuable but the teaching that is part of activism, is a small contribution to a better Chile, to greater awareness of what has happened that will eventually bring about change. That's the goal I feel I am missing at present and I've committed myself to another year of school teaching. I had to decide months ago and I thought it would give me time to know Mateo more. I can't just let everyone down now by walking away.*

*To be honest, can I just leave things as they are for another whole year? How am I going to deal with the issue of the false name? The teaching was just to finance me for a while. But because of my false identity, I can't remain in La Serena beyond this year, even if I wanted to, in case I am found out, let alone admit it to Mateo. I would like to know more about what went wrong with his wife whom he is separated from, as well as the disappeared uncle that seems to have been quite an influence on him. I need to think about how I am going to find out more. It would sound very natural, to describe to Mateo how my arrest here came about since we are in Iquique now and that way I could lead on to asking more about Mateo's uncle.*

As they walked through the town centre later that day, Isabel said, "It was just down that road there that I was arrested," She began to describe what happened. "It's so painful when they pull your hair, you know. There seems to me to be something almost acceptable about pulling hair in this culture, as a form of punishment. It is not seen as so terrible a thing to do, which it is. Even I've seen parents do it to discipline children but I think it is quite wrong. In Britain, it is seen generally as an absolute No, No. It has to be like that because it is so painful but that's only one of the things they did to me. I had a lot of kicks and punches too and I was covered in bruises, so they really didn't need to do the hair pulling which doesn't leave bruises, as if they needed to disguise the pain they were inflicting. We were entirely peaceful protesters, you know. How can they be allowed to do any of that? Was anyone able to tell you what they saw of what happened to your uncle? You must have speculated so many times and not knowing the truth is so awful."

"Yes, it goes round and round in your head, what might have happened. I never had any information."

"It's the same with the Why? questions. Do you know why your uncle was taken?"

"The only reason we could think of was that he was part of an Action Research project in education. There was an interdisciplinary programme of investigation into education under the auspices of the Catholic University. Action Research by its nature is critical, exposing ideology and the working out of vested interests."

"Wow, yes very much the sort of social science the regime couldn't tolerate. But it all sounds very interesting what your uncle was doing."

"I didn't understand what he was doing when I was only a teenager but I have been thinking about research in education recently and reading about the differing methods. It made me especially look at Action Research because I knew my uncle had involved himself in that."

"Are you looking for new opportunities in that field?"

"There are very few or no such openings here now, most of what I've read is happening in the States, but who knows in the future, perhaps participating in research whilst doing your existing job and after training and preparation in the vacations, it might be an interesting development. But we have to await a very different regime and a different attitude to education from the government here. There needs to be a great deal more money invested in education first, for a start."

"Julian's current social work job is as an Action Research worker in Social Services. It's quite a radical approach in the UK. I can't imagine that in Chile for a long time yet." Mateo stared at her. "Did you not learn from other prisoners what happened to your uncle?"

"No. We never had any final confirmation of his death, officially or unofficially."

"That's worse than knowing the worst."

"Shall we walk along the seafront for a while?" said Mateo.

"Yes, but wait. Don't avoid what I am asking. There was some sense of resolution when I learned from other prisoners what happened to my father. Not at first, but when my stepmother and I had met several fellow detainees, after five or six years, and we knew for sure it was him they had witnessed being taken out and he had never returned. Don't you want to try to trace others imprisoned with your uncle?" Mateo shook his head.

"It's too late now. No, it has to be left and put behind us."

"No. That's burying it, not facing it and it hurts you inside."

"No, it doesn't. I've already had the hurt of the loss. I know what happened to many of the disappeared. It's irrelevant which final act finished a person off. Just to accept and go forward is all you can do. And I'd be grateful if we could do that now and stop keeping on about it. I don't want to keep thinking about it over and over. Finish!"

"I want an official admission of what happened to my father. Without that, there is no proper recognition of the truth and no possibility of prosecutions." Mateo got up and began to walk away.

# Chapter 13

Mateo and Isabel walked along the beach without holding hands as they normally would and in silence. Eventually, they agreed to find a restaurant near the centre and walked the length of the attractive historic street of Baquedano with its 19th Century buildings, many fronted with wooden decking under porticos, acting as the communal pavements. A few people had brought chairs from within their homes to sit in the sun under their portico. It was very picturesque. After lunch, Isabel and Mateo enjoyed a brief swim and relaxed a while in the sun, but there was clearly something on Mateo's mind.

"I thought Julian was in Chile now and so he would have to give up the Action Research job you talked about."

"The local authority is keeping his job open for his return whilst he is doing voluntary work here. It's one of the employee's rights like taking unpaid leave to care for dependent relatives, children or adults. Up to five years maximum is allowed. One day we'll have such rights in Chile. Can you imagine? At present it seems unthinkable here, doesn't it? Of course, it isn't universal in the UK but most local government authorities allow it, so it would apply to teachers in state schools too."

"That's quite something. Are you in touch with Julian now he is here? Did you see him at Christmas?"

"No, no I did not see him but he had sent a letter or two to my mother's address and he gave me an email address, which I have not yet written to."

"So you intend to write? And what will you tell him? That you will see him soon?"

"No, no. I just thought I should let him know I am in the north for several weeks."

"So he needs to know where you are, to work out when he might see you?"

Isabel lay down fully to take the sun and ignored the last remark.

For *onces* that day they were meeting with Isabel's old friends and contacts. Some had been her students and all were keen activists. They were clear about the plans for the day Pinochet was to enter the Senate and were committed to the leafleting they had planned. They described their activities excitedly before the election in November and one of them, Ramón, said he and a small group had been able to go to Humberstone when *Quilapayún* had come to perform the *Cantata de Santa Maria de Iquique* in the abandoned nitrate town. Excitedly, Ramón described how he was standing with his banner listing their key demands when members of the music group came to talk with him. It was the first time the group had performed the *Cantata* in Chile in 24 years and they had chosen Humberstone as the place to begin their tour. They were dressed in black ponchos, just as they had been 24 years earlier, before the coup and their exile. Twelve thousand people, who had travelled from many parts of Chile, gathered to hear their presentation of the story of the massacre. The friends who'd attended described how moving it all was and tears came into Isabel's eyes.

Isabel was delighted to learn that her friends were starting a new education class on Political Philosophy after the summer holidays with volunteer teachers from the university branches in Iquique. They had negotiated these classes themselves and Isabel reflected on the growth in confidence, articulation and abilities that had occurred from when she first knew them. It really was remarkable, she said later to Mateo and just proves how much people can develop themselves, given the encouragement, opportunities and a few pointers. The meeting became a social occasion as they were so well organised and Isabel was glad to catch up individually with them all again. She had become particularly close to this group when she was working with them. There were young women, mostly young mothers, around Isabel's own age, some partners of theirs, a couple of older women, both grandmothers, six teenagers and four working men, including Ivan and Ramon, who were all clearly very intelligent and good at organising, though their job opportunities did not reflect the qualities they had. They all had proved loyal and determined in their commitment politically. Some were now studying for national exams and hoping to go on to more formal education, including one of the elderly women. It really was most impressive what members of this group had achieved.

"That's what education can do for you. It is the real liberator and can be revolutionary," said Mateo.

"Yes, Señor Plato. Education will solve everything."

"Platón - in Spanish," smiled Mateo.

-oOo-

Calama was reached by a further bus ride of over five hours, a distance which Mateo wanted to fly, but was finally persuaded by Isabel that the hassle of going to the airport with the usual waiting around, in the end, totalled as many hours as the bus ride, city centre to city centre. They agreed on an afternoon bus ride with *semi-camas* so they could be tipped well back for a siesta if they felt like it and they could "arrive in the town centre truly relaxed," as Isabel said. Isabel was keen to see the desert again too. She never ceased to be amazed at the range of colours and the variety of forms of the landscape of the desert. Calama was another of these surprising places that arise out of the desperate dryness because an underground river brings water from the Andes and a lush fertile plain is created. The River Loa descends from the mountains to the Oasis of Chiu Chiu which feeds Calama, giving a wealth of tropical fruits, wheat and vegetables. The long green tract of cultivated land along the river with total barrenness surrounding it was stunningly beautiful to Isabel.

Her friends were welcoming again in Calama and she always felt at home in the dusty, windswept *poblaciones* of this very working-class town, where the people seemed so genuinely warm and generous. The big local employer was the copper mine of *Chuquicamata* - then the largest open-pit copper mine in the world. The activists were planning a candlelit vigil with the families of the executed and the disappeared of the city, in *La Plaza de Armas,* the night before the ex-chief of the Army was to enter the Senate. On the day itself, they were planning to demonstrate again and all was prepared, they assured Isabel. There was a special determination amongst these people and they were not to be deflected. Their anger and hurt were very real as all had gone through the tough economic times in the early years after the Coup. Even if they had not lost a family member, they had all experienced the loss of the workers who had defended their trade union rights. They felt deeply about the words their posters demanded: job security, decent pay and pensions, good health services and free prescriptions, free quality education and an end to the dictator's life seat in the Senate and his Constitution. Some of the group started talking to Isabel about the price of medication and the excessive prices that some pharmaceutical companies charge.

"You really have to shop around, even to buy medicine your doctor is prescribing for you," said Luis, an old friend of Isabel's. "For the same medicine, you can pay very different prices in different pharmacies, sometimes almost double. Some of the more posh-looking pharmacist chains, the well-advertised ones, are making a fortune over and above what the medicine should cost and those are the shops already making a great deal of profit from perfumes, cosmetics and creams, and the rest. They don't need to charge so much extra - it's a real racket. And," continued Luis getting really passionate by this time, "an older person might be taking three or four medicines and even at the cheaper pharmacists, it's a lot of money out of their pensions. It's wicked the way people have to buy their medicines through *quotas.* It's health on hire purchase. It's not right. Some old people are in permanent debt. My mother fell on these rough pavements a while ago and she broke her arm. Her treatment at the hospital was covered by her monthly payments but nothing more. Afterwards, they offered her physiotherapy sessions in *quotas.* Can you imagine having an ongoing debt to pay off long after your physio sessions have finished? Each session for my mother was 10,000 pesos and I paid it for her because she wasn't going to attend and I insisted that she should."

Isabel and Mateo listened empathetically but they were encouraged by the enthusiasm of the group. They enjoyed a couple of days of informal and formal meetings with the activists, where they debated these issues and many others, including the serious limitations of the constitution. They were vigorous, valuable debates and Isabel was pleased to see Mateo getting involved with the new young people who had a lot to say about the inequalities in the education system. They were especially angry at the unfairness of how hard it was to get to university from a working-class background. Isabel could see this group lacked the contacts other groups in the northern cities had been able to make, with volunteer university lecturers and school teachers, who give free tuition to them to supplement the inadequate preparation for the national exams in their local schools. There were branches of various Chilean Universities in Calama and surely, Isabel imagined, there would be a few possible volunteers amongst their staff or amongst Calama's secondary school teachers. She and others had managed it in other towns, why not here? She decided that was something she would have to try to initiate but now was not the time to visit such institutions. They would likely be closed for the summer. Why were such valuable resources closed, she mused. What about using them for summer schools? She began to find out who might want to attend such classes and what they most needed that would help them towards national qualifications and pre-university entrance exams. Thank goodness for the Internet, newly available in these cities, thought Isabel so that it is possible to email schools and universities and ask for a text to be circulated to staff. Not as good as a personal contact but worth a try, she thought and without being able to promise success, she committed herself to do her best for them. She would have to return and make personal follow-up contacts in March, she thought.

After these intense meetings, the couple took a bus to the small town of San Pedro de Atacama, only an hour and a half away. San Pedro had become famous and had started to attract many tourists because of its historic and rare geographic features. The first and foremost of these was only possible to see by booking a tour starting at 4.30 in the morning, which Isabel and Mateo signed up for. They were to go to see the geysers of El Tatio and it was necessary to arrive before sunrise for the most impressive views. They were advised to take very warm clothing, overcoats or warm ponchos as the desert was very cold at that hour. Also, they were told they should bring swimming clothes and towels for later in the day.

As their range rover drew into El Tatio valley, 4,320 meters above sea level, just before 6 a.m. there were small wisps of steam rising from the brown desert ground. These grew in number as they walked around the flattened rocks, trying to avoid slipping on the thin ice covering much of the ground. The steam columns began to billow in volume and as the sun peeped over a nearby hill, hundreds of flumes of steam could be seen rising into the sky. The driver/guide boiled eggs for their breakfast in the bubbling water where it reached the surface at boiling temperatures. Here and there were forceful hot springs shooting up as natural fountains, heated by the geothermal system and they were warned not to get too near because the fountains could scald. They also learned these fountains were a major source of arsenic pollution to the river waters of the area. Mateo and Isabel recalled how they'd come across arsenic before in the history of this zone. They had to watch carefully where they walked but it was unforgettably exciting to see this rare and strange place. When the sun had fully risen and a hot summer's day had commenced, they were advised where there was a nearby volcanic *laguna* which was heated also by the geothermal system but this time to body temperature only, for an enjoyable swim.

At an altitude of 2,400 meters, San Pedro de Atacama itself was cold at night, the temperature dropping to zero even in summer, though in the daytime the temperature was of a warm summer's day. The desert encroached on the town, despite the fact that the urban centre had grown up around an oasis. The dust on the computers and keyboards in the local Internet Centre was testimony to the extreme dryness of the surroundings. It was clear the owners and the paid assistant at the Centre had long since given up on trying to keep the dust at bay. They knew they were fighting a losing battle and everyone appeared to accept as normal, the very visible layer of dust covering everything. Isabel wondered what it was going to do to the computers in the longer term but she was glad to find they were apparently working all right together with dial-up connectivity. She wanted to get her letter done to the various university branches and secondary schools in Calama, and this is what she told Mateo was her purpose in going to the Internet Centre. She wrote an email to Julian too. She wanted him to know she was thinking about him, which was true and she wanted to share some news about the mummies and also the activists she had been meeting. She described San Pedro and the El Tatio geysers and she knew that she should be showing these remarkable features of Chile to Julian. Much is new to me, she wrote, but I want you to see these amazing aspects of this country. Mateo was going to question her. Was she going to be able to carry off another lie and pretend she had only written to the schools and University branches under that close scrutiny?

-oOo-

Isabel and Mateo visited the archaeological museum named R P Gustavo Le Paige after the Belgium monk who had opened the museum in the 1960s with a massive collection of relics and artefacts that he and others had found in the local area from past pre-Colombian occupations over eleven thousand years. They also went to visit some ruins of ancient, native houses near the town as well. The hotel where they were staying in San Pedro had been built in the same style as the Le Paige discoveries of these ancient homes - circular stone buildings with conical thatched roofs. They learned that the pre-Colombian peoples had created terraced agriculture to prevent the precious water from the river from running off. They had grown potatoes and quinoa, corn and beans, also melons, courgettes, pumpkin and tobacco. They also appeared to have inhaled hallucinogens from the San Pedro cactus using ceramic tablets of human figurines and condors. Llamas and alpacas were important too for meat and wool and leather. They dried well-salted meat, which they called *ch'arki,* to enable them to store it and it is still made in modern times.

"Ch'arki is hard, salty and horrible," declared Isabel pulling a face.

"No, it's great and I'm going to buy some to take home," said Mateo, glad of some compensation for all the dust with which he was getting very fed up.

Isabel read out "'In the later pre-Colombian period, when the Incas dominated the area, the *Atacameños* were forced to worship the Sun God *Inti* and the people constructed alters high in the mountains, especially on the *Licancabur* volcano.' Look at the magnificent, snow-capped, conical peak over there. It's beautiful and displays itself to the whole town below. No wonder the ancients considered it sacred."

Isabel and Mateo needed their overcoats again for their venture that evening. They went to an astronomical centre created by a French amateur astronomer where they were able to use the several telescopes provided and observe the moon and planets and view globular clusters such as Andromeda. Isabel was thrilled with the view of Saturn with its rings that she was able to see so clearly and magnificently, better than she had ever seen it before. The Milky Way was, as usual in those clear, rainless skies, very visible to the naked eye and looked spectacular. A number of constellations were pointed out to them. Visitors were then taken into an *Atacameño* circular house and served hot chocolate and asked if they had any questions. It was Isabel who jumped in first.

"There is talk of a Radioastronomy Observatory of 50 antennas or a Large Millimeter/Submillimeter Array, to be built by North America, Europe and Japan and the Atacama is favoured for its high altitude and dry climate. If this goes forward and is constructed here, what will it show us? Will it give us more incredibly beautiful images, like *Hubble* has done but from even further into deep space than we have seen before, and thus further back in time?" The astronomer answered with a long explanation of the difference between observation of the universe by looking at visible light and the capturing of radio waves, which he explained are another, lower energy segment of the electromagnetic spectrum.

"The Radio Telescopes will receive millimetres and submillimetric wavelengths," said the Frenchman, "from between far infrared waves and radio waves of the spectrum. The high energy waves emitted by the universe are absorbed by the ozone layer of our atmosphere and are not able to penetrate it, thus they must be collected by telescopes like *Hubble,* outside of our atmosphere. The low energy emissions, which are not blocked by the earth's atmosphere, can be captured by a Radio Telescope here on earth. But we need a much bigger one than any we have at present. The new giant Radio Telescope proposed," the astronomer continued, "and by the way, it is definitely coming to Chile, will observe the light emitted by cold temperature objects in space to enable us to learn about planet formation back in time. It will be powerful enough to see the gas concentrations from which we believe new stars are formed. Even, it will be able to detect the unique wave spectra of different molecules, to enable us to know the chemical elements of the universe."

"Every element has its unique colour and characteristics, I know, so we are able to recognise... what is ...out there," staggered Isabel, "but did you say recognise molecules?"

"Well, yes, because each has its own wave spectra so we know what molecules are there." was the reply. "Eventually the 50 or 60, maybe more, high precision antennas that will form the observatory altogether, will be spread out across the desert at 5000 meters altitude. It will become the largest radio astronomical project in existence and produce, in effect, a single giant

16-kilometre wide telescope. A very large surface is necessary to pick up the radio waves of the weakest, most distant signals. The world has never had a telescope big enough before." There was silence under the conical, thatched roof. It was mind-blowing what they were being told and Isabel was glad of the much better understanding she then had. There were no further questions. The astronomer had given a very useful lecture to them which probably covered all he had intended to say, whatever the questions.

The next day a visit to the *Valle de la Luna*, seemed like a further astronomical adventure. The dramatic rock formations of the desert valley were aptly named after the moonscape and a visitor could well imagine he or she was walking on the moon. High overhead cliffs towered above them and then a challenging climb gave them a view of a formation called the *amphitheatre*. Vertical cliffs across the valley could be seen from above to make an almost a fully circular 'theatre', with a gently sloping interior bowl shape, just at the angle that makes the perfect acoustic shape of a Greek or Roman theatre. The small party of visitors were encouraged to walk along the length of a high ridge with a vast expanse of barren "luna" landscape before them, stretching to the distant horizon in one direction and to the foothills of the volcanic mountains in the other. As the sun was beginning to set and giving an orange, golden glow, they found themselves on the top ridge of a huge sandy slope, where a few young people were surfboarding down, just as they would in snow. They watched the lowering sun until it disappeared.

Mateo said, "I want to watch a great many more sunsets with you in the future. They are so beautiful and somehow they make me want to think about time, future and past and want the present to be endless."

Isabel didn't know what to say. She smiled and put her arm on his. "Come on, we have to get down before it gets completely dark." She responded to his desire to kiss her. She decided she must try to be very warm and natural with Mateo and fully relish his company. She was relieved she wasn't questioned about her email writing. She wanted to enjoy this time with this good man and to know him more. She had the impression something was missing in her feelings about Mateo but was that because she didn't yet know him well enough? Or was it that a long-term relationship feels very different from a new one? Is it the history that gives a relationship another dimension? *No, don't pretend, she said to herself. You would know at this stage if there was that special thrill and you feel yourself really in love.*

Another tour the following day took them to the *Salar de Atacama*. They would only be able to see small parts of this vast area, they were told, but the variety of landscapes they saw were surprisingly different and each of them stunningly beautiful in a distinct way. This time they saw deep blue lakes and natural moats, shallow and burbling, surrounded by vast areas of small white rocks, that, when up close, could be seen to be salt - pure, crunchy, white salt when walked on. It sounded and appeared like walking on thick, settled, crisp snow and vast quantities stretched as far as the eye could see. Bands of colour of orange-brown rocks with strips of blue lagoon, alternating with the white salt strips, gave the whole the effect of an abstract painting.

"Look at these last few photos I have taken. They could almost be Mark Rothko paintings," said Isabel.

"I'm sorry, I don't know his work, but your images are beautiful and abstract."

"I'll try and get you some copies of his paintings. The similarity with these landscapes of broad bands of colour is uncanny.

Isabel went back to her camera work again. Nearby there was a lagoon for bathing for those that wished. Further on, when they stopped again and descended from their *range rover*, after a short walk on salt, they were awed by a vast crowd of flamingos, paddling in the shallow waters. Most had their heads in the water much of the time and it appeared they were looking for the crustaceans they like to eat, the consumption of which gave the flamingos' feathers their bright pink colour. An occasional disturbance in the vast wilderness of silence, made groups of the flamingos suddenly take to the air and show off their huge wingspans of colour. Mateo was thrilled with this unforgettable display of nature. There must have been many thousands of birds and Isabel was enchanted to see his great delight and the beauty of the sight for herself.

For the five-hour bus ride on to Antofagasta, Isabel and Mateo had again made an afternoon *semi-cama* reservation. On arrival, Isabel considered it urgent to find a call centre with computers. She was disappointed to find she still had not had any electronic communication about the coffins' invoice or the investigation into what happened to her father. She had, however, had an email from Julian who was looking forward to knowing when she was back from her travels in the north and when he would be able to see her. Isabel was getting anxious to get back home and plan her activities leading up to the big day of demonstrations. She decided she would be in Valparaiso for the occasion of Pinochet entering the Senate and prior to that, she wanted to participate in various action days in Santiago. She needed to be in contact with Juan to know where and when the groups that Juan promoted in Santiago, like her companion groups in the north, would be demonstrating. It was essential, thought Isabel, to be in the capital and ensure the message there was loud and clear in opposition to the dictator entering the senate. She hoped the whole city would be out and she wanted to be part of that and she wouldn't be held back by Mateo wanting to limit her participation.

Isabel knew she liked being a teacher but she was very clear that her role had to be the political activist whilst ever there was the need and she knew she was animated and fulfilled through that activity. In the activist role, and promoting others to do the same, was where she found her greatest satisfaction. Whatever the risk, it had to be done and she must do it. Mateo, she thought, would always be inclined to discourage her in this. *Am I being fair? He has accompanied me on these visits to all my groups and never once complained about the political protests we have planned or the risks we are preparing for. But would he accept me just in that role, full time, without the school teaching, if that is what I told him I wanted to do for the foreseeable future - just when he's probably hoping it will all be over soon and we can settle back into conventional teaching. Whereas, I have come to the conclusion that now is the time for a big political movement to push for change. I've come to see that school teaching is not for me long-term and anyway I can't pursue it for much longer. I can't go on living under a false identity. The longer I do, the greater the likelihood of being discovered. I never intended it to be for more than a very brief respite to get a little money saved. If I tell Mateo about my true name, would he expose me to the Head and get me dismissed from my job? I don't think he would find that easy to do, nor would he want to do it. But he might feel morally obliged. He might be so angry and feel so deceived, that he would feel compelled to do it. What's in a name? Why is that such a big thing? My history, the person I am, they are still the same, all the past I have told him about, what I believe in. Does it matter whatever the name I'm working under? That's just a label for convenience. What I could do is participate in Santiago as Helena Garcia when on the streets and carry that identity card. That would put my job at risk but maybe that is a way out - the only way out of my contract for another academic year. It would save my previous detention from being linked with me now. Juan's people don't know me and if there is one name I can put at risk and want to get rid of, it's the false one. Juan will fully understand and assist me in that.*

Isabel had not yet broken the news to Mateo that she wanted to be outside the parliament building in Valparaíso on the big day and without Mateo. That had better wait until we are home, she thought. Mateo was busy at the hotel trying to catch up with news from the papers and TV since they checked in. There had been a lot of talk about the parliamentary activity of a libel action - a constitutional accusation against the ex-dictator but this would now be presented after Pinochet had entered the Senate. Would it ultimately fail like all the efforts to prevent him from becoming a Senator seemed to be fading away fast because the numbers to vote against him just do not exist in this loaded parliament? *They have been trying legal and parliamentary moves for months now and nothing has succeeded, which makes it all the more vital that the opposition shows itself on the streets and in large numbers,* concluded Isabel. That was where she knew she needed to be right now and she strengthened her resolve to get to Santiago as soon as possible. Isabel had other business to do there too like going to the Vicariate and developing a lot of photo reels but first, she must make contact with her closest companion of the street, her tower of strength, Daniela. She telephoned Daniela but she had heard nothing further about the coffins invoice, nor its revelation. She was told Daniela had arranged a meeting with the activists in two days' time and when this was done, Isabel wanted to hurry off to La Serena.

-oOo-

Sitting at Mateo's dining table after brunch on arriving back on the overnight bus, they took stock of all they had seen and done, including the activist meetings they had attended.

"They are undoubtedly an impressive bunch of people. I loved their enthusiasm and they are very fond of you and grateful to you and all you have done for them in the past," said Mateo. "They make a big fuss of you, don't they? But I want to tell you something."

"Yes, do," said Isabel a little fearful of what was coming.

"I hope you are not going to feel a responsibility to act as the main support and enabler for all those groups in all those far-flung cities in the next academic year. You can't keep travelling so often to all those places, as if there was no one else who could do the job." When there was no response, he continued. "I enjoyed our trip very much but I could see that there are others who could do the volunteer support job you've taken on yourself very well in your place. You've no need to push yourself so much to get round to them all frequently."

"I enjoyed the trip very much and I wanted to thank you, especially for all your support, practical and moral and immoral and..."

"If you are going to be so formal," said Mateo, ignoring the gleam in her eye, "it is a pleasure to be with you." He knew she wasn't going to listen to him. "I enjoyed not only the places we visited but the friends of yours too in the different cities. Look how capable Daniela has become as just one example. Maybe they weren't like that when you first knew them but they have grown and you can now leave far more to each of them. I bet you could find one person in each city whom you could consciously brief as a volunteer supporter and you could telephone them regularly to support them."

"Yes, I wanted to thank you especially for fitting in so well and being so nice to all the people."

"Well, you know me, good with women, children and dogs!"

Isabel smiled but she wasn't quite sure she liked that joke, which he had also made before. He did believe in his own charm and she didn't like the self-satisfaction.

"Oh yes, Señor Charmer."

"You're the only one I want to charm. In fact, you're the one I want to get serious about. Why don't you move in with me before the next term starts?"

"Wait a minute! We've only been seeing each other for six months. That's not very long to make a serious decision like moving in. And you want to make sure I'm not going to be disappearing frequently to visit the northern cities. Thank you very much." She wanted to add "Mr I-know-best," but she just managed to hold her tongue.

"Don't you think things are working out well between us? You have stayed here quite often so I thought you'd prefer not to have to go to your flat after an evening together. That can't be very nice to have to turn out again."

"That's not a major reason to move in together. That decision means a lot more, doesn't it? It means a long-term commitment in my book."

"That's exactly what I want."

"Is that exactly what you'll be willing to make?"

Mateo came around the table to kiss her and she stood up to respond. She put her arms around him.

"I'll stay with you tonight," said Isabel. "Look, I haven't wanted to push you and it's up to you, but if you want us to know each other better, why haven't you told me anything about why your first marriage went wrong, in your opinion."

"Yes, of course, I will tell you all you want to know but you will recognise that it is only my point of view. I'm very conscious of that and perhaps the church or the state would say I had no good reason to abandon the marriage. But it had become unbearable. I feel I stuck it out for nearly three years of hell. She had serious mental health problems, she was on medication which they kept adjusting but there was little change and it was so awful, with constant anger and physical attacks by her. I was frightened that on an impulse I could have hit back and I never wanted to be labelled a wife beater. I was determined that I wouldn't be, but I was so provoked so often. I had to keep leaving the house to avoid the violence by her and then she'd throw things at the door I'd just gone out of."

"Sounds like you had some really hard times."

"I used to try to calm her and hold her at first but it was no good. I saw her doctor and we discussed adjustment of her medication at length. She was finally diagnosed as schizophrenic and her medication was adjusted again to treat this and I had new hopes. At best there was paranoia and disorganised thinking. At worst it was frequent violent eruptions. Typically, there was a lack of desire to form a relationship, that's supposed to be one of the symptoms. She had periods of depression and anxiety and the general apathy was hard to cope with. I learned her mother had had depression and she had never told me that. Then I discovered she was having affairs, and I couldn't go on. Apparently, they were short and never long-lasting but intolerable for me."

"It all sounds unbearable and not what you signed up for."

"No, it absolutely wasn't. I felt I had tried but it was asking too much to sacrifice my whole life to what clearly wasn't going to be the marriage I had wanted. I just felt I couldn't go on. I felt I could live with my conscience because I had tried hard quite a long time."

"Yes, I understand. Thank you for telling me. Have you ever told anyone else? Do you not need to talk to a therapist, for your own health's sake?"

"Perhaps. I don't know. I don't feel a great need. I haven't told anyone else except my uncle, another of my mother's brothers. You'll have to tell me if you think I really should do that and why."

"Ok. I promise. If I see a real need and I can't say I ever have yet."

A couple of days later, Isabel went to have supper with Mateo and he reminded her after they had eaten that she had not given him an answer to his asking her to move in with him.

"It is a big commitment you are asking of me and I don't think I am ready to make that commitment. I'm sorry. I've enjoyed our time together in the north and all our time together. Thank you for everything but can we just remain, good friends, while I think about the longer-term much more seriously than I have so far. I'm not ready."

"I understand. No pressure. I'll wait. But I hope we can carry on being together often, as we have. I love you and I know that I want to be with you. You don't have that sort of certainty yet, do you? You are still thinking about Julian?"

"Why do you think that? Why should you say that? I…I…I have been affected by the fact that he is here in my country and looking for me but I've done nothing about it when I could have. I'm not rushing to see him, am I?"

"Well, we've been away more than a month. Thank you for sticking with that. It hasn't given you much chance to do anything else but I sense you've been a bit distracted."

"Have I? I didn't realise that. In fact, I thought I ought to be giving more time to serious thought about my future rather than sauntering about the desert."

"This was your Chile, that you are still discovering. There's more to see. There are the dramatic mountains of the far south you say you haven't

247

seen - a lush green spectacular contrast with the desert. Let me show you that too. I really want to."

"Well, not this summer. There's no time now. I have to go to Santiago very soon and in fact I'll be away until the beginning of the school term," she said. "I have to go to the Archive Foundation of the Vicariate in Santiago and find out what is happening about the coffins' invoice. There hasn't been a word more in the press about the coffins but that's probably because of the censorship rules. Nothing can be said if they want to keep things hidden. I want to follow up on the lawyer's promise to ask his people to investigate my father's disappearance too. And it's time to see my family again."

"You'll be going to the anti-Pinochet demos in Santiago, putting yourself at risk and you'll be going to Valparaíso, if you get that far, to reconnect with *el gringo*," Mateo said angrily. H*ow on earth did he know what I was only vaguely planning*, thought Isabel but then of course she realised it was a reasonable assumption. She opened her mouth to reply but then decided not to say anything. A moody silence on both their parts ensued. Mateo went to the kitchen and forbade her to enter when she offered to help. Eventually, he emerged and said,

"What did you mean about giving serious thought to your future? You're committed to a further year at the High School, aren't you? You won't let us all down on that will you?"

"No course not. I know that perfectly well, but I have been thinking about longer-term than that."

"Will you eat with me tomorrow before the overnight bus?" asked Mateo.

"No, thank you because I don't think I'm going to have time. I'm going to need tomorrow to wash and iron and pack, sort my photographic stuff and other things and finish the bits of food I have in the fridge. I want to prepare a couple of lessons for the very beginning of term. There does that sound like I'm leaving the school in the lurch?"

"Why not be honest with me and tell me that you've been thinking about the *gringo* and that is what you mean about seriously thinking about the future."

"No, you are wrong. At least, not principally. I've been weighing up what I want to be - a school teacher or a full-time activist. I'm looking not only at what gives me satisfaction and fulfilment as well as what's right. I know which gives me a regular kick of excitement which I confess I like."

"I can imagine which that is. You want the adrenaline rush but do you think that promoting violence is the ethical and best way forward?"

"What violence? Peaceful disobedience only. How else are the injustices here going to change and when?"

"You can't take on changing the whole political world onto your shoulders."

"Why not? What right have I not to bother? If everyone did that, maybe we wouldn't have the problems we have here now and I don't see a way out of them but for the people to rise up."

"How are you so sure you are right?"

"Well, it isn't just me who thinks all the issues on our posters must be addressed as a minimum and urgently. When are more people going to wake up? What can I do to wake them up?"

"Are you wanting to be an M.P? Is that what you mean about giving yourself full time?"

"No, what chance? I couldn't be even a member of any of the mainstream parties, let alone an M.P. for any of them. There has to be a serious grouping of the left that wants meaningful change. We need another Allende or a Pablo Neruda and that means waking up the population to realise it is in their interest. It is in fact the only way that is in their interest but all the propaganda vilifies anyone like that or worse - they kill them off. The current parties pay lip service to democracy and the good of the people but they allow the perpetuation of the current exploitation, as in all our five demands. These things have to change radically."

"Changing the constitution is fundamental to that."

"Don't I know that? And as the Senate isn't going to do that, what's the alternative?"

"What do you mean? Illegal means get you locked up and then see how far that gets you."

"How do you think Mahatma Gandhi or Martin Luther King felt when they were thrown into jail? But they weren't there forever and they achieved a great deal."

"And they both ended up getting killed."

249

"A mass movement for civil and economic rights using civil disobedience - that is the only way forward."

Mateo had no answer to that. He just stared into her eyes.

"I'm sorry I can't be what you want." She turned to go.

"You are what I want. I admire you but..."

"There is always a but..." She disappeared. In the *colectivo,* she thought, all I've just said applies to Julian too. I can't do anything much being stuck in England.

# Chapter 14

A t last, the day had come, just after the New Year celebrations. Julian was moving to live in Valparaíso. The people in Quillota had been enormously kind, generous and warm with him and he was sorry to leave them in many ways. Of course, he was urged to return to see them often and he did, including keeping up visits to the Old People's Home and his Spanish classes for a few months. He also agreed with the Youth Group that they would continue their monthly visits to the *Hogar de Cristo* children's home and he would meet them there. The home wasn't far from Valparaíso. Julian couldn't thank the Padre enough for the wonderful experience he had been given. Three students from his English class, Alvaro, and father and daughter, Javier and Catalina, insisted on coming with him to Valparaíso on moving day and they travelled with him, together with Mario, the driver, in the church minibus after *almuerzo,* which everyone insisted he must have before leaving. One church member had given him a table that she no longer wanted and someone else had given him a couple of stools, which were of course items Julian very much needed. Ximena gave him a set of double sheets which she said she no longer could use as all the beds at the Padre's house were single.

When the group arrived at the flat and they were helping unload the minibus, he found a corner shop open and managed to get some bread, cheese and ham and avocados and mangos and individual tubs of chirimoya ice cream, so he could give them *onces* before they returned home. They sat around the kitchen table together, two on the stools and three on the windowsill, with no plates and they ate from the papers the food came in.

Julian had saved a few plastic knives and forks and spoons and he had a pen knife with which he could cut the mango up and place slices on the ice creams. Fortunately, Julian had bought some pottery mugs at the artisan fair, and he had also bought an electric kettle to bring, having previously bought one for Padre Pablo's house. He felt that such a concession to modernity was lacking in the Padre's household. He'd bought a small portable television as well, the smallest he could find, but he knew he must keep up with the news and the language practice a tv offers.

Julian had also gathered a few pictures from *artesanía* fairs in Valparaíso and Viña to put on the walls. He had a large photograph of Isla Negra, Neruda's coastal home he'd not yet visited and he had posters of Victor Jara and Los Jaivas and an illustrated poster of words of the famous Argentinian writer Jorge Luis Borges. It read:

> "If I could live again my life,
> In the next – I'll try,
> – to make more mistakes,
> I won't try to be so perfect,
> I'll be more relaxed,
> I'll be more full – than I am now,
> In fact, I'll take fewer things seriously,
> I'll be less hygienic,
> I'll take more risks,
> I'll take more trips,
> I'll watch more sunsets,
> I'll climb more mountains,
> I'll swim more rivers,
> I'll go to more places – I've never been,
> I'll eat more ice creams and less lima beans,
> I'll have more real problems – and less imaginary ones,
> I was one of those people who live
> prudent and prolific lives –
> each minute of his life,
> Of course that I had moments of joy – but,
> if I could go back I'll try to have only good moments,

**If you don't know – that's what life is made of,**
**Don't lose the now!**
**I was one of those who never goes anywhere**
**without a thermometer,**
**without a hot-water bottle,**
**and without an umbrella and without a parachute,**
**If I could live again – I will travel light,**
**If I could live again – I'll try to walk bare feet**
**at the beginning of spring till the end of autumn,**
**I'll ride more carts,**
**I'll watch more sunrises and play with more children,**
**If I have the life to live – but now I am 85,**
**– and I know that I am dying ..."**

The pink walls didn't look too bare or too pink with these posters up and Julian had also bought a guitar and had a set of panpipes which Mario hung on the wall for him together with a couple of traditional knitted, *alpaca* wool, Aymara hats with cosy ear flaps and llamas in the pattern. He'd some other trinkets from Christmas presents from the Youth Group and the Padre's *equipo* as the Padre called his key workers, like Gabriela, Patricia and Fabio, who took part in the pool of shared present giving. The famous, very large annual craft fair held at Viña del Mar was coming shortly and he was told he should be able to buy there some *mimbre*. Wickerwork furniture sounded ideal as it was a modest price and he liked it. More immediately he would be able to get pots and pans and plates in the street fairs in Valparaíso. He had seen them and knew where to go.

Julian saw his helpers off and he was very grateful to them but rather relieved to be alone to think and to plan. He set up his CD player on the floor by the bed, put on an *Illapu* disk, took his bathroom things out of his rucksack and just lay on the bed with a book. *"Soy porteño"* - as Ximena often said - "I am from the port of Valparaíso."

Julian knew this city was the original home of Isabel until her mother took her to Santiago when she was seven. This was the city where her father and Constanza went to university and where they lived and worked and Isabel would visit frequently to be with them. Isabel might well have contacts here now and come here to see them. *Was that just wishful thinking?* he had to ask himself. *Why didn't I go to live in Santiago where there are contacts from her teenage years? But Isabel was never in Santiago when she was in touch with me in England. She's bound to return to Santiago sometimes, at least to see her mother. But I have no contacts there. I have to go where it is possible for me to go. Look how having contacts has helped me get this flat. And this sort of flat would be twice the price in Santiago without the view. Then there is my contact with the Catholic University here. I guess I started the evening classes in Spanish when Isabel first came to Chile because I needed to fill a hole in my life. But I've so enjoyed the studies since I signed up for a part-time Degree course and it has brought me here - to be a porteño for a while. Let's hope the other part of my purpose works out soon and Isabel rings Martina with a message.*

To make his whole living experience completely smooth, Ximena had arranged that the lady who looked after her house in Valparaíso, Martina, would do washing and ironing for Julian whenever he wished. With no washing machine, this was really valuable. Just a phone call to Martina and they would meet somewhere convenient. *It's who you know...*he thought again. Ximena had also given him the name of her niece who was a pharmacist in the town and she had made sure Julian was clear where her shop was, just in case he needed any medical attention. She'd thought of everything.

At the craft fair a couple of days later he found a lovely little two-seater sofa in wickerwork, four dining chairs, an armchair and a bookcase and they agreed to deliver them the next day. At artisan stalls, he bought table mats, cushions and a cloth with crochet edging to cover the kitchen table he'd been given for his living room. He also bought a wooden fruit bowl and a large ceramic serving plate and ceramic serving bowls, with which he was delighted. Very satisfied Julian returned home to await the completion of the furnishing of his Chilean home. When the furniture had arrived the next day he rushed out to find floor rugs for the living room and the bedroom. He was lucky to find a Mapuche traditional handwoven, large rug in the permanent Valparaíso craft fair for the living room and he bought simple woven rugs to go at the sides of the beds. He was also pleased to have found another wall hanging from the north of Chile or possibly from Peru, but certainly Quechua or Aymara tradition. It was a small tapestry of wonderful colours and intricate work which he loved but he thought the added bonus would be that it would hide a bit more of the pink, and it complimented the colour as well.

Julian wondered what Isabel would think of his flat when she eventually came to see him there, which he truly believed was going to happen. He'd done his best with 'the pink' but he could see it might still be too awful to be acceptable. Perhaps he could seek the permission of the owner to repaint it if Isabel strongly disapproved. For now, he thought he could live with it. There was an idea or an impression growing in his mind, that he so wanted to discuss with Isabel. He ached to know when that might be possible. Travelling up and down in the funicular railway frequently, to and from his flat to the town centre, afforded a very clear and close view of the parliament building. It dominated the view because of its overwhelming size and he was becoming aware that the parliament had absolutely no impact economically on the surrounding parts of the city. It was like the politicians were in a separate world, more so than might be true of most politicians in any other country, as here they were physically as well as socially and economically kept totally apart. The congressmen and women and the senators were literally, completely cut off from the city around them, into which they never ventured. The high metal fence through which garden shrubbery could be seen, around the perimeter of the Parliament might as well have been a ten-meter high, solid brick wall. The politicians' presence was not leading to any development whatsoever on this neglected port, which had been run down over the dictatorship years, whilst Santiago had received all the industrial investment.

From the market stalls at the foot of the *ascensor* to the cheap fast food cafés across the road from the parliament, there were no quality restaurants, nor attractive coffee houses opened up near the parliament where the politicians might socialise or even meet local people - heaven forbid. The nearby shops remained as poor, old-fashioned and run down as they must have been for many years. There were a few fast food outlets that would be considered well beneath the politicians' standards. There was a central covered food market just across the road, with its rough and ready stallholders shouting their prices and offers, which had been there for decades but along with it came a street where rotting fruit and vegetables got dumped and which always seemed to smell, along with the fish market next door. The parliament hadn't even had the impact of motivating that these streets were cleaned up. There were antiquated ironmonger shops and second-hand stalls in a street alongside the square next to the parliament, and that was where Julian had bought some of his kitchenware. The politicians would never have ventured to see those rough-looking stalls with their goods spread over the pavement. The *politicos* arrive from Santiago by car or helicopter and immediately after their obligatory visit is done, they scuttle back to the capital or off to their home constituencies without having to brush with the locals or spend any money from which the locals might benefit.

Julian was becoming quite friendly with the *ascensor* attendant Rafael and he shared these thoughts with him.

"Yes, you are absolutely right. And now, the *politicos* have agreed to spend 12 million *pesos* from tax-payers money, to build a restaurant, sauna and gymnasium for themselves on the very top of the Parliament building, so they will never need the city. There have been demonstrations against this extravagant cost, the protesters arguing there were housing and health priorities that weren't getting the funding they needed, but the building works are going ahead. Look you can see building work has started at the top."

"I've been thinking," said Julian, "it would be a good idea to restore and renovate the original parliament building in Santiago for the politicians and they could give this magnificent modern building to the Catholic University, which doubtless would be pleased to expand as that is the only place an expansion could be achieved in this neighbourhood."

"That's a great idea. The taxpayers wouldn't have to keep paying for the transport of the politicians to Valparaíso and the *politicos* would be in the centre of the action in Santiago, which of course is where they want and need to be."

"It is obvious that the dictator, when he was obliged to pay some lip service to notions of democracy and was forced to concede that a parliament was necessary, he wanted to keep it out of the way, in a secondary city, where it could do less harm. He didn't want any interfering politicians with their troublesome ideas that the executive should be subject to questioning and scrutiny, interfering with the smooth running of government."

"True and do you know that no parliamentary sessions are more than three hours long," said Rafael. "That's a full day in this parliament. Honestly, can you believe it? So they hardly need a restaurant. They certainly don't need a gym and a sauna offering a break before they return to work or a late-night session. They aren't there long enough."

"Amazing. So you would agree that they never step out onto the pavement outside the parliament, is a fair observation?"

"Absolutely!"

-oOo-

Julian wanted to get his voluntary work agreed with the contacts he had had from Constanza's friend Eliza and he had a couple of appointments coming up. He also wanted to buy an additional bed for his flat - a single for the third bedroom, a room which had nothing in it at present. His two younger brothers were talking of visiting if he stayed on in Chile and he had told them he had applied to his work for a further nine months extension to his unpaid leave. He was certain he wasn't going to be ready to return in June to England, right in the middle of the University term here and given he hadn't yet met up with Isabel. Julian was also thinking that if he sorted the single bed this week, it would be useful for friends from Quillota who were coming to see him on Friday and staying after the open-air concert on one of the quays at the port. Emiliano, Esmeralda and their daughter Ana were coming to the concert and Ana had said she'd bring a sleeping bag, but Julian thought it would be a nice surprise to have a bed for her and it was something he was going to need anyway. Valparaíso had a wealth of old-fashioned-looking furniture shops right in the centre of town and Julian was amazed at how cheap a very solid-looking bed with an oak headboard could be with a good mattress thrown in. At these prices, he decided to get a couple of bedside tables and two small chests of drawers and with these additions and a few more mats and pillows, all the rooms of his flat would be adequately furnished. The new furniture was promised for delivery on Friday, just in time for the concert.

What amazing musicians they are, *Los Jaivas* and *Congreso,* thought Julian and they were joined by two Argentinian music groups he didn't know but enjoyed. It finally all finished at 3.00 am and Julian and his visitors were relieved they only had to get to the top of the hill and not to Quillota. Despite the hour, Julian could not sleep initially and his thoughts turned to Isabel as always. He would go to an internet centre when he had seen his friends off in the morning, to see if there was any further news from her. He would enjoy writing to her again describing the concert and his thoughts on the parliament building. He could also say his home was now furnished and ready to receive her as soon as possible.

Emiliano shared some good news with him during the family's visit. Resources for the Youth Group's visits to the *Hogar de Cristo* children's home were pouring into the church at Quillota "from all sides" so the young people were able to develop their activities with the children and felt well supported. Julian was so pleased to hear this. Padre Pablo had given his full blessing to the work and when he sows an idea into the minds of his congregation they respond and the plan comes to fruition. Julian had thought it was his charisma, quiet and gentle though his manner was, but Julian had also come to recognise the people's empathy and great sense of solidarity and a willingness to respond to need and take action. Apparently, toys, paper, glue, pens, paints, storybooks, games, clothes, biscuits, sweets and chocolates had arrived and money was donated so that trips out could be organised in the summer months. This activity of the Youth Group was clearly flourishing with some of the adults in Julian's English class helping too.

A major social work organisation, Julian had learned from Eliza, apart from the church, was the YMCA *Asociación Cristiana de Jovenes.* The YMCA's Chilean headquarters had opened in Valparaíso in 1912 and when Julian went to visit its impressive head office, he learned that it ran children's homes, institutions for the disabled and community projects. He also learned that whilst the main commercial centre of Valparaíso was at sea level, the higher up you travelled into the surrounding hills, the poorer the communities became. The newest settlements and the most disadvantaged, those most deprived of resources and infrastructure, were at the very top. The headquarters organised visits for him to two community projects in the hills.

Julian's first visit was to a family centre in Cerro Las Cañas, about halfway up the hills, where the emphasis was primarily on education and attempting to compensate for that which the State educational facilities had failed to do. The educationalist Amanda explained, "40% of young people leave school in this *población* without completing their basic educational level and 80% of the adults we work with have not completed this basic level in the past. Nowadays it is illegal to remove a child from school without them achieving this obligatory level. But we have difficulty trying to persuade parents to allow a child to remain at school because of their poverty and their need for the wages the young people can earn. So the family centre tries to help get them up to standard before they leave. We also help with recycling uniforms to save that cost."

"What size are your classes?" Asked Julian, having seen some very large classes in Quillota.

"They are 16 to 20 in number. I empathise with the school teachers with classes of 40, but also I feel there was too much emphasis on formal methods of repetition and memorising. This is now considered old-fashioned in Europe but it comes from the dictatorship years. The teacher is a figure of power and the only one who 'knows' the right answers. There's no discovery by the pupils."

Julian was thinking that something about this should have gone into Isabel's video. This is relevant to returning Chileans with children unless they can afford private schooling.

"I also think the level of domestic violence in families is greater now," continued Amanda, "than it was before 1973 because of the brutality and anxiety that came about in the society as well as the greater economic pressures. They were worst in the early years of the military government when poverty was dire and now on average the pressures are not so great but there is greater inequality and the poorer families have not shared in the growing economic successes. Making ends meet, with their generally large families, isn't easy. One of the aims of this family centre is to try to reduce the extent of the *machismo* and family conflict, both verbal and physical. We often find that young people have suffered a lot of violence at home themselves and have seen a lot of domestic violence. We try to teach the young people there is another way to resolve disputes and how to articulate their feelings."

As Julian returned to his flat he noticed afresh the graffiti on the hospital wall behind his flat: *el mercado libre es fascismo*. The politicians' words are empty, he thought, when opportunity is denied through lack of education, poor housing, low wages and poverty and when a government tries to change that, to redistribute the wealth, bring dignity and more equality, it's crushed by extreme cruelty, as in the coup d'état with the help of the CIA. The people here know it, they've suffered it and Julian felt angry and incensed yet again for them. The family centre visit had had quite an impact on him and he felt the need of writing another missive to Isabel.

Later in the week, he went to another community centre, this time at the very top of one of the hills, *Cerro San Roque*. The community workers there were project manager Santiago, and Joaquín, assistant manager, and they gave an impressive account of their purpose and values. They appeared to Julian to have really thought through what social work was about and they were clear on how individual personal development can be promoted and facilitated. It was not something that could be imposed or resulted from telling people what was best for them. Truly democratic relationships have to be modelled, with open accountability to the community they serve. This project continued its work with adolescents, children and families through the summer holidays.

"The families here are unlikely to get any summer holidays away from their homes, even those families where there are wage earners, so we are arranging day trips and short camping stays at beauty spots in the forest or at the beach for all who want to come," said Joaquín. "We don't have so much formal work with the parents in the holidays but the day trips and activities involve lots of work and we get the parents participating in organising the days out. This in turn facilitates their skill development and taking responsibility and of course, it means supporting them with their various personal problems at any time. We are building relationships that are valuable for when we do parenting classes in the term time, on handling behaviour and avoiding violent conflict."

"We get the adults and the teenagers involved in the producing and presenting of reports to headquarters too," said Santiago, "when we request funds and report back on our activities and this further develops their skills and abilities and their knowledge and confidence when they have to go to face officials. The main aim of our work here is with teenagers to reduce drug misuse and related crime. The YMCA gets government money for that work, so we have to be accountable for what we are achieving. We aim to give them hope and purpose and help them with educational and job opportunities. It especially isn't easy for those who've already been in prison and many of the young people of this community have been to prison."

"Look, you can see the prison at the top of that hill over there," said Joaquín as he pointed through the window. "It's a good view from here and a constant reminder to the ex-inmates. "We've been able to help some young people get summer holiday jobs, despite high unemployment being a characteristic of this community. This means the full group of young people won't be around for the summer but those that are, generally help us with the community centre activities and with the trips away. They are so good with the younger children and great at organising and we need to keep them busy. This is another reason we feel this work needs to continue through the summer holidays. If you would like to join us in these activities whenever you can, you'll be very welcome."

Julian felt that definitely, this was the project for him to be involved with in the coming year, starting without delay. "I'll come whenever I can. Give me the timetable of the outings planned and the camps. I would love to join you in all I can." He was thinking it would be something worthwhile to do whilst Isabel was away in the north. He was appreciative of being able to see coastal and forested areas he otherwise would not have known but most of all he liked the companionship, the campfire gatherings, the sharing of food and its preparation, the mutual caring and the laughter. He also had the young people to thank for the growth of his knowledge of 'Chileanisms.' They took it on themselves to give him lessons in Chilean slang and expressions unique to Chile. They were able to talk to each other entirely in *Chilenismos* if they chose to and Spanish speakers from other countries would struggle to know what they were saying.

Julian enjoyed the interesting debates with these young people. He listened to the stories of the ex-inmates and the subculture of prison life - the world hidden from the warders. He tried to imagine their experiences and was fascinated greatly by their tales. He also loved the days out with the families and he would be able to join the family work with the children with behavioural difficulties in school when the term started again. It was good to get to know some of these children and parents on a social basis first. He liked the generosity of spirit and warmth, so typical of Chileans and this was shown too by even the so-called "toughest" of the adolescents.

-oOo-

One day that he found he had free, Julian decided to go to the famous book fair held every summer in a park in Viña del Mar. Writers were present signing books newly published and Julian looked for a novel by a Chilean author that he thought he would enjoy with lots of modern-day conversation that would be useful practice for him. He talked to one or two writers and booksellers and finally decided on *Patagonia Express* by Luis Sepúlveda. Then he came across a book he really had to buy by Franyo Zapata entitled *Myth and Realities of the Private System of Pension Funds*. Not the ideal subject Julian wanted to get his head around but his M.P. in London had asked him to look at the Chilean Pension Scheme that was being held up as a model to the world and advise him. Julian knew his M.P. quite well as he always got involved in campaigning in elections when they came around. Britain had just had an important general election bringing a complete change of government immediately before he'd set off for Chile in 1997. He found it hard to believe a pension scheme set up by a military dictatorship was likely to have much of a model worth demonstrating but as New Labour was interested in seeking new ways of getting private money into social schemes to reduce the demands on the public purse, they apparently wanted to consider this new model blueprint in Chile. Julian's M.P. was sceptical and he had never supported Tony Blair's leadership of their party. However, hopefully, important improvements were going to come about in Britain and Julian thought he could perhaps help from afar if there were lessons to be learned from the Chilean pension scheme.

Clearly, Zapata's book was a highly researched and a very recent document that had brought together far more information than Julian could ever have hoped to assemble on the *Administradoras de Fondos de Pensiones - AFP*. Julian discovered page after page of evidence of the massive exploitation of workers that had taken place and he read with more and more astonished incredulity. He was going to have to write a very strong warning that the Labour Party in Britain should not go anywhere near such a deception and "gigantic enrichment of the few that has ever been recorded in [Chile's] history," as the author concluded. The private pension scheme was not an option for anyone coming newly on to any payroll in Chile, it was a legal obligation to pay into it 10% of their wages or salaries. With no free press, no parliament, no political parties, and no trade unions, the regime was able to foist this major deceit on the public and the military government saved itself from an economic crisis in the initial year of 1980-81 by putting 350 million US dollars of workers pension contributions into the capital market. It also was used by the regime as a key mechanism to pursue the privatisation of banks and publicly held companies.

Investment in successful stock exchange companies is always risky because of volatility and the profitability of the scheme's investment in the private market was good in the early years but by the end of 1997, had become negative. When Julian went into the English Department Staff Room at the Catholic University around this time, he found them all having a heated discussion on their pensions. They had all received letters informing them of the values of their pension funds had fallen and that their pensions would be reduced from the previously anticipated level. They were furious, as they had gradually become aware of the deception that had been sold to them. Those that had had the choice initially of joining the new AFP were all regretting their decision to do so. It had, of course, been presented as highly desirable for its likely payouts and a "model for the world" which they now could see was just propaganda. The reality had been a gigantic enrichment of a number of AFP companies and the law never defined what those companies had to pay out.

Julian joined in the discussion with the English teachers, saying that removing the contributions that employers had to pay was a theft from the workers' salaries. They all agreed that was another aspect of the deception of the scheme. He recommended Zapata's book and quoted that three hundred million US dollars had not been paid in by employers but retained by them and not declared. The law has no sanctions, no fines, no investigative measures and cited that the system "increases and deepens the existing inequality." Incensed, Julian typed a five-page paper for his MP back home. Now he understood why Isabel had included the AFP in the injustices that must be changed.

Julian appreciated Isabel had good reason for her political activism but he was warned about the risks when the community workers at San Roque were discussing the protest planned for the day Pinochet was to enter the Senate. Julian was determined, however, that he would be joining them at the demo. Isabel and I should be demonstrating together. When is she going to reply to my emails? When am I going to see her? Perhaps she's involved with someone else. The nagging doubts returned to Julian again and again. *She's an attractive woman. Someone is bound to have approached her in all this time. I only want a straight and honest answer from her. If she was at all concerned about me, surely she would write more often, even if she is travelling around the north. But then I don't know how extensive is access to the internet in those northern cities. But I've had this experience before - waiting and waiting. Why don't I learn? Why do I keep hoping when there is so little hope? I came to Chile to resolve a deep emotional need - to resolve a life-changing encounter that had to be concluded with the experience of visiting the country that I had ached to see for so long. The political situation here fascinated me, the music of the exiled groups thrilled me, and the warmth and generosity of spirit of the people here have impressed me, but really I know I came to try to finish with this burning desire to not let go of this one Chilean or to find the truth of it all being over. I just need to know for sure.*

-oOo-

A visit to Pablo Neruda's house in Valparaíso was something else Julian felt he had to fit in during those weeks of waiting. He decided one morning he would visit *La Sebastiana*, the name that Neruda had given his house in this city. He caught the bus just around the corner from the front of the Parliament building, and it wound along the Avenida Alemania as it curved horizontally around the hills and valleys of the city a short way above the plane of the city centre. The views out across the bay between the buildings were magnificent and so of course was the panorama from Neruda's house when the bus arrived there.

Pablo Neruda apparently liked to be in Valparaíso to watch the firework display in the port on New Year's eve, which had long been a famous tradition. But also he had said he wanted somewhere quiet to work. He'd been looking for a house in 1959 in Valparaíso, to get out of Santiago. He asked a sculptor friend to search for him, saying he wanted somewhere not too big and not too small, not too high up and not too low down, where he couldn't see the neighbours but where he would be close to transport and commerce and a house that was cheap. Not an easy brief but a friend of his, Sara Vial and her friend Marie Martner, found a house they thought was in a suitable location but as it had been empty for ten years, it needed much work. Julian read on his visit that Neruda had found it too big but in the end, because the location was so perfect, he took the top two floors and Marie Martner and her husband Dr. Francisco Velasco bought the bottom two floors. Neruda later joked that he had "bought just stairs and terraces." He had the views though and he made a lot of changes to the structure. He turned the largest terrace into a dining room and added large, circular, shiplike windows when he had the terrace enclosed. Above the two floors was a tower to which he delighted in taking guests, as the whole of Valparaíso could be seen from its windows allowing 360-degree views. Julian also read an extraordinary story on his visit. After Neruda's death just after the military coup d'état, when Dr Velasco returned to the house, he found the neighbours anxious to talk to him about the noises they had heard coming from the house when it was supposed to be empty. They thought something very strange had been going on. When he went in, Dr Velasco found an eagle in the living room. He opened the window and let the eagle go but he recalled that Neruda had said to him that if there were another life, he would want to be an eagle. The doctor could find no way that the eagle could have got in as every opening was locked.

In the garden, Julian enjoyed contemplating these matters and sitting and staring where the great poet must have sat and stared. It had taken Neruda nearly three years to design and restore the building and it was clear that careful thought and taste had gone into it. Julian loved the window seats and the natural wood touches and he tried not to think about the place being looted after the coup d'état so that many of the ornaments and paintings couldn't have been those the poet had actually placed there himself. In the garden, there was a seat with a metal silhouette cutout of Pablo Neruda's famous profile at one end of the curving bench. So, thought Julian, we are invited to sit in the empty seat facing the poet as if conversing with him. Julian sat there at length and contemplated Neruda's poem about the north of Chile *Saludo al Norte - Salute to the North*. He knew he had another reason for thinking about the north, but he had written an essay on this poem and it was good to reflect on it on the bench in Neruda's garden. He remembered that Neruda is asking the reader to look at the world anew through a number of artistic strategies. The first of these is to address Chile as if it were a person. He addresses the North in the intimate, second-person singular because of the interconnection of the whole country. He likens the fertile middle part of the country with the waist of a person, who carries the *copihue* - the national flower of Chile - in her hand. Neruda makes reference to the body politique and says she carries a crown of sweat on her head. Chile exists because the industrial north, the head, works so desperately hard. Not only is the whole country's economy interconnected but he refers to how all countries' economies are interdependent. In this way, we are all drawn into concern about the conditions of workers in the north of Chile. Again he uses the *tu* form and the implication is the hard-labouring industrial zones are close and intimate to the lives of all of us.

Neruda reminds us that our wealth is built on the labour of others so that *"food arrives at our table."* He talks of the disfigurement of the land in the north in the process of exploiting the minerals that leave the 'person' of Chile full of surgical scars. He speaks to us of *"our metal brother"* who is the strong, metal worker struggling to feed the country and refers to "enemy metals" which implies the cruel conditions of work like the conditions of war. Neruda refers to the massacre of the nitrate workers at Iquique, *"bajo la metralla"* which Isabel had first told Julian about when she introduced the *Cantata* to him. Neruda says his thundering voice of anger will be louder than an explosion of dynamite at Chuquicamata for the devastated eyes, the collapsed lungs and the injured children of the North. Neruda's manner is not to preach or close down thought, it is to ask us to look at history with new perceptions whilst at the same time his political commitment is evident. He avoids an authoritarian polemic but his castigation of the causes of injustice are there, whilst his language is always suggesting a surplus, outrunning what he is trying to convey and thus opening up more questions. He presents hope and experiences, views and solutions through the voices of the people he refers to, without a claim of authority for one, or sermonising. Julian thought how wonderful it must be to achieve that "but that's the greatness of the man in whose garden I am now sitting."

-oOo-

One morning at the end of February, Julian received an email that Isabel was in Santiago and that he could ring her mother's phone number to speak with her. However, she said she would be busy and out most days and so it proved she was not there when he rang. It was then 11.00 am and Julian decided rather than go home, he would take a *colectivo* to Viña and look for a piece of jewellery for Isabel at the artisan fair in the main high street. He knew he was jumping the gun but he couldn't resist. He thought the present would be a loving gesture she would appreciate. The temporary international fair might still be there in the Quinta Vergara also and he was sure that he'd be able to find a necklace of lapis lazuli, in one fair or the other. She loved this national, semi-precious stone of Chile for its intense blue. Isabel had explained to him that lapis was the bluestone used in the funeral mask of Tutankhamun, though that lapis of course came from Afghanistan. Chile is almost the only other producer in the world and Isabel would say that the Chilean lapis was the best for colour. Julian appreciated that lapis lazuli looks at its best with gold, yellow and blue are exquisite together. But at the fairs, he found several set with silver and he knew that would be much safer to wear around Chile nowadays because it would be less likely to be robbed. He also knew that Isabel did not like to wear expensive jewellery when working with people for whom it would be far beyond their means.

Isabel had also told him that the gold necklace he had given her in the past, had been stolen soon after her first return to Chile. Such crime had risen inevitably when poverty had overwhelmed the people, Julian understood. Isabel had described to him how she was talking with some friends in the street and in broad daylight, she had suddenly felt a slight breeze at her neck and then realised that her necklace was gone. She said she had hardly felt anything, the theft was so swiftly and professionally carried out. Julian did not want anything like that to happen again. He found a pendant of lapis and a strong silver chain that was long enough to tuck the pendant into clothes in a risky area and which hung elegantly, he thought. Very satisfied with his purchase he made his way to the *centro de llamadas* in the shopping Mall in Viña. It was 2 o'clock and he hoped she might be home for *almuerzo*.

Matilda answered the phone and Isabel was not at home. He was to try after seven in the evening. Julian came out of the Mall and into the bright sunshine, which slightly dazzled him. A guitarist was playing and singing across the road, songs that he recognised from the *New Chilean Song Movement*. He stood for a while just to listen and to compose his feelings but the songs made him feel even more emotional about being one step closer to seeing Isabel, about the beauty of lapis lazuli, about being in *el ultimo rincón del mundo* as the people call their country, how lovely so many people were and how glad he was to be there.

Julian thought he should travel to Santiago very soon but he knew it would be best to coordinate with Isabel and fit into her plans. He had seen on the news that from the last day of February the Communist Party was staging a permanent demonstration in Santiago against Pinochet entering the Senate. It couldn't be only that party that was demonstrating. He knew other parties had been staging weekend demonstrations for many weeks against the dictator and calling for further protest. Isabel must be participating in some of these. There had been months of controversy about it in the newspapers, a debate about the constitutionality of it, complaints about the international shame of it, bishops divided over it, demonstrations in parliament about it and calls by even moderate parties like the Christian Democrats for a massive protest against it. Julian had kept a pile of newspaper cuttings since the previous November of the outcry against Pinochet becoming a lifelong senator. Demonstrations against the dictator in the Congress chamber were met with rapid eviction by the police but middle-class women in the parliamentary chamber holding Pinochet's photo in support of him were permitted to continue their cheering, it appeared.

Another incongruity was that the head of the secret police, the DINA was in prison for crimes committed during the dictatorship whilst the dictator himself was entering the Senate. The retired General Manuel Contreras was pointing out in his defence, very directly, that the real head of the DINA was General Pinochet. What an irony. The accession to the Senate could not finally be declared unconstitutional, despite all the debate, but what a pseudo-democracy it was for sure. The parties of the *Concertación* government had announced they were seeking support amongst parliamentarians for a constitutional reform to eliminate the institution of life senators. That had begun as early as the previous September and they had eventually won a majority in Congress. When the Upper House rejected this as expected, the government called for a plebiscite for citizens to decide on constitutional reforms where Congress and Senate differed. Even the Chilean justice system had admitted a legal procedure in February for a complaint of genocide against General Pinochet. The European Parliament by a large vote (another irony Julian thought, from a powerless institution) had condemned the arrival in the Senate of the Commander in Chief of the Chilean Army. Nothing had come of all these measures so far.

When he rang Isabel's mother's house in the evening, Julian still could not speak with her. She was not home. He went to the call centre to write to her and would try phoning again later. Still no luck. In his email, he had tried to pin down a time he would hope he could talk with her the next day. Had Isabel joined the permanent demo or another like it? That would mean sleeping out at night and Julian shuddered to think of it. That would invite the police to see who was there and it wouldn't be wise for Isabel to do that. He couldn't believe Isabel would join a 24-hour demo, so where would he find her? He contemplated going to Santiago to see but he wondered what time it would take to find her. His frustration with the waiting again was becoming intense. He decided he would not stay away from Santiago on Sunday 8th March, when he found that *Illapu* would be performing at a protest in the park and he invited Joaquín and a couple of young people from San Roque to go with him and hurried to get bus seats for them all. Sadly, amongst the thousands present, he never saw Isabel, unsurprisingly. The day prior to that there had been a women's march but with thousands expected at that, he doubted he would find her there and he had not attempted to attend. He would have to keep phoning and looking for emails but was without luck for several days. Finally, he had an email apologising for her being so busy and not able to read her emails every day. She told him not to worry and that she would see him very soon, but that was all.

The night before the day Pinochet was to enter the Senate, Julian was on the march from *Plaza Italia* to the Congress for the lighting of candles in the tradition of a wake or vigil in front of the Parliament building. Such protests and *cacerolazos* were taking place throughout the country. The centre of Valparaíso was quiet and subdued for the candle-lit remembrance of those who had died under the military regime. In the distance, in the communities of the hills, including San Roque, the banging of pots and pans was heard resounding their clear message of protest.

With his friends from the San Roque, Julian lit his candle outside the Parliament building. He thought his candle should stand for Isabel's father and a tear came into his eyes as he tried to think of the impact that loss had

had on Isabel. Suddenly there was a *"hola"* in his ear. He turned his head and it was Isabel. He flung his arms around her, hugging her for as long as he could and as best he could with the heavy rucksack she had on her back. She did return the hug and they kissed. She assured him she was going to go to his address that evening if they had not met up but she hoped they would meet. Julian insisted on taking the rucksack and they resumed the silence expected for the vigil but their eyes kept meeting and they placed their candles on the steps of the Parliament together. When the crowd began to disperse, Julian introduced her to his friends and as soon as he could he took Isabel's hand and lead her away and up to his flat. There seemed so much to need to say and so much news to share and yet all seemed unimportant compared with the sense of her presence and he wanted just to keep on kissing and hugging and touching her. Julian got as far as putting out wine glasses and spoke of cheese, when the hugging and holding lead them to be pulling off one another's clothes and hurrying to the bedroom in an embrace.

Julian brought the cheese and bread later and the wine as they sat up in bed and shared their news. It seemed like old times. Soon he was giving her the lapis lazuli which she seemed delighted with and she put on immediately with no other clothing and they both laughed. They talked till late into the night.

"I've dreamed of this for so long," said Julian "not just since I've been in Chile but for all this time I have known you, I hoped one day we would be together in Chile, especially all that time when you couldn't even travel here. Was it your dream too?"

"I'm sorry I didn't quite picture Chile with you. You are not part of this reality, but yes I am glad you are here and we are together here. For a while at least, this reality can include you. Thank you for coming to look for me."

"How could I do anything else? But what do you mean 'for a while'? I want you to be honest with me. You don't want this to be my reality longer term? Why did you not keep in touch? It hurt so much but I would not believe you wanted to end it all without telling me straight."

"I'm sorry. I don't know what happened. I got more and more involved in things here and I'm sorry I just couldn't see myself going back to England. Then I didn't think it fair to restart things with you if I was not prepared to return to England and I wasn't ready to go back with all there is to do here.

This is my reality and where I need to do things politically for a while at least. You know what Juan had proposed I do and I felt it was so worthwhile and the people were so enthusiastic, that I just couldn't see myself walking away from that commitment. So I didn't know what to say to you and the more I put it off the harder it became to say anything. I felt I had to go on with the promotion of direct action, even when I had run out of money and then I thought it would be a good idea to get a paid teaching job to keep me going. By that time I had to keep a low profile, in Iquique, especially where I was arrested and where I was getting known, but I knew I had to go on visiting the groups in the northern towns and try to keep them encouraged and committed."

"Carlos told me you had been arrested and I need to hear about that from you. Can I be part of this reality with you now?"

"Yes of course. It's great you are here. I only meant that you are going to want to return. You have a job and family to go back to. You can't be here forever."

"Can't we compromise on that? Let's think about it and see if there is a way around it."

"I think things have got to change here soon and then I won't be needed here so much. There are so many aspects of the political and economic spheres that are simply not sustainable. The people are losing their fear and with Pinochet entering the Senate and with so much opposition to that, it has got to bring things to a head."

"*¡Ojalá!* I hope what you say is true. How lovely it is to lie with my arms about you again. We've got to get up in good time in the morning for the demo outside parliament again. Let's get some sleep." Sleep evaded him, however, for a while. He knew he was thrilled to be with her again but how could the realities of two lands so far apart become one?

-oOo-

A good crowd of people had gathered the next morning when they arrived and more and more were gathering rapidly. Soon the demonstrators filled the steps up to the parliament building as well as the wide pavement below and they were flowing out into the road. Cars had been diverted and the street closed in anticipation of this. Julian was scanning the crowd constantly but holding Isabel's hand tight so as not to lose her. He saw his friends climbing up the few steps to the parliament entrance and suggested to Isabel that they join them on the steps for a better view. Joaquín and several young people from San Roque were there and greeted Isabel warmly. They pitched their banner "No dictator in the Senate" and Isabel handed around the individual posters she had brought. The crowd was brimming with banners and occasionally chants would start up in different parts. *"Asesino"* was shouted repeatedly and there they all waited. Someone, probably an opposition member of parliament, draped a huge lone banner out of a window of the parliament building about halfway up. It read *"NO! Nunca Más."* People milled around although it was getting difficult to move with the crowd swelling to thousands. Doing what was important - like demonstrating on this big issue - but doing it together with Isabel, Julian thought was perfect. He tried to get across to Isabel that his friends in San Roque would be useful contacts if she was going to do any further filming. Conversation, however, was now impossible over the noisy shouting and chanting.

Despite the noise, the demonstrators were peacefully standing and no one was causing any aggression. They awaited developments. The students holding candles for the disappeared were not permitted, as they had planned, to line the way to the back entrance to parliament, through which the dictator was escorted, and they were shouting their annoyance. Metal barriers had been brought in to pin them behind and away from that entrance. It was learned later that inside the building, opposition congressmen and women had held placards of enlarged photographs of disappeared persons inside the reception hall with the demand "Where are they?" and "Justice" as Pinochet entered. He was in a navy suit and was surrounded by his right-wing supporting senators. The ex-dictator, who in the Senate would have to listen to other points of view and respect other members instead of gruffly giving orders to all around him, put on a grim face and shook his head in exasperation. Members had been warned that protest would not be tolerated but some M.Ps broke into song with the National Anthem. They angrily gestured towards Pinochet when they came to the lines: "Chile, tomb of the free or refuge against oppression." One member shouted *"Asesino"* and was promptly removed.

Outside, suddenly a number of huge, ugly, armour-plated lorries began to drive around the corner from Avenida Argentina into Pedro Montt to the front of the Parliament where the protestors were gathered. Very soon the water cannons and the tear gas started. Julian grabbed Isabel's hand - determined he wasn't going to lose her in the rush and also concerned to protect her as he knew she had to be especially careful not to get arrested. The crowd spread in all directions and Julian rushed with Isabel across Pedro Montt and around the first corner. There they stopped with one or two other demonstrators in a shop doorway. By then Isabel was suffering quite a lot from the tear gas. Julian had contact lenses and was surprised at what great protection they were. However, his nose and throat were badly stinging and he was annoyed at the nasty, knife-like feeling, but he was glad that at least he could see. Then an army vehicle started to make its way along the street towards them, from the opposite end. They decided to cross Pedro Montt again further up and get into the plaza, where there were trees and bushes and where they hoped the military vehicles couldn't or wouldn't pass. By then, along the main road, a few protesters began to throw rocks and riot police with shields attempted to push them back. Julian and Isabel met up with a group of people discussing the events. Some complained that the whole of the city should have been out in protest and that there were relatively only a few. Others said how fearful people still are. Some were hoping the crowd would regroup and return to the parliament steps. Isabel felt she shouldn't do this. It was a bit too much like giving herself over to them. She and Julian decided to get further away by crossing a couple of streets that ran at the back of the parliament compound and, going a long way round, they could get back to Avenida Argentina and into a back street from there, where they could eventually climb the hill up Cerro Barón.

# Chapter 15

J ulian was so pleased to have Isabel in his flat again safely and this time she was looking closely at his furnishings and the decorations he had bought. She liked everything except the 'pink'. That was to be expected but she found it tolerable. Just in case, Julian had food in the flat and he started cooking. He had *reineta* which he knew she liked and he quickly made ratatouille and a salad. He defrosted some bread and warmed it as she always appreciated it warm and crisp. After eating they talked about the demonstration.

"They were bound to break it up that way. They always do and that's how they think they can silence any opposition. We have to just regroup and go in again and again."

"But that is bound to lead to your arrest. I'm so glad you didn't do that this time."

"There needs to be much bigger numbers. We have to be organised and with a clear plan to regroup and stay firm, again and again. I didn't want my week with you taken away this time. I wasn't going to let that happen. But when there are more of us…It needs a large-scale movement, a democracy movement which is going to demand en mass the freedoms we don't have now. I've got to keep working for that. To get the people to understand what they have to do. You do see why I am in Chile."

"Yes, but it can't be forever. There has to be a limit on how long you sacrifice your life in this way."

"I don't think of it as a sacrifice. It's a fulfilment. Honestly, I like the teaching at the school. Art is my subject after all and to try to enthuse children in appreciation of art and what the famous paintings have been about down the centuries, is very satisfying but I have decided that the political work has that extra dimension of fulfilment. It's teaching with a kick," she laughed.

Julian knelt down at the side of her and kissed her. He stroked her long dark curls of hair and hugged her as tightly as he could. "I know why I always loved you," he said between the kisses.

"Remember on holiday when we used to take a siesta," said Isabel and though not a normal Chilean habit, it seemed entirely appropriate on this occasion and they rushed hurriedly to the bed, rapidly helping the clothes off one another again. Late afternoon, sitting on the balcony and looking at the entire sweep of the bay and the sunset, Julian brought Chilean champagne mixed with chirimoyas and ice cream in tall glasses and they drank. He then ventured to ask if she would come to live with him there.

"Julio, for a week, yes, but..." Julian knew there would be a 'but.' "I have a commitment in La Serena and I can't let them down. I've promised them another academic year at the school and I have really enjoyed the teaching. But that will be the last year." She continued, "I've been to see my mother and my brother and I've seen Juan. I have this whole week free to be with you and then I am due back at school. But look, I don't have classes on Fridays next year, so I can get the overnight bus on a Thursday evening from La Serena sometimes and be with you for a long weekend."

"Can I come to you the other weekends?" he asked hurriedly, so the whole prospect wouldn't sound quite so bad. She gave a warm smile. I will have to continue my regular visits to the northern towns in the coming year. I'm just not going to be free every weekend to come to you. You do understand that, don't you?"

"I know how important it all is. But could you not do the same work here in Valparaíso or even in Santiago? We could see each other more and I could help you."

"Well, others of our organisation are coving these areas and I've built a lot of groups in the northern towns and now I want to maintain them and strengthen them. I can't abandon them. I must see them develop further and grow. That is my task with them and others are doing that here."

-oOo-

The days seemed to be racing by but Julian was very contented and he thought Isabel seemed so too. He felt he was falling in love with her all over again. To caress her and hold her body again to his, made him ache intensely that those moments would never end, just as he had felt so often in the past. All reasoning and his need to know why she had disappeared from his life, his desire to know what she really was thinking and how much she actually valued the relationship, dissolved away as it always did when he held her again.

They explored parts of Valparaíso he did not know, travelled in many different funicular railways, and walked the stairs and paths of different hills including Cerro Alegre, famous for its street art. They listened to violins being played from apartment windows near the Music Institute and they went to see the coloured houses of Cerro Concepción. They walked various *paseos* with their sea views, explored the authentic streets of Playa Ancha, visited the Barburizza Palace, now an art gallery and lunched on fresh shellfish in *La Caleta,* the fishing port. Isabel accompanied Julian on his first day at the university too. They went for interest to see what the Professor who headed the Faculty of Literature and the Science of Languages had to say when welcoming the new students. The day began with coffee and breakfast in the student dining room with all the students of this faculty and all the teachers. The Professor spoke of "us", the students and staff, as not living in *una Torre de Marfil,* especially in the coming period that he anticipated would be difficult politically. However, he asked the students to avoid violence and damage to the property of the University and not to throw the seats out of the windows, because the university has to pay for these and he stressed, "it's your money and your property." Isabel and Julian smiled at each other. The Professor then made a general invitation to the students to feel free to consult their teachers and that they were there to help.

They were then asked to make their way to the theatre where one of the literature lecturers made a presentation on the significance of *la palabra* this being the faculty of several modern languages and Latin and Greek, as well as the Faculty of Literature and Philosophy. The presenters used stories of Benedetti, Cervantes and others and illustrated clear and direct "words" of political commitment or of love, as in Benedetti's case. Isabel related to Benedetti especially as he had been many years in exile from a military government in his native Uruguay. Isabel liked his word "dis-exile" and the presentation used exerts from his only novel published in exile *'Springtime in a Broken Mirror.'* The principal protagonist goes into exile after five years in prison and joins his family, already in exile. "I am the same person but another person too," he has to recognise, as are all the characters of his family also changed. They all find themselves isolated from each other and unable to communicate. His spring, after his winter of prison, has a broken corner like the cracked mirror, but still, it has some use, though it is not all that the spring should be. The couple thought the presentation was powerful and very well done.

In the literature department, Julian made a note of his timetable for the classes he was attending and then did the same in the social work department. He didn't have any classes on a Monday, so that would enable him, he said to return from a weekend in La Serena on the Monday night bus, so he could have long weekends with Isabel.

"I'm going to have classes on a Monday and you are going to be busy with essay writing and your voluntary work. You have to take care of yourself. I am going to be visiting the cities in the north, like last year, so I will be very busy too. We'll see how it goes." she added.

Whilst in Valparaíso, Isabel wanted to visit the mother of a friend of hers in exile in Sheffield. Julian had met this friend Diego several times when he came to London and when they went to the Chilean reunions in the Peak District. The Sheffield City Council had made the largest number of council houses of any council, available to refugees when many Chileans sought asylum in the UK after the coup. Julian used to enjoy their visits to the Chilean gatherings in the Peak District and he readily agreed it would be good to visit Diego's mother, who lived alone in Playa Ancha. Emilia gave them a warm welcome and was delighted to see them. They came around to discussing the psychological shock for people in the early days of the coup d'état. Emilia talked of how Diago was working in Santiago on the day of the coup and another son was working on a ship in the far south and she was so fearful, not knowing where they were.

"We couldn't go out of our houses, there were soldiers in every street and almost the only sound was the noise of machine guns." How vividly Emilia recalled this nightmare and Julian couldn't imagine the process of adjustment, the anger at the injustice and the anxiety she must have felt. Diego was arrested and she asked Julian to imagine living two years not knowing if they are going to kill your own son. "Imagine the effect on your body, twisted up with this fear and your head full of worry." It clearly brought very painful memories for Isabel too and he realised she had never told him in this sort of detail what happened to her and her family when they had not known where her father was. Julian felt the visit brought him closer to understanding the experience of the *golpe militar* on individuals and on Isabel in particular.

Emilia was a very strong woman with much courage and determination. When her eight children had all grown up she began to study to qualify as a nurse and she began to work in a medical centre of the Red Cross in a poor *población* that was suffering from scarcities as well as the great fear that the dictatorship provoked. Just to speak of the coup showed Emilia's courage because the majority of people don't want to remember, thought Julian and he had never heard anyone speak so graphically and express their feelings so fully. They agreed that the common custom of keeping these feelings to yourself becomes a forced habit under a dictatorship and that it is now part of a cover-up. The authorities want to keep the lid on dangerous emotions or they might burst forth with consequences threatening to the establishment. Isabel said this was very much what she was trying to get across to people. In seeking change they needed to express their injuries in a constructive way.

"It makes me think of the death of Martin Luther King," said Isabel. There were angry reactions that were dangerous and destructive but because of the massive outcry, there were some changes, like black children going to white schools en mass and winning scholarships to white colleges. Not enough was achieved but something was gained."

"Yes, but the inequality has got worse since then in the US and in the UK and in Chile. The result of neoliberalism and the Chicago Boys," responded Julian.

"All the more reason to blow the lid off, but constructively," she replied.

"That's what I have to try to do here in Chile," Isabel told him on the way back to Julian's flat. She asked if he understood why she had to stay and try to do some more in the coming year, continuing with what she had started. He tried to look understanding. "I have to keep alive the action we've done and planned for the coming year. I need to build on the history and political awareness classes and plan further political activism with them. We have to keep on demanding a new constitution, changes to the education system and pensions, etc. I hope we are going to move on to greater acts of civil disobedience or these things will not come about. That's why I'll have to travel to the north some weekends and won't always be able to see you. It is also why I want to be in La Serena to be halfway to those places but at a safe distance." Julian remembered something he had thought of when Emilia was talking, by Octavio Paz.

*"The injuries are in the blood."* he quoted.

"But you have to go further than just accepting this, you have to take action to heal the injuries," she replied.

"You are taking big risks in this society if you get into acts of civil disobedience. You will be arrested and the consequences of that will be far worse here, I imagine than in England."

"Don't worry. I know how to be very careful."

-oOo-

With the relationship feeling tentative again and fearful of what might happen to Isabel, Julian tried to be accepting of what Isabel had explained. He was deeply moved by their week together and was head over heels smitten again. He returned to his commitments and the opportunities he had created in Valparaíso, with a degree of relish, he said to himself, as interesting times are coming up. The first of these was that Julian had the opportunity to visit the parliament building. He was taken by his student of English, Alvaro, and Julian really appreciated going into this architecturally impressive building with someone who knew many of the procedures and the significance of the decorative symbols and the Constitution. Firstly they entered an enormous chamber that had been constructed for both the senators and the deputies to assemble together and to receive visitors of state. It was impressive and beautiful but for the majority of the time, this magnificent room remained without use. Julian thought that was symbolic in itself.

By contrast, the chamber of the Deputies and especially the chamber of the Senators were quite small but clearly comfortable for debate and obviously adequate for the current number of members involved. Both chambers were dominated by a large wall of copper. In the Deputies chamber, the wall of copper is green, the natural colour of copper as it is found in the ground and in the Senators' chamber the wall of copper is a glistening brown, the colour of manufactured copper and its shine had the effect of illuminating and animating the chamber in a way that was not realised in the larger lower house, beautiful though the natural green copper was. For each law or constitutional change to be sufficiently worked upon before the approval of the Senate was possible, was the obvious symbol that could never be lost on the onlooker. Furthermore, it was like a pictorial representation of the binomial system of seats in the Senate that the military regime had integrated into their 1980 constitution. This ensured that it would be almost impossible to get radical change passed by the Senate, including any reform of the constitution. The Senate would always bring a careful, conservative moulding to legislation passed by the Deputies. It was there to work on, correct or reject, whatever comes forth from the Lower House and to "manufacture" it suitably into the shiny copper the establishment required.

Alvaro was able to explain that the constitution was a response to a particular interpretation of Chilean history between 1960 and 1973 held by the legal advisers to the dictator and the military. It was an institutional framework of limited democracy, designed to ensure presidential control of the legislative process and ensure "military tutelage and veto power over the decisions of the civilian authorities." They called it 'protected democracy.'

"That had other consequences, even after Pinochet was no longer the president," continued Alvaro. "One-third of the Senate is nominated and not elected so that the majority will always favour conservation of the present, rather than change. It is designed to keep rightwing dominance and this is reinforced by the binomial system of two senators coming from each region. The first is elected with 33% of the vote and the second can only come from the same party if, overall, that party and its two candidates together, have achieved 66% of the vote. This is difficult for any party ever to accomplish anywhere and it means that a right-wing candidate can take the second seat with far fewer votes than the second candidate of any winning party would need. This actually is what does happen," continued Alvaro getting even more agitated, "And, in addition, the Right and Pinochet have more support in rural areas than in urban districts so the Constitution writers gave the 20 rural, least populated areas 20 electoral districts and thus 40 deputies in the lower house whilst the seven most populated urban districts with the same total population as the 20 rural districts were given just 14 deputies. The whole constitution is rigged to assist the right-wing parties."

Shaking his head in despair, Julian replied that the electoral system in the UK, through the Boundaries Commission somewhat favours the right, "but here this is so blatantly gerrymandering, it's staggering."

"Yes and another key point," continued Alvaro with great emphasis, "this 'protected democracy' forbids the President of the Republic from removing the commanders-in-chief of the various branches of the Armed Forces - Article 93 of the constitution."

"So a democratically elected president," said Julian, "does not have control over the military, a basic aspect of political democracy!"

"Right. This non-removability of military commanders made sure that even if Pinochet should lose the 1988 plebiscite, which he never expected he would because he had total control of all political propaganda, but if he did lose," Alvaro went on, "All he had to do was to move his office across the road to the Ministry of Defence and continue to be Head of the Army, which is in fact exactly what Pinochet did do!" There he was part of the National Security Council, charged with maintaining "institutional order" to which the government's every move had to meet with the Council's approval. The next elected President Patricio Aylwin and his successor Eduardo Frei called for Pinochet's resignation several times but they were simply ignored. Aylwin said the constitution did not have "a road to full democracy" but he said he had compromised in favour of a gradual and peaceful 'transition'. However, he knew there was no endpoint of arriving at democracy with this constitution."

This is a deliberate failure to allow a return to full democracy, pondered Julian as the enormity of the situation began to dawn on him. No wonder there are calls for a new constitution! Alvaro also talked about the Constitutional Tribunal.

"This is charged with restricting the powers of the President and the lower house of Congress."

"So it cannot impartially decide on issues of the constitution or its change. I've read that some Deputies have attempted to get the Tribunal to declare that Pinochet could not be a life peer on the basis of having previously been president because he had not been an elected President, which the constitution requires. The Tribunal did not even uphold that requirement of the constitution."

"That's right. There are many contradictions in all of this," agreed Alvaro. "When Pinochet claimed that the "Armed Forces have reconstructed an authentic democracy" everyone knew it was a lie but it was enough for the outside world to largely believe it. They weren't going to look at the detail."

"It takes your breath away" Julian staggered. "This perpetuates to the outside world the lie that Chile is a democracy. It is a *seudodemocracia* even moderate politicians have called it that but, more importantly, this will surely be destabilising at some stage in the future."

"Precisely," said Alvaro, "it can't be accepted forever. There has to be a mass outcry. A constitution like that has to be changed, but its essence is to make it incredibly difficult to change." Julian shook his head, thinking now he fully understood why Isabel says a mass movement of civil disobedience is the only way forward.

"No wonder many aware people are calling for a new constitution. No wonder so many young people seem so entirely disillusioned and cynical. It's just impossible to believe that changes could be made through this Parliament. The system makes for cynicism."

"Absolutely," agreed Alvaro. "But will the people accept it forever? I think sooner or later there will have to be an uprising. You're right, it's very unstable but fear will keep the lid on for quite a long time."

"The booming economy and the growing consumerism will help them to get away with it further too, but eventually..." Julian suddenly felt very fearful for this little country of which he had become very fond. He feared more, even than he had done before, for Isabel and wondered what chance he had of getting her out of this country before the worst happened. Not much chance at all, he realised, because that will be exactly when she says she cannot desert the people and must stay to help bring about a new reality. That is what she's working for even now. His heart sank and he wondered why he had not been able to see the problem of the constitution so clearly before. Isabel had tried to explain but never with all the detail that Alvaro had given him. Julian also began to wonder if he himself could live in this country, long term.

-oOo-

Julian was attending classes in *The Sociology of Development* and was particularly impressed with a recent book by a leading Chilean intellectual, who was coming to a University in Viña del Mar very soon and the class had been invited to go to hear him. His name was Tomás Moulian and a key part of his argument in his book *Chile Actual - Anatomía de un mito - Chile Today - Anatomy of the Myth*, published a few months earlier, was perfectly illustrated by the current debate about the legitimacy of the ex-commander in chief of the Army going into the Senate. Moulian had written, before Pinochet declared he was entering the Upper House, that the ruling elite, "inspired by the tactic of appeasement and with fear still strong within the masses, the elite was acting with a strategy of 'whitewash,' presenting the transition from dictatorship to democracy as cleansed white and made pure for the common good and the necessity of Chile." He says that with "plastic surgery" the government of the Transition converts the dictator into a Patriarch, legitimated by new powers and his atrocities whitewashed and totally covered over.

In the weeks that followed the dictator's entry into the Senate, Julian noticed the newspapers continued to be constantly dominated by the arguments over its legality and the political parties themselves were preoccupied with the effects on their parties of what they called the "Pinochet factor." The Right was concerned that their parties had become, in the eyes of the electorate, *"pinochetistas"* and that their leader had now become the ex-dictator instead of their pretended candidate for the presidency, the mayor of Los Condes - an upper-class area of Santiago - Joaquín Lavín. The Centre and Left were concerned that their parties were divided into those who would sign the Constitutional Accusation and those who would not. The latter, who were not supporting their colleagues to act against Pinochet, seemed to want precisely the "whitewash" Moulian had predicted, so as to "move on" and "face the future" rather than the past, as their complicit President of the *Concertación* had asked them.

There was at last to be a vote in the Chilean Parliament on 9th April, the day after Julian had visited, on the constitutional accusation that the dictatorship had violated the constitution. There were 55 votes in favour of the accusation, one abstention and 62 votes against the accusation of violation of the constitution. From the outside, it looked like a foolish denial of the reality of the deaths, torture and imprisonment of thousands. Julian thought with scorn that it couldn't surely be credible that the so-called "democracy" could approve in this way the conduct of a particularly cruel dictator, who tore up the constitution and imposed his own and who had whitewashed the sins of any official or Army officer, none of whom could be held accountable for any action, however abusive. Was this the approval that the majority of the politicians felt it necessary to give to the dictatorship? Julian found it incredible and was glad to be able to get hold of Isabel on the telephone the next evening to talk with her about it.

"Of course, it does not represent the voting population," said Isabel. "The latest polls show the people 60% in support of the accusation of violation of the constitution and only 30% rejecting it."

"It's all exactly as Moulian said. This is legitimising the dictatorship through a whitewash. And, as if to make sure of the total whitening effect, the very next day after the vote is Good Friday, that is today. I have noted all day that there was almost no news on the television at all and certainly no commentaries or debates on the vote. At the normal times for news on all the channels, they were showing instead, the Easter passion story, courtesy of Hollywood or other foreign interpretation or a children's version of it. Thus there was little reporting and absolutely no discussion at all about the consequences of the vote in parliament. What perfect timing they had chosen to ensure the total *blanqueo*, the cleansing of the dictatorship."

"That is the technique, that is exactly how the news was handled in the dictatorship. They have not moved forward or democratised it at all."

"The whitewash, Moulian says, was necessary so that the people and those outside the country could recognise a mature capitalist democracy. Moulian also says the whitewash is like the iceberg that Chile took to the heat of a Seville summer for the Expo exhibition in 1992. You remember it was to show Chile's technological capacity and achievements, that Chile could preserve an iceberg dragged from the Antarctic, through the Equatorial region and maintain it frozen in the Andalucian heat for the Expo. Moulian called it a 'sculpture of our metamorphosis'."

"He's good Moulian. Can you get me a copy of his book? I could use that sort of stuff in my 'extracurricular' teaching," said Isabel laughing at her newly invented name for her direct action groups.

"Yes, you could, in your rebellion seminars, you mean. I know. I'm sorry you don't get any Easter holidays as you've only just started the school term, three weeks ago isn't it? You'll come next weekend won't you?"

"Yes I will, on the overnight bus on Thursday evening. I'll be at the bus station by 8.30 am."

"I'll be there to meet you. Lots of love."

Julian returned to his reading when he reached his flat again. He found again where Moulian had referred to the iceberg for the Expo. He read, 'it established before the eyes of the world, the transparency of Chile today, the footprints of blood and the torments were the white veins of the ice which demonstrate the New Chile. Chile has been made clean, sanitised, purified and the damage transformed into dry blood and the pain of those who wait for the disappeared, the exiles and the unemployed - all had been metabolised in the pure ice.' Julian thought that analogy illustrates that Chile today is based on the absence of truth. Chile can't be the democracy it pretends to be and the constitution makes it not possible to have the 'purification' from the years of terror that Moulian is calling for. Julian was making notes and writing ideas for an essay. He wrote 'there is no historic responsibility assumed by the Armed Forces nor the businesses that have benefitted exploitatively from the Pinochet capitalist revolution. With this constitution there never can be accountability for past atrocities, so they'll just believe they can go on getting away with it. But will the people tolerate it forever?' Powerful stuff, this Moulian, thought Julian and he looked forward to hearing the famous man that everyone was talking about.

-oOo-

Julian threw himself, not only into his classes at the university but into his voluntary work and Isabel continued to visit every fourth weekend or so. He had not yet visited her in La Serena, there was always some reason that made it impossible, according to Isabel. Each time they came together it seemed to Julian as exquisitely desirable and as enticing again as it had been when they were newly in love. When separated, between her visits, he rationalised in his mind all the unchallenged behaviours, that in the past had made him question the saneness of their alliance and its suitability. He alternated between wanting to face these doubts with her and rehearsing how he might approach them with the decision to just forgive and forget and offer unquestioning affection and sexual desire. In practice, he was anxious not to spoil those precious but brief few days together every month. He did enjoy as well the catching up they would do, talking of all they had been involved in since the last visit and the discussion of ideas, there never seemed to be time for analysing the past.

Julian was assisting in the parental classes for the children who had been excluded from normal school because of behavioural problems. He was able to contribute to the preparation and presentational form of these classes from his group work experience in England, with children in care whose placements in families had broken down, with his training of foster carers to handle difficult behaviour and from his experience of group work with parents at risk of having their children removed. The handling of damaged children's behaviour had become one of his special interests. He wondered how well he would be able himself to put the theory into practice. *It is one thing to know the most effective ways to handle bad behaviour. Actually doing it is another matter. If Isabel and I have left it too late for us to have children of our own, we might look at fostering or adoption of a child in care. Any older child will have to play out the damage and loss they have suffered, to a greater or lesser extent, depending on the degree of harm. Would we be able to manage that? It requires a great deal of insight and patience. Would Isabel consider such a life-changing commitment as taking on a child who, however difficult, must never suffer rejection again? We are a long way from being able to seriously contemplate that now. I had better apply myself to the present.*

Around the same time, a major theme of the Literature course he was attending, was concerning the level of violence in Latin America and how it is reflected in its literature. The professor who was taking this class had just written an article on this subject and for Julian, three points stood out: Spanish America had, since the conquest, had to deliver its "people's sweat and its natural resources" to cultures economically more developed; secondly, that violence envelops the South American man "from the past like original sin," as wrote Chilean author Ariel Dorfman; and thirdly that the violence appears to be a self-defence mechanism in a system where insecurity reigns. How then, the professor posed, could the Latin American man be asked to reject violence? Julian recalled some of the debates he had had with Isabel over the use of violence to overcome injustice. It was something she would never renounce because she ultimately saw it as the final solution, but what would that violence then lead to? There were no good examples from history, he argued. In contrast, that very week, news had came through of the violent killing of a bishop in Guatemala by death squads. The killers appeared to want to impede the peace process that the bishop had been engaged in. So concluded Rigoberta Manchú, a Guatemalan activist who had gained some international fame and Julian had been reading about her. The bishop was a pacifist, an ethical choice very few would subscribe to in Latin America. What happens to peaceful attempts at real change to overcome injustice? Chile's military coup was an example of how peaceful radical change is violently crushed. Is it inevitable?

An additional disillusionment began to penetrate Julian following the vote on the constitutional accusation, to which he kept returning in his mind. *The ethical cowardliness, the way the 'dead and the disappeared' of the dictatorship have been let down by the politicians yet again and the irrationality of all that seems to be going on around me, makes me feel at times deeply troubled by the weight of it all.* His lecturer in sociology had opened his class one day with the remark that there was no critique in the country today. Passive attitudes play in favour of the people in control and those in control are the friends of the dictator. They are the ones that have benefitted from the exploitation and the injustice and they continue to perpetuate it to benefit further. A giant enrichment of the few had occurred like never before, as Zapata had shown in his book, and the low wages after the years of the dictatorship were still the combustion for the exportation of natural products. The owners of the country were still taking advantage. Julian had read that the difference between the incomes of the rich and the poor had augmented 40 times during the few years of the so-called *Transition to Democracy* governments. How could the *Concertation* go on letting that happen? Added to that, Julian felt the weight of the harshness of life he could see around him, the cruelty of capitalism without a Welfare State to soften its worst effects. He thought it was something very ugly to see. "Never, never forget," he wanted to shout at people back home who could not understand the importance and civilising effect of the welfare state. A new generation in Britain had been dismantling the welfare state built by those who remembered the 1930s.

The Epistemology of Social Work lecturer reminded Julian's class that day, that Neitzsche said we have to learn to see, learn to think, learn to speak and learn to write. The students in the class confirmed their experiences in all of their own schools, that the presentation of what currently exists, is presented as a singular and absolute, unquestionable truth. They recognised now that this positivism demonstrated in the classroom is repression and intended to make the population not think and not question. Critical awareness has to be learned.

-oOo-

One of Julian's favourite singers, whom he had come to know through Isabel, was Patricio Manns and Julian noticed a few A4 size posters around Valparaíso advertising that he was to appear at *La Piedra Feliz,* a music and dance venue serving food, near the port. He thought it would be great to take Isabel when she visited and he talked with Joaquín to invite him to go with them and suggested others from the Community Centre might like to go too.

"You'll probably need to get tickets in advance. It will be very popular and it's not a big place," Joaquin advised. Julian offered to get tickets for them and he was told the only sure way was to go to the venue earlier in the week. "I don't know of any other place that would have tickets for that kind of "alternative" music. *La Piedra Feliz* is of course a commercial centre but it does give a room to artists of the *New Chilean Song Movement* from time to time. They still make enough money because it is usually very full and they have several rooms so two or three concerts are going on at the same time. You'll probably have to book a table but we can just have drinks and eat later somewhere else.

"Patricio Manns is more than a singer you know," continued Joaquín. "Apart from writing many of his own songs, and they are very poetic - he's probably the best quality songwriter - he is also a novelist and a non-fiction writer and a poet. He had a book of poetry come out two or three years ago inspired by the Zapatista uprisings in Chiapas in the south of Mexico. He wrote in poetry the history of the Mayas from the fifteenth century to today, recording the impact of the Conquest upon the Mayan people and the consequent injustices, which are still unresolved. He shows how current inequalities and discrimination leave the people no choice but to be obliged to struggle for social justice. Patricio Manns shows the roots of their struggle. It is an impressive *poemario*."

"I didn't know all this about him. Wow, I must look for this book. Do you know the title of this book of poems?"

"*Memorial de Bonampak,*" said Joaquín. "I'll lend you a copy. It's profound and moving. He even describes the Mayan architecture which is quite something in poetry! It has been compared with Neruda's *Canto General*."

The evening of the presentation was powerful for Julian and Isabel was thrilled with being present. *La Piedra Feliz* was packed and Julian was so glad he'd been told to get tickets in advance. He and his friends had a table close to the front and Julian felt excited to be in the thick of the enthusiastic atmosphere created by Patricio. Clearly, the audience really valued this man and all he had achieved. The applause was tumultuous. His voice was rich and deep and his songs and music gentle and beautiful. The friends all ordered *Pisco sours* - a very Chilean drink made from distilling fermented Moscatel grape juice, combined together with lemon juice, egg white, ice and cinnamon.

"I'm so happy to share the real Chile with you," said Julian to Isabel, in the interval.

"Yes, this is a rich cultural heritage and all the striving for justice it represents is the good side of Chile and just what I have always wanted to share with you." Julian squeezed her hand and looked lovingly into her eyes. He wanted to say how he hoped that being together would be extended soon and he didn't like all these separations. He determined he would try to talk with her that weekend about the longer-term future. After the performance, the friends invited Julian and Isabel to go to one of the cafés open in the port for the workers who work late into the night and early morning, including fishermen returning from their fishing trips. The café served a very large plate of fried food for all of their group to share.

Julian also wanted to discuss with Isabel an essay he had to write about Chile's identity and he hoped it might be a way of leading into a discussion of their personal future as well. He recognised he had to go very carefully or he risked an argument developing and after an enjoyable lazy morning, most of which they had passed in bed, and the joy of all the weekend, he didn't want to spoil the atmosphere. He doubted very much that Isabel was likely to agree to return with him to the UK at the end of the current academic year, in a few months' time. Yet Julian knew he was becoming more impatient with living in Chile because of many of the thoughts on his mind recently, especially the pseudo-democracy and the likelihood of an uprising. What about those for whom there was no escape? He knew that would be Isabel's first thought. But it didn't apply to either of them. They did have an escape.

Julian was preparing an essay on Chile's sense of identity, its meaning and expression, which the Literature professor had asked the class to write. He had thought long and hard about this issue. He saw history and historical buildings as a very important part of the identity of European countries. He loved to feel all around him the architectural history of cities like Salamanca, Cordoba, Oxford and Bath. Could identity be, in part at least, the feeling of being surrounded by history and its connection to its current residents? Is that more obvious in Europe where people are more able to live amongst their history? There were of course a few centuries of history reflected in the architecture of Santiago and Valparaiso. But pre-Colombian architecture has been so much destroyed by conquest or earthquake and what was left was very remote from where the people now live, like Machu Picchu in Peru and the Inca remains within Chile.

"I'm sure identity is more than history but do you think this physical remoteness from historic representations contributes to a feeling of a lack of identity for a country?"

"You think Chile suffers from a lack of identity?"

"Well, I think there is a searching for an identity and an insecurity about what it consists of. People love their country but there is a lack of critique that is holding back the change you are working for. I think it is also why people turn to extreme excitement over football matches. I've seen them when the whole town seems to go mad. But if there is an absence of certainty about who they are, the people are likely to turn to false values like football and also flag-waving and militarism."

"Yes, I agree with that," said Isabel. "But history is more than architectural remains. When whole cultures have been repressed and are still discriminated against, like the Mapuches, the essence of a historic identity is missing. The imported music and films which are so popular here and the lack of many cultural programmes on the TV, add to this absence, I guess."

"There are rare excellent exceptions, like a few Chilean-made films or concerts by Chilean music groups or orchestras or dance companies. In contrast, the constant TV diet of North American police or horror films and Mexican soaps, I find really upsetting. When a country's sense of its own distinctiveness and background is fragile and it lacks confidence in itself, it can't develop the cultural identity it should have. I can see that. The Andean and Mapuche cultures have been pushed to the margin by invasion and conquest but if Chile could recover them and value them, it could restore a sense of Chile having roots and heal the subconscious feeling of insecurity, that comes from having been torn away from everything that went before."

"Wouldn't it be wonderful if these minority races and tongues became integrated into modern life, not as tourist spectacles but as history and culture that makes one country distinct from another nation?" Isabel said.

"Exactly. Colonialism has caused an economic dependency which is maintained to this day. Primary goods are sent still to the ex-colonial powers and manufactured goods come back in return at a high cost. Colonialism causes as well a seeking for a missing identity because it has destroyed the indigenous roots. Imitating North American popular culture will not satisfy this need for a native culture."

"Yes. That's why what Violeta Parra started is so important. The Andean instruments used by the folkloric groups in their music have had an important role in connecting the people to their roots and the music has contributed to a Chilean culture."

"I guess confidence comes from building on a country's own history, its own culture and its own science, although lots of international collaboration is needed for that nowadays. They all are about creativeness and all can then build further on the past achievements and produce more achievements."

291

They sat quietly for a few moments and then Julian said, "Pablo Neruda in *Las Alturas de Machu Picchu* likened the history of South America to the struggle of an enslaved people creating the architecture of Machu Picchu. He wants their voice never to be forgotten and calls on today's labourers to be born again with him to build a new future, likening that future to the 360-degree stunning vision possible at the summit of the mountain. Inspiring, no?"

"He's about building a new identity," said Isabel and Julian nodded. Julian was thinking about how well they can develop ideas together when they discuss something like this. It had happened before, he remembered, in England.

After a pause in the conversation, Julian decided to test the water. "I was walking out of the class with the *profe* the other day and he made two interesting comments. He said the situation in Chile is becoming very dangerous and the conflict between the classes is very apparent. He called the conflict strong and ready to explode and he added 'Marx was right.' He also said that the phenomenon of forced entry into private houses for theft, is a new phenomenon in Chile, and it is a symbol of the growing conflict."

"Well, that's what you get if you increase the gap between the rich and the poor so much. They've only themselves to blame," responded Isabel.

"You will be careful won't you every day, if this is true things are getting more dangerous or conflictive here. I hope you will return to the UK with me next February. You won't sign up for another year at the school, will you? I want to be with you and I want you to be safe." Isabel only looked pensive and gave a weak smile. Ignoring this theme she returned to the former.

"I'm glad the middle classes are getting rattled. If they don't want to pay reasonable taxes and the wealth is not distributed fairly, they'll reap the consequences." She walked out onto the balcony, seemingly ignoring his first point, but she returned to say, "I am giving my notice at the end of this semester in a week or two before the next semester begins in August. The next will be my last semester." Julian got up and wanted to put his arms around her. "That isn't a promise to return to the UK, just a definite decision I will no longer go on with the teaching at La Serena."

"Well, I'll settle for that." He hugged her tight, knowing that everything will depend on the political situation at the end of the year. *"Algo es algo,"* he said and in his mind, he continued the well-known Chilean expression. 'Something is something, said the devil, carrying away a couple of nuns under his arms.' Such a wonderful image and it made Julian smile again remembering it, despite that Isabel was making no promises.

-oOo-

From late autumn, Julian had noticed the dogs who live in the streets were curling themselves into perfect circular shapes on the pavements, just as he had noted was their habit on his arrival in the country, a year before. In the summer they laid out flat to stretch themselves out as much as possible, like dogs in England living with central heating. *The dogs are curling up again'* Julian said to himself when the weather had cooled a lot. He thought it remarkable to see these circular furry shapes dotted around the pavements. There had been local government efforts to remove the street dogs but he was told there was an outcry from the citizens. The people were fond of their street dogs. They fed them and made sure they were well looked after. Julian had not seen a mangy cur and he was almost fond of hearing them howl at times during the night. He wondered if they sensed an earth tremor when humans couldn't. They certainly howled when there was a recognisable trembling.

Now, with all he had learned, the word *dogs* had a double meaning. *Los perros don't curl up out of fear, nor do the powerful "dogs" - the owners and leaders of the country - they curl up with indifference and ignorance. What a metaphor!* Julian was currently reading Vargas Llosa's famous novel *La Ciudad y Los Perros* where the micro-world of the young students at a military college represents the wider reality of the city and the society. Both are worlds of violence, injustice and degradation where brutal control, ingrained with class and racial prejudice, maintains the hierarchy of the military school and the pyramid of social control in Peruvian society. Could it be much different in Chile, coming out as it is from a military dictatorship? Julian's literature professor ran a discussion amongst the students in his class on "institutionalised violence." One example brought up was that a person under suspicion by the police in Chile could be kept in a cell for seven days without communication with anyone, denied even a lawyer. In addition, there

293

is an assumption of guilt until the accused can show his innocence. Julian gasped in horror. I've got to get Isabel out of this, he determined.

Isabel would not engage in any further conversation about the future and left it vague about when he would see her again when she left after her weekend visit in July. Julian knew he couldn't keep trying to pin her down to a commitment to return to England yet and he would have to leave it but it continued to trouble him. She was due to come to Valparaíso for at least a week in the winter break between the academic semesters in August but she said that she would not arrive until after the first weekend. She had not stated clearly what she was planning to do that weekend nor where she was going but Julian imagined it would be a weekend of political activism in one of the northern cities. He had not attempted to persuade her otherwise and she had become impatient with his repeated calls for her to be very careful. He offered to join her too but she would not hear of that nor tell him where she was going to be.

"This weekend is an opportunity I can't miss," was all she would say. His worst fears that she was deceiving him with another person emerged again but he had constantly pushed them aside. This time he told himself that she means a political opportunity or she would not have said that. He had no choice but to hope for the best and he felt mad that she made him feel so powerless and excluded. When he could not reach her to confirm that she was getting on the overnight bus on the Sunday and again on the Monday evening, Julian started to be really concerned. He had rung the La Serena phone number several times and had no reply and then he finally was able to speak with the landlady. She only could confirm that Helena was not there at the flat and had not been all weekend, nor had she returned there. What had she been doing? Where was she? What was she up to?

# PART 3

# Chapter 16

I sabel had decided that the first weekend of the two-week break between the semesters in August, was when she could give herself to modelling the direct action she had talked with her groups about and if the worst should come to the worst and she was arrested, well it was a couple of weeks before she was due back in school and hopefully, she'd be out and no one there would be the wiser. She thus prepared with Daniela and others in Antofagasta, on a previous visit, all the details of their plan and she was satisfied they were well-rehearsed. She decided not to tell Julian because she would be annoyed at his repeated attempts to tell her not to take risks. The activists' group had debated the tactics and agreed on non-violent action that would border on civil disobedience but they would avoid damage to property. They would sit at the entrance to the *Intendencia* Regional Government offices in the town, refusing to move and regrouping if they were moved by any means, including tear gas. They had the banners, posters and leaflets prepared together with their strategies ready should arrests take place.

A large group of about 100 mostly young people assembled on a Saturday morning and as the offices were not open that day, they thought they could argue they were not obstructing the highway, although that is what the first police who came along to talk to them, said they were doing. However, they had already had nearly an hour standing on the steps of the building and shouting the demands written on their posters and handing out their leaflets. They made a lot of noise in that time, blowing bugles and banging drums and they had captured the attention of the public to advertise their demands. There had been lots of supportive feedback from the public. The offices were very central to the town, a stone's throw from the central square, *Plaza Colón*. The press had been informed in advance and several reporters and cameramen had come to record events.

As a large group of police approached them, the demonstrators sat down on the pavement and steps, in defiance of being moved. An officer tried to reason with some of the group and threatened what would happen if they did not respond without delay. They all remained seated. The police withdrew and collected batons and shields preparing themselves to approach again. First, however, came the vehicles with the tear gas and the water cannons and the activists were forced to move. Within a few minutes, they all returned holding one another's hands to assist their companions. All were coughing and spluttering and struggling to see with the tear gas and they were drenched. They sat down again, linking arms. This time, the police in twos, lifted the demonstrators one by one, who became limp, making themselves difficult to handle, and the police dragged them away and attempted to forbid them to return. As the demonstrators pressed forward again to return to their sitting positions on the steps, a few slipped around the containment line that the police were attempting to make. Isabel was one of those who again took up a sitting position on the steps. Five police vans were now arriving and all the demonstrators were taken, handcuffed and roughly thrown into the opening rear doors of the vans. Isabel was delighted that almost all of them had stood their ground as planned but all of those that did were arrested.

Daniela and Isabel had planted in the crowd of onlookers, several witnesses who observed all that had taken place. They included Daniela's mother and immediately the witnesses began telephoning all those they had been detailed to contact. Thus relatives knew what had happened and the law students supporting the manifestation sprung into action, though little response was expected from the police that day. The police, in fact, claimed for days that they were currently processing the detainees and could answer no questions. It was useful, however, that there were people aware of the detentions who would be pressing for information, not only about where they were being held but articulating to the press who had been taken and how they were being handled as soon as that was known. Isabel's brother was among those who were telephoned by Daniela's mother.

Being squeezed up in the police van with others was unpleasant with not enough height to stand up and not enough space to sit down without pressing unduly on others. Their proximity together helped keep them a little warmer than they might have been as it was mid-winter, although the temperature was above zero but they were wet. Pushing against one another was also the only way to manage the twists and turns of the van as it sped away and with their hands not free. It occurred to Isabel that the literal physical closeness symbolised the solidarity they felt with one another and she shouted out to those in her van,

"Hermanos y hermanas, ¡solidaridad!" They all cheered. "At least rubber bullets have not been used, perhaps because the press were present."

"Or perhaps because we all remained calm and our absolute non-violence stance gave them no excuse," Daniela struggled to say from the floor of the van. "Well done everyone." Several cheered.

"I think we were just lucky. They often use rubber bullets without any excuse. You know they have metal inside. That's why they are so dangerous, so we were very lucky," said Isabel.

"We are being taken out of town," said a voice from the other end of the van. "We are not going to the local police station."

When they arrived at a compound in the desert, they were driven through several gates in convoy and finally, the demonstrators were ordered to get out of the vans. That, they were not reluctant to do as everyone had aches and pains from the way they had had to crouch and bend. They were directed into a hallway and each searched and asked for their names and identity numbers before being told to pass along a corridor. The men were directed to a different door from the women. They all remained in their handcuffs. Isabel happened to be one of the first of the women who was ordered to proceed along a corridor. Soon the corridor became dark and when a corner was turned, there was practically no light at all. Isabel slowed and told those near her to slow because she couldn't see. Guards shouted for them to move on faster and Isabel stumbled on something in her pathway. It felt like a wooden bar, dark in the shadows. She lost her balance and twisted herself to get alongside the wall and avoid being crushed by the person pressing on her from behind. Then she heard the crack. She shouted out to warn the others,

"There are obstacles, I've fallen. Take care. Put your feet out as much as you can." She was in excruciating pain. "I've broken my ankle." She shouted as a guard approached to force her on. "I can't move." He pulled her up and pushed her forward. She staggered and screamed out again. Another guard came and the two of them yanked her under the shoulders, her legs trailing behind and they bumped her head through double doors to open them at the end of the corridor. One of the guards pulled Isabel's hair for good measure and then they dumped her to fall on the floor and the other guard gave her a kick in her kidneys. Others were piling into the room now and names were being called. Daniela was called along with Isabel and together with ten others, they were ordered through another door. One guard pulled on Isabel's arm as she had not moved and dragged her after the others in her group to a cell. The door slammed shut. The handcuffs were removed from each of them in turn by the two guards remaining in the cell. Isabel was ordered to stand up and she had to be pulled up by two companions. Her handcuffs were removed and she told them her ankle was broken.

"I must have medical attention. It is urgent and cannot be left."

The guards completely ignored her. They left the room and they all heard the key in the large padlock on the door slowly turn. Isabel pulled herself towards the wall so she could sit perched up against it and Daniela put herself alongside her. Others found themselves a space. They had about a square meter each and would have to encroach on each others' spaces for lying down. There were no seats or benches nor anything that could be called a bed. One young woman began to cry and Isabel suggested they sing Victor Jara's song *Levántate y Mira a la Montaña* Isabel was worried that she might not get her leg plastered or not get it set in time to do it correctly. It could leave her crippled and that scared her.

"Come on let's sing, *Stand up and look at the mountain,*" she said and they all joined in. Then they settled to rest and wait for what would happen next. It was three hours before a guard appeared and large enamel cups were passed around. Isabel put her hand up.

"I've broken my ankle. I must have it set properly, please get me to a hospital." The female guard listened and appeared to be uninterested. She went out of the door and reappeared with another female guard who had a large enamel jug in her hand. It contained only water and the women were grateful for that. Isabel directed another request to the second guard, asking for hospital attention.

"I will report it," she said coldly.

Several hours later the door opened again and blankets were thrown into the cell. Everyone scrambled for one and Daniela brought one for Isabel. Then they were all ordered to form a line as they went out of the door. Four women guards awaited them in the passageway outside. Two of them dragged Isabel behind the rest of her prison mates. They were marched to a room with 10 loos and one sink. The room was entirely open with no suggestion of any means of privacy. There was one loo roll on a string, of the shiny, non-absorbent type. Isabel had to drag herself across the floor of the room and she hated the smell of the place. They were marched back when all had finished and ten minutes later the dismal light bulb in their cell went out. Sensing that it wasn't late, Isabel suggested they sing again and most of the women joined in *Venceremos:*

From the Deep crucible of the homeland
The peoples' voices rise up.
The new day comes over the horizon
All Chileans begin to sing.
Remembrance of the courageous soldier
Which his example has made him immortal.
First we confront death,
Our country we'll never betray,
We shall overcome, we shall overcome.
A thousand chains we'll have to break
We shall overcome, we shall overcome.
We know how to overcome the fascism.
We shall overcome, we shall overcome.
Peasants, soldiers, miners,
And the women of our country as well.
Student, employees and workers
We will do our duty.
We'll sow the land with glory
Socialism will be our future
All together, we will be history's completion
To fulfil, to fulfil, to fulfil.
We shall overcome, we shall overcome.

A loud bang was heard on the door. The prisoners could hear other cells had joined in the singing. *"Silencio"* came the shout again and again. The women shuffled around to accommodate themselves between one another lying down. None of them could sleep for quite some time. Isabel reminded them of what she had told them before to expect.

"We have to expect a week of this, minimum. But we will be all right. We will support one another and stand together. Don't worry. Just keep your cool and don't do anything to provoke them, even though you feel angry with them."

*"Silencio"* came again with a loud knock on the door. They whispered after that. One or two said how hungry they were and that feeling made it difficult to sleep.

"There will be food tomorrow, I think. They have to give us something," said Daniela.

"Yes, I think so," said Isabel but her tone wasn't very reassuring. "Just think, we can all lose that bit of weight we wanted to lose and when they allow visitors after a week, we can enjoy what they bring. Take courage. *Venceremos.*"

The next morning the procedure to visit the loos was repeated and then they were ordered to clean the loos, a trolley of floor mops and brushes having been brought in. Daniela tried to act for Isabel and others joined in to help too. On returning to their cell, water to drink was brought to them again and then individuals were called out and interviewed during the morning. Each time the door opened Isabel shouted that she must have medical attention and that her ankle was broken. Then, with fading hopes, she started to shout for a bandage and a splint. To her surprise, by late morning a bandage and a piece of wood appeared. Daniela knew how to do a professional ankle bandage and she bound Isabel's ankle as best she could, attempting to use the splint to straighten the heel. There was quite a discussion on how best to place the wooden splint and with that and the ankle swollen, it looked a very odd shape when the bandage was done. Isabel just hoped desperately it might do some good but she did not give up demanding to be taken to a hospital at every opportunity. Several of the women were called and taken out individually to be registered and interviewed, but Isabel was not called, which she hoped might give her a chance to be heard about her foot. If only she could get a message to her brother but phone calls were denied them as well. No one could have any contact with the outside world.

Everyone was feeling very hungry by the afternoon when a couple of jugs of pumpkin soup were brought to them and bread. At least they thought it was supposed to be pumpkin soup but it was very thin though the flavour wasn't bad.

"At least they thought of the garlic and the herbs," said Isabel.

"It's just so watery."

"The bread is practically passed. It's so hard you can hardly bite it."

Isabel wondered what they could reasonably discuss to pass the hours or how they could entertain themselves to try to get through the long hours of doing nothing. *That is the worst aspect of all this,* she thought. *You move from a busy, stimulating life, rushing about all the time, to wondering what on earth to do, what to think about, hour after hour.*

"Can't we do our own little *peña?* We could all recite a poem or sing a song or tell a story," suggested Isabel.

"You could tell us a story, summarise a book or an interesting event in history. You are good at that," said Daniela to Isabel.

"I could try and tell the story of the slaves in Haiti, as Carpentier wrote. Some of the graphic details will make us feel a lot better about our position," she laughed.

This made several women willing to tell the story of books they had read, from Jane Austen to Isabel Allende. So they passed the hours until the shouts of silence came again for the night. Isabel was contented that spirits were lifted the second day and the following days. The detention centre routines didn't vary day after day. Eventually, Isabel was called for a registration interview and she could only hobble slowly to the desk where she was asked to stand. She asked that she be taken to the hospital before she would answer any questions. Her interviewer ignored her and demanded she answered.

"Will you get me to a hospital if I answer," she demanded and her face was slapped.

"Answer and then we will see if you have a medical condition."

"Sure I have a medical condition caused by you."

303

"Full name?" Isabel answered the questions. As agreed before, she gave her address as Daniela's."

When asked what organisation she belonged to, Isabel did not answer. When pressed she said, "I am a citizen and a democrat. I demand a just society, dignity for workers and pensioners, free education and health care and a political system without military control."

*"¡Silencio!* What is your medical condition that needs attention?" Isabel explained again she needed an X-ray and a full plaster for her ankle. "It is urgent, it has been three days now without attention and soon it will be too late to set right." As she was dragged away Isabel shouted that they all needed to telephone their lawyers. She was pulled back to the cell by two women guards.

-oOo-

Isabel was to learn later that her brother Carlos had been in touch with Julian. Carlos only had the phone number of the woman who did Julian's washing, Martina and she had gone to Julian's flat to find him, having no other way to be in touch. He wasn't at home and she had left a letter under his door. Julian was so grateful to her when he later learned how important it was for him to ring Carlos. Her note only said, "Ring Carlos urgently."

Making his way to the call centre, he became more and more anxious and frustrated by the time that it took to wait for the *ascensor* to arrive up the hill and to take him down again. "Carlos, what news do you have," he burst out on finally getting through to Carlos' office. It was a receptionist on the line, who asked him to wait.

"Isabel has been arrested," he finally heard. "I know very little but she and her friend Daniela were taken at a protest rally in Antofagasta last Saturday. The mother of Daniela telephoned me but I cannot get any confirmation or information from the police. I'm afraid I have no other news than that yet."

"Are you going to go to Antofagasta?" asked Julian.

"Until the police confirm they are holding her, there's no point."

"But surely we should go and demand an answer. Wouldn't it help for a lawyer and perhaps a foreigner to be there in person demanding information and her release."

"They won't give us any information if they choose not to and we'd just be waiting around. I have got work commitments."

"Yes, of course, but I could go. They do have to be a bit careful how they deal with a foreigner and whether news of their behaviour will get out of the country."

"It will be difficult to track her down until I get more information from them. We don't even know which station she is held at."

"Well, the nearest to the city centre where the demo would have been."

"Not necessarily. You know they can hold her a week without any obligation to let even her lawyer see her."

"Yes, I know. It's disgusting. That's an abuse of human rights and *habeas corpus.*"

"Julian, that may not be the worst of the human rights abuses. She's likely to be covered in bruises. You'd better prepare yourself."

"I realise that and the conditions people are held in aren't good either, are they?"

"No, they are not. Look I will go to Antofagasta as soon as they will allow me to see her. They haven't even acknowledged they are holding her yet. I'll be ringing them constantly to demand that but at the moment I've only got a general city police number. I've not got a specific police station number. Also if many people were arrested, they may have moved them to other detention centres."

"What like the sort of torture centres, seemingly ordinary houses, used in the dictatorship."

"Look, calm down. Stop letting your imagination run away with you. Yes, they do use other centres, and yes, sometimes there are false accusations and they knock people about, but let's not speculate about the worst until we know. Things are better than they used to be." Julian didn't feel that sounded very reassuring.

"I'm getting the overnight bus to Antofagasta tonight. Have you got Daniela's phone number and the mother's number? Presumably Daniela's husband and family are looking for her? Oh, and yes, she's Isabel Helena Henriquez Navarro, right, in that area?" Carlos confirmed this and obliged with the phone numbers.

"Keep ringing me, I don't mind how often or what time, in case I get some news for you."

On arrival in the town the next morning, Tuesday, Julian immediately searched for a call centre and rang the numbers for Daniela and her mother. There was no reply at either number and Julian had to assume that everyone was at work or at a police station demanding information. He was agitated as he sought a place to have breakfast and to find out where the nearest police station was. He received some very unfriendly looks when he asked this question in the café. He knew he also needed to find somewhere to stay overnight, but he didn't think that would be a problem as tourism was beginning to develop in this seaside town with its stunning coastline and hotels being built all along the beachfront. As this was winter he guessed there should be some vacant rooms. Julian decided he should arrange a hotel room to start with, so he wouldn't have to take his rucksack of belongings with him to the police station. From his map, he could see there were a few hotels not far from the *Plaza Colón* which looked like the central square where the cathedral was and he was halfway in that direction already from his search for a call centre.

At *Plaza Colón* he found the clock tower which symbolised the town in the tourist leaflets he had collected at the bus station - that is, apart from the famous arched natural rock formation jutting out of the sea, known as *La Portada*. Making sure he had the location of the central police station and ignoring the surprised look on the hotel receptionist's face, he set off to talk with the police. He explained what he had come for and he was asked to wait. After nearly a quarter of an hour, when it did not appear that the policeman on the desk had made any enquiries but merely talked with further people waiting in the queue, Julian stepped forward to ask what was being done about his request.

"I am a British citizen and I need to have confirmation if you are holding Isabel Henriquez," he said forcefully. He was told he would be seen shortly and must wait. After another quarter of an hour, he tried again, this time demanding to see the superior officer of the policeman on the desk. Others looked around and Julian shouted his demand again. There was a flurry of activity and an officer asked him to step into another room.

"I need to know if Isabel Henriquez is held here, or where she is and why." The officer sat down at a computer and stared at the screen, saying nothing. Julian waited again for what seemed a long time to him. Eventually, he was asked for his name, address in the UK, his address in Chile and he had to produce his passport and his Visa of Temporary Residency. His heart sank. He might be in trouble as his visa had recently expired. Julian explained that he went to renew it in good time at the *Intendencia* and they had told him to go away because they were overwhelmingly busy with Peruvian immigrants and they could not deal with it at that time. The officer raised his eyebrows and gave no clue as to whether this was an acceptable explanation or if consequences were to follow.

"It only ran out four weeks ago. I tried to renew it a second time and was told the same. Please, that is not the issue that brings me here now. I will go to the office again as soon as the issue which brings me here is dealt with. That is something much more important: I need to know the whereabouts of Isabel Henriquez please, please."

"It is a very serious issue that you are in the country without a Visa," came the reply.

"Look I can be here for three months as a tourist with no visa, so let that be my status now until I am able to sort it out in Valparaíso. It's not my fault, I went twice to the office and was told the same thing."

"I will have to talk with my senior," said the police officer and disappeared out of the room. A further endless wait left Julian wondering what to do again. Shall I go out and demand attention or do I just wait and wait here? It could be ages. We have not even got to the issue of Isabel, he despaired. Another uniformed officer entered and booted up the computer again. Finally, he turned slowly to Julian and said,

"You must go to the *Intendencia* in Valparaíso within the next two weeks. I am reporting this matter to the police there and they will be checking out that you have done so. Right, so that is all, you may go."

Julian was incensed. "I came here to find out what has happened to my *companera*. She was arrested last Saturday in this town for participating in a demonstration perfectly peacefully. I want to know where you are holding her and I want her released as she has done nothing wrong."

"How do you know that? Were you at the demonstration too?"

"No, but I know that she would be a peaceful protester and any democratic person with any courage would do what she has done. I hope she has not been harmed." Immediately Julian thought he's said too much and again there was silence and a wait. The officer attended to the computer once more.

"What is the nature of your complaint?"

"I haven't made a complaint yet. That depends on what you tell me. I want to know where is Isabel Henriquez?" The officer started typing.

"Her full name and ID number." Julian gave the name in full and then said that he didn't know her ID number.

"We can't proceed without that." Julian saw it as a provocation but realised he should go carefully.

"A person is more than a number. You have the full name, and date of birth. Do you have any protesters held here from Saturday's demonstration?"

"You have no right to ask that and you will not be told."

"Do you have Isabel? You must inform her family."

"You are not family."

"Well, her brother then. He is a lawyer. Here's his number. Ring him please and tell him."

"Not everyone from the rabble on Saturday has been processed yet. I cannot see her name on the list so far. Come back tomorrow if you must and we'll see then."

"Who do I ask for? Can I see you again please?" He was ignored and the officer made his way to the door.

"What could be happening to her whilst she's not on the list. It's like she's a non-person. Anything could happen to her." He was further ignored.

Julian felt there was no alternative but to leave the room as well. He slumped into a chair in the waiting area at the entrance corner of the large room, which was busy with police talking to one another, or on phones or moving hurriedly about. How long should he sit there? Was there any point? What should he do? Eventually, he was asked to leave as the door was being locked for the lunchtime closure. He was ushered out with a queue of other people, who he soon realised were also seeking information about relatives arrested. Julian staggered out into the bright sunshine and pushed through the group standing on the pavement, to a man who had shouted "Where's my daughter?" on being escorted out.

"Was your daughter arrested in the demonstration last Saturday?" he asked.

"Yes, and there is no news of where she is since then. It's an abuse of human rights. They still use the same tactics as under the dictatorship. There's been no reform. I'm so worried..."

"Let's stick together. We have to demand news as a group. Is the police station open to the public to go in later?"

"Yes. We'll have to reassemble at 4.00 pm," he shouted to the whole group.

"They told me to come back tomorrow, but I'm willing to assemble with you this afternoon. The more the better."

"We weren't told when to come back. I'm Leonardo, by the way."

"I'm Julian. I'm English. They might just have been a tiny bit more helpful with me as I'm a foreigner. I don't know for sure. I can only hope. But I'll stand with you till we get some news on all our relatives."

"Who are you asking for news of?"

"My Chilean girlfriend, Isabel."

"Was she a refugee in London for several years?"

"Yes, that's where we met."

"My daughter has spoken of her. Isabel is like a sort of regional organiser."

"Yes, she can only visit from time to time."

"My daughter is Paula. She's in the group of activists. Her mother has always been worried that something like this would happen. I've always rather admired her courage but now I feel I must do something. Her mother will be going mad, let alone what might be happening to Paula."

"I know, it's scary. Look, I'll have to see you later because I need to phone Daniela's family. You'll have heard of her. I couldn't get them earlier and they might have some news. Do you know where the closest call centre is?"

"Come to my house. We've got a telephone. And you must have some lunch with us."

"Oh no, I couldn't do that. It will worry your wife more."

"No, no, there's safety in numbers. Come with me, please. I'll be glad to know if Daniela's family know anything yet. I know them."

"Thank you. Chilean people are so warm and generous. I don't feel hungry at the moment but I'm really glad to be with you. We must stick together. I need to phone Isabel's brother too. He is a lawyer and when we make some progress about where the arrested are being held, then I think Carlos will be able to help as a lawyer." At the same time, Julian was thinking that perhaps Carlos was right, that it is all a waste of time till there is recognition of the arrests and charges made. He followed Leonardo to a bus stop and after a 10-minute bus ride, they arrived in his *barrio*. His wife, Pati was welcoming but she glared at her husband when he said they couldn't get any news and she disappeared into the kitchen. Julian was shown the phone and he was soon talking with Daniela's family. They had no news yet and had been to three different police stations so far. Julian told them his news that he had been told to return the next day. The Chileans were again surprised at this. Julian knew it might be just his optimism but he had hopes. Leonardo asked to take the phone. He talked a while and then, putting the phone down, he said,

"Her mother is called Juana, I know her and I know Daniela. Daniela's father was a disappeared person. Juana stayed in the crowd to watch all that happened at the demo."

"Oh, what did happen," asked Julian.

"Most protesters returned and sat themselves down in front of the Regional Offices and refused to move. They were lifted up into police vans."

"Oh no, I thought Isabel wouldn't ask for trouble after having been arrested before. They are bound to keep her longer this time, she always said that. Why on earth did she take the risk."

"I bet she was so frustrated that nothing changes. The sort of action they are trying now, the activists call civil disobedience. I think they feel they have to do more because marching hasn't got anywhere. She's got guts though."

Julian then rang Carlos's office but was told he had gone to lunch. Julian explained to Leonardo and said he would ring Isabel's mother's house as that is where he usually goes for lunch.

"Hold on, wait. Do you know if Isabel's mother knows she's been arrested? Is she supportive, will she understand and is she strong enough to cope with the worry?"

"Ah! you're right. She may well not know Isabel's in custody and she will be angry but anxious too. No, I had better speak to her brother first. Thank you for making me think, I could have caused some serious problems there and Isabel would be furious."

"Best she doesn't know until she has to know and when we have some news." A part of Julian thought it would do her good to face the reality of the dictatorship and its legacy, instead of denying it but he knew it would be a harsh way to learn. He said nothing and agreed he shouldn't phone.

After lunch, in which Pati served a tasty *cazuela,* Julian returned to the phone to try to get Carlos at his office. Still, there was no news but he confirmed that Esperanza had not been told about Isabel's custody. Carlos said he would take an overnight bus on Friday night unless she was actually released, but he thought that unlikely. He thought he should be able to see Isabel as it would then be a week. Julian took down Isabel's ID number from Carlos.

The new friends returned to the police station at 4.00 pm and a group of at least twenty people was gathered. Julian was introduced to Juana. When they marched into the police station as soon as the door was unlocked, they were not treated with any tolerance and ordered to get out, *"al tiro."* Threats were made that they would be down in the cells if they hung around any longer. One young man said he was not leaving until he had news of his brother. He shouted he would rather be in the cells because there he might find his brother or people who could tell him something. He resisted as others tried to pull him out with them, as the whole crowd was being bundled out. He insisted he must stay and two policemen came and grabbed each of his arms.

"What do you think might happen to him? What offence could they charge him with?" said Julian to Leonardo when they were outside.

"He could be held a week and then just let go or he might be charged with obstructing the police in their duty. They'll find something if they want to. The trouble is the false accusations they can make."

Julian felt he just wanted to be alone with his thoughts until the next day but as Leonardo had been so kind to him, he didn't want to just leave. He said, "Can I take you to have *onces* at a café."

"Thanks but I think I should get home to my wife. She'll be worrying about me as well as our daughter now. I have to go to work this evening on the night shift."

"Oh no, what is your work?"

"I'm a manager of a team of copper miners."

"You'll be knackered tomorrow. Did you work last night?" Leonardo nodded. "Did you get any sleep today?"

"I had a few hours. I can manage."

"Can I ask about Paula tomorrow for you so you can sleep a bit longer tomorrow? Give me Paula's surnames, I.D. number and your phone number and of course, I'll ring if there is any news."

"Ok, thanks that means a lot and it would help. I'll be here at the end of the morning." Julian obliged with a paper for the full details and soon he was alone. He decided to take a long walk along the seafront before going to his hotel room. He thought the hotel room on his own might be quite depressing. He would avoid that as long as he could. After his long walk, he returned to the main square, having found a modest-looking small hotel a couple of streets from there. He had a look at his tourist leaflet and it told him that the clock tower in the square was modelled on the clock tower of the Palace of Westminister with the four faces of the clock resembling Big Ben's clock and made by British clockmakers. He learned that there was quite a sizeable number of descendants of British colonialists in the town and he didn't want to be regarded as a British Chilean and not a foreigner when he returned to see the police. It prompted Julian to take his passport with him the next day.

-oOo-

Julian arrived at the police station the next morning at 9.30 am. He didn't think there would be much news any earlier. A few other relatives he recognised from the day before were there. He asked them if anything had happened this morning so far. They said they had not been permitted to go into the station as yet and the officer at the door had said that there was no news and for them and to go away. Julian thought he would wait a while but he would attempt to enter at the latest by 11.00 am. That he thought should be after their midmorning breakfast break and with a good amount of time before the lunch closure. He was hoping that something might go forward this morning. He talked with the others a little and went for coffee with a couple of them. At 11.00 am he attempted to enter the police station. He was not stopped at the door but the desk officer, after checking all his documents said there was no news and he should not wait around.

"I was told by your senior officer to return today. There should be some news. I want to see the most senior officer here, please." That at least caused the policeman to go to speak to a colleague and then to pick up a phone. Half an hour later he was ushered into the room he'd been taken to the previous day. The same senior officer came in.

"It does not appear they have processed Henriquez Navarro yet. She is not on the list but I have requested that they give us information as soon as possible and told them who you are. You can try this afternoon if you wish but it may be another day yet." He stood up to go.

"Can you tell me if Paula Jimenez Gomez is on the list? I am a friend of her parents and her father is at work. Please help me." The officer took his seat again, looked impatient but booted up the computer again.

"Yes, she is here. She's at *Retén La Negra, Ruta 5 Norte.*"

"Where is that? Can she be visited? When will she be released?"

"When she has been charged. No one can see her yet."

"Can a lawyer not see her?"

"No. No one."

"Is that legal? Do you think that is fair and democratic?"

"I don't care what it is. I've told you all I can. Now go." he shouted. Julian hurried out and in the entrance hall wrote down the address the officer had said.

He told the others outside what he had learned and asked where there was a phone. He was told there was a phone he could use in a café they pointed to and he rushed to ring Pati and Leonardo.

"What does *Retén* mean? Does it have a meaning or is it just a name?" he asked when he had told Pati all he knew.

"*Retén* means police station but the word has another meaning: lock." Pati began to cry. Leonardo came to the phone. *Retén Ruta 5* is perhaps 15 kilometres out of town. I might be able to get a *colectivo* to take me."

"Can I come with you?"

"Ok, but they won't let us see them before they are charged. It's normal procedure and yesterday they said it takes a week. Saturday afternoon is probably going to be the first chance to see them and it is the usual visiting day."

"I feel we've got to try to see them today though."

"Yes, I know. I'd like to try this afternoon. Make sure you have a good meal before we go so you are in your best state if we have to wait a long time."

"Ok, thanks. Where shall I see you?"

"I'll come to the police station in town. I'll be there at one o'clock. We must take food for Paula, Isabel and the others. If we do get to see them, we will need to give them food because they won't have had anything much and prisoners depend on what is brought in for them. They share it of course between them, so get as much as you can carry but stuff that can be eaten immediately without cooking."

"Oh, of course. I didn't think about that. Of course, I'll get whatever I think will be suitable and good for them."

Julian rang Carlos and told him what he knew. He hoped to see Isabel at the *Retén,* but he hoped too that Carlos would be coming Friday evening on the overnight bus. Carlos confirmed he would as he would expect to be allowed to see Isabel by Saturday. Today he doubted Julian would get to see her. They would talk later. For now Julian had a rushed shopping trip to do and a good meal to consume. He found a new supermarket in the centre of town and laden with bags he entered a serve-yourself café. He didn't feel like eating but he supposed he should as Leonardo had advised. Laden with shopping bags full of fruit, vegetables that could be eaten raw, like carrots, avocados, peppers, washed green leaves, tomatoes and a pile of bread rolls and ham, cheese, butter, milk, mayonnaise and tins of sardines, anchovies, muscles, *almejas* and *navajuelas,* all with pull-off lids, Julian found an empty table and stood up his bulky bags by a wall and went to the counter to take a meal from what was on display in the glass-fronted showcases. He noticed they had hard-boiled eggs and he asked for a dozen of these, to the great surprise of the shop assistant and that was all they had cooked. He had wanted to get eggs to take with him and these, already cooked, were just what he needed. He asked for portions of salad mixtures, prawns and gouda cheese for himself and hurriedly ate them. It was time to meet Leonardo.

As Julian approached the police station he could see Leonardo up ahead almost arriving there. He shouted him and many people looked around but so did Leonardo, who hurried towards him. He had a load of food bags too and they bumped one another with their bags as they embraced. They made their way to the next corner to be on the main road and the *colectivo* routes and Leonardo was soon hailing a car. In 25 minutes, surrounded by the sombre brown hills of the desert, they walked towards the entrance gate with a reception hut.

Leonardo said, "We'll have to hand this food to the guards. We just have to hope they will pass it all on to our people, but they may keep some stuff themselves. The girls will probably only have had some thin soup at best, so far."

"You'll have to wait till 2.00 pm," said the policeman in the hut. It was 1.40 pm.

"Can you look at our documents now so we can go straight in at 2.00?" said Leonardo.

"No, 2.00 pm. and you can't take all those bags in."

"It's only food for our relatives."

"They will all have to be checked."

"Can we start that now, please?"

"No" and the small opening of the hut window was closed.

# Chapter 17

A s they waited a few others came to queue behind them. At 2.05 another officer came out of the hut and asked that they empty the bags.

"Where?" said Julian. The officer grabbed one of the bags and tipped it upside down and the contents fell out over the dusty road. Oranges and apples rolled away and tins from the bottom began to fall on the other fruits and vegetables. Julian didn't dare say another word of complaint.

"I.D." demanded the officer as Julian was running after oranges meters away. "Who are you to see?" Leonardo stepped up.

"My daughter Paula Jimenez Gomez."

"And you?" The officer looked at Julian.

"Isabel Henriquez Navarro," and he gave the I.D. number

Leonardo also gave Daniela's name. "I'm here on behalf of her mother."

The policeman disappeared inside the hut and when he was satisfied with the contents of the other two bags which he also tipped out, they were told to go forward to the long hut a little way ahead. They were body searched again at the door of the hut, had to give the prisoners names again and the food bags were taken from them. At last, they were allowed to pass through. Other visitors arrived behind them and then they heard the door lock behind them and they were all ushered out of the other end of the hut. They entered an open yard, surrounded by wire netting and then some women began to run towards them from the other side of the yard. The visitors hurried across and Daniela and Paula arrived, recognising Leonardo, they both hurried towards him. Julian rushed up to them and demanded to know if Isabel was with them.

"Yes, yes she is but she's hurt her ankle. It's probably broken. She can only come very slowly." And then limping and clearly in pain, Isabel appeared with her arms around the shoulders of two other women and they made their way slowly towards Julian. Isabel's and Julian's fingers touched through the wires. Words were impossible and Julian cried along with Isabel.

"How did it happen? Did they hit you?"

"Many times, my arm is killing me. Look at the bruises. But my ankle is broken, because I fell. They made us walk down this completely dark passage and they'd put obstacles in the way and I fell over something."

"Won't they let you get medical attention for that? It needs an X-ray and plastering."

"I keep asking and they should get me medical attention. I think Carlos might be able to make that happen."

"I'll ring him. Leonardo and I brought a pile of food. I hope it all gets to you. Have you had anything to eat here?"

"A bit of thin soup and hard bread. Nothing much."

Julian listed all he had brought and told her about the eggs from the café and the woman's surprise when he asked for twelve.

"I hope there are some lemons to go with the fish," Isabel said a little indignantly but with a smile. Julian looked a bit sheepish. He confessed he'd forgotten lemons.

"The tins of fish were a bit of an afterthought. Sorry." Suddenly a whistle was blown and they were ordered back to their hut and the visitors were told to leave on their side. The prisoners were desperate to eat and all ran back to their hut, except Isabel and Daniela. She helped Isabel hop back and Julian watched them. He felt ready to explode as they left but Leonardo wouldn't let him say a word until they were out of the gates.

"I can't go without demanding she gets medical attention for her ankle."

"You are so mad you'll end up inside. Her lawyer brother is the best person to demand that."

Leonardo had arranged with the *colectivo* driver to return at 3.00 pm. He thought there was no chance of being able to stay longer than that and there were no *colectivos* doing a routine pick-up in this remote place on the Route 5 South highway. They would have to wait and Julian kept opening his mouth to begin to speak and then closing it again and shaking his head. There was no point in stating the obvious or everything Leonardo already knew. Julian felt helpless and despairing. He thought Isabel should not be putting weight on her foot. On arrival in the town again Julian asked Leonardo to wait while he rang Carlos and told him all that had happened.

"I'll ring immediately to demand medical attention for her ankle. It could affect her all her life if it is not dealt with now. It mustn't reach the limit of being able to be set."

"Should I go now to the police station to demand she be taken to the hospital?"

"No, let me try first. Ring me back at 6.00 pm and if I haven't achieved agreement that she'll be escorted to the hospital, you can go then to chase it up." He continued, "she could be done for obstruction of the highway, that can apply to sitting outside a public building where people go in and out."

"But she sat down outside the *Intendencia* Regional Offices on a Saturday when it was closed so she wasn't obstructing anyone."

"That doesn't matter. It's the act of doing it. And possibly obstructing the police in their duty. Depends if she resisted being arrested. Going limp makes it harder to be picked up and that could be seen as obstruction."

"That is not obstruction in the UK - just going limp. I know that for sure."

"Well, it can be here. It's a fine line between going limp and resisting. I'll get the overnight bus on Friday evening. I'll go straight to this *Retén* and I'll see you in the town after that for lunch.

"I believe we can visit Saturday afternoon and I've arranged to go with the father of one of the detainees I've met."

"Yes, ok, good. Of course. I expect I can see you by 12.00 noon or perhaps sooner. Do you know a good place, that everyone knows and I can't miss you?"

"*La Torre del Reloj,* Plaza Colón."

"We can have lunch together before you go to visit. That's if they'll let you see her again so soon. Don't bank on it."

"Ok. Can I cause you some more hassle?" Julian asked and proceeded to tell Carlos about Leonardo and his family and about Paula and Daniela. I doubt if they can afford lawyers. Can you do anything for them as you are going to be there on Saturday?" Julian called Leonardo to the phone to give the girls details.

-oOo-

When Julian rang Carlos in the evening when he was home, he learned that the *Retén* authorities had agreed that Isabel would be escorted to the hospital on Wednesday but she would be returning the same day and not permitted to stay overnight in the hospital.

"I'll try to check it has happened tomorrow."

"Don't make yourself a nuisance. It is best she'll be at the *Retén* on Saturday. They have agreed I can see her then."

"It's now urgent to get her leg set - I hope it really does happen. How can I best be sure?"

"Ask at the police station in the city by 1.00 pm. That should give them time to act and time still to take action if they haven't done it. But be polite and don't keep pestering."

Julian promised to calmly check and thanked Carlos. The next morning, the senior officer at the police station who knew him confirmed that Isabel had been taken to the hospital and Julian gave an enormous sigh of relief. The officer noticed this and with a wry smile and a friendly *"Vamos,"* hurried him out of the room. It was Thursday and Saturday seemed a long way off. He thought he shouldn't go shopping until Saturday morning so that the fruit and veg would be as fresh as possible. Two days to kill seemed an endless amount of time. He pondered how the prisoners would be passing the time and he judged that every hour would probably seem like two to them. He could walk the length of the seafront and this is what he did with a newly found appreciation. He would remember the lemons this time, and be ready for the Saturday afternoon visit, if they would allow it. He thought he might be just accepted along with the other visitors and Leonardo hoped the same and they agreed to meet up Saturday in time for Leonardo to meet Carlos before their visit. After another long walk, Julian decided to ring Daniela's number and her mother's number to be sure they had information about the *Retén*. Juana had learned that day about where the detainees were held and had been told she could visit Saturday.

"Come and have supper with us tonight," she said and Julian was grateful for the friendliness, generosity and recognition he was alone. He tried to express some of that and Juana cut in.

"We are very fond of Isabel and all she has done for us and I am sure she is helped by your support of her. It will be great to see you."

Julian took down the details and was pleased to meet Daniela's husband and her children as well at Juana's house that evening.

Carlos attended on Saturday morning at the detention centre and secured an agreement that Isabel and the other girls would be released the next week when the paperwork was complete and they would only be charged with obstruction. He explained when Julian and Leonardo met up with him.

"What will be the consequences of that? Will they be fined?"

"Probably not, but they will have it on their record so they no longer have a clean record."

"What time of day do you think they will release them?" Carlos and Leonardo just shook their heads.

Leonardo said, "They'll have no phone and no transport. We'll have to go and just wait and hope, from Tuesday onwards, you say?"

"Yes. They won't have managed the paperwork by Monday for sure and Tuesday, well… it will be very lucky if they were let out by then."

"I'll go in your place," said Julian to Leonardo. "You'll be working, won't you?"

"I'll go early in the morning because I am on an afternoon shift next week."

"Ok, and I'll be there from 11.00 am when you need to get back and get some lunch."

They did manage to get access on Saturday afternoon and the visit went in a similar fashion to before but the food was not tipped out all over the road. The bags were only looked into. The time with the prisoners was brief as before, but Julian was able to hear all about the hospital visit under escort and that the X-ray confirmed an ankle bone was fractured. He was relieved to see Isabel in a plaster up to the knee.

"I didn't care about the stares of people seeing me sitting in the waiting room with a police officer at my side. The radiographer wasn't happy that he insisted on coming into the X-ray room with me. He was told to sit in the corner and she whispered to me, "What have you done?" I told her I stood for democracy and a new constitution, free education and good health provision and after that, she was really nice with me. She kept smiling and taking her time. She showed me the X-ray and explained she had good hopes it would repair well. The bone hadn't moved out of shape, just cracked. The bit of wood had helped a lot." Julian just shook his head with relief. The consequences could have been much worse, he thought. "She hid me a little by pulling a curtain a short way over and she gave me her sandwiches to eat. I was ravenous and so grateful to her. I managed a few bites before the officer shouted to open the curtain, though he could see I was there from underneath the curtain. She shouted that she was adjusting my jeans and dressing me again and it seemed to satisfy him. I had to agree she cut my jeans to go over the plaster and she helped me into them. All the time I was attempting to bite into the sandwiches. She made the jeans a bit of a performance to give me more time to finish the sandwich. She was really great."

"She was," agreed Julian.

"Then she said I had to wait while she got me a plastic cover for the shower and she slipped a little cake into my hand. The officer was none the wiser but by the time the plastering was done, he started to get really impatient. We'd been hours, five or six I guess," she laughed.

The whistle to end the visiting session was loudly blown. Julian asked hurriedly,

"Did you get all the food that I told you I'd brought? That was the day before the radiologist fed you at the hospital, wasn't it?"

"Yes, what luxury two days running. I never saw the clams you mentioned you'd brought."

"There's the same stuff again today with lemons," he smiled as they were ushered away from each other to different exits. "I love you, take care. I'll be here to meet you next week, whatever day."

On Monday Julian went just in case the women should be released, though everyone thought it was hopeless. He took a book to read and just sat by the roadside. He was told if they were released early, there were buses along that route, especially early morning, so they wouldn't be entirely stuck. He returned to the town centre at 5.00 pm when a return bus came. Tuesday he was more hopeful of success and he did want to be there to meet Isabel, rather than her having to get the bus. Leonardo was already there. Julian was there by 9.00 am with food and drink as well as a book and he waited. Leonardo had ordered a *colectivo* for 12.00 so he could get to work and Julian was sorry to see him go. It was not until 1.00 pm that a small group of women emerged from the gate. Isabel was amongst them limping slowly, with one arm around Daniela's shoulder and the other around another woman's shoulder. Two of the detainees were met with cars and others of the group piled into the cars with them. Julian asked one of the drivers to request two *colectivos* for him and the girls that were left. Julian gave him enough money for two collective taxis to pay them in advance, so the drivers, he hoped, would trust that it was worthwhile to come to collect them all.

Julian took a deep breath when he finally sat in the front seat of a *colectivo* with three girls in the back, Isabel, Daniela and Paula. When eventually they were alone, he asked Isabel "What did you mean by 'you couldn't miss the opportunity.'"

"Well, I can't be so defiant when it's school on Monday but with two weeks off I thought why not. I should be out by that time and school will never know."

"They will when you appear with a plaster cast up to your knee."

"I can just say I fell on an uneven payment. You know what some pavements are like. And the police don't know my school name Helena Isabel Garcia Sepúlveda."

Julian just shook his head. "I hope you are going to be Isabel etcetera., etcetera. and stay at my place for the rest of what is left of the two weeks you should have been there. First of all, we need to get you crutches or you'll be putting too much weight on your foot. Then we need to get bus tickets. Do you want to stay in my hotel room or sit on the seafront while I do that?"

Isabel was adamant she could not stay beyond the following weekend once they were in Valparaíso again but she was very appreciative of being looked after, as she was in quite a lot of pain when she moved about. She worried about having done no preparation for the coming semester at school but Julian managed to get a couple of books she needed from the Valparaíso library. He enjoyed cooking for her and he was so thrilled to have her safely in his flat again. He felt it easy to be attentive and affectionate with a joyfulness he sensed from deep within himself. Isabel was responsive and grateful. He wanted to accompany her on the bus to La Serena to assist her there but Isabel insisted that she would have a friend collect her in his car.

"His car?" remarked Julian. "Who is he?"

"Yes, his car. He's the only person I know well enough to ask, with a car. He's a teacher at the school. The one that I helped over the trips to the flowering desert. I'll have to go down to the call centre to ring him and I need to ring my brother and my mother. Do you think we could go down in a taxi so I can do all that this evening - when Carlos will be home from work. I don't want to trouble him at the office if I can help it and he can talk more freely at home."

"Ok and we'll book your *cama* seat on the bus too. You know the full bed seats get booked up early. But I am worried about how you are going to manage in the shower when I'm not there to hold you. You can smile. I know it's nice but seriously you are in danger of slipping so easily."

"I'll be super careful. I'm managing quite well with the plastic covers the friendly X-ray woman gave me."

Julian knew that she would not be able to be dashing about in her usual fashion. He worried to let her go but it was hopeless to try to stop her. He resolved to make the most of the few days they had together. It was the weather for being safely ensconced at home. Julian remembered he'd been warned about how heavy the winter rains can be. Now he saw for himself and he hurried to buy an umbrella - something he'd never needed before in Chile. The sea, which he had only seen as a beautiful blue/turquoise colour or gold and red when reflecting a fabulous sunset, now looked an evil, dark, browny green and it was very choppy. Julian shivered even to look at it from his apartment window and he was glad he had managed to buy an electric heater in time for Isabel's return as she had to rest. However, the flat's construction was not great. The winds howled and drafts entered every window and door.

They regularly watched the television news and Julian was so pleased that they could discuss the news together. That week the news was filled with children in the hospitals of Santiago with difficulties in breathing because of bronchial pneumonia. There were images of parents with children and babies waiting in corridors, coughing, crying and breathing with medical masks fitted to oxygen cylinders. The numbers had now reached the point where there were no available beds for them all. This apparently was a regular phenomenon. One mother interviewed declared angrily, "The World Cup doesn't matter, the restaurant for the politicians overlooking the sea doesn't matter, but more resources for the hospitals is the only thing that does matter." Julian and Isabel cheered the mother together.

"There have been a lot of references to the high levels of pollution in

Santiago, contributing to the problem of the children's breathing and I bet the elderly are having problems too but they don't seem to be mentioned," said Julian.

"Yes. The air over the city is particularly trapped within the two mountain ranges and industrial and traffic pollution are the actual causes of the widespread bronchial illnesses. Clearly, no one wants to address the real cause of the problem. They address the consequences by restricting the traffic by not permitting cars with particular numbers in their number plates to enter the city on particular days. Things have now become so bad that there was even a march of protesters through the streets of central Santiago demanding action against the contaminated air of the city."

"The environmental damage is contributing to climate change too and that is another reason they have to prevent the pollution. You know, I was thinking. You know what a close view we have of the parliament building when we go up and down in the *ascensor* just here. It's so big it's in your face. I can't help thinking about the total inappropriateness of that building, every time I see it. I was thinking the other day that the giant arch of that building, makes it a structure with a giant hole in the centre. It has always looked incongruous because of its sheer size and alienation from its surroundings but now the hole under the arch strikes me as symbolic of the hole in the centre of the capitalist revolution, a revolution made worse in Chile because the Right forced it through so violently. I was reading Marshall Berman, the American Marxist humanist writer recently. He said the bourgeoisie has "alienated its own creativity" because it is not able to look at the moral, social and psychological abyss of its own creation. We could add, its own environmental abyss. Capitalism doesn't look at the consequences of the abyss it creates, the damaging pollution and the climate change."

"It doesn't want to stop production or make payments to heal that damage. Only government can make it do that and that doesn't happen when the government is composed of puppets of the capitalists," agreed Isabel.

"What a perfect summary of the symbolic meaning of that excessively large building, in the wrong place with a gigantic hole in its centre." Julian went over to Isabel's chair and gave her a long kiss, hugging her and kissing her on the neck too. How he loved to feel they were united in their view of the world and fully understood one another's perspective.

"It's great when we can communicate and share our thoughts…but I wish you would stay longer. You could have a bit of time off work without messing them around much. You haven't taken any sick leave yet for your ankle. You need to rest to get better more quickly than if you push yourself too fast."

"I know, but don't spoil things by starting again about my staying. You know as soon as I can hobble around I have to go back to the job."

"I think you will be exhausted. Just one more week till you've got a bit stronger and hopefully you're in less pain."

"Ok," Isabel said to his surprise. "I've been thinking that too. I do think I need a bit more rest and recovery time. I feel so knackered. I'll have to go to the call centre again though and tell the school."

"Of course. I need to ring Joaquín too and see all that has been going on. We'll have to change your bus ticket too."

-oOo-

Joaquín, who had become Julian's closest friend in Chile, came to visit them both a few days later. He had talked with them both before about a new project that he was planning with others and now he was excited to tell them it was coming to fruition. He was planning to leave his paid community work job very soon and transfer all his time, to the development of this new project, unpaid. Joaquín was to initiate a self-build scheme for homeless people and he had identified some empty land above the *barrio La Isla*, which would become a *'toma'* for the new community. Homeless participants, with whom he had worked closely for many months of planning, would contribute to the communal construction of homes. They would prepare food communally too as a regular principle of mutual sharing, so he could be sure he wouldn't starve without a salary, he said when Julian expressed concern about how he was going to live.

"I trust the people involved and that's enough for me. The essence of the project is mutual self-help. I will share my knowledge and experience of building wooden construction homes and vegetable cultivation and the learning I've been doing recently on creating ecologically sustainable houses. I can enable those who join the project to acquire skills and we will together create a mutually supportive but outward-looking community. You know Pedro the electrician who is a resident of *La Isla*. He is keen to make his family a participant household. He would supervise all electrical installations of the project but he will still do his outside job.

"What other people are interested at present to join the project?" asked Isabel.

There are low-paid workers in insecure and unskilled work who are jumping at the opportunity to join this project. We have had to make a waiting list. There are young men and their girlfriends with no other prospect of a home of their own through to older people who want to give their time and learn skills. There are grandmothers and grandfathers willing to give their all to this collective community. One is Catalina who you know. She is very active at the community centre."

"She told me she had never had a home of her own," said Julian. "All her life she said she had always had to live with in-laws, with all the tensions that involves, especially when bringing up children. Now she is on her own and renting and just caring for one of her grandchildren. I'm so pleased for her if this will bring her a home of her own."

"She was keen to join the project from the very start. There are students too who want a home where they can study, away from the clamour of a busy household, overcrowded with younger brothers and sisters. They all have in common their commitment to making decisions in partnership with one another, through an *Asamblea* of the whole community, which will have various subgroups for organising requirements like finance, social needs, materials acquisition and educational needs. They will all pay a minimum for food purchases by the people in charge of the communal kitchen and we've agreed always to eat together at least twice a week to develop the sense of solidarity. Based on the principles of equality and self-help, participants will solve their housing needs and climb out of poverty. We will create a collective life and a home for each family in compliance with ecological sustainability and mutual self-help."

"Wow! Impressive," declared Isabel. As soon as I can walk about properly I want to be filming the development of your project. Can I, as you go along?"

"Yes, that would be great for us to have a record of the development and to spread the word to others about how this can be achieved."

"Exactly. That is essential and you must explain the philosophy of the project and demonstrate how you are practising equality and democracy. You are very articulate. It will be a great video."

They promised to see Joaquín soon and be there when the first sods of earth were to be dug to begin the work. Julian returned his attention to the present and said he was reluctant to see Isabel off on the next Saturday overnight bus to La Serena.

"Look. I am very interested in Joaquín's project so I have been thinking that instead of going to one or two of the northern cities each month, I will come to you in addition to my usual monthly stay here."

"Oh, I see. The project will bring you more often and you are not coming for me."

"Don't be silly. Yes, I am coming to be with you but I will talk to Juan about reducing my commitments in the north. I don't want to let them down but with this broken ankle, we have come to a natural pause. I also think they are very able to go forward now without my visiting so often. I can regularly phone people like Daniela and support from a distance. It is so limited what we can achieve. I mean I wouldn't mind a broken ankle if it got us somewhere but what has it achieved? I think we need a rethink about how we go forward. We need to build a national mass movement and we seem such a long way off that." Julian was relieved to hear Isabel talking in this way.

"The demos are one way to influence people towards that national movement but there are other ways," he said. "The demos do seem at present rather isolated and limited in what they can achieve." But then Julian was more concerned when she continued,

"I know. The publicity we get is only local and soon forgotten. Maybe damaging property or stopping traffic would bring forth more attention, put us more in the limelight."

"But what about antagonising people too?" Julian tried to keep calm and rational.

"If people see our cause is just, it won't put them off. It will build momentum and eventually the government will have to give in to our demands, as with the suffragettes."

"Well, I hope so but I feel it is early days. Do enough people yet see how unjust the constitution is?"

"We have a long way to go to build enough support, I know. Juan will certainly be impressed with Joaquín's project and he'll agree a video is vital. I think I can best use my time on that and combined with coming to see you..." she smiled as Julian made his way towards her to throw his arms around her. He showered her with kisses. "I really have enjoyed being with you, you know, not just because you have looked after me so well. I'm just glad you are here in Chile and that you understand so much of what is going on. To share my country with you is great. I never thought you would see so clearly what is going on. Your analysis of things is very good you know when there are people here who don't see half that."

"Well I didn't want to tell you but one of the English teachers at the *Catolica* said to me exactly the same the other day. For me it is nothing, there is much more I should know, no doubt, but if you learn and listen and analyse with the right values, you can't miss what is going on."

"Come here, I want to give you a big kiss. I am so pleased we are here together. We do share the same values and that is the most important thing for me."

"Me too." After a passionate kiss, a little awkwardly with Isabel's foot on a stool, Julian said, "That same teacher told me an awful story of what had happened to him during the dictatorship. He had been the Dean of a Faculty in a university until 1978. One day he arrived at his office as normal and found a military officer sitting in his desk chair. The Dean was ordered to write his resignation there and then and he knew that doing that meant he would lose his pension at the same time as losing his job. He had four young children at the time. The military man took out his pistol and placed it slowly on the desk. 'Write your resignation *al tiro,*' he shouted. I can hardly imagine a fraction of what so many people like this have gone through in the dictatorship. He was telling me this story because he wanted to explain a new law that had been passed. Anyone who has lost salary or pension under the military regime could now claim their losses through a judicial process. A few already have been compensated and the lawyers took half of what they were owed but Ronaldo, this lecturer, said he could retire if he could win such a case. He is now 70 years old and still working to get his youngest children through University."

"It's another limited law. You'd have to show loss of an actual job, not for example what you might have earned if the dictatorship hadn't blown your life apart or what you might have had if your husband hadn't disappeared, like Constanza's."

"No, true. Let's hope it is only a start. I want to show you something else we have in common and both enjoy."

"What's that?"

Julian hurried to the kitchen. "Look at this." And he held up a large spider crab.

"Wonderful."

-oOo-

Mateo was at the bus station to meet Helena, with his car. He hugged her but she avoided his kiss to her lips.

"Thank you so much for meeting me. I can't even manage with the convenience of a *colective* taxi, I'm afraid, great as they are. But changing routes and a short walk and luggage are just beyond me at present."

"I know. I'm taking you to my place first for breakfast," said Mateo.

"Oh no, you don't need to do that and I have so much to do at home."

"Well, the first thing you need to do is eat and I want to hear all about everything that has happened to you."

"Look I haven't even a pair of trousers prepared that I can wear to school tomorrow. I can't go in jeans and these jeans are the only ones that are split to go over the plaster. I normally wear dresses or skirts to school but I'd rather cover the plaster with trousers as much as I can. Do you think it would be acceptable in this situation?"

"Yes I think it would but there is no reason not to wear a skirt and let everyone see the plaster in all its glory."

"I'd rather not. But I don't know what would be best. I was only planning to cut open one pair of old trousers. I think I should do that and see what the Head's reaction is. At least there will be a day with it more or less covered for everyone to get used to the idea."

"Helena, have you got your story clear, with some details. I assume this is something to do with your demonstrating rather than a genuine accident." Isabel was a bit taken aback. She hadn't thought of herself as Helena for a while, let alone that he had guessed what she had been doing.

"Breakfast would be great and I'll tell you all about it and test out my cover story with you." It was a while since Isabel had been to Mateo's flat and she was pleased to see its cosy space again. Breakfast was one of Mateo's special brunches and they talked and drank coffee all the morning.

"I'd love you to stay, you know that and I could happily look after you. You won't manage very easily, be honest, will you?"

"I believe I can manage. I've only done some lesson planning and I need to sit quietly and do some more preparation. I need to sort out clothes, I've only a few in that case."

"Do you want some washing doing?"

"No, no thanks. That's all done."

"By the *gringo*, I suppose." Isabel scowled in a joking way.

"No, someone called Martina. Look, I've tried to be honest with you. That's how it is. You can't just wipe out ten years and anyway I don't want to."

"Ok. Don't worry. Let's just get you sorted, *cojo.*" Isabel had to smile at his slang reference to her limp. "And how are you going to get to school in the morning?"

"I'm going to have to take a taxi while I have this plaster on. I can't walk much yet."

"I could come and collect you."

"That's really nice but it would look a bit odd and might start tongues wagging."

"Well, I don't care. I just wish they had something to wag about."

"Let me go by taxi at first and then let's see how I go on walking around the school and whether that's too much in one day or if I could do a bit more. I'm sure in another week I may find I can walk from the *colectivo* stop. Will you take me home now please?"

"And what about shopping? Unless you are going to let me feed you every night and morning, which means you'll have to live here." As Isabel shook her head, he said, "You are going to need some food in the house but promise you will eat with me sometimes."

"Ok. Fair enough. Thank you. Take me to a supermarket now please and I promise to eat with you twice a week."

"It's a deal."

At the school the next day there was much empathy for Isabel and she had to tell her story of falling where the central market was held in La Serena, which everyone knew was very uneven ground and the drops and holes were largely hidden from view when the market was in place and crowded with people. Mateo had stayed well back when teachers gathered around her in the staff room. She was very tired at the end of the first day and when Mateo offered, witnessed by other teachers, to give her a lift, she willingly accepted the offer.

"I know we did a load of shopping yesterday but I'm going to feed you tonight. You look really tired."

"No, I can't," said Isabel thinking that Julian was bound to ring to see how her first day back had gone.

"Yes, you can," he said driving off in the direction of his flat. She was grateful and said no more.

An enjoyable and familiar evening for Isabel followed and when she asked to be taken home, she was taken without delay. As she stood ready to go out of the door, Mateo put his arms around her and hugged her and then released her and she proceeded to the door. The next day he took her directly from school to her flat as requested. He leaned over to kiss her before she left the car. She thanked him and got out. The following day after school, he drove her to his flat and again cooked for her.

"All this kind treatment is very lovely," she said. Mateo smiled.

"Have you seen the paper today? A minor move forward in the so-called transition to democracy was achieved by parliament. They agreed, mostly through Zaldivar, President of the Senate, who secured Pinochet's and other senators' agreement, that the bank holiday which celebrates the anniversary of the military coup, is to be abandoned and the first Monday in September, substituted in its place, as a 'Day of National Unity.'"

"But people still need to protest on 11th September and I'm sure the usual protest groups will be out. They have to remember those killed, imprisoned and disappeared. 'Never will they beat us with torture nor death,' we always shout. We must go on declaring that. I suppose there will be a few people out in La Serena. I should like to be there."

"Oh yes, in your state? At least the Army will no longer parade their triumph on that day. That is something to be grateful for."

"What do you mean, my state? I'm perfectly able to stand in a protest."

"And when they put on the water cannons, how are you going to run away. You'll just be knocked over, have some sense."

"Will you take me home please, or I will go to find a *colectivo.*"

"I'll take you, wait a minute."

-oOo-

The telephone rang at Isabel's quite late that evening and it was Julian for her.

"Where have you been. I've been trying to get you for days. Well, no, I'm sorry I couldn't try yesterday after school because I had commitments at the Community Centre. But I have been worried about you. How have you gone on?"

"Not bad. I have been tired at the end of the school day and on the first day apparently, I looked so tired, I had an offer to drive me home and the teacher insisted I went to eat with her first. Which was very nice of her. I was here Tuesday but this afternoon, she took me home again to eat with her family."

"Well, that's great they are looking after you. What about if I come to La Serena to look after you there at the weekend?"

"No, really, please. There is no need and I must get more preparation done. Look I was thinking that instead of coming to you the following weekend as I normally would, that will be my last week with the plaster on and by the weekend after that, I should be free of this plaster and in a much better state to travel."

"Well, ok but let me come to you, when you would have come here."

"No please, go to Joaquín's project and let me know how things are developing. I should have left my cameras at your place, so you could take a few shots, while I'm still carting this plaster around."

"I could come and get it."

"Please, leave it."

"Um. Ok. My brothers are definitely coming to Chile in November. They have booked now, so I need some help with where I should take them. I think it ought to be the north as it is so very much different from Europe and you know it well."

Yes, great. Without a doubt, right now I suggest San Pedro de Atacama and Tatio and the flamingo salt lakes. Are you going to travel with them?"

"Yes, they have deliberately fitted the dates around when I will be freer because there won't be any Uni classes, as the students have exams."

"That will be great for you. Unfortunately, I will still have teaching commitments. Only the national exam years have no classes."

"Of course. Take care of yourself. It sounds awful I won't see you till October."

"It's only a couple of weeks."

"Nearer three. Much love and kisses."

# Chapter 18

When Isabel came next to Valparaíso, plaster free, they went to visit the new project together without delay. It was now calling itself *Bello Barrio* and a principle ecological measure they had taken was "sawdust" toilets. Joaquín explained.

"We can buy the sawdust very cheaply, it's a waste product of course and there is a sack in each of the communal loos we have created here with canvas divides. They are all we need at present while we are building our houses. A covering of that sawdust into the dry toilet works perfectly and then we bury the waste." Julian and Isabel looked into the loos and were amazed that there was absolutely no smell coming from them.

"We've also rigged up a shower and we recycle the water for our vegetable garden. I have a little wooden house to sleep in now here but others are building more elaborate homes for themselves and their families."

"What about obtaining state subsidies for housing for homeless people," asked Isabel.

"So far, we've had nothing but rejection. The subsidy authorities will only consider houses with conventional connections to sewage pipes, even though the local authority will not permit this in the case of 'taken' land for many years to come. It seems that the state is not prepared to assist self-built housing either and it has no interest in the efforts to be ecologically sustainable. They will finance registered building firms in the construction of traditional homes and there have been in the news some corruption scandals of builders receiving large grants and misusing them or building below-standard homes."

"I know. It is awful and short-sighted."

"It's best for us. It leaves us free to do what we want and not to have to conform to their regulations. Come and see the houses being started." Most were only in the stage of foundation ditches being dug but large piles of wooden pallets stood at the side of several plots. Isabel wanted to be busy with her camera as some project members were digging. She captured Joaquín also saying, "These wooden pallets were to be thrown away, and we acquired them at no cost. They will form the structure for walls for some of the houses, filled with mud and straw between the two levels. Some members are planning to make handmade mud and straw bricks which they bake hard. Look here are some and the mould they make them in. Thanks to you Julian, we have learned that you need double walls to ensure the insulation from the cold and from the heat."

Isabel stopped filming and said, "I've a friend in Arica who has been investigating how to improve the earthquake resistance properties of mud and straw *adobe* traditional houses. They have had no earthquake resistance in the past, but there are ways to greatly improve them. I gather they should have buttresses at the corners and extra strength through pilasters mid-wall. The walls crack in earthquakes at the corners, so these measures prevent them falling on their occupiers. Wooden beam frames help too. This could be really important for you and avoid dangerous collapses, I'll try to find out more. It is the son of my mother's friend so she will still have the contact details for his mother."

"That will be a big help before they go any further," said Joaquín. "I've always said they need to investigate this further. I've always been worried about the risks of earthquakes on mud and brick houses but I think with a good structural frame, they could be much less dangerous."

"Yes definitely. My friend also said large bricks too are important so there's less chance to crack between the bricks. Your idea of stuffing pallets with mud and straw would, I think work best of all because the pallet is a frame to a large solid brick inside, providing they are well packed.

"Where are you getting some funds from? You are going to need money for wood, not to mention food at some stage," asked Julian.

"Do you remember my friend Andrés? We were at school together. He was here last summer but only visiting because he is studying architecture

335

in Germany. He's really committed to helping the project and he has set up a savings/donor group in Germany, 'Homes for Chile' they call it. His friends and anyone he can interest in the project make monthly savings so that they can meet any savings the people here make with an equivalent amount in euros. They are each linked with a family here. Saving is nearly an impossibility for the poorest but a scheme that assists them when extra expenses come along, like new school shoes, and a scheme that doubles their own efforts, helps them make real strides towards saving. There are government schemes here too that enable people to get housing subsidies if they can show evidence of saving in a scheme systematically, so we are using them and hoping we can argue later about the sort of housing they can purchase. Hopefully, we'll win acceptance eventually but the savings will be doubled by the German donors anyway."

"I must see if I can get you some money from England," said Julian. I think friends and relatives and my Dad's church will give something but also I will try my Trade Union. They do give to charities and I think it is reasonable to ask them for a modest monthly payment to you Joaquín whilst you are developing this project full-time and unpaid. A food and clothing allowance, for example."

"That would be wonderful as a safety net, should I need it but also it can be saved for costs like electric lighting along our pathways and some paving slabs because these paths will become mud in the winter rains. We also want to build a log cabin as a communal room with a kitchen and an office. We know that preparing food together helps a sense of collectiveness and solidarity and we want to do that very regularly, not just on special days, so we need a communal kitchen and the room for all year round eating together." They continued walking around the site.

"Over here we plan a visitors' house so that foreign students can do placements here eventually. We've been talking with various academics who do voluntary teaching for us and they seem to value what we are doing and want to make placements here for ecology students and climatology students, social work and international relations students. Watch this space."

When Isabel and Julian were alone, Julian speculated on what he might do to seek funds. He thought he could produce a little leaflet with photos to give out to the people in the UK and he hoped he could get his Dad's church members interested in a scheme similar to the one in Germany. He also had a friend from school whose life had gone in a very different direction from his but they had always kept in touch.

"He's made a lot of money in the City. I think he would make a donation to *Bello Barrio* and he is talking of visiting here before I leave. I'm going to write to my Trade Union rep too. She works in my office and I know her well."

"Could you ask your brothers to bring some children's books when they come? You know how few children's books there are about. It doesn't matter if they are in English, the older children can translate them with the help of the volunteer students that run the homework club and they can put stickers over the words and then we could have a good supply of books for the children when the nursery can get going."

"That's something else my brothers could ask for from the church congregation. It might be a good start to enthuse them about the project. My brothers won't need their allowance of two large suitcases each to bring, so they could both bring a case of books with them."

"They'll have to watch the weight and split the books between the two cases," said Isabel. "It really is impressive what Joaquín is achieving. The philosophy and the practice are very much what I tried to promote. Perhaps, I spread myself too thin over too many areas, though some friends in those northern cities have achieved a lot. They made great strides in giving children some of the opportunities that normally only go to middle-class children. I've seen the adults grow through education and studies that took them on to better lives. But the truly collective nature of *Bello Barrio* and its mutual self-help, its participative democracy, are something very special and rare."

-oOo-

Within a month of the creation of the new Day of National Unity, the calm routine of life and any possibility of national unity, was suddenly, blown completely apart. Late in the night of the 16th October, agents of Scotland Yard informed the ex-General Pinochet, in a London Private Clinic, that they had received an order for his detention from the Spanish Judicial authorities. Pinochet was recovering from an operation on his spine and doubtless, the news was an uncomfortable shock. More than half of Chile, on the other hand, exploded into celebrations when the news broke. The highest legal council of Chile sent a formal protest to Great Britain that Pinochet's diplomatic immunity as a Life Senator had been violated and the Army declared his detention "irregular and unacceptable." However, large anti-Pinochet crowds in Chile were soon out on the streets in all the major cities marching in support of the detention and demanding the ex-Commandant be brought to justice. Four hundred Pinochet supporters attacked the British and the Spanish Embassies in Santiago with stones and eggs and other objects. The leaders of the Christian Democrats and Socialists rejected any defence of the dictator but the country's President, attending a summit meeting in Oporto, Portugal, declared that the Chilean government did not recognise the authority of a Spanish court to judge Pinochet and the President cancelled his planned visit to Madrid.

Day after day in the following week the embassies continued to be attacked, each time more violently, resulting in more and more arrests. The Catholic Church pleaded for calm whilst opposition senators created a "Crisis Committee" and boycotted the legislature. President Frei returned from Portugal to make a call for tranquillity and a plea to not paralyse the country because of the situation of Pinochet, but supporters and opposers were out on the streets even on midweek working days, protesting or celebrating. Chile was in chaos and the tragic divisions of the society, created by the dictatorship, made themselves painfully clear.

The courageous Spanish judge Baltasar Garzón, who had brought this all about over the killing of a number of Spanish persons under the dictatorship, including priests, then demanded an investigation of the Swiss and Luxemburg bank accounts of Pinochet. Margaret Thatcher publicly defended Pinochet for the help Chile gave to Great Britain during the Falklands War. The Chilean government evoked humanitarian reasons to obtain the liberation of Pinochet because of the delicate state of his health but the European Parliament backed the detention and France and Switzerland asked the UK also for Pinochet's extradition for victims from their countries that had disappeared under his regime. The allegations against Pinochet in the High Court in London continued and the UK Law Lords' decision regarding extraditing him to Spain or returning him to Chile, was speculated about in all quarters. Fifty thousand people attended a *fiesta popular* to rejoice at the detention in O'Higgins Park in Santiago.

Julian, Isabel, Joaquín and many others from *La Isla* and *Bello Barrio* happily joined the marchers celebrating on the streets whenever possible. Nothing else seemed so important and the joy was palpable. Julian wrote to his MP again asking that he encourage or support any actions regarding the case of Dr Sheila Cassidy, the British medic who was detained by the military government, as detailed in her moving book "Audacity to Believe." He also mentioned how active and supportive backbencher Jeremy Corbyn had been in recent developments over British detainees during the dictatorship. Julian was of course suggesting his MP should do the same.

Julian's jubilation was rather dampened when he rang his brother Luke in England and Luke had been informed by their travel insurance company that they would not cover them for travel to Chile at this time because the Foreign Office was advising not to travel to Chile. "What nonsense," Julian said. "Now is a great time to travel to Chile when the people are at their most joyous and especially affectionate and grateful to the British. Chile isn't represented by the upper-class areas of Santiago where ignorant and privileged people are storming the British embassy and burning Union Jacks," he assured his brother. Luke, in turn, promised to go on searching for insurance and thought things would calm down before their trip.

Isabel sent a message to Julian that she would not be coming directly to Valparaíso the last weekend in the month as she thought she should take some video of the demonstrations in favour of Pinochet in the capital and then come to Julian's Saturday evening. A demonstration was planned in Vitacura, an affluent part of the capital, in support of Pinochet and it was being organised by the Right's presidential candidate, Joaquín Lavín and Senator Sebastián Piñera. Julian was extremely worried, on getting the message, because she could be putting herself at risk. He rang her that evening and he was relieved to find she was there and answered the phone.

"You could easily get so angry with the supporters of Pinochet and you'll be walking alongside them to take your video. Do you want to look like a supporter? That's crazy and risky, aligning yourself with such people, just to take a few film shots."

"I don't want to be with such persons. I know what they are like and how they upset me, with their posters of *El Salvador* Pinochet. I despise them but I think I should have some video of those in favour of Pinochet to illustrate the huge division within the country. And there have been a few demonstrators in favour of the detention too at the embassies."

"Then there could be clashes. That's even more risky."

"Listen, an idea has been going round in my head this last week that I must make another film. I've already filmed our demonstrations in support of Pinochet's detention and I need the other side. Also, I saw in the paper yesterday a photo of a pro-detention poster, outside the British Embassy, which I thought was superb. It showed Chilean inventiveness at its best. It said, *Gracias Ladi Di por el favor concedido* - 'Thanks Princess Diana for the favour conceded.' You know the princess is known here in Chile as *Ladi Di.*"

"Yes, I know. She died soon after I arrived in Chile and everyone was talking about her. But you're right the poster is clever and makes you smile."

"I'd love to be able to capture that poster on film and I hope it might be on show again this weekend. I'll come to you in the evening. Don't worry. I'll see you soon." In the event, there were 30 to 40 thousand people protesting at the dictator's detention - the organisers said 50,000 and the police estimated 30,000 but Isabel wasn't able to find the witty poster.

The initial decision of the Law Lords on the twelfth day of the detention may have calmed the travel insurance companies somewhat but the mass of the people, knowing Pinochet would not be judged and prosecuted in Chile, was bitterly disappointed when the English Lords initially declared that, as a head of state at the time of the allegations, he had diplomatic immunity.

"That's typical of the British legal system," said Julian, when next on the phone with Isabel. "It's all based on tradition, but to say a head of state is immune, above the law, what principle of democracy does that uphold? It's typical, making a decision on past tradition and not on moral principle."

"The sovereignty of this country is threatened by a colonial power," came the reply.

"You do surprise me in saying that. That's the argument of the Right and even the centre seems to have bought it, but you! And sovereignty equals dignity and democracy does it? What national dignity will Chile have if Pinochet is returned and isn't put to justice? You know that he won't be tried in this country. There aren't even any promises that he will be taken to court here."

"Yes, yes I know that, but it is not a political matter where a principle of modern democracy can be argued. It is a judicial matter, as the UK government keeps saying and so they can't interfere. Legally he has to be judged in Chile and we will make sure it happens."

"Aren't legal decisions disguised power politics in the end?"

"It's our matter to deal with - here in Chile."

"But this country won't deal with it. Fortunately, the Law Lords recognise they have to hear the arguments of Baltazar Garzón, so they aren't letting the dictator go yet. They have to recognise international laws like Nuremberg."

"Ricardo Lagos, a candidate for the Presidency, has pointed out that the English Court has recognised the immunity of the Head of State but not his innocence. Things are starting to change now I'm sure, so we have to have the chance to deal with him and bring all the Chilean cases against him."

"I hope you are right! But I doubt it."

-oOo-

Before the end of October, Isabel received word from Juan, that a new satirical pamphlet was being clandestinely passed around amongst students in the capital. It was called THE CLINIC, named precisely after the Harley Street Consultancy where Pinochet was arrested. Over the door of this privileged private hospital, carved in stone in large letters, it read THE CLINIC. The paper took the English title because of the obvious association but also, Isabel explained when she was with Julian, because the word has a particular significance in Chile.

"A hospital is translated *hospital* when it is a public medical facility for the masses but a hospital is called a *clinic* when it is a private medical treatment centre of much better standards for the fee-paying/privately insured classes. So the pamphlet is a great mockery of the privileged. The founders of THE CLINIC paper are fed up with the timid coverage of Pinochet's arrest in the mainstream Chilean media and they hate the ultra-conservative nature of Chilean society. Like Private Eye, they want to combine serious social analysis with humour, ridicule and mocking of political figures like Pinochet.

There is no tradition of such satire in Chile, no *Spitting Image* sketches of Chilean politicians. This is a big step forward."

"I'd love to see a copy. It's genius to name it THE CLINIC."

"THE CLINIC's first print run was distributed free around the bars of Santiago and then the three founders paid $2000 US dollars each, to get their pamphlet distributed in news kiosks around the capital. Some have called them terrorists but it's a breath of fresh air, Juan says. There are many people glad to make fun, at last, of their leaders and to see a critical analysis of what is happening in Chile, including the failure to transition to democracy. I've asked Juan to send a copy here and perhaps we can make some copies and distribute it about."

"Joaquín and *Bello Barrio* will be glad to see it."

When the paper arrived at Julian's, he was daunted by most of the jokes which were beyond his Spanish. He tried to read a few to Isabel over the phone and get her to explain.

"The whole concept makes me smile but many of the jokes are too difficult."

"It's not just that jokes are the most difficult thing in a foreign language. I don't get all the jokes because I don't know all the references. That's what happens when you are away from your country for a while and you miss so many details. But it's good to see them tackling subjects that no one else seems to dare to touch like Chile still does not have a divorce law and the TV censorship."

"I like the way they call Pinochet *Pinocchio*. He was a puppet of President Nixon. The amazing thing is my Dad always refers to Pinochet as *Pinocchio* and has done so for a long time. Perfect description - he was used by US foreign policy."

"But he was also a representation of the Right in Chile. Sad but true! They were a minority but they were the powerful ones and they couldn't tolerate the democratic result of Allende's election. Did you see the special report in *La Tercera* this weekend, that a UDI party senator is saying Pinochet is a victim of the hatred of the Left who are motivated by revenge because they couldn't "get the power?" The Left had the power under Allende by democratic means and it was seized from them by military force! See how they totally reverse the truth and lie so blatantly!"

"I saw the photo in the paper of the British police outside of THE CLINIC," said Julian smiling, "the real clinic at 20 Devonshire Place, Kensington. The policemen had such looks of consternation on their faces and the heading was that the Rightwing Opposition in Chile is claiming a conspiracy of the socialist left of Chile and Europe together. They can't bear to accept that a Spanish lawyer is just doing his job on behalf of Spaniards killed by Pinochet."

"Things are going to begin to change from now on, I'm sure," said Isabel again with such conviction. "With the detention and THE CLINIC taking off as a newspaper and articulating what people are feeling, the people will be less cowered now. THE CLINIC is demystifying the military facade and its absurd symbols. I'm told the journalists plan to do more investigative work and the paper will question the current politicians and question the pseudo-democracy and all that is happening or failing to happen in post-Pinochet Chile. I'm sure it's a big step forward. I only hope it is the beginning of some justice in Chile and that the cases of torture and the disappeared are investigated properly. Now is our chance. We have to demand that."

Julian could hear in that optimism of Isabel a clear vision of what had to be the new petitions of her political activities and the future of which she would undoubtedly want to be a part.

"I'm sorry but I don't believe it will happen. No one believes he will be prosecuted here for anything."

"Well, Contreras, Head of the *Dina* - Secret Police - is in prison for the killing of Orlando Letelier, a cabinet member under Allende and Ambassador to Washington. It can happen and there will be more prosecutions."

"Contreras was let out on bail and then given protection by a military unit until eventually he was imprisoned but he only got seven years. The CIA wouldn't reveal all their evidence. They would do the same with *Pinocchio* or their part in the whole affair would look so bad. But can you imagine the manoeuvres that would let Pinochet off the hook?"

"You've always got an answer. Things are going to change, I'm sure. We'll get them. We are preparing our case, getting the evidence, my brother and I. You wait and see."

"Don't forget as well, that the prosecution against Contreras was made outside the country, in a foreign court or they wouldn't have him. Chile's gone along with it by making him a scapegoat."

"I've been thinking more and more about the post-detention-of-Pinochet film I want to make. It was only an instinctive notion when I went to video the crowds in Santiago protesting at the detention and our marches in support in both Santiago and Valparaíso. I'm going to have to research in the coming months what is behind all that has happened since. Things are very different from when I made the last film throughout 1995. There's much more chance of international interest too now and the diaspora also needs to know what's happening here just as much as ever. They were the main ones who saw my last film on the private circuits in the UK and in several European countries. The film can begin with the celebration marches in favour of Pinochet's detention and those against it. Then I should like to examine the whole issue of whether justice could be done here if Pinochet was to be returned to Chile. Even our professional body of teachers has delivered a letter for Home Secretary Jack Straw to the UK Ambassador, saying the conditions do not exist in Chile for the dictator to be judged here. They, therefore, supported his extradition to Spain and regretted the position of the Chilean government in its efforts for his return. I could get an interview with the Director of the teaching body. I could represent both sides of the argument with some *Concertación* politicians too."

"Sounds good."

"I could also get an interview with our M.P. for the La Serena area, Isabel Allende. Did you read eleven socialist deputies, including her, sent a similar letter to that of the teachers' but they were in opposition to their leader and presidential candidate? It was to his profound annoyance. Ricardo Lagos is part of the *Concertación* and he pronounced that he would "put in line" the socialist MPs. He declared their actions were undermining the government's efforts to assure the British government that the Courts and Judicial Power in Chile would act and resolve the cases against Pinochet. He said the missive of the socialists suggested that they had resigned themselves to there being no justice in Chile and this is unacceptable to the *Concertación*. This issue is becoming massive and dividing the country, just as much as the dictatorship itself has and I want to get to the truth of these arguments. I think I could get one of THE CLINIC journalists too on film."

Julian reflected on the number of months he had left in the country; only four. Doubtless, Isabel means that for more than just four months she will want to watch developments, do her research, do her filming and then get any political action instigated that she can. All these actions flashed through his mind. He said, "You are never going to stop and summer is coming when the people you need might not be around and not much happens. Surely the political demos demanding a new constitution, are the most needed now, more than ever. You'll need at least to change the amnesty for crimes by officials. That would be the minimum change to the constitution needed to get any convictions here. With that law in place, any conviction is impossible."

"There you go again - pessimistic as ever. The College of Journalists has presented a complaint about illegal detentions, deaths and disappearances of journalists to the Court of Appeal and other groups. Something must come of this. They've been accepted by the Court. They can't be ignored. It can be done, we must do it."

"I know, you have to do it. I just hope you keep safe."

"Well you wouldn't want to stop me would you?"

"No, no of course not. I couldn't."

"No, you couldn't."

-oOo-

Julian was in the north with his brothers Luke and James and his older brother's girlfriend Olivia in late November, when he read in the papers of the further judgment of the Law Lords of the House of Lords. Two of the five had rejected the Appeal of the lawyers representing the Spanish Judge Garzón and three ruled in his favour, stating in their verdicts that immunity is not absolute and that the power of the state was used by Pinochet for the aims of abduction, torture, disappearance and death, which are not the state's function. Excitedly, Julian translated for his brothers the article about the great parade of thousands in Santiago.

"'We cried with happiness because justice has been done,' said the President of the Organisation of the Families of the Detained Disappeared. 'Seconds after the pronouncement of the judgement, at our headquarters we did not have a big collective hug, the majority of us remained crying quietly or taking the hand of the person next to us. Then more and more friends and relatives began to arrive so that soon we could not all be contained in the patio of the building. We could not quite believe what had happened and we came out to start a march. Students and trade unionists were summoned and members of different political parties and we finished by making a massive demonstration of five thousand at least.' Look at the photo of one of the banners that must have been quickly made for the march," continued Julian, "'Now Pinochet to the prison', it says." That evening when they went to a restaurant in San Pedro de Atacama where there was a concert of Andean music, the compere asked each table in turn where the diners were from. When Julian and his brothers' table was reached and he shouted *"Inglaterra"* the whole restaurant erupted into cheering, clapping and stamping with shouts of *gracias* on all sides.

"Thank goodness it wasn't the *vergüenza* I thought at one point the Law Lords judgement was going to be," he said later to Isabel on the telephone.

"They are still going to fight his extradition to Spain like mad. We'll see what happens. I know the humiliation to the country's dignity and its sovereign immunity are arguments of the Right, but there is something in the argument that a country like the UK, which created so many atrocities in India and other parts of its Empire, not to mention the holocaust of the Spanish conquest of South America, that these Europeans think they can be judging our leaders and treating us again like a colony. It is an outrage. I want my father's case and the thousands of Chileans with similar cases, to be heard here. Pinochet cannot just be tried on a few European cases and get away with all the rest."

"Yes, but if he's locked up for the rest of his life because of those cases, it comes to the same thing. Better a bird in the hand than two in the bush."

"Oh, you've always got an answer." Julian wondered where that aggression suddenly came from. He said, "You think I've not understood how you feel?"

"You can't know what it is like for a people suppressed under a colonial power." She paused. "There's been a settlement of the teachers' strike today." Isabel was keen to change the subject. She knew it was very unlikely Pinochet would ever be judged and sentenced in Chile but she was more determined than ever to fight for it.

By Saturday Julian had more arguments to put to Isabel. He understood what she wanted regarding the full weight of justice being brought upon

Pinochet and though things were becoming tense between them over the issue, he felt a need to quote a prominent person, who would always be listened to by Isabel, in support of his argument. He'd found in that day's paper a quote from Eduardo Galeano. He said that Augusto Pinochet "did not appear from nowhere." He was the fruit of an "imperial veto" imposed in the 1970s by the United States on the Latin American democracies. Galeano said he had received the rejection of the immunity of the ex-dictator with immense and unexpected happiness. "This is good news for those who believe in human rights and in the necessity of finishing with the impunity of power." Julian was ready to deliver this quote with a note of triumph in his voice, but there was no reply on the telephone when he rang that day and nor was there an answer the whole of the next day when he tried repeatedly to ring. She wouldn't have gone to any of the cities in the north without contacting me to perhaps see me up here, would she? And she wouldn't have gone to *Bello Barrio* without letting me know, even though she has a key to my flat. Where has she gone?

Julian tried several evenings in the following week to be in touch with Isabel but she was still not at home, according to her landlady. The family party, having flown to Calama and visited San Pedro, Tatio and Iquique, were flying back from Antofagasta to Santiago after the next weekend. Daniela and Leonardo had been true to their word and were laying on a *fiesta* in Antafogasta for their last evening in the north. Julian was so excited about their trip and so delighted to be with his brothers, but a sad concern about Isabel increasingly dampened the proceedings for him. He had loved it when they were all together when his visitors had first arrived. Friends from San Roque came to meet his brothers and Olivia and a great Chilean evening of eating and singing was enjoyed by all. Isabel was there to greet the family too. She knew them all in England and they had acted like long-lost friends. Julian recalled a joke his friend Joaquín made that evening. Luke had brought a full-sized circular *Cambazola* cheese with him, knowing it was Julian's favourite cheese and having heard him complain of little variety of tasty cheeses available in Chile. James had brought White Stilton, remembering how Isabel was especially fond of that. When the cheese was passed around, Joaquín loved the new flavours and said, "You Brits, you can keep Pinochet, just keep on sending the cheeses!" How they had all laughed together. Julian knew the coming weekend in Antofagasta would be a similar warm Chilean event and he had hoped Isabel might travel from La Serena to be with them and her friends there but he could not get hold of her and he didn't even know where she was.

-oOo-

The twice-weekly meals at Mateo's flat had continued after Isabel's plaster was removed and she was very happy with the regular attention and companionship. She knew that the nature of the relationship might change or rather revert to what it had been before, once that plaster was off. She had not fully prepared herself for that moment with a firm decision of what she was going to do. Rather she had postponed the decision in her mind several times. It wasn't that the disagreement with Julian over Pinochet's return was sufficient reason to bring that relationship to an end, it was rather a feeling of dread and dislike about returning to Europe, that was growing in her. If the Brits or the Spanish or others were going to gloat about dealing with "our dictator," she felt angry, shameful though it was to have such a thing as a dictator. The Spanish hadn't even dealt with theirs. Instead of a feeling of warmth towards the U.K. and Julian, she felt an uncomfortable shiver at the thought of returning.

When they arrived at Mateo's flat one evening after school, there was a beautiful orchid plant in the middle of the dining table.

"It's for you," said Mateo as Isabel gasped at its beauty.

"Oh, how lovely. Thank you so much. You are really trying to spoil me."

"Yes, and why not? Will you let me spoil you rather more?" he said coming close to her and putting his arms about her.

"Look, you are very lovely and I confess I don't know what to do. I thought I had thought this all through…" She resisted his attempt to kiss her.

"I want to take you out tonight instead of us cooking here. What do you think about going to the Italian restaurant we went to when we returned from the flowering desert. It's almost a first anniversary for us, only a bit overdue."

"No it's not an anniversary because there has been quite a gap."

"Don't I know it. Come on. *¡Vamos!* Let's go and look at the sunset before we go to the restaurant, as it's quite early."

When they came to the bay of La Serena, looking across to Coquimbo bay, the sky had just enough clouds to reflect additional patterns of golden yellow and red into the sky with patches of intense shades of turquoise and deep blue. The sea was a lustrous silky gold, shading to maroon. Isabel adored to see a sunset over the sea. As they sat on a sea wall Mateo put his arms around her and she turned her head towards him. They kissed and he drew her to him and kissed her again. He jumped off the wall to pull her close to him and with all their bodies touching one another they kissed again.

As they returned to Mateo's flat after their meal, Isabel thought to herself, I do want this and I want to be here in Chile, but I already know I cannot carry on in La Serena as teacher Señora García. I can't let Mateo go on thinking I'm normally called Helena. What a mess. I can't resist this guy. I'm just going to enjoy him and worry about everything else later.

"Penny for your thoughts?" said Mateo as he pulled into his parking place. Isabel smiled and took his hand as they walked towards his flat. "No excuse that you need to start a school day from your flat tomorrow morning. You don't have any classes tomorrow. It's Friday." As soon as they entered the flat they were kissing and taking off their clothes. They tumbled onto the bed and how right and familiar and delightful it all seemed to Isabel.

Whilst Mateo was teaching the next morning, Isabel returned to her flat, gathered papers and books for preparation of various lessons and packed a case full of clean clothes. They had not discussed how long she would stay, it just felt right to her to be there for the coming week. Mateo was delighted to find her at his flat when he returned home. Isabel had been shopping too and had prepared a seafood soup for that evening. After the meal, another passionate evening followed.

On Saturday morning they went together to the seafood market. It seemed later to Mateo that Isabel was able to produce a banquet with oysters, clams, *picoroco,* scollops, mussels and prawns with pasta in a cream sauce. Isabel also bought some seafood unfamiliar to Mateo, *erizos* and *puire* for the following day. The latter, a Chilean shellfish full of iodine with a very strong taste, Mateo found he did not like, but Isabel clearly loved to indulge. The other, the sea urchins, had a smell that was reminiscent of the elephant house at the zoo but Mateo could accept that and didn't dislike it. They were quite a delight that evening as was the swordfish they bought for Sunday. Thus Isabel and Mateo passed a lazy, romantic, indulgent weekend together.

The pleasures of the weekend extended into the following week, although they were both teaching but by the next weekend, Isabel had decided she needed to talk to Mateo, trusting for the best.

"I have to explain something to you. You won't like it."

"You want to go and find the *gringo* again."

"No, that's not what I was going to say, although I ought to see, what are in effect, my "brothers-in-law" before they leave the country really."

"I thought so."

"Listen. I have loved being with you this last week or I would not have stayed. It has felt right and beautiful. I have no doubts about the rightness of being with you."

"So stay. Move-in with me properly, as I asked you to before."

"Listen. You won't like what I have to say and it does cause a serious problem about what I am going to do in the future."

"I hope that future is going to include me or do you want to say it can't?"

"No. Mateo, listen. You know all the political work I have tried to achieve in the northern towns and you know that twice now I have been arrested. I've got 'form,' a record." Mateo looked serious and worried. "I have a false identity, which I only did to try to separate my teaching life from the one with the record. It was just to protect myself and try to get a job when I needed the money to survive. My organisation said they could get me the I.D. papers I needed and it seemed a good idea on just a temporary basis. I never envisaged getting involved like I have with you but I can't just go on being an art teacher in La Serena, with a false identity forever, even if I wanted to. I fear it may catch up with me some time."

Mateo just stared at her. He started to feel angry at the deception but didn't want to express that yet. He shook his head.

"You mean you are not Helena García Sepúlveda? You mean the Isabel they call you up in the north is your real name with different *apellidos?* What are your real last names?"

"Henríquez Navarro and I'm Isabel Helena." Mateo now glared. "I believe I can trust you with this information. My bother is the only other person who knows…"

"And you wait till now to tell me. You didn't trust me for all this time?"

"How could I tell you? And how important is it anyway? What difference does it make? At the school, I'm Helena García...and with you..."

"It makes a hell of a difference. You couldn't even be honest with something as basic as your name."

"It's just a handle, a label."

"No, it's not just an unimportant thing. What else can't I trust? What else is false about you? What else have you not told me?"

"Absolutely nothing."

"You might not have anticipated getting involved with one of the teachers but when that happened, did it not cross your mind, to be honest with me then?"

"Well, I'm telling you now. Now that perhaps we, I at least, am further on in our relationship."

"What on earth does that mean?"

"Now we are involved again, my feelings are deeper and I am taking it more seriously than before."

"Well, I took it seriously before. You clearly were just messing about."

"No, but I couldn't decide."

"Oh, so now you have and I'm supposed to just brush over that. Don't worry Helena or Isabel or whatever, that's all right. That's fine. You've ruined everything."

"I'm sorry."

"And you can't just tell the Head and stay on with a new name. *¡Dios mio!* Have you any idea how serious is the offence of false identity? Then you'll really have 'form'."

"I'm trusting you never to reveal this." Mateo angrily shook his head. You can't stay in La Serena. You can't get a reference from the school. And I can't be with you unless we go far away somewhere completely unknown. No, it's not all right."

"It's been an awful shock for you. I must go." Isabel gathered her things together and he did not attempt to stop her. She looked back at Mateo as she went out the door but he did not return her look.

Isabel returned to her flat and felt very alone and somewhat depressed. Mateo did not talk to her the following week in school and she was alone every evening. She prepared herself to take the overnight bus to Valparaíso on Thursday, at the end of her teaching week.

# Chapter 19

The travellers had returned from the north that week to Julian's flat and there was much-animated talk of the geysers, heated lagoons, moon-like desert landscapes, the French astronomer and the flamingos. Isabel shared photos of the dessert in flower and the *Chinchorro* mummies. She had brought her slide projector with her. They all visited *Bello Barrio* together and delivered the large quantity of children's books brought from England. The construction of the communal room, kitchen and office were now well underway. The building was an impressive log cabin built of regular-sized tree trunks, which were purchased with donations collected from Chilean supporters. Luke and James were also able to present donations from their father's church congregation and friends. They were so enthusiastically welcomed and thanked, that Julian was delighted his brothers had experienced the full Chilean warmth and understood better what he was doing in this country and why he loved the people so much.

Joaquín had a story to tell them. They had already recognised that the nursery and after-school club they planned would have to have their own premises because the equipment, toys and tables and chairs donated would take up space and now the children's books needed to be displayed to invite the children's interest too. They had been given some logs and made a start on this new construction but the wood they acquired free turned out to have a wood termite eating it away. The trunks were only fit for firewood, so the further donations from England enabling them to purchase some good logs would save the day. The termite, however, would give its name to the children's nursery. They had decided to call it *La Polilla*. The *Asemblea* had also decided the after-school/homework club would be called *La Biblioteca*. The English brothers had another surprise for them. They were able to tell them that so many books had been given them in response to their *Libros para Chile* campaign, that there were a great many more books on the way by cargo ship.

The visitors also went to Pablo Neruda's house in Valparaíso before Isabel had to make her goodbyes and take the overnight bus to La Serena. Julian took his brothers and Olivia to various seaside locations along the coast in their last few relaxing days of their holiday. Everyone seemed very satisfied with their holiday in Chile. Julian had a strong desire to return to Britain with them and missed them desperately when they were gone. However, they had bought him a dial-up modem and a second hand laptop, so he would more easily be able to keep in touch with them and his friends by email and Skype.

Julian had not wanted to ask Isabel where she had been when he had tried to reach her by phone, until after the visitors had left. When she next visited and they had made a further visit to *Bello Barrio* for her to do more filming, he felt compelled to bring up her disappearance but received no satisfactory reply.

"You must be able to remember where you went, if it wasn't possible to get you even quite late at night and all week, you must have been away," he argued.

"I am allowed to stay out late at night if I wish," she retorted. "I do have a social life in La Serena and you wouldn't ring too late to upset my landlady would you?"

"True, but you were never there. I did so want to talk to you."

"To keep going on about Europe deciding on our affairs."

"Well, you must be glad he's not strutting around the Senate but a worried man under house arrest. It's all in the hands of the Home Secretary Jack Straw now. By the way, Jack Straw's son was on my Social Work training course and we did a community work placement together. I got to know him quite well. I'm sure he would expect his father to do the right thing."

"What is the right thing?" said Isabel as she rather sulkily threw herself into a chair. "The Pinochet family are trying to get it accepted he isn't fit to go before a judge because he's under psychiatric care for stress and depression. Nothing like the stress and depression he put a lot of other people under. They want him to have the right to respect for his state of health and the right to a fair trial. What rights did thousands of defenceless people have when they were tortured, executed and disappeared, without trial..." She was so angry she couldn't go on.

A while later Julian tried again. "I just wanted to talk to you and it doesn't seem like much of a relationship if we don't know where each other is any time and can't get to share things."

"Do you always share things with me?" Julian was a bit taken aback by this. He had always thought he was open and willing to share everything when she would let him. Was it just a ploy to deflect from looking at what she had done and her not being honest with him about where she was?

"Yes, of course, I do share things when I get the chance. If you will let me get hold of you. I'm pretty fed up with you not answering the phone or not being in touch for ages. Do you think that is a right or fair way to conduct a relationship?" His voice was rising and he knew she was switching off.

"You're fed up are you." Isabel was clearly going into another silent sulk and Julian hated these. He knew if he spoke in that way, her sulking would be the result. He also knew the sulk was an avoidance and they had not discussed all those months the previous year when she had not been in touch at all with him and he hadn't known where she was. He had tried to put that behind him but he recognised he felt resentment and out it had come. Now it was hopeless to talk further. Isabel got herself a book and went out to the balcony.

After dinner that evening, when there had been little conversation, he tried some reconciliation. "I want so much to be with you and for us to be together in every sense." There was no reply. "There always seems to be something missing. Why are you so distant sometimes with me even when we are together? Does it make sense to carry on like this?" He realised he'd said the wrong thing again in her eyes and being accusatorial wasn't going to get anywhere. However, he wanted to shout about the months when she'd not been in touch and he'd been worried, frightened for her safety and he had felt abandoned. It hurt. Why did he always feel pushed into a position where he had to either ignore what she had done or have to complain about it? It was always the same. If he complained, he was in the wrong for "blaming and moaning". If he said nothing, her behaviour was never held accountable and she was always ready to hold him to account for the slightest mistake.

There clearly wasn't going to be any coming together that night, let alone discussion about the future, nor resolution of the issues. They remained outstanding as always, Julian was thinking. He knew he should make a definite decision on the whole affair. Would it not be better for him to return to his home country having resolved the whole matter with a definite end to it? Isabel was bound to stay on in Chile in the light of political developments and all she now was set on achieving. They had been invited and accepted an invitation to a family Sunday lunch with Emilia, the mother of their friend Diego as Diego was in Chile, or Isabel would very likely have left on the overnight bus that evening. He dreaded their relationship falling back into the worst of times that it had reached in Britain. She seemed no more contented here in Chile recently and it couldn't be that forced exile was the reason. What was really the cause of her lack of commitment?

Diago and his large family were gathering together the next day. In the event it was a very happy day for Julian and Isabel and it avoided conversation between the two of them. Julian laid his worries aside to enjoy the Sunday *almuerzo*, as he felt he had done too many times before. Emilia served the best whole salmon baked in the oven he had ever tasted. It really was perfect and he was assured by Diego's brothers it was because it had come fresh from the south of Chile. The families of Emilia's children, all crowded into Emilia's small bungalow, made a warm, friendly and numerous gathering. Some were keen to give advice as to where Julian should visit in the south of Chile before he returned home and the suggestion of a trip was put to Isabel by them, immediately. Isabel carried off her response beautifully without a hint of problems between them. She said that she had always wanted to go to the *Torres del Paine National Park* and how they should do that to complete Julian's visit to Chile. So what did that mean, Julian wondered, but he would have to wait before he could discuss it with her.

"You should see the south, its true," and "let's see," was all he could get out of Isabel when seeing her to the overnight bus.

"When can I ring you?"

"Anytime but I don't promise to be there waiting for you." It felt like an unpleasant note Julian had hoped to avoid.

-oOo-

"Can I see you at the weekend," said Mateo to Isabel when he managed to catch her alone, having followed her out of the staff room.

"Is there any point?"

"That's exactly what we need to talk about. Will you come to my flat on Saturday. I'll sort all the food. Don't bring anything, only yourself."

"I'm feeling a bit low, a bit vulnerable. I don't want to get hurt further. I have to protect myself."

"Can we meet to discuss all that. You know we can't here."

"What about on a neutral territory?" Isabel was thinking at the flat she could be persuaded into a sexual encounter when she had determined in her head that it was all over. "I could meet you where we go to see the sunsets. Don't worry about preparing food. It will be helpful just to talk."

The sunset is worth seeing at least, thought Isabel as she got out of the *colectivo* Saturday evening. She went to sit on the wall above the beach and watched the golden waves of the sea. Mateo arrived very soon after her. He put his arm around her and kissed her on the cheek and asked how she was.

"Thank you for coming," he began. "I just didn't feel we could simply leave things as we had and go on seeing each other all next year, whilst not speaking having not parted well."

"Yes, I think you are right."

"I was shocked and I confess, very cross. Now I have had time to calm and to think. I just want to say that I admire your courage. I understand how things came to be the way they are. I wanted to apologise for being angry."

"No, no need for that. I don't blame you. It must have been a shock."

"There would be no harm done if you remain on the path you had intended. It is only if you want to choose a different path that everything becomes very complicated."

"I know. I can't ask those complications of you. I thought perhaps I could expect them, but that was so wrong of me. I see that now. I had some fantasy that we could escape somewhere far away. It was madness and a moment of mature thinking makes it plain, that it would never be all right - we would not be all right in the long run."

"Sadly, I think that is true. Wherever it was, even in Chile, it might be like you described exile."

"It would be exile."

"I think we have come to a similar conclusion, which perhaps says how right we are for each other. We can't run away, like in some Ana Karenina and Vronsky passionate affair and expect it to all be roses."

"I know. It wasn't roses for them."

They sat quietly on the wall.

"Look the sun is touching the water now. It sends a bright golden line across the sea directly to us, as if reaching out to us to bathe us in warmth," said Isabel.

"It is like the sun is telling us to be warm and caring to one another."

"I thought we had that. That is why I felt I could ask you for help when I needed it and I trust you."

"We do have trust and you can ask me any time for help. I want there to be friendship between us, that there won't be a coldness every time we see each other."

"I want that too."

"I felt I had to apologise for being so angry and let you know I have not maintained that anger and it will not return. I'm sorry that you said you felt depressed. How do you feel now? Can our ongoing friendship help you with that?"

"I was hurting a lot at first but knowing you don't think too badly of me helps."

"I know what you did was not with bad intention. I really meant it when I said I admire you. I realised it took courage, though I can't say I agree with you doing it. I do agree with why you did it. If I can help you in any way in any political work you do or any trouble you get into, I am there and willing to help in any way I can.

"I appreciate that. I will feel very alone next year."

"You are assured I won't betray you to the Head or anyone else. You know that I hope."

"Yes, I know."

"Let's find a restaurant. I don't want to ask you to my place, though I hope there may be occasions in the future when you might come."

What a decent guy, thought Isabel. Mateo took her hand as they walked along the seafront, through the crowds to select a restaurant from the many available.

"This one is supposed to have a good reputation. Let's look at the menu."

They stayed at the restaurant until late into the evening, talking very freely about many different topics. It all seemed so natural and easy. When Mateo had taken Isabel home, she went immediately to bed, though her head was full of thoughts. If only things could be different. She did not think she would have been able to be so resolute if Mateo had not been so resolved. He was strong and firm but very affectionate and tender in a caring, loving manner. She was going to have to do the right thing and stick to her decision to maintain her relationship with Julian and go to the south with him. She had not done what was right in the past but she had been weak and indecisive and created a mess, not only for herself but for Mateo. She'd taken it as fun but she knew she had hurt him and now she had a taste of that hurt when she had wanted it to be more serious. It was her not knowing or not being able to decide what she really wanted that was the route of her problems - as if she had not found herself. She could see that now. *Have I really confronted who I am and what I want*, she wondered? *I am very sure of my political values and I can articulate them clearly, but they were societal. What about my own personal values - my practice of my values in individual relationships? Am I sure I can spell those values out and not find them wanting ethically? I have focused on my own need and what I have wanted at any given time. I have not focused on the other person, their needs or the hurt inflicted if I was not taking a relationship seriously. Only by doing that, I now realise, would the values by which I live my personal life, be consistent with my commitments at the political level.*

*I always valued an idea I learned from Julian and he learned from his study of the Spanish philosopher Miguel de Unamuno. We both had similar values we thought but Unamuno articulated them more fully for us. I remember the discussions we had more than once, that were so illuminating. Unamuno said we only know and feel humanity in and through ourselves and when we find our brothers and sisters within ourselves, we come to love them, because they love life as each of us do. In a deep examination of our own selves, our needs and our passionate love of our own lives, so our thinking broadens and flowers into a love of all that lives. These values drive our political ideas and actions to care about what happens to our fellow human beings. But what about on the individual scale - the humanity of Mateo or*

*Julian? What have I done in not loving as I could and should? What self-centred values have driven my behaviour?*

-oOo-

There were three more weeks of the term before classes broke for Christmas and the summer holidays. Julian was glad to be with some of his student friends again and enjoyed the celebrations with them when their results came through at the end of the academic year. He had another interesting conversation with the Literature Professor when collecting his latest essay from him. The professor said something that really troubled Julian for some time. He said that a culture takes centuries to develop the separation of the three parts of government and that this does not exist in Chile. "But," Julian responded, "Surely the old constitution, like that of the United States, had the separation of powers concept deeply embedded in it and there must have been a tradition to that effect."

"No, that was the theory but it was not practised by the privileged in judicial and political positions and with the recent military government, it was all lost completely. The judiciary is sadly not independent and certainly wasn't under the dictatorship," said the professor. Julian went away saddened again by another lack of a basic principle of democracy. *If they ever write a new constitution they had better get the separation of powers very clearly written in,* he thought. *But how separate would they prove to be in Britain where the judges are supposed to be independent, if it came to a crunch decision on a governmental action? How independent would the final decision by the U.K. on Pinochet be?* Julian wanted to share all these thoughts with Isabel but decided that he should not at present. *She'll only be more antagonistic if it looks like I am criticising her country yet again. But she was incessantly criticising mine, the country that took her in, in the first few years I knew her. I was critical of many things in my own country of course but nothing was right for her. She seemed quite surprised when I agreed with her critical comments on much about Britain, especially the racism. Was she testing me to see if I would stick with her? They were valid arguments and I guess they represented how alien she felt at being in the U.K.*

Julian decided to mention to Joaquín what the professor had said, the next time he saw him at *Bello Barrio*. It was after Julian had spoken to his brother Luke that day.

"Luke tells me that Jack Straw, the Home Secretary, says he can't send Pinochet to Chile because Chile has not asked for an order of extradition, but I thought there was no extradition treaty in place between the UK and Chile."

"I think it can still be asked but they'd have to admit a case in a Chilean court on behalf of a Chilean disappeared person or an imprisoned and tortured person like Garzón has done on behalf of 90 Spaniards. "The problem is, under the present constitution, it is not possible to bring a case on behalf of any individual Chilean in a court here," said Joaquín.

"So this means that Isabel, even if she had the money and all the evidence she'd need, couldn't bring a case about her father?"

"No she couldn't, it would need a political agreement in Chile first to change the constitution."

"That seems hopeless but it was quite clever of Straw or the UK government to leave the door open for that. Perhaps Chile could be nudged into doing the right thing about changing the constitution."

"But it won't happen, they must know that. The Right isn't interested in changing the Constitution. Nor are they really interested in Pinochet, they only want to maintain the system as it is now. No one in power has said that Pinochet should be judged in Chile. On the contrary, it is the basis of the Transition Government that 'Pinochet *no se toca*', the promise that Pinochet is never to be touched."

"And Pinochet has just sent a letter to the people in which he calls the country 'a truly democratic regime in which all the institutions function fully,' meaning the judiciary, the parliament, everything. *¡increible!*" said Julian.

"'*No se toca*' applies not only to what senior members of the Armed Forces were up to but applies to secret pacts that surrounded the dictatorship when leaving the presidency and the *Transición* government was coming in. I was reading an article in *Punto Final,* one of the few left periodicals. There were many areas that the military regime wanted to keep secret and a major one was the hundreds of hectares of land, hundreds of properties, houses and flats that the Armed Forces had acquired and the huge profits made by them in secondary sales. The journalist was quoting from a book recently published by Dauno Tótoro who says there is an unknown mountain of these operations that have made senior military and civil companies a massive amount of money. We know Pinochet became very wealthy but these operations have continued in the *Transición* time, although the author says there have been ministers who've tried to put an end to this embezzlement and fraud. They've failed because the military remains so powerful. He also makes the point that this is an 'insult to the population' affected by severe cuts in health, education and housing budgets, taking place at the same time as the generals have gone on enriching themselves."

"Wow, Isabel ought to try to get hold of this author for her film."

"Yes, she should. And, you know that the President and members of the government have to meet with the National Council, the senior Army and Navy personnel whenever the military demand it. Well, yesterday they met again and that was for the third time very recently."

"As Moulián says, the Armed Forces in Chile are politicised and the people are depoliticised."

"They want to keep firm control in this fluid situation of Pinochet's arrest and the impact that has had on the country. They are leaning on the government even more than usual."

"What a tragedy. What a democracy!"

-oOo-

Julian attempted to ring Isabel, twice without success. He was so frustrated and felt there was much to tell her about. Eventually, he was able to get in touch with her and he also wanted to get a plan about Christmas and the New Year out of her.

"You know this flat offers the best view that you could wish for, of the fireworks in Valparaíso Bay on New Year's Eve. I hope we'll be here together to see them."

"Yes," she said, rather to his surprise. "I wanted to know if you want to come to my mother's house at Christmas. My brother will be there and his family."

"Wow, yes I'd love to."

"Well, don't sound so surprised. What do you mean 'Wow' it's perfectly natural isn't it unless you have something else in mind."

"No, no. Yes of course I would like it very much."

"We could stay from Christmas Eve to say 28th December and then we could go to your place. I won't be able to see you this coming weekend though. It's the last one before Christmas and I have a lot to do."

"Oh yes, ok, I understand. I was hoping to put a tree up with you, but I'll get that done so the place is decorated for when we come from Santiago. Shall I try to arrange a bit of a party for New Year? I could see if Joaquín and the others would like to see the fireworks from here too."

"Yes, nice and my brother and family might want to come over. It'll be the best view they could hope for the children to see the fireworks without having to take them into the crowds down in the port."

Julian went to the Christmas fair in the park next to the parliament building at the weekend to try to ensure he had all the decorations, lights and a tree that he thought were necessary. There were a huge number of stalls to choose from and amongst them a number of artisan craft stalls too. The Chileans certainly seemed to make a big thing of Christmas. He felt he had to choose carefully to find a tasteful set of baubles and reject a lot of brash plastic stuff but he did like the beautiful handcrafted wooden toys on the artisan stalls. He realised he ought to check the ages of Carlos' children before deciding on any of these as presents for them. He thought they were probably a little old for these wooden toys now. He would have to ask Isabel. He tried throughout the day and into the evening to ring Isabel but there was never a reply. The next day it was the same. He was troubled again because she had not said she would be away this weekend.

Julian went to a travel agent's whilst out Christmas shopping and obtained some information on getting to the National Parks in the far south. He thought buying an air ticket for Isabel would be a great Christmas present but he didn't want to make a plan for her before she had agreed to go with him and confirmed the dates which suited her. Where was she on these unexplained weekends? There was little time to worry, however, with preparations and parties to attend to in *La Isla* and *Bello Barrio*. The crowd in the communal kitchen was full of excitement and the children's party was a great success. Sitting around the campfire with a large cauldron cooking supper, together with the music, the singing and the chatter was the best of Chile, thought Julian, but for him, there was one ingredient missing.

For his personal Christmas celebrations, Julian bought a butterfly broach in gold with lapis lazuli for Isabel to open on the day, still with the hope they could travel to the south soon after the New Year. He decided to disguise the apparent size of the present by wrapping the broach up in a box with a lot of leaflets he had found on tours to the National Parks Laguna San Rafael and Torres del Paine. For her mother, he bought a blouse and for Carlos's wife, Mariana he bought a lapis lazuli necklace. He bought a shirt for Carlos and after consulting Carlos on the ages of the children, he found a beautifully carved wooden chess set for Antonio, now seven and a put-together wooden train set for Liliana, four years. He was looking forward to seeing Carlos again after the very warm conversation they had on the telephone.

The days of Christmas in Santiago passed with Isabel's family were very enjoyable for Julian and the only uncomfortable moment was when Isabel smashed a book down onto the kitchen table when all the adults were together sharing the food preparation for the Christmas Eve dinner. The book was by the journalist Patricia Verdugo and the title was *Los Zarpazos del Puma* in which the journalist details much of the *'caravana de la muerte'* that massacred 72 prisoners when a special armed commission journeyed to the provinces on board a military helicopter called *the Puma*. Isabel had been given the book as a present and she made a remark about the courage of the journalist to speak out when so many don't. Isabel's mother looked so angry and let out,

"Don't you start. I'll…," waving a finger in her face. All such subjects were then given a Christmas break and proceedings went on smoothly after that. Julian wondered in how many households there was a fragile truce in the terrible divisions of many Chilean families after all that had happened.

When Isabel and Julian were alone, Isabel said, "I really do appreciate time with my brother and the children you know, and Mariana too of course. I mean I must stay in touch with my brother and these children and see them regularly over the coming years, wherever I am. Perhaps they could afford to come to England sometime. It would be a great experience for the children. When they are older they could perhaps stay a school term and attend school there."

"Yes, I think that would be possible. And absolutely we must see them all frequently. That's essential and we can come to visit here often. I like being with the children. They are very lovely and Antonio is pretty good at chess for his age. I didn't know he had already learned to play. They have a chess club at his school but he told me he'd never had a chess set of his own before, so I think it was a good present for him."

"Yes, it was perfect. He puts my chess skills to shame. He knows he can beat me and so he wants to keep on playing with me. His dad won't let him win if he can help it because it's the only way he will get better."

"Yes, I agree, I do the same but he's beaten me once."

"Liliana is good at her numbers and she's learned to read a lot of words from the flashcards. If only all children could have this early stimulation, what a creative and talented society we could be. When is it going to happen?"

"Come on, don't get sad. It's Christmas."

"At least I beat you all at Monopoly," Isabel said. "You have to be ruthless like the capitalists are."

"But there's lots of luck involved in that game, it's not just skill."

"I know, you're right, but that reflects reality too. "Mostly, those who get all the wealth and privilege are the ones who already have it by luck of birth."

They climbed into bed and Julian put his arm around her as Isabel snuggled up to put her head on his chest, but she was sad for another reason.

"It's a whole year since I went to the Vicariate and since I met the famous lawyer. When I went there two days before Christmas, there was still no admission that the coffins were ordered by the military even though various human rights organisations have demanded that acknowledgement and they have not proven them to be old. The police have never come up with a scientific report on the age of the coffins, nor permitted an independent examination of them, which of course the lawyer asked for."

"Do you think they found they were recent and not 100-year-old nitrate company's coffins and this meant they could never publish their findings?"

"Yes, I think so. They just put a blanket ban on any statement and they have left it at that. That's what I was told. How can they get away with that? But they do. There is no accountability. It's like the disappearance of my father. I told you when I last rang a few months ago, the farthest the investigating lawyer got was a recognition that my Dad had been held at the concentration camp and they said he was then released. That is what they do. That's all they say and apparently, that is normal. No liability - only lies. They pretend they had let him go and have no further news of him. Sometimes they say a prisoner's own party killed him, but that's not true and couldn't apply to my Dad - a Trade Union representative in a Teachers' Union. It's not like a revolutionary party they want to discredit. So they just say they let him out and know nothing." Isabel began to weep again.

"I suppose it's something that you have an acknowledgement that he was held there. Could that not be used? Used for wrongful imprisonment with a large number of other acknowledgements of people detained?"

"Not under this constitution. It is so awful and just brings us back to when are we going to change the constitution?"

"I know, I know. Don't be sad. You are going to be tackling that issue again next year and nobody is doing more than you. Don't be downhearted when you are with your family, with people who love you." She snuggled into him more and they lay quiet.

On Isabel and Julian's last day in Santiago, they went to the *Parque Intercomunal de la Reina* with all the family. It was good for Julian to see a large green space in the city, although it was situated amongst the more privileged areas of Santiago. With a magnificent backdrop of the snow-capped Andes, the extensive grassy areas and the trees gave ample space to the walkers and joggers, the families picnicking and the groups of teenagers playing football. Their family party enjoyed a walk in an area left to grow naturally and Isabel and Julian chased the children, rolling in the long grass with them, tickling and being tickled. Julian and Mariana went to buy *asado,* served with a variety of salads and vegetables, from the stalls barbequing meat on the edge of the park.

In the few days when the couple were alone in Valparaíso between Christmas and New Year, they agreed on a plan for a trip to the south and made the appropriate bookings. Julian was so happy and excited with anticipation and the trip was to begin on 1st February. Meanwhile, there was the New Year's Eve fireworks party at his flat to organise, followed by summer activities, trips and camping with *Bello Barrio* he was to assist in. Isabel said she needed a visit home to get more winter clothes for the trip south and another visit to Santiago to do an interview and some editing of her video of *'The Chilean Divide.'*

"*Bello Barrio* wants to arrange a leaving party for me when we return from the south. I really would like you to be with me for that," said Julian. He thought it was time to face the issue of whether Isabel was coming with him to the U.K. - a subject he had put off long enough.

"I'm going to stay with you when we come back from the south, until your flight and see you off."

"But you know I want you to come with me to England. We really should be together if this counts for anything. You know I can't ask for any more time off from my work. I've already had an extension."

"I'm going to do another year at the school in La Serena. This is going to be an important year in Chile politically. I feel I can't do anything else but be part of the changes that have to come about now, following the *huevon's* arrest."

"So that's it! And it's definite and all arranged without saying a word to me before confirming with the school."

I haven't confirmed anything. I just haven't given in my notice. I would have to have done that a whole semester ago. Anyway, would it change anything? Wouldn't you still be determined to go back? I can't go now. I will next year. I promise. I've got to try to achieve something in the coming year."

"If only you had told me sooner. I knew what you were thinking but it's wrong you don't say honestly what you have decided."

"Look, I've thought long and hard about it. It was not a quick decision. *Mamadre* desperately wants me to return and now Eugenio doesn't want to come back to Chile, like many such young people now settled there, she feels she shouldn't come but stay in England where he is. Then there's the issue of what chance of employment she has here and what pension would she get here. It's hard for her to return."

"So coming back to England finally matters not for me but for your stepmother," said Julian.

"Don't be silly, but it is part. of my thinking, of course. I should like to come with you but you must see that I can't, with all the possibilities about what might happen here now after the detention. I must try to do my part in the political agitation we are going to need to change the constitution. I've all those contacts, all those people committed to action and with Pinochet in custody, there is less feeling of fear. I know we can build up more numbers and really make our demands heard now. I can't fail to work at this now that there is the opportunity."

"What opportunity? It could take years. It took Mahatma Gandhi's non-violent protest years and many imprisonments."

"It had better not take the twenty years it took him! No, no, I promise I won't stay more than one more school year. I must try this year to make sure the activists are building up momentum and check out what I can for the legal case of my father, to help Carlos. Also, I've two films to finish that I am in the middle of making. You must see I can't leave in March." Julian came around the table to give her a hug and a kiss.

"I do understand, with the detention, you are going to have to be here. But one year only, yes? Come what may, because there will always be more to achieve." He pulled her to him again and they kissed.

"Honestly, I do want to be with you. We are going to have a wonderful holiday together before you go." Isabel licked what she could reach of his chest and began undoing his shirt buttons. He responded by caressing her neck and began to undo her blouse. Soon they were in bed. If only it were all as exquisite as this, thought Julian as they rested, lying together after making love.

"I had hoped we might want to have some children before it's too late."

"Perhaps. I…" she raised her eyebrows and gave a slight smile. "We should have done that a few years back if we were going to. I know, we were always unsure of where we were going with the relationship. We never seemed to settle down to anything stable, or rather, I didn't, I'm sorry but it's not too late."

"I know, I hope, or we might think about adoption. We know each other much better now. I'm sorry for my part. I do understand the pressures on you in the past and your priorities right now," said Julian, very surprised that she had apologised for the first time ever. "I never have wanted to let you go. I came to Chile to complete and finish the Chilean interlude of my life. Now I am even more in love with Chile and swept up in it and in love with you. We'll work things out, together. We can come here every year in work holidays and you might stay a bit longer - but not too long. We have to be together."

"Yes, but you do understand the duty that I feel I have to my people. You do see why I need to get things achieved here this year and out of my system."

Julian couldn't see that the situation here would ever be out of her system. "I knew you'd want to be here longer now. I understand that completely with all that is going on. I'm not surprised. But it was a bit of a shock to know it was all definite. I thought you'd arranged it with the school without saying a word. We must be more open about our thinking in the future. So, to give a semester's notice you'll have to give notice this coming August. Well, that doesn't sound so bad. Maybe I could come for Christmas and have a few weeks in January here and we could return together. But for now, I want to be with you as much as I can, so I want to go with you to La Serena for a few days when you go to get your things and I want to go to Santiago with you."

Isabel looked a bit doubtful. "You'll be bored hanging about whilst I'm editing video at the studio. I was thinking of a week in La Serena, so I could do a bit more preparation for next term rather than leave it all till after you've gone. Anyway, you'll have too many commitments with *Bello Barrio*."

"Well, can't we make it a long weekend like Friday to Tuesday in La Serena and then you could bring some of your preparation here, while I go alone to some events with *Bello Barrio*. Let's not be separated at all whilst we don't need to be. I've done my full year's commitment to La Isla now. *Bello Barrio* will understand when I can't be there and they don't depend on me. It's just a pleasure to be with them but it's more important for me to be with you. You know I love capital cities, so if your mother or Carlos will have me - I know Carlos will - *'mi casa es tu casa'* he always says to me, I would be happy to see more places in Santiago whilst you are busy there."

"OK. Let's stay with Carlos, but we'll go to La Serena first."

# Chapter 20

C arlos and family came to stay for the New Year's Eve party and more than a dozen came from La Isla and *Bello Barrio*. Santiago, Director of the La Isla Project and his wife came and four of the teenagers who had been especially friendly with Julian. The volunteers there, Alejandro the guitarist and Victoria, the electrician Pedro and his wife and two teenage children, grandmother Catalina and her teenage grandchild as well as Joaquín and a volunteer at *Bello Barrio* from Spain. Julian did a round of champagne with ice cream and chirimoyas and the Spanish girl passed around grapes for them to all eat twelve with the twelve strokes of the clock at midnight in the Spanish tradition. Everyone had brought food, Isabel made a ceviche of *reineta* and put out several plates of seafood and salads. They brought wine and beer and juices and cheered and oohed on the balcony watching the spectacular fireworks display. They all hugged each other after the fireworks and filled their glasses again with champagne. They then danced the conga around the flat.

Isabel and Julian enjoyed a long lie-in the next morning. They had seen Carlos and his family off quite early when the children woke up and had decided to go back to bed. They chatted and cuddled and reflected on the party. Julian wanted to thank Isabel because for him it was a perfect atmosphere to have her there with his Chilean friends, but he didn't know how to say anything without sounding gauche and foolish. Finally, he decided he must say something whatever the risk.

"You know it has been such a good experience to know these people and to be with you and them together is sheer happiness for me."

Isabel smiled and climbed on top of him to kiss him. "I'm glad. I thought my brother got on pretty well with the others. Did him good to meet some working-class people for a change, other than as work clients."

"Oh yes, I hadn't thought of that. Everyone seemed to get on ok and they are an intelligent lot and your brother is a very good soul. The four lads from La Isla are a witty and jovial bunch. I still struggle with their Chileanisms and the way they speak but your brother seemed to understand it all."

"Yes, of course. He said he would come to visit us in England.

"Great," said Julian feeling grateful for the confirmation she would be coming, yet feeling he should not have to be thankful for snippets of reassurance. He pulled her body down onto his horizontal torso and kissed her passionately as if to seek to deepen the bond. They rolled over several times in their love-making. It was gone midday before they faced the clearing up from the night before.

Isabel had arranged another filming day with *Bello Barrio* when they were to run a day of children's activities, inviting the families of their neighbours in La Isla and another nearby community. The day finished with a student band singing and playing songs of the *New Chilean Song Movement.* Joaquín was very skilful in his capacity to win publicity and voluntary help for the project, at home and abroad. It was a useful 'public relations' day to introduce who and what *Bello Barrio* was, to the neighbourhood and other contacts throughout Valparaíso. Isabel tried to illustrate this and their community spirit in the video. She also talked with Joaquín about the wealth that the senior officers of the armed forces had made and determined to contact the author of the article he had mentioned. Joaquín gave her the cutting.

A week later Julian found himself on a bus with *camas.* He was next to Isabel and on his way to La Serena. After a quick visit to her studio flat the next morning and breakfast at a café, they were strolling along the half-kilometre walkway known as the Museum of the Open Air with its 34 classical statues in the centre of the city.

"This walkway was created in the nineteenth century and named after the sixteenth-century founder of the city, Francisco de Aguirre," said Isabel. "It's lined with acacia trees, alamos trees from Mexico and look, these are banana trees." Julian didn't think he had seen banana trees before.

"Do they produce bananas? It's not tropical here." Isabel thought not but it was just warm enough to grow a few tropical trees.

"I've never seen them with hands of bananas," she said.

"These are Greco-roman style statues," said Julian. "They seem a bit pretentious."

"Incongruous, I know. They were put there in the twentieth century." The statues continued the length of the walkway towards the sea and towards the famous lighthouse which has become the symbol of the city. Julian wanted to go into the lighthouse and they climbed the squared tower to the top. Seeing the whole city from above, he was amazed at its size. He also thought the city centre was very attractive and he began to think that here was a city in Chile with a historical feel and real elegance.

"Maybe the statues are not so over the top after all," he admitted.

"Well, the city was founded in 1544 and is the oldest after Santiago. So much for your theories then! If you want more history - there was a village here before that, which was called in Mapudungún, Snakes and Condors. Pedro de Valdivia wanted to link Santiago with Lima by sea and he chose here for his troops to rest. They established a permanent base but five years later there was a native uprising and the new town was burned to the ground and nearly every Spaniard was killed. Valdivia wasn't here and he ordered Capitan Francisco de Aguirre to re-establish the town. It became famous for its pirate attacks, including the most famous pirate of them all, Frances Drake. Drake wanted to open up the Pacific route to the English."

They walked back towards the town centre.

"Of course, the city suffered from a massive earthquake, inevitably," said Isabel. "It was in the eighteenth century and it wiped out nearly all of the many buildings. Most of these historic and elegant buildings including the cathedral, only date from the nineteenth century."

"I like it - the city I mean, not the pirates and the earthquake. If you want to do some work tomorrow I will be happy walking around this town. There's a Japanese garden to see and the cathedral of course and several universities."

"Let's enjoy the beach then this afternoon a little, after some lunch. Actually, a day sorting myself out would be very helpful."

That evening, after they had eaten, the phone rang and the landlady knocked on the door, shouting "Helena, *teléfono*." Julian only heard Isabel say "see you tomorrow" and he wondered who it was.

"Everything ok? Who called?"

"Oh, just one of the teachers from school. Apparently, they've arranged some extra days we have to be in school before the term starts for planning and training meetings. He wondered if I'd got the letter because I've been away so much."

"Well, you've got your post now you are here, haven't you?"

"Yes but apparently he rang my mother's and was told I was coming to La Serena, so he thought he'd better follow it up and explain before my mother talks to me."

"You must be quite friendly with that teacher for him to know you are away a lot and to have your mother's number. Is it a special friend?"

"No, no, it is just the teacher who I helped with the trips to the flowering desert. I told you about him and he met me when my ankle was in plaster. So yes, I have got to know him more than most of the teachers."

"You said you would see him tomorrow but I thought you were doing work at home tomorrow."

"Yes, but one of the things I have to do is clear my classroom of last year's stuff and put up new things for the start of this year. I said I'd call in briefly. Several staff are in school doing the same."

"Well, I'd like to go with you. I'd love to see the school where you have been working. I know it's quite a posh and a long-established school."

"No, I can't take strangers in."

"Really, I'm hardly a stranger."

"I can't. Leave it, please. Let me have a day getting organised and you do what you said you wanted to do in the town and leave it at that."

They each did their own activities next day and Julian asked no more questions. The day after that, Isabel was keen to take Julian to Coquimbo, the port that had now grown and merged with La Serena.

"There are copper mines near here and shipping that copper away has long been the purpose of this port but a lot of industry seems to be developing here now and many people are moving into the town for jobs. What I wanted to show you was the penguins that can be seen just a little way along the coast. I thought you'd like that. By the way, they are starting this year to build the tallest monument in South America here - goodness knows why. It's going to be 83 meters high. I can only assume they want to compete with Rio de Janeiro's Christ the Redeemer. That's supposed to look very big when you are up close and it can be seen from all over the city, but it's only 30 meters high. Imagine 83 meters," said Isabel as they left the house the next morning.

"We need to get a couple of *colectivos,* one to the centre and one to go to La Herradura Bay to see the penguins." Julian was delighted to walk on the rocks up close to the penguins. They seemed unafraid of humans and some waddled up quite close to him as he stood still. He loved to see them diving and swimming too. The sea lions lounging on other rocks looked so enormous that he didn't think it would be wise to get too close to them. They seemed to be continually swopping places by pushing one another off the rocks and then they had such a struggle to get back onto the ledges. They would repeatedly fall back into the water before finally making it onto land again or before seeking out an easier ledge to conquer.

"I really could do with one more day working tomorrow and then we can take the overnight bus to Santiago tomorrow night, ok?"

"Are you going to the school," asked Julian.

"Yes, I need to finish my classroom but I want to work here in the morning. We could meet for lunch."

"Ok great, if you've time. What if I bring something in for you?"

"Great but the facilities aren't very brilliant here for cooking."

"I know. Don't worry." Julian had spotted where he could get homemade food nearby. "What would you prefer *guatitas* or *Pastel de Choclo?"*

*"Guatitas?* You don't eat tripe, do you? I can't stand it."

"Oh, it's wonderful Chilean style, mixed with loads of vegetables to make a lovely tomatoey sauce. I never minded my mother's tripe, English style in a white sauce, but I prefer the Chilean way. It's delicious."

"Well, not for me, thank you very much. Anything else but not that."

-oOo-

In Santiago, Julian heard a little of a conversation Carlos and Isabel were having in a small room, off the living room, where the telephone was.

"I was there when he rang" Julian heard Carlos say, "when *Mama* picked up the phone and he asked for Helena. *Mama's* voice rose like a question, repeating 'Helena?' I was trying to get the phone from her and mouthing to her 'it's Isabel.' It was ok, she got it eventually." Isabel said something but Julian couldn't hear her nor Carlos very clearly for a while and then Carlos said, "He's a nice guy - a good guy and it's obvious he is so in love with you. Don't mess things up and don't hurt him. I've become very fond of him. That's not the point but hurting him and hurting yourself is the point." Again Julian could not capture what Isabel replied. They were coming out and Julian hurriedly moved away to the other side of the lounge.

Saddened, Julian decided to carry on as naturally and as normally as he could. He wasn't sure he could do anything about his fear. Was he being cowardly to say nothing? What could he say? He was beset with doubts but the holiday in the south was booked and he was determined not to upset that and to hope that would be a good experience for them both. The next day, when Isabel was at the video editing studio and Julian was on his way to visit the *Pre-Columbian Museum,* on Isabel's recommendation, he came across some open-air stalls of second-hand books and he found a Spanish copy of a book he was especially fond of: *The Art of Loving* by Eric Fromm. Julian recalled that he and Isabel had both said they thought highly of the little book when they had discussed it years before, but Julian was not sure, on later reflection, that they understood it in the same way. He bought the book and began reading it avidly and he made a great many notes in Spanish over the coming days. Repeatedly, he came across parts that he wanted to discuss with Isabel but finding the right opportunity seemed increasingly difficult. I've got to make the time he told himself and he questioned whether he was being timorous and spineless, as time seemed to be rushing by and so far he had said nothing. In the Spanish version, he hoped the words of Eric Fromm would have more emotional meaning for her. *We would both agree that Fromm is right to say that to love is to give and not to receive. To give love, to give of yourself includes respect. Respect, says Fromm is to concern yourself with the growth and development of the other. How can I bring this up with Isabel knowing she had a differing view? Isabel once said that respect is something you have to earn - you have to be good enough to deserve it, which is not the same as Fromm is saying at all. We are all worthy of concern for our growth and development, whatever our mistakes and faults.*

*What does 'respect' mean I must do? I have to accept that Isabel needs to do what she feels she must achieve in this coming year and I have to hope she grows, learns and becomes fulfilled through that work. If I am to love and respect her I have to let her do what she needs to do.* But another of Isabel's ideas troubled Julian and seemed to contradict what Fromm was saying. *I remember I was not happy when she said that their relationship had to fulfil her needs and only by believing that it could, would she commit herself. That was years ago. I wonder if she still thinks that right because, as Fromm says it is the wrong way to look at a relationship. He said that you only get your own needs met when you try to meet the needs of the other and occupy yourself with their fulfilment rather than your own. I'm sure that is right, but is it all too idealistic? Doesn't one person's need come to dominate, especially when two people from different countries have to decide in which country they want to live or when a couple both have career ambitions and one has to be sacrificed for the other to succeed?*

*How can you give yourself to the fulfilment of the other if you are living thousands of miles apart? Have I ever tried hard enough to ensure her needs are met? That is what is being asked of me now.* Julian also thought that trying to have a philosophical discussion with Isabel is always hard because she is quick to call such ideas empty words. *She wants action, not words, she always says. But we need to think through what we should do and what is right in a given situation. There is another useful idea in Eric Fromm we should discuss. He says we are habitually conscious of when we are not loved, but we are unconscious of our fear to love. Is this our real problem as a couple? We have to commit ourselves without guarantees, to give ourselves completely in the hope of producing love in the loved person. That is not easy. It is an act of faith and if we have little faith we have little love, says Fromm. I have to make myself vulnerable and trusting and leave her behind in this country.* Julian determined that he must find the opportunity to show Isabel the book and try to talk with her.

They returned to Valparaíso together and Julian got immediately involved again with *Bello Barrio,* whilst Isabel did a couple of school preparation days and a couple of days researching and setting up contacts and interviews in March that could contribute to her film. She sent an email to the author Joaquín had told them about and had received a positive response to meet with him. Isabel was especially excited about that. She had also had an answer from Isabel Allende.

"My MP, daughter of President Allende, not the writer, who is his niece." she explained to Julian. Julian was currently tackling one of the latter's novels in Spanish. "I will be able to see her in La Serena in late March and she's agreed to be videoed."

At *Bello Barrio,* they were working on clearing a garden area outside the children's nursery where the children would be able to plant seeds and grow vegetables, fruit and flowers. They were also preparing for another camp for five days and Julian and Isabel were invited to join them. They agreed to join over the weekend. There were summer activities for the children in the *barrio* La Isla whenever they were not away camping and Julian joined them when they were planning a Children's Rights march around La Isla. They had been doing work on the UN Declaration of Children's Rights to enable the children to be aware of what their rights are. The children had done drawings to illustrate the rights and they were adding cardboard and sticks for handles to use these as posters for their march. Julian joined the discussion groups on their rights and the children were copiously expressing feelings and experiences. Some children clearly needed further follow-up as some painful feelings were expressed about incidents at home and these couldn't just be left and forgotten. In the small group, which Julian was facilitating, the children were supportive and empathetic to one another and their seriousness and maturity were impressive. Julian made careful notes afterwards about who should be given an individual opportunity to talk further and gain therapeutic support.

Joaquín had acquired some UN leaflets on Children's Rights to give out and some balloons stamped with 'Children Have Rights' from his YMCA supporters. The 'Y' was no longer his official sponsor and supervisor, as it had been when he worked at La Isla Community Centre, but he could turn, for informal support, to his old boss and friend at the 'Y'. He had previously been his 'father figure' when he was in a YMCA children's home. In San Roque, the children, together with Julian and Joaquín and volunteers, formed an impressively long line as they marched through the streets making as much noise as they could with toy trumpets, drums and whistles and carrying their banners and posters on each of the Children's Rights. People came out of their houses to see them and leaflets were given out. Families began to applaud them and Julian thought yet again he had learned a new lesson to take back to England.

-oOo-

Finally, Isabel and Julian were away and they flew to Puerto Montt from where they could take a ferry boat through the fiords and islands of Chile's southwest coast, calling firstly at Chile's largest island Chiloé. They disembarked at the small port of Quellón for a brief glimpse at the beautiful green island and its traditional wooden tiled houses. The hand-carved, elegant, decoratively curved-edged tiles of wood covered the top half of the walls as well as the roofs of the traditional houses and they were to protect the buildings from the winter rains. The cafés they went into all had wood-burning stoves alight and this was summer. Julian shuddered to think of what the winters would be like when the rain hardly stopped, they were told. The snow-covered Volcano Corcovado on the mainland facing this part of the island was an impressive sight. They bought roasted *piñones,* called locally *pehuen* in Mapuche - the fruit of the *araucarias* and found them good, like chestnuts. They are a principal part of the diet of Mapuches, they were informed.

The journey on the ferry continued between a series of small islands and the mainland, making for beautiful views of green hills and dramatic coastlines with sandy and rocky coves on either side of the boat. Occasional conical, white volcanos gleamed in the sun on the mainland side and the distant Andes mountains remained a continuous backdrop. The couple had the cheapest double cabin available because the luxury cruise cabins were way out of what Julian could stretch to, but it was adequate though very small and simple. It would have been cheaper to fly but he was advised the views were magnificent from the boat and he had to agree on that. Also, they were to get up close to a glacier, where no car or plane could take them. Arriving at Laguna San Rafael they boarded small boats to get closer to the extensive cliff edge of the San Rafael glacier where it reached the sea. Their little dinghies looked like miniature toys against the huge backdrop of the glacier. They weaved their way between the icebergs and these were mostly an intense blue in colour, like the glacier itself, indicating the hundreds of years of age of the ice. They watched new icebergs being formed as large chunks of the ice cliffs fell from the glacier into the sea. The tradition was to drink whiskey with ice in it from the icebergs and as glasses were passed around, a hunk of ice from the sea was chopped up by a crew member and celebrations were called for.

"Salud," said Julian to Isabel, raising his glass. "Much love, success and happiness. This is great to be here."

"Salud, salud," said Isabel and she turned to other passengers to wish them good health too.

"What is not so great is the retreating of the glacier. There are date markings on the cliffs at each side of the glacier where the glacier ice once reached. Look how much it has shrunk," said Julian. From the 1960s to the 1990s various dates had been carved in the rocks and the distances between the dates were growing. "It's imperative that every world leader should come to see this view of the melting glacier and perhaps then they would take seriously the warming of the planet."

"But they only think short term. It's the people that think longer term and they need to know. But isn't all this blue sea and ice beautiful?" said Isabel. "Look at the expanse of it."

Arriving back in Puerto Montt, they flew to Puerto Natales, the most southerly town before Punta Arenas. Julian had explored whether it was possible to go from San Rafael to *Torres del Paine,* without returning north. However, a glance at the map showed it to be impossible. He learned there was another expensive boat trip that was possible but that there was nowhere else to begin such a trip but Puerto Montt. There were no towns, no roads, no human civilisation in the intervening wilderness of snow-capped mountains, fiords and islands. By road the only way south was through Argentina, the highest peaks that divide the two countries being so close to the sea at this point, that Chile becomes very narrow, mountainous and empty of human life. Flying south from Puerto Montt was the best option.

"It looks like we are looking at the sea but it is only an inland lake," said Isabel as they looked out to a wide expanse of grey, cold water from in front of the port of Puerto Natales. The sky looked grimly dull from when they arrived and that continued. From the ambient temperature, they felt they were a long way south. The next day they went by bus a couple of hours to the edge of the National Park *Torres del Paine.* They wondered then where to go and soon learned from the hikers who looked fully prepared in their walking boots with sticks and rucksacks, that walking was the only option. There was no more public transport but Isabel and Julian were far from their hoped-for destination. There was a view from the back of the famous three, mile high, granite peak towers - the *Torres* and hikers were setting off for the *refugios* they had reserved in advance, for their three-day hike to the towers. Isabel had been keen to avoid paying for a private minibus tour overland to see the famous peaks from their best view, so now she insisted they set off with the hikers, to see where it took them and make the best of the day that they could. She enjoyed chatting with the hikers and they separated off from them when they came to the spectacular view of *Los Cuernos,* impressive high, pointed horns in this dramatic countryside. She and Julian were ready for a rest and they said goodbye to their new friends. It had become clear they were not going to get to see the towers that day, so Julian insisted that the next day they take a private tour.

"We can't be sure we'll ever be here again. We can't miss the best view now we are this close," he said.

"We'll doubtless come again, why not?"

Julian thought that was not very realistic, at least for a long time and he thought of the cost and the distance from the UK. Then he realised he was centred on another reality and clearly Isabel was centred on a Chilean future, but he said, "The location is so remote. It's 2000 kilometres from Santiago. You can't just pop down for a quick visit."

"This is beautiful and the sun is shining. Come on. You can see the different strata of rock in such contrasting colours."

They resumed their walk and it was rigorous at times as the wind was bitter and strong, but when a beautiful blue lake came into view, they agreed on a sheltered place behind a rock to have their picnic. They appeared to be alone in that wilderness and both agreed it was a magnificent experience of nature. They then made their way back to be sure of catching the last bus to Puerto Natales but they called first at the public facilities open at the first refuge of cabins and restaurants on the hiking route. Isabel came from the loo with a cunning look in her eye. She had seen a hiker's walking stick propped up against a sink when no one was around and it remained there abandoned when she came out of her cubicle. She did nothing but asked Julian to wait at this place a further half of an hour and suggested they take a hot chocolate. When she then went into the ladies' toilets again, the walking stick was still there and no one was around. She decided to take it.

"You would think somebody would have missed the stick and gone back by now, wouldn't you," she said to Julian. "If I didn't take it, someone else would." Julian knew that argument was a dubious basis for action but decided not to look in judgement. "It makes a difference walking these rough paths with the stick. It gives you more security and helps you up the slopes," she claimed.

That evening they both took advantage of the opportunity to have spider crab for dinner. It was clearly the main delight of the menus in all the restaurants in this part of the world and was served in many different ways, hot and cold, in sauces or alone, in pies or soups.

"Exquisite," said Julian, taking a fresh piece of spider crab with lemon juice.

"*Esquisito,*" said Isabel. At least they agreed on it being their favourite food and the best-tasting type of crab you could get.

The next day Julian paid for a private day tour that took them in a luxury car to the lake where the dramatic vertical rock towers are seen to their best advantage and he was so glad he had insisted. They had the chance for some walking and a picnic lunch was included. Isabel couldn't deny she had loved the photographic opportunities and the most impressive natural surroundings she had ever seen.

-oOo-

The last two weeks in Chile for Julian became very busy and seemed to rush by. He visited Quillota with Isabel for lunch and saw Padre Pablo, his sister Ximena, the secretary Claudia and housekeeper Emilia. Gabriela from the Old People's home and Patricia, the nun, also came for his lunch send-off. Alvaro and Javier, two of his students of English came in to have *onces* with him. On another day Julian caught a few teachers in the English Department of the University, returning to prepare for the new term. He loved the party with *Bello Barrio* and very much appreciated the illustrated book of Bernadetti's poetry that Joaquín and volunteers Victoria and Alejandro, gave him.

The couple had agreed it would be better to spend the last night at Carlos and Mariana's house in Santiago before going to the airport. That way they could do the final tidying of the flat the day before and not have to rush it on the morning of the flight. They need not have been concerned as the three friends from *Bello Barrio* wanted to help in the final clean-up and with carrying cases, so these tasks were quickly executed the day before Julian's flight and they had time for *onces* all together at the corner shop.

"I'll be at the demonstrations against *el huevon* in England. You can count on that," said Julian as they waved him off in Carlos' car. "The Chilean community are always out there. Now they gather every weekend as near as they allowed, at the private estate where he's under house arrest, at Virginia Water and they bang loud drums. Thank you for everything, for so much. Keep in touch."

That night in Santiago, when the children were in bed and Esperanza had said goodbye to Julian and gone home, Isabel wanted to get the lawyer's point of view on the recent developments with the ongoing detention of Pinochet.

"Have you heard that the judgement by the Law Lords," began Carlos, "which was set aside because one of the judges was said to be potentially biased due to his historical ties with Amnesty International, has been reversed? Just this week it has been confirmed again that a former head of state cannot claim immunity. But now there is a big 'but'. Now, Pinochet can only be prosecuted for crimes committed after 1988, when the UK ratified the UN Convention Against Torture. The UK embodied the Convention in a Criminal Justice Act in 1988 which means that most of the charges against Pinochet are invalidated. But it also gives the green light for him to be extradited to Spain."

"How can they come up with a 'get out' like that?" said Isabel, staggered as she had missed the latest news. "Is Spain still able to try him for the 94 Spanish cases brought against him there? Isn't there some international law that could be used for cases before 1988?"

"Well, the UN High Commissioner of Human Rights - Mary Robinson has said the Law Lords ruling was an endorsement that torture is an international crime and so subject to universal jurisdiction. That means anyone can be tried in any country and not only in the country in which the crimes happened."

"Can we then bring Chilean cases against him in England under this universal jurisdiction?" asked Julian.

"The problem is that although some legal scholars think this is very important in legal history - the biggest development since the Nuremberg Trials and that some crimes like torture and genocide are crimes against humanity, the UK and the Spanish findings were based on domestic statutory law and not on universal jurisdiction."

"Oh no! So it all gets watered down again," said Isabel. "So what's this big legal step forward - this universal jurisdiction?"

"The scholars are still arguing about that one. It is the first time that a current or former head of state was arrested in a foreign country for international crimes." "But what have they achieved, in all this legal wrangling? What do you think would be the likelihood of prosecuting him if he is returned to Chile?"

"There would be great efforts to avoid it. The Constitutional Tribunal, for example, could recommend to Congress a special status of 'ex-president' and grant immunity but it is just possible the Supreme Court might vote the other way."

"So it would be a political vote and not a legal finding? Under the present constitution, it's clear what way that political vote would go. "The Supreme Court could not overrule a Congress vote, could it?"

Carlos shook his head and Mariana came in to say the supper was ready.

"It's all very depressing," said Isabel, "and now there is so much talk of him not being medically fit to go before a Court."

"The British Home Office Secretary of State, in the end, has to decide whether to extradite him to Spain," said Julian, "but the British Government keeps saying it is a legal matter, not a political one. It appears to want to separate itself from the case but it so obviously will be a political decision. Do you remember last year Margaret Thatcher said the Home Secretary Jack Straw had wide powers to finish with this episode and Tony Blair rejected that saying it was judicial, not political? It seems amazing to me the way the legal and the political are so intertwined and used whatever way they wish when it suits them. There is no separation of powers anywhere." Again Carlos responded only with a gesture. He shook his head as they all sat down to eat.

When they were alone, Julian ventured to tell Isabel he had found a copy of Eric Fromm's *The Art of Loving* and he would like to leave it with her as a leaving present. He fumbled trying to say that he hoped the year to come would be a great fulfilment for her and that she can achieve all she needs. Isabel didn't want to say anything too controversial on their last night together and was anticipating the lovemaking that was to come. She did say, "Thank you."

"I don't know what for."

"For the book and your wishes for me this year. For being patient again and giving me another year. I do know what I want now. I do know I want to be with you in England, having done all I can to move this country forward to a new start. I confess I was not clear in the past on where I wanted to be. In England, I wanted to be here and when I was here I couldn't face going back. But now I know I want to be with you and I am content that it will be in England. I know what that means, in a way I did not, when I first went and I won't be taking a fantasy view of my country back with me either. I know that I love my country but not now with an idealised view of what it could be. I will not be totally cut off from here either, like in the past. I know the country's strengths and weaknesses and I will be able to keep coming and checking it out."

At the airport, Julian said, "Promise you'll keep in touch and we won't have any more of these times when I don't know where you are and if you are safe. At least we've got email nowadays and you've got the modem now. And promise I will see you soon. I love you. You must take great care in whatever you do politically and tell me where you are."

"Well, I can't advertise my plans on insecure emails all the time. Don't expect you will always know where I am or where I'm going. You must see that." She gave him a kiss.

"Yes, yes I know but write to me and tell me you are safe whenever you are back from a demo. Ring me often too and I'll ring you." She covered his face in kisses as he was trying to say this.

Julian kept looking back as he made his way through Departures as long as he could but she was no longer watching him.

The long flight home made Julian feel he couldn't dodge the inevitable questioning of where their relationship really was at. *I came to Chile with my hopes of any future relationship crushed. I came to grieve and resolve the loss as I felt I had to.* Julian took out his notes on Eric Fromm's book. *Perhaps I could write to her with some of Fromm's thinking and now she has the book, perhaps she'll read it again and respond to what stood out for me. I never seemed to have the right opportunity to talk with Isabel about it. I'm a coward. Why didn't I make the time? Have I always hung back for fear of love not being reciprocated? Am I fearful of love itself, as Fromm says we often are - of being exposed and insecure? If I am, then I am as much to blame for the failures in our relationship in the past. I had to leave her to be free but is it my little faith that is the cause of my worry? I had no choice but to leave her now. I ache for her to come back. I've read it was said of Violeta Parra that to love her was like chasing a hurricane. No matter how hard you tried, said a lover, she would always go away. Not because she didn't love back but because she needed her freedom. But is that freedom or is it really her fear? Fear of love, fear to have faith and to trust?* Julian pulled out from his hand luggage the latest CD he had bought of Patricio Manns, attached his earphones to his portable disk player and listened.

| | |
|---|---|
| Porque te amé | Because I loved you |
| Las flores enviudaron, | The flowers were widowed, |
| Cayó una estrella | A star fell |
| Herida por los celos, | Wounded by jealousy, |
| Entró el verano en mi alma | Summer entered my soul |
| | |
| Y murió el hielo | And the ice died |
| Y suaves picafloras | And gentle hummingbirds |
| Me injuriaron. | They reviled me. |
| Mi invierno se fue al sol | My winter went to the sun |
| | |
| Porque te amé, | Because I loved you |

| | |
|---|---|
| Retrocedió la noche atormentada | Receding the haunted night |
| Como una negra copa ya vaciada, | Like a black cup already emptied, |
| Porque te amé, porque te amé, | Because I loved you, because I loved you |
| Porque te amé. | Because I loved you |
| | |
| Porque te amé | Because I loved you |
| Dormí en el paraíso, | I slept in paradise |
| Rompí los nudos, | I broke the knots |
| Liberé el secreto. | I released the secret. |
| Me hice visible, | I became visible |
| Cómplice y concreto, | Accomplice and concrete, |
| Y me dejé caer bajo tu hechizo. | And I let myself fall under your spell. |
| Y anduve mundo acompañándote, | And I walked the world accompanying you, |
| Con una mano | With a hand |
| En que cabía tu mano, | Where did your hand fit, |
| | |
| Al paso firme de mi amor pagano, | At the firm step of my pagan love, |
| Porque te amé, porque te amé, | Because I loved you, because I loved you |
| Porque te amé. | Because I loved you |
| Nació tanto rosal y todo fue | Both rosebush was born and everything was |
| Casas amadas, lechos y ventanas, | Beloved houses, beds and windows, |
| Y cada vez que abría la mañana | And every time the morning opened |

385

| | |
|---|---|
| Despertaba feliz, | I woke up happy, calling you. |
| llamándote. | |
| El mar me descubrió | The sea discovered me |
| Porque te amé | Because I loved you |
| | |
| Me descubrió la hierba | I discovered the grass |
| Y el rocío, me descubrió lo | And the dew, I discovered |
| ajeno | the alien |
| Y lo que es mío, | And what is mine |
| Y ya nunca te irás, | Although you are not here. |
| Aunque no estés. | |
| Lancé al abismo el corazón | I threw my heart without |
| sin fe, | faith into the abyss, |
| Abrí mi pecho | I opened my chest |
| A la dulce aventura, | To the sweet adventure, |
| Y te deberé siempre tanta | And I will always owe you |
| altura, | so much height, |
| Porque te amé, porque | Because I loved you, |
| te amé, | because I loved you, |
| Porque te amé. | Because I loved you |

-oOo-

*He really has been very understanding,* thought Isabel as she sat on the bus back into Santiago. *It is going to be tough for me now to be on my own again after all that has happened. I'm going to be busy, that will help me just get on with what I have to do.* But facing the political activism all over again on her own without Mateo to smooth the path, arranging the comforts to escape to and showering affection on her, she knew would be hard. She knew she would miss him. *I am going to feel more alone than I have felt before in La Serena, except perhaps at the beginning. And without Julian to discuss it all with and offering forgiving love and level-headedness. I could just bring it all to a crushing end by getting myself arrested when using my false identity and the school would be informed. I can then run back to England, assuming they let me out quickly but*

386

*there are protesters held for months. Could I withstand that? Well, I would have to, but it wouldn't be easy. What if I was injured again? No, I've got to be more constructive than that and I must keep open my permission to return regularly to this country without difficulties. I couldn't bare it if I wasn't allowed into my own country, like during the dictatorship.*

*It was a great idea that we have arranged with Julian's landlord that we will rent his flat for at least a month during the university vacations. We've left all the furniture Julian bought in exchange for a reduced rent and the landlord gains a tenant when the flat would normally be empty. I've got the pictures and posters, the pottery and the books all dumped in my room at my mother's. We'll be able to put them back when we are there but I must try to organise my room a bit better tomorrow. I still have many of my father's books kept there stored in boxes. I must get another bookcase and get that room looking decent again.*

Isabel was on her way to see Juan at the bus station and she went early to the tiny café to have a bite for lunch before they met. The café owner greeted her warmly as always and soon brought her a toasted cheese sandwich with salad. When Juan arrived and they moved into the back room, the owner brought coffees for them both.

"It looks very possible that they might return Pinochet to Chile soon, rather than extraditing him to Spain and we have to be ready with how we are going to receive him."

"We are going to prosecute him with all our might," responded Isabel.

"But you know why that is a long way off here in Chile. How are we going to respond on the streets, I mean, when he first comes? We have to send the message we don't want him here. We want him prosecuted in Spain."

"No, we don't. We, the Chilean people must prosecute him here."

Juan shook his head and didn't want to argue that point with Isabel. "Shall we try to make a rejection demo at the airport when he arrives? Security will be tight. It won't be easy."

"We'll need new posters declaring: PROSECUTE and TO THE PRISON."

"But the posters we have on needing a new constitution will be relevant. Without that, we won't get him prosecuted. I'll get the local groups doing new posters as you say. We may only get a few hours' notice that he is being released and put on a plane."

"I think there are going to be legal arguments for a lot longer yet. I'll be in La Serena when the schools are back, but I could come Fridays to Sundays. We would need a big demonstration in Santiago if he suddenly arrives back. But what do we do in the meantime, if it takes weeks or months before he is sent back? I have the awful feeling that if we just wait, momentum will be lost. Right now the people are more divided than ever but the inadequacy of a constitution that doesn't permit prosecutions should be clearer than ever. Now is the time for dramatic action to hammer that home."

"You are absolutely right. The alternative will be drift achieving nothing."

"I think we have to go on showing support for the detention. Pinochet's supporters are still out shouting for his release. They are still burning Spanish and British flags outside the embassies. There is a better chance at present that we could get convictions abroad, as much as I want him to be prosecuted here. He has to be held until we are sure he'll be tried here or until he is tried in Europe. What can't happen is that he is just released home. I'll talk to our key people in the northern towns and see what they think about continued demos about the need for change to the constitution. We could aim for a nationwide coordinated strike and manifestation. What about that?"

"It all seems so hopeless to expect that any officials could be brought to court for misdemeanours when Pinochet has so many supporters in the Upper House. I think we have to demand of the country an uprising for a new constitution."

"Yes, you are right. OK, that is our demand - a whole new constitution. We won't get that without the entire country showing it demands that. We'll call for strikes and manifestations and I'll let you know the response in the northern towns."

Isabel pondered again the conversation with Juan on her return to La Serena. *I have to throw myself into achieving everything that I can but I must set a time limit. I have made a firm commitment that I will return to the UK in a year and I must stick to that - like, in a way that I've not stuck firmly to any personal relationship before. That is how I have got hurt and I have hurt others. I know I will not find happiness and fulfilment unless I do the right thing. I do have a stronger sense of myself now. I don't feel so lost and hiding behind, not one but two apparent identities which gave me the feeling I was play acting in either role. I've also felt that I have two countries and I didn't seem fully to fit into either. I've grown up in these recent years that I've spent in Chile. That was a process that needed to happen because my growing up was cut short when I had to search for my father and Raúl and then go into exile. I think emotionally I was frozen and my growth was stifled.*

*I've done some soul-searching over my mistakes. I know where I have failed to put my professed values into practice on the one-to-one level. The humanitarian values, and the caring for others' futures, have been missing in my personal relationships. Have I acted too impulsively and given in to immediate gratification? I've always thought of myself as conscientious and determined in what I want to achieve. Have I been determined enough about my love relationships? I want a future loving relationship that is richer than I have allowed in the past because I have always held myself back and protected myself through fear of giving my all. I'm glad Julian made me look at Eric Fromm again. I see now that whenever Julian and I have renewed our involvement, I have held back in part, fearful as Fromm says.*

*I've valued the friendships that the political teaching and the demonstrating have given to me. I feel I found the real Chile in those friendships but my personal reasons for being so involved have to be on a sound footing and perhaps they have not always been. We have to keep up the political protests this coming year but I will go into them more rationally, as the ethical thing to do and not for the excitement and the status that I get out of them. I have to give what I can and then call a stop at the end of the year. There has to be a limit and that comes when I have done all that I have promised for this coming year. Julian will be here again in ten months' time. We'll enjoy the summer together and then I'll go back to England with him, satisfied I have done all I can. I see now that my emotional growing up was stifled here by the coup. I lost my youth, I lost persons very close to me, I lost my country, my possible career here, but now I can envisage another future happily. I have to bring harmony into my life, into my relationships. I'll make more efforts with my mother whilst I am here. I want to choose my future and not feel I only have a future thrust upon me. Knowing who I am, involves knowing what I want for the future. Julian has allowed me to fulfil my need to finish my work here. Now I have to think about fulfilling his needs as well as my own. We've agreed on yearly holidays here but to live in the more stable and safe situation of the UK to bring up a child. That is what I want.* Isabel finally dropped off to sleep in her *cama* bus seat.

# Epilogue

A
t the beginning of October 2019, Isabel and Julian arrived in Chile for a planned, extended stay, following their recent retirement from work in England. Isabel now owned a small flat in Valparaíso, which she had decided was essential for spending large amounts of time of their retirement years in Chile. Much of the time of their last visit to Chile had been spent in searching for a modest property and finally, they had settled on a flat within an older building in historic Valparaíso. It had the required view of the magnificent bay and was not far from an *ascensor* to the commercial city centre. This was the couple's first visit since the purchase had been completed and it had been made possible through the inheritance, with her brother, of her mother's house in Santiago.

Carlos had agreed that much of the furniture of their mother's house should go to Isabel and so they had a beautiful *lingue* dining table and a sideboard, of which Isabel was particularly fond. She had learned that the *lingue* forests of Chile were now endangered because of habitat loss and so Isabel caressed the attractive, curving markings of this beautiful mid-brown wood as they began to arrange their new home. They had acquired beds and chests of drawers too but were going to need new mattresses and more bookcases. Isabel began to put out the books that were her father's, on the bookcases brought from her room at her mother's house. She's not looked at the books properly since the time that she made the decision to go into exile with Constanza and she was taking her time. Julian was busy making measurements for the new kitchen that the flat needed.

On the morning of the 11th October Isabel switched on the radio and listened with growing excitement but with trepidation, to the news that a large number of secondary students were avoiding paying fares in the Santiago metro by jumping the turnstiles. This followed the steep rise in fares imposed for public transport users from 6th October and had now become an organised protest with thousands taking part. Tempted to rush off to Santiago immediately, Isabel reluctantly decided to see how matters developed and to try to organise protests in sympathy in Valparaíso and to suggest such ideas to her contacts in the northern towns.

"The cost of living is becoming impossible for so many families. It's not just transport costs, it's food and electricity," said Daniela, with whom Isabel had always kept in touch through the long, intervening years. They had met up occasionally on some of Isabel's many trips to Chile in the last twenty years.

"I agree. We must show our solidarity."

"We could call for a strike and organise a protest march for next Friday against the government for their cost of living increases and in favour of all we've been asking for all these years, a new constitution, etc. We'll use our posters against the *AFP* pension scheme and against education and health as businesses. They are all part of the terrible costs people have to pay. I'll get in touch with all my contacts *al tiro*."

Isabel had similar conversations with her contacts in Iquique, Arica and Calama and she and Julian went to visit Joaquín at Bello Barrio. The community welcomed them as always and showed them the latest developments, extended houses, an additional meeting room to the communal hall, an impressive, octagonal visitors' accommodation house of wood and substantial fruit and vegetable gardens. Joaquín had taken to beekeeping and gave them a jar of his excellent honey. They also kept rabbits and chickens. Broad plans had already been made by the residents of *Bello Barrio* to make protests in support of the students in Santiago and they were hopeful of a large turnout for a day's strike and march through the central streets of Valparaíso to the Parliament on the following Friday.

During the coming days, the news come through of more fare dodging, occupation of Metro stations and violent clashes with police in Santiago. By 18th October, some groups in the capital had begun the destruction of Metro stations and infrastructure on such a scale that the underground trains were totally suspended. The government declared a state of emergency in Santiago but that was incendiary and much of the country reacted with even greater numbers taking to the streets. Huge protests, *cacerolas* and rioting crowds were out Valparaíso, La Serena and Concepción and within a day or two more, in every major city throughout the country. Within days the state of emergency was extended to all the cities and their surrounding 'greater' areas because incidents were spontaneously taking place in so many suburban communities.

"The people are incensed. There are years of anger bursting out at the injustice," said Isabel to Julian, "they are smashing the pavements with hammers to make rocks as ammunition to throw at the police. Perhaps, at last, it is the moment we have waited for."

"It has taken the twenty years we said it must not take."

"Yes, I thought the protests a few years back about the reforms to education were going to become the trigger to wider changes but it all calmed eventually. Everyone knows a big uprising must come eventually but you don't quite expect it when it starts. We must make sure that this time, this really is it."

"You mean instability and rioting on a big enough scale because these things will have to precede any major change."

"Yes, I do. If they won't listen to huge numbers of peaceful protesters, what else can the people do? The government is clearly very rattled, bringing out the Army to try to prevent damage to businesses and the scale of the looting that is going on. But that seems the only thing they listen to."

"You're not advocating looting, I hope and don't you think the damage to the Metro stations and digging up pavements is a terrible waste of the country's resources?

"It is a waste but 20 years of peaceful protests haven't been listened to. We've been marching and banging pots here in Valparaíso this last week and because of the large turnout, I hope it may be enough without needing to turn to criminal damage. What an amazing number of people we have had out. The squares have been full of people banging their saucepans. The people have been happy, playing music and dancing as well as marching. And it has been the same in all the other cities. Many schools are closed. At night it's different. That is what the government cares more about. That is when the sacking of shops takes place but notice it is the big supermarkets and the expensive pharmacies which get attacked. The ones that take such massive profits whilst the old people can't afford their medicines. Also, it's the branches of banks and AFP that are being attacked and I can't say that is wrong. The AFP companies have been stealing from the people all along. These attacks on businesses are what is making the difference this time. Now the President says we are at war! We have to show him what war is," insisted Isabel.

"The head of national defence, very soon after that speech last night by President Piñera, said that he was 'content' and 'he's not at war with anyone.' Thank heaven this time it sounds like the Army won't carry out the repression the government wants. At least that's a step forward!"

"It doesn't seem this time that the majority of the population have been alienated by the damage done to the Metro stations. Radical actions that bring about arrests can lose the support of the majority but it seems this time that so many people are so angry about the cost of living and the inequality in every sense, young and old are all coming out in support."

"I don't like the taking of risks, as you know," said Julian. "I fear for you especially but I know you were right when you always said that history shows us that it is only with civil disobedience that change has ever occurred. Social change comes through conflict, unfortunately, but people get hurt." Julian shook his head.

"I want to go to the march organised for 25th in Santiago," replied Isabel. "I feel I should be part of what is happening in my capital city sometimes and this march is to demand the resignation of Piñera. After that, we'll see what is needed. More drastic civil disobedience will be needed to keep up the pressure, I expect. I must go to see Juan too, though he's old now he's still organising and coordinating and supporting others."

"How are you going to move about the capital? It won't be easy."

"The *colectivos* are still working, so I should be fairly safe in them. They will only go where they feel it's safe."

"The President has already apologised for not recognising the issues that trouble society and promised a lot of new measures, like increased pensions, reduction in the price of medications, making up workers salaries to a guaranteed minimum. Even a promise to tax at 40% incomes over £8000 a month."

"Wow, who earns that amount? All of it is too little too late and the people want more than that. They don't trust the President to implement and enforce anything. He's promised things before and nothing has come of them. We've still got to go forward demanding his resignation."

"There's a march to take place here as in many cities of the country. Why go to all the trouble and risks of going into Santiago?" But Isabel could not be dissuaded.

On October 25th, over 1.2 million persons, according to official estimates were said to have marched in Santiago, the biggest march ever held in Chile and there were massive manifestations throughout the country. Hundreds of arrests were made and Isabel had become very frightened when rubber bullets were flying around and she tried to ensure she kept well away from looters. She confirmed later that the rubber bullets used still had metal pellets inside but these were later banned. The authorities were also accused by human rights groups of torture and sexual abuse following arrests.

By 28th October, President Piñera had sacked his Interior Minister and changed seven other cabinet ministers and still the protests continued. Bank branches and shops, especially branches of electricity companies and pension companies continued to be burned and cars set alight in residential streets. Doctors and nurses were out on the streets to aid injured persons and lawyers were assisting those arrested by the still militarised police. At last, one of the biggest demands was heeded. By 15th November, Congress had agreed to a national referendum on whether a new constitution should be created.

"Things are moving fast," Isabel was surprised to hear herself saying. "Thanks to social media, which we didn't have in the past, everyone has reacted fast, got information about what is going on and when and where to join a demo. That will be our main tool for campaigning hard for a vote for a new constitution. The Right, who can throw lots of money at the vote, will try desperately hard to avoid any change. The constitution suits them and their money-making so well. The campaign will have to be like the "No" vote against Pinochet, a massive grassroots effort.

"But at least this time you'll have the social media to spread the word," said Julian. "the Right owns most of the traditional media and tied it all up for Pinochet that last time."

"The plebiscite will be in April next year. I can't bear the idea of returning to England at the end of March and not being here for the final push and the result of the vote."

"No, I know. Fair enough, we'll extend our stay. Of course, I know you'll want to be here to be part of that campaign to the last. I do too. I can't see us getting this kitchen sorted before then anyway."

Isabel had secured some funds from Juan for her contacts in the northern cities to get leaflets printed for distribution in the poorer *barrios* about why a new constitution was vital. They had debated whether it was still worthwhile to do paper leaflets but they knew social media could not reach everyone, especially the poorer, older persons and their votes would be needed. These were to be ready for the next semester when student volunteers were organised to distribute them. All of Isabel's contacts were deeply committed yet again, she was so proud to see.

Later in November, Isabel's friend Silvia, the nun, was in touch with her to tell her that in Temuco the head of the statue of the *conquistador* Pedro de Valdivia was removed in a demonstration and the head hung from the hands of the statue of the Caupolicán, the Mapuche leader of the resistance against the Spanish in the 16th Century.

"The Mapuches have been out in force, like never before, demanding their rights to decent education and health services and the restitution of their lands," said Silvia. There were 5000 marching last weekend and they flew a Mapuche flag above the head of Caupolicán's statue. They have to have their rights respected in this new constitution we are to have, hopefully. They need a say in its writing too."

"It's good to hear they are finding a voice in larger numbers now. You must keep me in touch."

"The Mapuche's are demanding the demilitarisation of their communities. The repression in recent years has been awful. I've had many an argument with the local police chief."

"Well done, Silvi. Keep it up. *Hasta la Victoria.* Perhaps we could come and see you in the summer. You're in Temuco itself now aren't you?"

"Yes, you must come. I can find a room for you. Take care of yourself."

In early December, *Bello Barrio* organised a large *peña* for all the local neighbourhoods, supporters and volunteers to raise funds for poor arrested persons to be helped to pay court costs in fighting their legal cases. Some young people were being held for lengthy periods, weeks going into months and anxious parents were being helped to speak out against such inordinate detentions of a few youngsters. At the concert held in the open air, Julian was reminded of Angel Parra's voice when a young singer performed and sang some of Angel's songs.

"What a pity Angel Parra has not lived to see what was going on in Chile now," Julian half-shouted to Joaquín, trying to compete with the volume of the music. He knew that Angel had died in France a couple of years before.

"He worked so hard to keep the *New Chilean Song Movement* alive," said Joaquín in Julian's ear. He went to perform to all the exiled Chilean communities in Europe during the dictatorship years. Let's go to my place and try to talk."

Julian was glad to have a conversation with Joaquín again and they entered his ramshackle but colourfully painted wooden house, near the communal facilities of *Bello Barrio*. "This is more of an office now and an overflow visitors' refuge occasionally," said Joaquín. I've converted a very old bus into my living quarters and I've got a workshop too, both are at the other end of the land. We now have legal possession of this land, by the way, after quite a struggle."

"I remember you were in a battle with the local authority in the past when we visited. Well done then if you finally succeeded."

"But things have been getting worse for people in recent years, it isn't surprising there has been an outcry. Take healthcare as one example. I remember one year when you came with your arm in plaster a few years back. You had broken it and you'd had it sorted at the clinic in Álvarez, Viña del Mar."

"Yes, the taxi driver refused to take me to the local hospital in Valparaíso. He said that the clinic was the best place for me after he had asked me if I had travel insurance. The quality of service with state-of-the-art medical facilities was perfect. There was no waiting but immediate attention too."

"You know that the quality of the *clinics* is excellent. The medics are trained in the United States and the best possible equipment and treatment are available. In the *hospitals* for the masses, the latest equipment is not accessible and did you know that the patients have to buy their own medicine and syringes and bandages?"

"Do you think the inequality has got even worse over the post-dictatorship years?"

"It certainly has. Poverty is supposed to have been reduced with the economic boom but the wealthiest 10% receive 40% of the income now and there is still no safety net of a welfare state for the unemployed, the disabled or the elderly or the sick. The rich and the corporations have enjoyed very low taxes for so long. No one believes the government will enforce the higher taxes promised now. They are so corrupt they'll find a way around the new taxes. We were one of the most equal countries in the world in Allende's time and still after thirty years of so-called democracy - that isn't a democracy of course - we are still one of the most unequal countries. We have fewer regulations on the worst excesses of the capitalists than even the United States. Can you imagine?"

"That's terrible. The States don't have enough controls."

"But this time, in this *estallido,* this social outburst, as it has come to be called, the anger is even greater," Joaquín continued. "The people trusted that Michelle Bachelet would achieve the reforms she promised after the 2011 to 2013 student disturbances. But she couldn't in the end achieve much. The vested interests are so great and the corruption hinders every good intent. You remember how cynical the people were, especially the young. Now the people can see clearly that neoliberalism has not brought the promised goods. The banking crisis and the ongoing failure to deliver better housing, better pensions, better schooling, better health services are really clear now. The people aren't prepared to wait and see any longer. They know they are being deceived and no one believes this president will do what he says. The people have abandoned their fear now."

"But people are getting killed in the protests and that fear doesn't seem to stop them."

"36 people have died so far and over 427 have lost an eye - these are the latest UN High Commissioner for Human Rights figures as of yesterday. But we have to go on. You know this *peña* is to help with legal costs of the poor who are arrested. Did you know that 28,000 have been imprisoned so far? It's big this time. Come on let's go back to the music."

-oOo-

"What about a New Year party in our new flat?" Julian suggested. "We've got the view for the fireworks. Wouldn't that be great again, twenty years on, to have Joaquín and the *Bello Barrio* crowd and your brother and your niece and nephew if they'll come. They've got their own circle of friends now of course, as young adults but we could ask them."

"That's a great idea. I'd like to ask some of my contacts here in Valparaíso and it will help with future action here with the vote on the constitution. Yes, let's do it." And Isabel went to work without delay inviting friends and contacts. Joaquín was keen and said he would invite all the members of *Bello Barrio* that would have known Julian from twenty years before. The couple began planning the food they would serve and both Julian and Isabel, when they cooked on alternate days, prepared large quantities of food so as to put portions in the freezer for the party. Carlos and his wife said they would come but weren't sure about their son and daughter. In the event Liliana, their daughter came with her boyfriend.

There was already a sense of celebration in the air because of what the social outburst had achieved already, so the New Year party became a double celebration. Much of the conversation referred to the vote on the new constitution and the party-goers kept wanting to toast the new Chile that was coming with the New Year.

"One of the most remarkable aspects of all these demonstrations is that all the traditional political parties have been excluded from what is going on," said Carlos to Joaquín and Julian. "The parties have tried to get in on the act but have been prohibited, by the young people especially. The only flags that have been seen at the demonstrations are the Chilean flag and the Mapuche flag. The banners and posters have been about the demands for better pensions and health services and without-profit education and of course the need for a new constitution. Never have flags representing political organisations ever been seen."

"It's not surprising," said Joaquín. "The mainstream political parties have so let the people down and achieved so little in the so-called transition."

399

"That is exactly what Isabel always did with all her groups in the north," said Julian. "They didn't want to be tied to a particular party and all the banners they have made over the years have been about the demands and not for particular parties or politicians."

"I think that was right and the only way to present the concerns of the people," said Joaquín. The traditional political parties are so discredited, so despised as professional politicians. Their representatives were literally expelled from the streets by shouting when they attempted to show any party symbol. I saw it happen at a recent demonstration. It was great the way we brushed them away."

"I'm impressed that there is a real understanding amongst the people of why we need a new constitution and banners demanding that have been more numerous than any other demands, I think. We have even had street meetings debating what is wrong with the constitution and academics, lawyers and teachers answering questions. Like street seminars. I've been doing some of those in Santiago," said Carlos.

"How great," said Julian. "Yes, I've noticed the demand for the constitution is very prevalent on the recent demos we have joined," said Julian. "The constitution is at the heart of all that is wrong but the arguments are complicated and it is so good if it is now better understood. All the matters that should be the responsibility of the state were put in private hands to make a profit or they don't get done and just don't exist - like minimum wage protection or adequate unemployment benefit."

"Let's drink a toast to celebrate the end of a dark era. Here's to a new age coming soon." Everyone around cheered and hugged and raised their glasses.

"To a new Chile," shouted Isabel and everyone cheered again and drank. "The other thing that is very different from past social outbursts is the amount of video footage that we have of every incident," Isabel continued to those around her. "The young people can show atrocities by police or show they were peaceful and unarmed when the police are claiming the opposite. They get them sent out on Twitter and Facebook before the police can stop them and some go viral."

"You can imagine," said Carlos, "I've been involved in quite a few cases, defending people arrested and the video has proved really useful to show the arrested person was peaceful and not pointing a weapon as the police have wanted to claim. The violence and the brutality of the police have been awful."

"Piñera promised that peaceful demonstrations would be respected," said Joaquín, "but he was obliged to say something more conciliatory after saying 'we are at war.' A militarised police force isn't going to have the right mentality to respect legitimate protest, is it? They have carried on in the way they did in the past, even the dictatorship past."

"Come on, it's nearly time to eat the grapes as the clock strikes midnight. Take twelve each." Isabel took around a large bowl of red grapes. "Did you keep in touch with the Spanish girl, Joaquín? What was her name?"

"Azucena. I went over to stay with her family and I toured a little, not only around Spain but in other parts of Europe and I went to visit Andrés in Germany. He married a German girl and he stayed there. I also stayed with Azucena's family in Granada and she arranged for me to go to various projects to demonstrate the techniques of mud sculpture. Do you remember all the cupboards and desks I sculptured in *barro* in Bello Barrio?"

"I do. They are still good. I've seen them. All the communal kitchen cupboards and the office and nursery storage cupboards and the beautiful wall you made around the well are still great."

The clock began to strike and, eating grapes like mad, they all went outside to the front garden to view the fireworks. They began to embrace each other and wish one another *"Feliz año nuevo"* and cheered and shouted to neighbours who came out too.

"To a New Chile," Isabel shouted again and again to the whole street and their neighbours responded, "To a New Chile" and the fireworks began.

-oOo-

The social outburst quietened somewhat in the new year but there were students who demonstrated by tearing and burning their university entrance exam papers in the second week of January. Isabel reluctantly accepted the argument from Julian that a brief holiday before the campaign about the constitution came into full swing and they made a plan to visit a friend of Isabel's, now in Valdivia and to go from there to the Lake District and spend a few days in Villarrica and then to go on to stay with Silvia in Temuco.

"We could pull in Concepción too if you would like to. I could contact

Marita, my vet friend there. I think we'd be able to stay there with her." Julian was delighted at the opportunity to see another part of Chile he didn't know. Julian and Isabel had been very regularly to Chile since they were living in Chile in the 90s but their visits had been as brief as work holidays would allow and they had spent their time mostly with relatives and friends in Santiago and Valparaíso. They also had had their adopted child David with them and they had managed to show him the rare sights of the geysers and moonscape of the desert together with the oldest mummies in the world and the desert when it was flowering. Twice they had visited the huge telescopes and David was very interested in astronomy as a child.

"The fewer short flights the better nowadays, I know," said Julian. "But we'll fly to Valdivia to start the tour, won't we?"

"Yes. Any decent government should think of opening up the railways again and sleeping compartments are a great way to do these long distances. Trains are the least polluting. Another of the awful damages that Pinochet brought about was closing nearly all of the railways."

I shall never forget when the British Government let him go free to return to Chile on the grounds of ill health and when he landed he jumped out of his wheelchair in triumph on the tarmac outside the aircraft. What ignominy. *¡Una verguenza!* The Brits should never have allowed such a disgrace. I was so ashamed of my country and my government."

"I know, it was wrong. It happened even before we could test if we could get convictions in another country. Certainly, Carlos believed there could have been convictions in Spain. Nothing worked out as I hoped. And now we've got Piñera, the first and only right wing president since Pinochet. He should be done for crimes against humanity, for the deaths that have occurred recently and the injuries done by rubber bullets with metal pellets."

"I read the injured now total over 30,000."

"Yes, Piñera's war on his own people! How can such atrocities be allowed again? How could the people ever have voted for a man who is one of the richest in Chile? He's a billionaire, you know - I mean in dollars, not pesos, of course. He was fined by the securities regulator for trading after receiving information about LAN Airline stock, like insider trading. He was fined 680,000 US dollars! All this was long before he was elected president. He made a lot of his money from his LAN Airline stock and also from introducing credit cards to Chile. What an achievement! I'm not saying credit cards aren't useful but it's not much to feel you have done for the world. It's a way to cream off a great deal of money from a lot of people and that is where he made most of his fortune."

"When is Chile going to have limits on what parties can spend on elections? That's something else that should go in the new constitution," added Julian.

"We've got to win the plebiscite for a new constitution first, under these unfair rules. *Dios mio*."

"Come on, don't get downhearted. The people aren't going to let go of the chance of change this time."

"I hope you are right. I must FaceTime David." David had been placed in foster care with them when he was five years old, three years after Isabel's return from Chile in 2000. Isabel recalled the quiet and intimate celebration they had made together when David came to them and then the long, drawn out process of being able to adopt him. "I hope all is alright in London. I did miss him this Christmas and New Year."

"Yes, I did. It was the first time we've not been together at Christmas since he came to us. All will be well at home. He's a great lad and hasn't he done well. There aren't many kids who were in care that get to achieve Ph.D.s."

"I know but he hasn't got it yet."

"He will do, difficult though it is in Maths to know how your proposition is going to work out."

"Well we've had a few years since he was five to give him that second chance."

"But you remember it wasn't easy. It took him a few years to get over the loss he had suffered and he did test us to the limits."

"I know, but I always empathised with his loss. I think he did better than me really and he was just a child. Loss and change when they are of that emotional intensity, are so hard. We talked together about it for hours and hours."

"I know you did. I remember. I think that really helped because he knew you had been through loss and a complete sudden change in your life."

"I was old enough to have had chance to think through my values and to

403

know what my purpose in life was to be. They helped me find my identity. A child suffering major change is groping in the dark for his identity. When you think about it it's very terrible to have that change forced upon you so young."

"Yes it is. How can a child's sense of self remain stable when his whole world changes?"

"I don't think my sense of self remained stable with the total change of my life and I was an adult. I didn't know who I was for a long time. I needed to achieve something in line with my values and you were very patient with me as you were with David."

"No, I wasn't as patient as I should have been with you, not at first anyway but I wouldn't give up and when I understood better, I had more patience. I think that was good training for taking David on."

"I think it was."

"Remember how hard we worked at finding ways to develop his self-esteem and all the dilemmas about handling his behaviour?"

"Do I? And I think both he and I had to learn to not live in the past. I think I could help David with that. It was hard for him to start loving and trusting again because he was scared of the pain of loss from his past."

After graduating from Oxford, it had made sense to all of them that David move into his parents' flat in London when he had begun his doctorate as Julian and Isabel were going to Chile. David's intention was to move out on their return but as that had not yet happened, he had remained in his family home.

"I think we can be very proud of David," said Julian taking Isabel in his arms and kissing her. "We must be with him next Christmas."

The holiday passed very enjoyably with warm welcomes from Isabel's friends, new places explored and quite a lot of walking done in some of Chile's beauty spots in its Lake District. Julian especially liked the modern wooden houses with their brightly coloured, laminated log walls, the type that Silvia used to live in. Now Silvia was living in a brick house in the city of Temuco and she took them to all the sights and even took them to an Illapu concert in Lautaro, an hour north of Temuco. Silvia herself had not been to a concert in decades so it caused considerable excitement for her. Sitting on top of the hill *Cerro Ñielol*, the friends talked of the forthcoming plebiscite on the Constitution and Silvia told them more about all the Mapuche demonstrations that had been going on alongside the other protests in the country but for even longer, since a Mapuche farmer was shot by the police in November 2018. Locals of the town said the "Jungle Commandos had entered the town firing bursts of bullets without provocation." They were said to be "investigating" the theft of three cars.

"The Mapuches have a grave sense of injustice. So much of this sort of abuse has happened under the militarised police force. Some Mapuches are wanting the return of all the lands south of the BioBio River," said Silvia, "but if their rights were respected and the unused land and forests made communal with free access for gathering fruits and herbs, I think most would be satisfied."

"Yes, with a state that doesn't discriminate against them but promotes the wellbeing of all, it would be a very different Chile for the Mapuches."

"You know in one demo they destroyed the statue of José Menéndez in Punta Arenas," said Silvia. "He was a sheep farmer and with others built a sheep empire in Patagonia a hundred years ago, but they denied the indigenous people their traditional rights and took their lands. It wasn't until the twenty-first century that the truth about the genocide of the Selk'nam people was fully known. They used to inhabit the Tierra del Fuego Islands and Menendez and his men were found guilty of genocide. I guess the few remaining Selk'nam descendants, together with some Mapuches, feel it is time to put right the historical narrative."

"There were quite a lot of actions against statues of authoritarian and military leaders," said Isabel, "including the statue of Bernardo O'Higgins, revered as the founder of Chile, who freed the country from Spanish rule, but of course, he was an autocrat."

The next day, news came through that opposition to the protests had shown itself in the form of an arson attack on the Violeta Parra Museum in Santiago. Eyewitnesses said that at least six tear gas canisters were shot into the building by the police but officially the cause of the original attack was never established and always doubted by witnesses. This was the second of two incidents against the Museum during February 2020. The friends tried not to let sadness about this type of incident depress their spirits. Isabel was getting anxious to get back to continue the campaign for a new constitution.

"We've still got to fight passionately. It won't just happen without effort," she insisted. They first had the planned visit to Marita in Concepción coming up, and this included another new experience for Julian. Marita took them to a friend's house where the father of the family made a *curanto* in his garden. This was a meal cooked in a traditional manner in a deep hole in the ground. Previously heated stones were placed at the bottom of the hole and then pork and chorizo were added and then mussels - the huge southern Chilean mussels known as *Choros Zapatos,* shoe sized mussels, together with *picaroco* and *almejas.* Large rhubarb leaves were then placed on top and to Julian's surprise, they added a further covering of wet sacks and then soil and clods of grass. After an hour the food, pressurized in this way, was ready to be "dug up" and the family and friends enjoyed a delicious meal in the garden.

The holiday was, however, overshadowed by the increasing dominance in the news of the spread of the global pandemic from the time of the first lockdown in Wuhan on 23rd January 2020. The few attempts in Chile to continue the protests after the summer holidays were soon repressed by the lockdowns. By mid-March, the first cases of coronavirus in Chile were confirmed and these were in persons who had travelled to Europe or Asia. Early cases were thus in the *barrios altos* of Santiago. Lockdowns in these areas began on 20th March, the government having declared a 90-day state of catastrophe two days beforehand. The promised plebiscite on the constitution was postponed from April to October. Isabel was bitterly disappointed with this news and suspicious at first of the motives. Doubtless, the government were delighted to have a reason to postpone the vote.

Depressed and frustrated at times, Isabel made herself very busy in lockdown, putting out short videos with the demand for a new constitution and illustrating the faults of the old one. She also achieved something she'd been looking for time to do for a while. She studied online a UK Open University, non-examined course in Astrophysics. She was eternally grateful for electronic communications and had various zoom meetings with activists and enjoyed zoom lectures from the Astronomical Society, of which she was a member in London. Julian researched and wrote a detailed proposal for electric, collective taxis which would solve, he became convinced, the pollution, the congestion, the road accident levels and the inadequacy of public transport in the UK as well as enable low traffic neighbourhoods with adequate transport. He wrote to various politicians and transport academics with limited response. He could see such electric collective taxis as the solution to so many problems, but a scheme required government backing. So the months in and out of lockdowns passed and finally the lead-up to the plebiscite was upon them again. Julian went to visit Joaquín.

"The political class are trying to take over the vote for a new constitution," declared Joaquín. "Without doubt, those whose interests the current system serves, of course, want to prevent change. But the *estallido* has been a people's movement. They have risked life and liberty in the social outburst to achieve this change and the power to bring about a new constitution must not be lost."

"At least there is going to be control of the money that can be spent on publicising a viewpoint. I gather that many different registered and enrolled groups are being given television time by the Electoral Registration Commission. The groups are limited to that allocation so that a reasonable balance of views can all have their share of screen time and the Right can't buy extra time."

"Yes, hopefully, all the criticisms that can be made of the present constitution will all be heard and given their fair time in the media. There are still a lot of pandemic restrictions in most parts of the country, limiting the number of people that can meet together. This campaign will be like no other. No one is going out door-to-door and calling meetings. It's all happening online or in airtime."

"Voting will be very strictly controlled at the polling stations with social distancing and the hours that different age groups of voters can attend at the stations in two-hour slots. Everyone has to take their own pencil," added Julian.

In the event, 78% of the voters voted in favour of a new constitution being written. The turnout was voluntary and not a legal obligation. In answer to the second question put to the voters, 79% chose that the new Constitution should be written by a directly elected convention and not by a body of existing members of Parliament and elected representatives. In May 2021, 155 persons were elected by popular vote to the Constitutional Convention and the rules of this vote included that half the Convention should be female and 17 seats were given to native peoples' representation, 7 seats to the

Mapuche, 2 to the Aymara and the remaining 8 seats to eight other ethnic groups.

"The traditional political parties have again sought to dominate the vote but," Isabel said to Julian as they watched the results of the vote coming through, "the people showed their determination and prevented the Right from having sufficient votes to dominate the Convention, voting most of all for independents."

"I gather the Right did not win enough votes to prevent a two-thirds majority agreeing on a new constitution."

"Thank goodness. Come on, we have to go out and celebrate," insisted Isabel.

These overwhelming results brought people onto the streets in cities and towns throughout the country. The government, it seemed to many, wanted to use the pandemic as a means of preventing celebration, but pandemic or no pandemic, the people were out to rejoice at the triumph of their will having been done. Isabel and Julian met with Joaquín and other friends in Plaza O'Higgins, the square next to the Parliament building, on the night of the vote. What ecstasy the crowd felt. This was a real triumph of the people. How they shouted and sang, masked as they were, but nothing could dampen their joy, not even the pandemic laws, which did not permit their gathering in such vast numbers.

The next day, Isabel drew the attention of Julian to an open letter written by Miguel Lawyer Steiman to Salvador Allende, the President elected in 1970 and overthrown in the military coup on 11th September 1973. Miguel Lawner Steiman was a prizewinning Chilean Architect who had been a member of the cabinet of Allende. He was executive director of the Corporation to Improve the Urban Environment. He was detained in various concentration camps under Pinochet and when freed he went into exile in Denmark until the late 1980s. Since then he has worked on many projects of social architecture and has investigated and denounced human rights violations committed during the dictatorship.

"Listen to this, said Isabel to Julian, "his letter to Allende begins with a quote from Allende's famous last speech to the people of Chile when the bombing of *La Moneda* had begun. You'll remember it. Allende said, 'You continue to know that, much sooner rather than later, the great avenues

through which the free man passes, will open to build a better society.'
Lawner has written:

*"Dear Chicho:*

*What an unforgettable joy Companero. Last night's victory is your own victory. It is the triumph of the convictions that you taught us to sustain in the hard times and in our maturing years.*

*You were present since the popular uprising in October 2019, as you have always been with us in the battles against the tyrant, in the search for our detained, massacred and disappeared comrades, in the denunciations of those who were lowering the flags that you raised with so much conviction. The Piñera government was greatly defeated last night. Along with him, also defeated were those who aspired to achieve 1/3 of the Convention in order to veto any attempt to end the Pinochet constitution - that lock that guarded the validity of the most fanatical neoliberalism to this day.*

*The former Concertacionistas have also been defeated, those who managed to administer the model in the best tortoise style, so that nothing would change. The citizen movement triumphs, which in October 2019 mobilised one million two hundred thousand people in Santiago and the same in the rest of the country. Those who raised thousands of counsels to develop our future in search of the common good. The innumerable community cooking pots triumph that conquered hunger, to which the callousness of an insensitive and arrogant government condemned us.*

*The political Left triumphs. Yes, the true Left, heir to the best traditions of the Chilean social and political movement. What satisfaction! How much effort we had to carry out, to educate and win consciences in the midst of so many adversities! I end by quoting your words, when you closed your victory speech, on the night of September 4, 1970 and which have a full effect today in this new historical victory:*

*"Go home with the healthy joy of the clean victory achieved. Tonight, when you caress your children, when you seek rest, think about the hard tomorrow that we will have ahead when we have to put more passion, more affection, to make Chile greater and greater, and life more and more just in our homeland.*

*Miguel Lawner 17/5/2021"*

When the Constitutional Convention began its work, Silvia rang Isabel to tell her about the person who had been elected President of the Commission.

"She is an amazing Mapuche woman," said Silvia. "Her father was a bullock driver who learned to read by his own means at age 17 years. He later learned furniture carpentry. Elisa Loncón's mother grew vegetables to feed the family and produced some to sell. Elisa grew up in poverty but her father did buy books for the family, mostly on history and philosophy. Her father had a vast knowledge of the oral history of the Mapuches and her mother read her poetry and taught her to read. She attended the *University of the Frontier* and studied English and when Pope Francis II visited Chile she acted as an interpreter for the VTR television company. She continued post-graduate studies in The Hague, in Canada and in Mexico and gained a PhD from Leiden University in the Netherlands and then a further doctorate degree in literature at the Pontifical University of Chile." Silvia was clearly most enthusiastic about Elisa Loncón Antileo. "I've met her, you know," she said finally.

410

"That's an incredible story. Thanks for letting me know. You must be pleased with the recognition already given to the Mapuches. Things can never go back from here. What hopes we all have of this Convention. None of us can be let down again by injustice, discrimination and unfairness."

"Let's hope not. Are you planning to return to England soon?"

"Well, I want to stay now till the Presidential Elections are done, so there's plenty to keep us busy here."

"I can imagine."

Julian could quite see Isabel's need to stay for the election but he did insist on being home in the United Kingdom for Christmas 2021. He organised the bookings once the quarantine restrictions were dropped. Isabel was increasingly excited at the prospect of real change at last in Chile. They were delighted with the news that in September, the street outside the University of Santiago, from where Victor Jara was taken on the day of the military coup, 11th September 1973 and to which he never returned, was renamed Victor Jara Avenue. The next day Victor Jara's English wife was given a National Award for Performing and Audiovisual Arts, for her "outstanding career in the development of dance in Chile, and her tireless work as a choreographer and teacher for generations." Joan Turner left Chile after Victor's death and after attending Pablo Neruda's funeral. With her two daughters she returned to England. However, she returned to Chile in 1984 and founded a School of Dance and eventually founded the Victor Jara Foundation in 1994.

Some sadder news came through towards the end of September. It was the death of Patricio Manns. He had been born in 1937 and was the son of a jazz musician and his mother was a concert pianist. Joaquín told Julian more about him.

"He tried many kinds of jobs, including coal mining and journalism, before meeting up with the Parras and Victor Jara and becoming part of the *New Chilean Song Movement*. As well as being a singer and guitarist and, you know we have talked before about his poetry and novel writing, he also wrote two plays for the theatre and he was working on his memoirs until just before he died here in Chile on 25th September 2021."

The first round of the Presidential elections appeared a severe blow to the hopes of change. A right-wing candidate, son of a German Nazi, and a man who had defended and supported the Pinochet regime appeared to be the leading candidate, though he had not won an outright majority Isabel saw it as essential to get the vote out for the alternative Gabriel Boric Font the candidate of a left coalition *Apruebo Dignidad*. He would be Chile's youngest president ever if he won and he had been a leading protester in the student movement of 2011 - 13 for an end to for-profit education and improvements in funding for higher and secondary education and student grants.

Julian heard Isabel talking to David on her smartphone. "Boric studied law and after finishing his studies he became a Member of Parliament. He was key to the negotiations for achieving the plebiscite for a new constitution." Later she added, "He has included in his presidential campaign an impressive green agenda." Julian went to put his arm around Isabel so he would appear on David's screen as well.

"I knew you'd be glad about the green agenda. If only all world leaders would join Boric. Let's hope he has some influence."

"Let's hope he wins first," said David.

Despite continuing restrictions, there were great celebrations in the streets and squares of the country when Gabriel Boric won the largest vote ever achieved for a President. Isabel and Julian hugged and danced and sang with friends from *Bello Barrio* and others, almost not able to believe all that had been achieved in the last few years. The following day, when they finally emerged from a short late sleep, Julian received a telephone call from England.

"Isabel," he called, "It's your son. He's ringing to congratulate you and wanting now to see you." Their eventual reunion that Christmas was emotional and joyful. David did not think he had ever seen his mother so happy. The Chilean president would not be inaugurated until 11th March but news kept coming through that maintained their hopes and expectations.

"Boric has appointed the granddaughter of Salvador Allende as the new Minister of Defence and she will preside over reforms of the military. They are long overdue. To his female-majority cabinet Boric has also appointed Camila Vallejo, who was president of the University of Chile Student Federation, previously to Boric himself and she was very active in the student protests for reforms with him ten years ago. Once described as the world's most glamorous revolutionary, Camila Vallejo is to be the official spokesperson for the Boric government," Isabel informed them all.

In March in the UK, the family watched together online, Boric's inauguration. It was conducted in the principal salon of the Parliament building in Valparaíso - one of the rare occasions of its use. Boric paid tribute to Salvador Allende on his arrival at the *Moneda* by walking to and saluting Allende's statue, which now stands in the Square in front of the Palace.

"Boric and his partner are not going to live in the Palace but in an ordinary *barrio* of Santiago but of course, the *Moneda* will be his office," Isabel told the family. They all went to meet with Chilean friends that evening for a joyful celebration at a Chilean restaurant in London.

By May 2022 the new draft constitution was published and the final version by July. The country voted in a referendum on its adoption on 4th September. The new constitution proposed fundamental rights to be guaranteed by the State, a welfare state, which includes access to water, housing, and decent employment with free higher education but it recognised pre-existing rights to property and free enterprise. It gave gender parity across all government and state institutions and declared the State to have absolute, exclusive, inalienable and imprescriptible control of all mines and mineral substances but without the nationalisation of mining. It also was to make the state responsible for the prevention, adaptation and mitigation of risks, vulnerabilities and effects produced by climate change. It proposed a state of autonomous regions with a president and congress and a senate of reduced powers representing the regions.

Incredibly, when the plebiscite on the new constitution came, it was rejected by 62% against and 38% in favour. Isabel, Julian and others like them were stunned. It just did not seem possible after nearly 80% had voted for a new constitution. Rejection meant the 1980 Pinochet constitution continued in place and it was unbelievable that the country did not want to be rid of the dictator's sham of a democracy. How could it have happened? Were the Right so powerful and with so many resources, they had manoeuvred their way into persuading the people it would not work for them? Had too many believed that the Senate becoming a body of regional representatives would divide Chile? Was gender parity across government and guarantees to a minority of indigenous peoples a step too far? When mainstream traditional political parties and their leaders were critical of aspects of the proposal, had they been greatly influential? Was the commitment to free health and education and access to decent housing, pensions and mitigation of climate change risks all thought to cost so much that the people had been cajoled into not voting for them? How could the majority not want these? Why not? It made no sense and like so many others, Isabel and Julian were staggered. No one could explain what had happened. The result was an incomprehensible and complex mixture of many factors. Even the Mapuche-dominated region of *Arucania* had rejected the new constitution by an even greater proportion. Nothing made sense.

"The vote that a new constitution should be produced still stands. It is just that this one was not thought right or good enough. The President says he will require a new constitution to be drawn up by a newly elected convention. But I still can't believe what has happened," Isabel added to Julian and David.

"There could be another social outburst," said David.

"How will they agree on what basis the new convention will be formed and the constitution will be written? It's daunting," said Julian. Isabel suddenly recalled her first visit back to Chile after years in exile and her "search" for the old 'real' Chile.

"I only know we can never give up hope nor can we wish for what we used to have. There never has been a perfect time in the past that we should want to return to. A golden age does not exist. I had to learn that lesson. We can't look back and wish we could return. We have to look forward to creating a better future. That is all that matters and that is what we are here for."

15th September 2022

# Glossary

*abrazo* - a hug

*Adios* - Goodbye

*adobe* - mud and straw bricks for housing

*aislamiento* - isolation, insulation

*al tiro* - immediately (Chilean slang)

*almejas* - clams

*almuerzo* - luncheon and main meal of the day

*Altiplano* - Andean Plateau

*apellido* - family name, surname

*artesanía* - craft work

*Asamblea* - assembly

*ascensor* - funicular railway

*Asesino* - Assassin

*Atacameño* - people of the Atacama desert

*bajo la metralla* - under the machine gun

*baños* - bathrooms

*barrio* - neighbourhood

*barrio alto* - upper-class area of a city

*barrio popular* - working class neighbourhood

*Bello Barrio* - Beautiful Neighbourhood

*Biblioteca* - library

*biblioteca de la calle* - library of the street

*bienvenido* - welcome

*blancos* - voting papers left blank

*blanqueo* - the whitewash

*cacerolazos* - the banging of pots and pans

*cama* - bed seat in a bus which tips back to near horizontal

*Camanchaca* - sea fog

*cariños* - endearments, affection, caresses

*cazuela* - casserole of beef and vegetables

*cena* - evening meal, supper

*centro de llamadas* - call centre

*Cerros Pintados* - Painted Hills

*charango* - a twelve stringed, instrument in the form of a very small guitar

*Chile Actual* - *Anatomía de un mito* - Chile Today - Anatomy of the Myth

*cojo* - one legged, limping, disability to one leg

*colectivo* - shared taxi

*compañera/o* - partner

*Concertación* - Coalition government post Pinochet

*copihue* - the national flower of Chile

*cordillera* - mountain range (Andes)

*cuidate* - take care

*desaparecidos* - *disappeared*

*desierto florecido* - the flowering desert

*detenidos desaparecidos* - detained disappeared persons

*día feriado* - public holiday

*Dios* - God, *Dios mio* - my God

*diputada/o* - Member of Parliament of Lower House

*educación sin lucro* - education without profit

*el dinero llegará* - the money will arrive

*el inglés* - Englishman

*el mercado libre es fascismo* - the free market is fascism

*empanada de pino* - Chilean pasty of minced beef, hard-boiled eggs and olives

*equipo* - team, usually sports

*erizos* - sea urchins

*Feliz Navidad* - Happy Christmas

*fiesta popular* - popular party or celebration

*Fiestas Patrias* - Independence Day celebrations

*garabatos* - swear words (Chilean slang)

*Garra de León* - Flower named after a lion's paw

*geoglificos & petroglificos* - geoglyphs & petroglyphs

*golpe del estado* - coup d'état

*golpistas* - coup leaders

*gringo* - foreigner, especially Northern European

*guardería* - children's nursery

*hermanos y hermanas* - brothers and sisters

*hogar de ancianos* - old peoples home

*¡increible!* - incredible!

*Inglaterra* - England

*Intendencia* - Regional Government Headquarters

*jaivas* - crabs

*la boina gris* - the grey beret

*La Ciudad y Los Perros* - The City and the Dogs

*La Moneda* - the Presidential Palace

*la palabra* - the word

*La Tercera* - National newspaper

*lacrimógena - tear gas*

*laguna* - lake

*Las Alturas de Machu Picchu* - The Heights of Machu Picchu

*Las Venas Abiertas de América Latina* - The Open Veins of Latin America

*Levantate y Mira a la Montaña* - Stand Up and Look at the Mountain

*locos* - pacific shellfish that cling to rocks like limpets

*Los Sabores de la Abuela* - The flavours of Grandma's cooking

*mi casa es tu casa* - my house is your house

*micro* - local bus

*mimbre* - wickerwork furniture

*miseria* - *the misery of extreme poverty*

*muchisimas gracias por todo* - very many thanks for everything

*nana* - domestic help who care for children when they are young

*navajuelas* - Chilean seafood

*Norte Chico* - the Little North - the southern area of the Atacama Desert

*Norte Grande* - the Large North - the northern area of the Atacama Desert

*nulos* - spoiled voting papers

*Nunca Más* - *Never Again*

*ojalá* - would that it were so

*onces* - elevenses

*papas chuños* - sun-dried potatoes

*paracaidistas* - the parachutists

*pasean* - they walk about

*paseos* - promenades

*peñas* - musical events

*perros* - dogs

*pesos* - Chilean currency about 1000 to the pound sterling

*Pinochet no se toca* - Pinochet is never to be touched.

*pinochetistas* - Dictator Pinochet supporters

*pituto* - contact or relative who speaks for you to get a job

*piure* - a pacific seafood rich in iodine giving a very strong distinctive flavour

*Plaza Colón* - Columbus Square

*población* - poor urban area

*poemario* - book of poems

*polilla - wood termite*

*profe* - commonly used term for teacher or lecturer, short for *profesor*

*Punto Final* - Final Point (newspaper)

*¡Que lindo!* - How beautiful!

*quotas* - hire purchase payments

*rabia* - anger

*Salar de Atacama* - Atacama Salt Lake

s*alud* - health

*Salvador* - Saviour

*semi-cama* - semi-bed, adjustable seat in a bus

*seudodemocracia* - pseudo-democracy

*Sol y Lluvia* - Sun and Rain

*solidaridad* - solidarity, empathy, mutual bonding and sharing

*te amo* - I love you

*terca* - obstinate, stubborn

*toma* - taken land, a neighbourhood created by rural poor flocking into cities

*Torre de Marfil* - an ivory tower

*Torre del Reloj* - clock tower

*Transición* - Transition

*Unidad Popular - Popular Unity* - alliance of Left parties which won the 1970 election

*Valle de la Luna* - Valley of the Moon

*Vamos* - "Let's go"

*venceremos* - we shall overcome

*vergüenza* - shamefulness, ignominy, disgrace

*Vicaría de la Solidaridad* - the Vicariate of Solidarity

*zampoñas* - Andean musical pipes

*zinc* - corrugated iron

Printed and bound by CPI Group (UK) Ltd, Croydon, CR0 4YY